MW00490025

Paperback: 978-1-7362987-0-1

First paperback edition December 2020.

Edited by Alyson Montione
Cover art by Jake Bartok

Schara Reeves Press

ScharaReevesPress.com

ACKNOWLEDGEMENTS

Editor:
Alyson Montione

Cover Artist:
Jake Bartok

General Support:
The Lord
Family
Friends
Schoharie Library Writing Club

Beta readers:
Amelia Couture
Heather Heckman
Becky Rowling
Emma Panzera
Khristich Schmid
Jubilee Schmid
Zebulun Schmid

PRONUNCIATIONS

Aelor Ven (AY•lor vehn)

Alarune (al•uh•ROON)

Ameri (uh•MAYR•ee)

Anahli (ah•NAH•lee)

Asher (ASH•er)

Astra (AS•trah)

Baeno (BAE•no)

Bandon (BAN•dun)

Belayr (bell•EER)

Beclian (BEK•lee•un)

Cadbir (CAHD•beer)

Ceryn (Sir•IN)

Cheyd (SHADE)

Cithan (SIGH•than)

Coryn (COR•in)

Dannsair (Dan•SAYR)

Delnor (DEHL•nor)

Destrin (DES•trin)

Drogan (DROH•gan)

Eatris (EE•tris)
Entrais (ENT•rays)
Ethian (EE•thee•uhn)
Euracia (Yur•uh•KY•uh)

Farian (FAIR•ee•un)
Flawkey (FLAW•kee)

Gavin (GAH•vin)
Graece (GRACE)
Geltum (GEHL•tuhm)

Hyperyn (HY•per•inn)
Hyperxelobane (hy•per•ZEHL•oh•bayn)

Ilnorian (ill•NOR•EE•en)
Ivinon (IHV•ih•nohn)

Julyn (JOO•lin)

Kaeden (KAY•den)
Kayliene (kay•lee•EN)
Keeshiff (KEE•shiff)
Killyan (KILL•ee•an)
Krysophera (kris•OFF•er•uh)

Leyda (LAY•dah)

Ligrean (LIG•ree•en)

Litash (lih•TASH)

Louko (LOO•co)

Lucian (LOO•shee•un)

Macridean (MACK•rih•dee•un)

Malnimar (MAHL•ni•mar)

Mariah (mah•RY•uh)

Melye (MEL•yay)

Merimeethia (mer•eh•MEETH•ee•ah)

Merym (MER•im)

Miadoris (mee•ah•DOR•is)

Nodroit (NO•dro•it)

Nythrian (NITH•ree•an)

Nythril (NITH•ril)

Omath (OH•math)

Pershizar (PER•shih•zar)

Ravyen (rah•VEE•en)

Rednimaen (red•NIH•main)

Rheritarus (Rur•i•TAR•us)

Rhumir (rue•MEER)

Rufio (ROO•fee•oh)

Salah (SAH•lah)

Se-Ednian (seh•EHD•nee•un)

Soletuph (SOUL•tuff)

Tallaman (TAW•lah•mahn)

TaReev (tah•REEV)

Triscri (TRIS•cree)

Tyron (tie•RON)

Verzaer (Ver•ZAYR)

THE EXILED:

OF SHADE AND SHADOW

A DAUGHTER'S RANSOM: BOOK I

BY NIAMH SCHMID
AND REBECCA SCHMID

CHAPTER I

<u>**Astra:**</u>

Two hundred eighty-four days since The War had ended, and Astra wished to find herself anywhere other than sitting outside the Proceedings Hall. She was too sad to cry, too scared to run, and too loved to be able to tell anyone. None of it made sense. Astra had exhausted herself trying to figure it out in words. Now, she didn't even bother to try.

Astra adjusted the strap of her leather tabard for the third time, wondering again if she should have just worn a dress. It would have been more formal—more acceptable in the Court's eyes. And yet, she reminded herself that she had given up on being accepted. All she could do was try to be noticed. It was the closest she would get to being truly heard. That's why she had chosen the armor she'd worn in the last battle against Euracia: maybe it would make her look older than sixteen.

Again, she shifted in her seat and tried not to disturb those that sat on either side of her on the wooden bench. The thing was as long as it was uncomfortable, stretching down the entire back hallway. It was almost entirely full. Hearing Days were always busy. But Astra had been prepared for this and had arrived well before the hall was open. Even then, there had still been others before her. The official who had taken down her name had been shocked to hear her title, but had not questioned her. After all, anyone who came on a Hearing Day had the right to present their case to the King and the Court.

It had been over three weeks since Astra had spoken to Ent—

1

King Entrais as everyone else called him now. She had tried many times, only to be turned away by the guards at his door. It seemed that his new duties as king left him too busy to be a brother. Any time he did have to spare went to caring for his still frail wife.

Astra understood this. Truly, she did. She did not resent her brother, however, she did miss him. She missed having a friend. Someone to talk to. Someone to hug. And while she agreed with all her countrymen that Ent was the best person to lead this new Litash, she couldn't help but worry over the toll it would take on him.

The herald called for the next person, and Astra was drawn from her reverie. Only two people left before her. She needed to focus. Mentally, she reviewed her case. Perhaps if she was able to articulate it better, and in a clearer way, Ent would believe her. At least he could no longer dismiss her. And while Astra doubted the Court would care, she knew that Hearing Days were often attended by large audiences. Maybe someone would hear and take action.

The only thing Astra was sure of was that she couldn't simply sit and do nothing. Not when Tyron could still be out there. Not when she relived Euracia's last words every night in her dreams. *"Do what you will to me—I don't care. You're much less imaginative than my brother."* Ent had replied that Tyron was already dead. But Euracia had just laughed. A horrible, twisted, gurgling sound that had turned to choking, and then to silence.

"Miran Terost," the herald called, making Astra jump slightly.

So much for focusing. Now she only had one person left before her. The girl forced herself not to look at the other end of the hall, where the door led away from the Court and her brother. She tried to make herself relax with much less success. She settled for gripping the edge of the bench instead; her fingernails digging into the wood hurt much less than having them dig into her palms.

At least her parents weren't here. They were busy trying to calm the Elves off in Cithan. Astra had caused them plenty of trouble with her Gifting and her inability to master it. Even they had given up and simply given her a red bronze cuff to suppress it. Astra didn't want to cause them any more stress than she already had. The years of separation during The War made things awkward enough as it was.

The one person left in front of her was called, leaving Astra increasingly nervous. The other case must not have been heard long if they had moved on from it so quickly. Her stomach twisted and she tugged on the strap of her arm bracer. She ought to have tried harder to contact Ent and at least warn him. She had tried to write to him, but she was sure her messages got lost in the endless pile she'd glimpsed on his desk; he never wrote back. When she had broached the subject of Tyron during those rare moments they were together in person, Ent had always looked troubled. He would listen, then say that it was not the time for such things. He told her not to worry so much.

And now she was only worrying more. The temptation to slip away before her name was called only grew. But what choice did she have? Could she remain silent and so bear the responsibility of anything Tyron might do? The girl shivered. No. She had to tell them. Even as hard it was. Even as hard as it was for her brother.

"Princess Astra," the herald called, causing every head in the corridor to turn her way.

Astra swallowed, took a deep breath, and stood. She ignored the

3

stares and nodded to the herald. He gave a little bow and motioned her through the doorway.

The passage between the waiting hall and the Proceedings Hall was much shorter than Astra wished. It seemed like she had just stepped into the narrow corridor when she had to step out again, this time into overwhelming sound. To her left was a teeming crowd, held at bay by a wooden rail that ran across the length of the huge hall: the commoners' observation area. Above was a sloped balcony with row upon row of nobles. Lords and ladies, all in bright silks and satins, with fans and even food as they watched the proceedings.

But the front of the room to her left was what made Astra's heart drum faster. Tiered seats formed a half circle, facing towards the wooden booth where plaintiffs made their case. Court members filled these ranks. But in the middle of a raised platform sat two thrones with royal guards on each side. One throne was empty, but not even her obscured view could hide the tall figure of her brother sitting on the other.

Astra waited as the herald instructed, then watched him as he walked out onto the floor and bowed towards the Court. He straightened and made his announcement with a voice so loud that Astra was sure he used Gifting. "Princess Astra Verzaer, Princess of Cithan and Sister to the King, General of Dragons from The Great War."

That was a much longer title than the one she had given the official that morning. It made her cringe, especially when the whole room went completely silent and she could feel a thousand eyes fix on her. As the herald passed by and motioned for her to go forward, Astra told herself that at least the title might help them take her seriously.

She focused on simply getting to the wooden booth. She did not look at anyone—courtier or commoner. Once there, she bowed deeply towards the one occupied throne and gave the traditional greeting, "May the king live long."

But once she straightened, she could avoid it no longer. She looked up to see her brother's face, entirely overcome by shock. He looked pale as he gripped the sides of his throne, his bottomless grey eyes filled with confusion and the ever present hauntings of unfounded guilt. Barely, he was able to respond with a respectful nod and release his grip on the arm of his throne so that he might motion for her to enter the booth.

Astra did so. Shame swelled within her as she climbed the short stair and then turned to face her brother again. She should have found a better way.

"What is your complaint, Princess?" Ent's voice was stiff as he gave the traditional cue for her to begin.

The girl's words nearly escaped her. She had to grab hold of them, give herself mere seconds to compose herself, and then throw herself into them.

"I come with no complaint, my king," Astra began in what she hoped was a full, calm voice. "I come with a warning, which I believe has as much of a right on this Hearing Day as any complaint." Astra registered motion and shifting expressions but did not dare stop to observe. "And my warning is simply this: I believe that the Prince Tyron is still alive. And knowing his ways, I cannot help but also believe that he will be back. The War which we have all fought so hard to win may not yet be over."

The hall was oddly quiet. Only subtle murmuring threaded its way through the commoners' area, echoing up into the balcony.

"Are you prepared to bring forth evidence?" Ent's voice held a secret strain.

Astra hated herself for putting it there. "I have not yet been given permission to investigate," she clarified for those listening. "But the facts I do have are thus: Prince Tyron was known for his particularly strong Gifting. After the siege on his fortress in Alarune, no body was ever recovered. Would it not have been easy enough for him to have cast an illusion of his own death? We all know him capable of the planning that such a ruse would take."

Astra's intention had been to allow a few seconds of silence for her point to sink in. Instead, the pause gave a Court member enough time to ask, "But, Princess Astra, were you not the one who killed him?"

The question took her away from her planned speech. "I," she tried not to think of that dark night. "Yes. But he did not—"

"Then how can you ask us to believe he's alive?" the man asked, sounding somewhere between amused and exasperated.

Astra's tight stomach was already tying itself in knots. "Because when I ran him through, he, he," The vivid image of the man, grinning as the sword protruded from his chest, was sickening. "He simply smiled. And dissipated. He did not bleed or grimace or fall. How else could that be explained?"

Now the courtiers were exchanging glances.

"And have you any other witnesses of this?" the first man asked dubiously.

Astra had to consciously relax her fists. "No, but there—"

"Princess," now his voice was patronizing. "The battlefield is, well, quite heated. It was never meant for children."

A blonde lady on the other side of the tier picked it up. "We all know what happened to you," she said with a thin smear of pity. "The torture you endured during your capture is beyond what even the most hardened warrior ought to endure, much less a little girl."

Astra stuttered to a stop, feeling ill. "That is not what this is about," she choked.

"Enough," Ent's command cut through the hall. "Will you really treat her—one of the very people who helped free you—worse than the stranger who was just arguing over his cow?" The question held an unfamiliar hostility as he stared at the blonde lady.

Astra looked back at her brother, trying to fight the icy feeling that was growing and threatening to paralyze her. Her throat felt tight and a tremendous pressure was growing in her chest. But she knew that Ent had it worse. She knew he remembered that week as vividly as she.

"It is only my intention to show her that we understand her trauma," the lady replied, oblivious. "We do not blame her for her paranoia."

There was an odd twinge of energy about the room as Ent's eyes lit in anger. "Oh yes, of course you understand. You were there, weren't you?" His voice dripped with biting sarcasm. Astra had only ever heard this dangerous tone from her brother once in her life. "She has a valid point and, perhaps if you had ears, you would listen. Euracia himself didn't seem to think Tyron was dead."

"Euracia?" someone in the back scoffed. "The one you

7

overthrew? Since when, exactly, did we start going by his witness?"

A muted chorus of agreement rippled around the room. How could they be so openly disrespectful to Ent?! The tension within her grew and Astra couldn't hide her clenched fists.

"He was in league with Tyron," the girl interjected. "He would have known the prince better than any of us."

"Please, Princess," came a dry voice. "Your age hardly qualifies you for politics."

"And your treason hardly qualifies you to be free, and yet *I* allowed it." Ent's temper audibly shortened.

The blonde woman spoke again. "But, Sire, this outburst of hers is only reenforcing what I have been saying these past few weeks: that this girl is clearly sick and in need of help." Her voice was sweet to the point of sickly. "She doesn't need to investigate, she needs time to heal. If we are to act in her interest, perhaps we ought to be prescribing her a physician and some extended seclusion."

This was going wrong. All wrong. This was a mistake. Astra tried desperately to speak, but nothing was coming out. All her words stuck in her throat. All she had managed was to make herself vulnerable, another target for anyone seeking to hurt Ent. And just like with Tyron, she couldn't stop it. She was captive. Trapped again.

It was as if from a distance that she heard Ent's low, hard voice. The clamor of the Court members was even further away, blurred together and yet still overwhelming. It was too much. Too much. Astra clasped her hands to her ears, but it was too late. It was building inside her like a scream.

And then it came out. All the Gifting she had suppressed for long months burst out in a great wave, shattering the red bronze cuff that had been meant to keep it in. It hit the room with a rolling shock, knocking all those who had been standing to the floor. The massive stained glass windows that lined the back wall fractured and sent broken glass raining down with a clatter. Screams erupted amidst the chaos. There was a thunder as the panicked crowd pushed and shoved and tried to push through the hall's double doors.

"Astra, stop!" Ent's voice pierced the roaring that filled Astra's ears. "You are going to get someone *hurt*." The voice was much closer to her than it should have been.

Hurt....hurt...no! She had to stop. She was going to hurt them. The yelling, the fear, the trampling—it was all too much. The screams echoing in the hall were matched by those in her own head. The overpowering memory of Ent pleading with Tyron to stop pulled her down to her knees. Ent. She was going to hurt Ent.

"*No!*" The cry left Astra's lips as the whole world gave way to blackness.

Whether the dark lasted seconds or hours, she didn't know. All she knew was that when she opened her eyes, she was still in the hall. It was completely empty, and completely unrecognizable. Chairs were strewn everywhere, many charred or blackened. The very air smelled burnt. Tapestries hung in shreds on the cracked walls. The now empty window frames let in shafts of light that only served to highlight the thick dust which filled the room.

Horror made everything seem to be in slow motion as Astra staggered to her feet. She turned in a slow circle, glass crunching beneath the soles of her boots. No one. They were all gone. Terror struck deep: what had she done? *What had she done?!*

A sound startled her from behind and she swiveled around instantly. She could barely even hope to believe what she was seeing. "E-Ent?"

He stood before her, the edge of his green coat singed. There were waves upon waves of emotions warring in his eyes, but all he said was, "Astra…" He looked her over as if worried she was the victim—the one hurt.

Astra's chest burned and she realized her breath was coming in gasps. She didn't dare move towards Ent. "Did, did I hurt you?" Her shaking hands and thudding heart told her this was too real to be just another nightmare.

He crossed the distance between them in quick strides and put both hands on her shoulders. Then suddenly, he pulled her into a tight hug, squeezing her as though afraid she would slip away. "No. Not hurt. Not hurt. Not me, not any of the others." He rocked her gently. "Oh Astra, what are we going to do?"

"I am so sorry," the words poured out like a sob. "I didn't mean to. I, I was just, I thought that…" Her breath caught and her voice died away to nothing. "I'm sorry," the girl whispered. Fear told her to pull away, to run, to get far away where she couldn't harm anyone else.

But Ent only held her more tightly. "Shh," he soothed. "We'll figure it out. We always have."

A sound made them both jump and Astra felt her brother's embrace grow protective. People were banging on the somehow locked doors, yelling indiscernible orders as they did so. Astra's trembling increased.

"Let's get you out of here," Ent said. "Hold tight."

Astra obeyed as her brother Gifted them away from the room.

***

Astra was nervous. Entrais had barely been able to keep the news of Astra's catastrophic episode from spreading all through Litash and its surrounding countries. Yet even so, rumors were beginning to circulate. It felt as though the entire planet of Eatris knew. Now it was at the point where she wasn't even allowed to leave her quarters. It had been only a week—a horrible, painful, slow week, riddled with solitude and whispers—and Astra wanted to scream. But she couldn't. She had to keep *it* under control and herself quiet so that she didn't hurt anyone. While no one had been killed in the Proceedings Hall, they might not be so lucky next time.

Today held a different kind of anxiety, for today was the first time Astra had been allowed to leave her room since the incident. Eight palace guards had come to escort her, saying only that the king had summoned her. The only time Astra had seen Ent since that day had been in secret, and then only for him to make sure she was alright and being taken care of. It was a wonder Astra hadn't been thrown in a dungeon or in some physician's laboratory with the way she had completely destroyed the courtroom. She probably would be now if it wasn't for her relationship to Ent.

Astra was somewhat relieved when they turned towards Entrais' quarters instead of heading south to the throne room. She feared another direct encounter with courtiers, or any of the nobles or...or anyone. Though she feared she might do something to Ent if she wasn't careful, the fear was significantly less without a crowd intent on provoking her.

The princess and her escort arrived at the chambers Ent shared with his wife, Jade. A page went in first to announce them and the wait stretched Astra's nerves even further. The guards were of no help, staring straight forward as if she weren't even there—yet she knew that all she had to do was slip off her red bronze cuff, and their swords would be drawn. The cuff was much heavier than the previous one, though she knew it would be just as useless. Even with its ornate words in thousands of languages that curled around in beautiful patterns, its rich red color that matched her hair, and its mirror-like polish, the thing felt like a manacle. And Astra knew exactly what that felt like.

Finally, the page returned and the group entered. Ent was standing in the middle of the room, having obviously just stopped pacing. The evidence was written all over his face and taut posture, making Astra even more anxious. Her brother looked so tired and stretched thin. She wondered if the nightmares had grown worse for him, too.

Ent motioned for the guards to go and received only stubborn silence in response. His face hardened and he said in a deadly, even tone, "I made a deal. Now you will either move, or I will move you. Don't tempt me."

Soon, the door closed and the room was empty.

Instantly his shoulders slumped, "Oh, Astra. I am so sorry. I'm so sorry." Ent waved his arms in the air and started to pace.

Astra felt nearly sick. "What is it? What is going on?"

He stopped and stared at her, taking a deep breath. "You're going to hate me, Astra," He whispered.

"I don't understand." Astra wished he would just tell her already.

The rare, dangerous light of fury sparked briefly in his eyes before he hid the emotion."They want me to lock you up—after everything you've been through. They want to throw you away like some toy they've gotten bored with. I told them I wouldn't. They say you're delirious and paranoid. Dangerous, even. If anyone is, they are," he finished with an angry mutter, feet scuffing the floor as he fought the urge to pace.

The last bit did sting. Dangerous. She knew others thought it and, after last week, she agreed. But did Ent think it, too? Did he fear what she could accidentally do to his wife? Jade was still frail after all she had endured in The War.

"What are you going to do?" Her voice sounded far away.

"I..." He apparently couldn't stand it anymore and started pacing again. "I'm going to send you to Merimeethia for a little bit."

Astra began to put the pieces together. The possibility of what might be happening hit like a wave of cold water, leaving her numb. "You mean, I'm being exiled."

"No. I... I'm letting them think that. It's somewhere they can't get you, and where you can still study. Some of them even want to *experiment* on you, Astra! I don't understand how they can even think about it, after all you've done for this country." His fists balled, and with a weighty sigh, he looked down at the ground. "Your sacrifice is what did this to you in the first place." His voice changed then, holding a quietly confidential tone, though he didn't lift up his eyes to meet hers. "I just need you to know I believe you. I don't think he's dead any more than you do. Jade keeps saying to just leave him in the ground...but I can't. You and I both know he's not dead, but I think you'll have a better chance finding information up in Merimeethia—where he was banished before The War."

The mere mention of Tyron sent a shiver down her spine. But her mind was, for once, focused on other things. Still trying to process, she quietly asked, "I can't come back, can I?"

Ent's brow furrowed and he knelt down, bringing his face level with hers. "I'll figure out a way to get you back, Slip, I will."

The nickname made Astra want to run into his arms as she always had. Through all the war-torn years of her childhood, Ent had been her one refuge. Being near him was the only thing that let her feel safe, and now she was being sent hundreds of miles away. Even though Ent was with her now, he couldn't do anything. He had fought for her, and it had still come to this.

"Okay." Astra managed to say. She felt like she was choking. "I trust you." It was a moment before she found her voice again. "When must I go?"

Ent's face turned sour, and he got a very pained expression. "Um... Well. There is a ball coming up. A lord that lives on the east side of the Sea of Triscri. I have.... unfortunately been invited to go. But you have as well." Then he took a deep breath and the pained expression grew deeper. "As has...well...Louko."

"You're sending me with, with *him*?" Astra shook her head now. "Please, don't. I can take care of myself." She understood that exiling her wasn't Ent's choice, but this was different.

"Astra. As capable as you are, you are yet sixteen: I'm not letting you go by yourself, and as much as you don't like it, he's the only one that has really shown himself capable of defending you. As long as he doesn't know what's going on, anyway..." The way he trailed off didn't convince Astra. "And Merimeethia owes us enough that they won't argue with your presence there." Ent sighed again and moved on. "I've only been allowed to bring you to the ball as long as Soletuph comes along as a guard. He's powerful enough that they trust him."

Astra suppressed her aversion to being watched and secured. At least Soletuph would be much better than the strangers who had been watching her night and day. Jade's younger brother—however solemn and gruff—was still an improvement.

Astra swallowed her frustration, asking instead, "When did you talk to Louko?" How had Ent arranged this? Somehow she couldn't see Louko being able to sit still long enough to write a letter.

There was an awkward pause. "I haven't exactly told him yet. I wrote King Omath, and he assured me Louko would be at the ball to escort you to Merimeethia—under the presumption you are conducting research, of course. No one will know of your exile. But I am sure Louko has been informed of his role."

Astra wasn't so certain. She couldn't see Louko being any happier with this arrangement than she was. He had always—when it truly came down to it—proven himself loyal. But he had always kept strictly to himself and Astra doubted he'd be thrilled over having a travelling partner. Especially one he hadn't gotten to pick. If Louko hadn't expressed his displeasure over this already, then Astra had a feeling she would hear all about it at the ball.

CHAPTER II

Louko:

It was wet, cold, and utterly miserable. That pretty much summed it up for the soaking Prince Louko. It hadn't even been so *very* bad until now. Granted, the rain had been atrocious… *granted,* his skittish nag had gotten stuck in the mud and thrown him off….but even that had been rather fun compared to this.

And what was *this?* What could be so much worse than battling bandits or getting stuck in the rain for hours? Something terrible. Something so terrible he would rather be hung upside down and fed as live bait to a ligrean. Something so truly petrifying that he would have fallen on the nearest sword—had he not been too much a coward— even after living through the bandits and ligrean, to escape it. Something so terrible he would rather be home… Louko's train of thought came to a screeching halt at the thought of home.

Perhaps not that.

But that was beside the point… What was this he was so against tonight?

People. Lots and lots . . . of people. And that wasn't the worst of it. He had actually agreed to go to this meeting of people, this—social gathering. . . So, technically it was a ball, but it was still possibly the worst day of Louko's pathetic and boring life.

Well aren't we just in an especially dramatic mood this evening? He chided himself. The prince let out a shiver, half from the rain and half from the pleasant reminder of what he had gotten himself into. *Ick. What*

17

were you thinking, idiot? All this to get out of the palace? You could do better. No matter how untrue the statement was, here he was, standing in front of the mansion of Lord Helmir of Litash. And the best part? He was being interrogated—*interrogated!*—by an equally wet and annoyed guard.

"I'm sorry, lad. Last time I checked, we didn't allow dir'y scoundrels inta nobles' 'ouses." The guard's jeer prickled Louko's very twisted sense of fake pride, and the prince put on his most grating smile. He was *not* in the mood for this.

Louko cocked his head, causing water to cascade from his black hair and form puddles on the cobblestone. How pleasant. "I wasn't aware nobles let their houses be guarded by rusted, talking cans, though I must admit it is a rather amusing" He stopped himself, realizing his stupid mouth was getting him in trouble. "But really, if you just let me exp—".

"Ey'! How dare you! I'll 'ave you taken in for such open disrespect!" the stubby guard interrupted, wearing a puckered expression.

Oh, if only Louko had bitten back the words. *Idiot.*

"What's the matter now?" Another man with a spear appeared from the small guard house, and *he* looked grumpy *too.*

Well, why don' t we all just forget the dancing and sit around and complain instead? Who needs a ball? Louko thought, hardly the most optimistic in the group and still debating whether he actually would prefer a night in the manor's dungeon to being allowed entrance to the party. The idea was tempting…

"Sir." The first guard's tone turned from scorn to respect. "Was just bout' ta throw this scamp in a nice cold cell for the night so he learns a lesson, sir. 'E's been rilin' me up and disrespectin' the nobles' judgment, sir."

Deciding against the pleasant isolation of a cell, Louko rolled his eyes, annoyed with the guard's description as well as the unnecessary use of 'sir'. "Oh please, if you'd—"

"Shut up, I didn't ask you," 'Sir' Guard spat, turning back to his bumbling idiot of a companion. "Did he give a reason for the intrusion?"

Louko's lips pressed tightly together in forced silence, all too used to being told to shut up. Oh, if only Kaeden was here… Louko had never tried to go to such a gathering without the advisor—and he definitely wouldn't be doing it again. Honestly, it was a surprise Louko's father had let him go to a gathering without supervision.

Or that he'd been allowed to go at all.

"Sir? Oh, he wanted to get into the par'y, sir." The guard reported.

Again, Louko tried in vain, "If you would just give me the chance —"

"Will you be quiet? If the rain and cold wasn't enough, now I have to deal with this instead of staying somewhere nice and warm!" Sir Guard thumped the butt of his spear into the cobblestone.

Louko wished he could just finish his sentence. Actually, he wished he had ignored the impulse to speak in the first place. Or at least the impulse to insult the stupid guard. *Blew it again, idiot. When are you ever going to get it right?* Probably never. He knew part of his reason for being so difficult was the inkling of a desire to not actually be able to go to the ball at all. But after all the trouble he'd gone through to be allowed to come, he knew it would be stupid to throw away all his effort at the last moment. He hadn't realized just how nice it was to get out of the stuffy castle, and if he didn't behave his father would be less likely to let him leave if another chance arose.

Once again the annoying guard broke in, "Sorry sir...would you like me to put 'im in a cell for the night, sir?"

"Yes! Just get him out of here and do your duty!" Sir Guard huffed again and turned to leave.

Now desperate—as well as tired, irritated, wet, and grumpy—Louko's mouth twisted open in disbelief, "Would you *please* just stop a moment and let me speak! I have an *invitation!*" Because...as much as he would *love* spending the night in a cold...damp...rancid cell...he really didn't want to have to explain such a thing to his father. Especially if it was his own stupid fault for opening his mouth in the first place.

Both guards froze, then Sir Guard turned around, "What?"

Louko rolled his eyes and sighed. "You know, the little piece of paper that announces that you are *actually* invited?" He waved his hands violently.

Sir Guard came forward, eyeing Louko very suspiciously. Seeing he had the guard's attention, Louko pulled a soaking piece of parchment from his leather coat, all but throwing it at him. He knew he shouldn't take his own frustrations out in such a way, but Louko was beyond the point of caring. It wasn't like the ill-tempered buffoons were helping.

The grump of a man looked over the half-readable parchment, then threw it back at Louko. "Who in Eatris is Prince *Louko?*" The guard said his name like it was some made-up word in a made-up kingdom.

The prince resisted the sudden urge to turn around and leave after all. "It says right there the youngest son of King Omath of Merimeethia…." He said, trying to suppress the irritable tone seeping through.

The two men scoffed and Sir Guard gave Louko another suspicious glance before looking at the invitation again. "Well, check on the list, then" He elbowed the other guard, who took out a thickly rolled up parchment and muttered through the long list of names.

"Keeshiff o' Merimeethia….Mariah o' Merimeethia…" Louko heard him mutter, "Oh. Louko. Huh. Fancy that."

"Yes, fancy that." Louko sighed, not sure how glad he was that his name wasn't known much. Litash was quite isolated, and even though he had been instrumental in helping Entrais and Astra win The War against Euracia and Tyron, Louko had made a point of trying to remain under the radar.

Now realizing their mistake, the guards quickly allowed him through.

"Sorry, Your Highness."

"You know how it is, people tryin' ta always git in—"

"Tis' only been a year since The War n' all, Sir—"

"And—"

They continued to babble on apologies and fall over each other as they bowed and scraped, but Louko just gave a smile and walked by, about ready to get out of the rain. He passed through the gate and walked across the courtyard to the marble stairs leading to the doorway of the Litashian mansion, knowing he wouldn't be as fortunate as to have the nobles in this stupid ball not recognise him.

All the servants had apparently fled either to the dryer stables, or inside the mansion. So after taking a deep breath, Louko knocked on the door, this time having his precious parchment in hand. Even before the door opened, he chided himself to hold his tongue this time. Better not have a repeat offense.

A dark haired man opened the door a crack, opening it further and looking cordial at the sight of the invitation.

Louko gave him a humorless smile and held up his parchment, wishing back the days when the most complicated thing he had to do was plan an attack, not some elaborate trip to some ball just to get out of his *boring* life routine. It even *sounded* pathetic.

The man read the invitation, and his demeanor turned to aversion at the sight of Louko's name. Yes. It would make sense a household servant would get more gossip. Finally, Louko was allowed in, though completely soaked to the bone and regretting every decision he had ever made leading up to this. Why, oh, why had he ever willingly accepted an invitation to this stupid ball!

Oh...right. Because you couldn't stand home any longer. Idiot. It seemed he was reminding himself every five minutes.

But then there was the reminder of how easy it had been to convince his father...

"May I take your coat?" The servant looked at Louko hesitantly, and his eyes seemed to mask suspicion.

Louko doubted he would ever get the leather coat off in its condition, and shook his head. "Thank you, but I have it under control. Do you have a fireplace I could just get a little drier by before I join the festivities?"

The man simply pointed down the hall, "Second door to your

right. Would you like me to lead you?"

Louko shook his head, "Oh no, I can find it myself. Thank you." He gave another fake smile and, without another moment to wait and regret, walked down the hall, every movement feeling terribly uncomfortable. He arrived at the fabled "second door on the right" and, after listening to make sure it was unoccupied, entered.

It was a small, simple room with a stone hearth and a warm fire going—most likely commonly used for servants to warm themselves, and perhaps the occasional hunting party. If Litashians...did that sort of thing...Louko really wasn't quite sure. His exposure to Litashian culture consisted of the language—which Kaeden had taught him—and what he learned while fighting their tyrannical shape-shifting king Euracia while trying to avoid contact with Tyron...

"Don't go there," he warned himself, not really meaning to mumble aloud. Fortunately, he was alone.

Louko carefully peeled his jacket from his embroidered white tunic, wringing the stupid thing out in a nearby spitoon. Waste not, want not.

Then he rolled up his damp sleeves and put his hands in front of the fire, waiting for the flames to return life to them. Perhaps the fire would do the same for him. Such a silly thought, but all the same, Louko's life *was* in need of kindling. In fact, in Louko's opinion, it wasn't even much of a life. But perhaps it was just him. He had, after all, been spoiled thoroughly by being allowed to tag along with King Entrais and his sister. He looked down at the beautiful blade Ent had given him, and thought again of the lost times—so recently passed. He was dangerously close to wishing them back, if only to maybe try harder...do

23

something different so that—

"You are insufferable," he interrupted himself.

Rubbing his hands together, Louko decided he was dry enough to be let into society. If only he had gotten wetter… then he would have an excuse.

He let out a sigh. Of course things couldn't work out *that* perfectly. Louko uncomfortably tugged at the formal shirt he'd had to borrow from Keeshiff. It was so uncomfortable that Louko no longer wondered why his brother had been so willing to lend it… Louko hadn't attended a ball for years, and had long since abandoned such fine clothes.

Collecting his half-dried jacket from before his feet, he left the room and walked back to the doorway, handing it to the servant.

"I'm back again." He announced, seeing the servant was clearly *very* happy to see him… "Is there a back way into the room?" He turned and looked at the large doors that stood before them, directly across from the entrance to the mansion. The music and laughter emanating from behind them was an obvious sign that the ball was in there.

But Louko knew if he went through that door he would be announced… and stared at… and then talked of…. an involuntary shudder shot through the prince. Yes…. he definitely wanted to avoid that.

Turning back to the servant, Louko saw him giving another look. "Beg your pardon?" the servant said in confusion.

"A servants' passage or something? So I can avoid being announced?" Louko cocked his head, wondering if perhaps not every place had as many back passages as his father's castle.

Yet another confused look from the man…

But the man seemed to finally get it, pointing down the hall again. "It's the first door on the left."

Louko nodded and took his time getting there, sweeping his hand through his snarled hair as he approached the small servants' door and marveled at how it wasn't hidden like so many of the ones at home. *You can still turn back, Louko. You don't have to go through with this idiotic idea…*

But why not? *'Cause you're an idiot.*

So with that cheery thought, Louko opened the door and went down the dimly lit passage. The noise of the ball got louder and louder, and he soon found the door leading to the room. Rolling his eyes at his own hesitation, Louko opened the door and was greeted with light and beauty, and most horrifying of all, people.

At least no one took notice of him immediately, as the door was probably often in use tonight. Louko took advantage of this, assimilating as fast as he could into the crowd. Of course, his less than pleasant appearance did him no favors. Perhaps he should have at least tried to comb his hair… but nonetheless, most were busy in conversation, and he was invisible for the moment.

Now for his real reason for coming… if he could find them. Actually, if they really were here at all. What if it had really been just a rumor?

Then you would get what you deserved, believing Mariah's gossip.

That thought didn't last long, however, as he soon caught sight of King Entrais' towering figure, sticking out like a sore thumb as usual.

But where was Princess Astra? Maybe she hadn't come with her brother after all.

Louko intended to find out, and made his way to the king, finding Entrais in the company of a young, red-headed lady standing next to Ent's brother-in-law Soletuph. Wait….was that? *No.* Not Astra. Not in a *dress.*

With an ill-repressed smirk, he approached the small group. They seemed to notice Louko, and Entrais nodded in greeting. "Oh, Louko! There you are."

There he was? Louko was confused. Had Entrais been listening to gossip lately? Louko wasn't sure whether he was more concerned at the king's apparently new habit, or the fact that Louko was still a center of attention in the higher circles.

"King Entrais." Realizing how he had not yet responded to Entrais' greeting, Louko dipped his head in response.. As much as the tall half-elvish king made Louko feel exposed and awkward, Louko *had* explicitly come to the ball to see him and his sister.

An uncomfortable look crossed the king's face, and Louko realized with a wince that he had done it again. Stupid, Entrais hated titles and formality. How quickly Louko fell into old habits.

Then Entrais smiled and gestured to Astra. "*Prince* Louko, this young lady is greatly in need of a dance partner, would you do the honor?"

Louko was about ready to throw up right there. WHAT?! Noooo. Louko never went to these parties for a reason… *dancing.* And *especially* not with Astra. "Oh no, I really couldn't." Louko gave a brittle smile.

"Oh come," Entrais pressed. There was something behind it, and the king gave a glance at the stern-faced Soletuph who was standing by as he wondered what was going on. Meanwhile, Entrais continued with, "I am the guest of honor, and will make a scene if you refuse."

It didn't encourage Louko to see Astra was equally discomfited, but Louko was taken by the preoccupied way she rubbed the bracelet on her wrist. He wasn't sure whether it was the nervous habit that distracted so, or the fact that she was *wearing* jewelry again. Or maybe it was the fact that it was the *same* bracelet he'd seen at the coronation. Of course, it did look rather nice, and he realized she'd never had a chance to wear dresses or jewelry before because she had always been on the run. For some reason, the thought struck him as odd, and it was only Entrais' threat that brought him back from the rabbit trail, as Louko did not want to run the risk of being the main attraction. Not that Entrais really *would* make a scene. Entrais was possibly the least likely of anyone in the room to do so.

And yet, however much he'd rather be impaled with a spear, Louko got the feeling that he ought not to refuse. So, Louko nodded, staring daggers at Entrais even as he offered his hand to Astra.

Astra whispered something to Entrais, but he just shook his head and prodded her on. With a huff she obeyed and put on a smile which, all in all, looked less friendly than her frown. Well, this was going to be an awkward two minutes.

Louko took her hand— like it held a disease— and led her to the dance floor.

That was about the moment Louko remembered he couldn't dance.

With that now in the forefront of his mind, Louko should have been thankful for the slow waltz, but all he could think of was how embarrassing it was going to make this.

Suddenly, his partner's voice broke through his thoughts. "...did you brush your hair?"

Louko was bewildered, and looked up quickly at her with a mystified expression. "Um....no…" He tried to return to his usual unaffected expression, but unfortunately he had to return his eyes to his feet, trying in vain to mimic Astra's footsteps in a way that didn't make things worse. *Wow, what a way to be an idiot, Louko.* "I just got it wet, is all." The silence between the 'no' and the rest of his sentence was extremely awkward, and the abruptness he'd at last finished it with was even worse. Where *was* a sword when he needed one….

Oh right, on his belt… but of course, falling on one in the middle of a dance floor was hardly an acceptable pastime.

"Such manners and grace." Astra's voice was somehow both sarcastic and teasing. "I see you've been busy, Louko."

Finally Louko was able to look up and, feigning astonishment, said, "Astra……? Is that you?" I didn't recognise you under that very blue, very big...dress." A small, smug smile appeared on his lips.

"No. Of course not. Soletuph shape-shifted like me just to test your dancing skills," Astra said dryly. "Of course, this shade of blue looks so much better on him."

"Actually, if you put a few more frills on the hem, it could be *just* your style." Louko grinned, unable to remain unpleasant any longer.

"Funny, I was just about to say the same for you." Astra didn't appear to be joking anymore. "I must say, I'm disappointed—you cleaned up."

"Well, blame the rain." Louko narrowed his eyes then, "At least I'm not wearing a dress."

Astra smiled icily. "That could be arranged."

"How kind."

They danced in silence for a few moments after that, until Louko's gaze caught on Entrais and Soletuph, both staring at them with a grim sort of approval.

"So... Entrais' and So-tough are happy." His voice held no humor, even as he used his old nickname for the Ethian Guard.

"Yes... should we kill Ent now, or later?" Astra asked with sincere interest, singling Entrais out as the culprit. "Or is death too kind...?""

With a raised eyebrow, Louko cast another glance at Entrais and Soletuph before answering, "Hmm...Well, we want him to regret it. That will require skill. Stares while we dance, then how about you start choking and I pretend I poisoned you. Then when no one's looking, we deal with him."

Astra considered this a moment. "Perhaps. The only issue is when they drag you away for execution."

At this point, Louko would rather have the excitement. "Hmm....that would put a damper on things...Wait." He paused for dramatic effect. "What if *I* faint and then you save me? He comes over to help, and then we make our move."

"Sure...but I am not catching you," Astra stated. Then she paused. "Not in this dress."

Louko sighed. "Ha. Ha." *Unimpressed, Astra. Unimpressed.*

However, as the minutes went by, Louko felt less anxious than he had in perhaps months. It could be very calming to plot assassinations. He should do it more often. Too bad that sort of thing was frowned upon in polite societies… But then again, looking around the room, he noticed the odd stare or condescending glare here and there, and realized *he* was frowned upon in *all* societies, so who cared?

Miraculously, the dance ended and they were saved. Astra was quick to return to Soletuph's side, making Louko further suspicious of...well, he didn't know. But something.

"I didn't know you could dance, Louko." Entrais broke into those ever churning thoughts, and Louko looked up at him and gave the best overpowering, obnoxious, annoying, angry smile he could muster, and said between his clamped teeth, "I. Don't." Then his smile disappeared and he glared at the king and added, "Thank you very little, *King Entrais.*"

But Louko's attention wandered as he noticed the growing collection of sideways glances from others as well as the occasional whisper. At first dread settled in his throat, but as he paid closer attention he realized the majority of stares weren't at him...but at Astra. Dread turned to confusion as he wondered: what had he missed?

An conspicuously loud cough brought Louko back. It was Entrais —big surprise. He always was good at being awkward.

"So Louko, when are you intending to leave tomorrow?" Entrais asked.

Now he was baffled. "Um...why?" Were they really in *that much* of a hurry to be rid of him already? He wouldn't be surprised. And yet, the way Entrais had said it...suspicion crept in.

"Should Astra meet you at the dock tomorrow, or are you leaving tonight?" Another pause as Entrais appeared to realize Louko's growing confusion. "I had written to your father and arranged it all...."

"I'm sorry?" Louko's words were terse and impatient amid his rising sense of panic. "Why does Astra need to meet me? What has been arranged?"

"She's going to Merimeethia with you. To. Er. Research in your...library."

Louko had no idea what to say—he was too upset for something as simple as words. Astra?! Going...going to *Merimeethia*? Poking around the library?! It didn't *belong* to her! It belonged to someone else. The thought of it made him irrationally indignant, and he was already in an irritable state as it was. Even more than that, Louko felt panicked. What if she saw... what if she found out about him? She would be under his father's hospitality for who knew how long...

And then, anger. *This* had been why his father had let him come. He would have been made to go anyway. Of course.

Then he realized he hadn't replied to Entrais, and the king was starting to look awfully uncomfortable.

Not that Louko's delayed reply was going to set him at ease. "I'm so glad you asked me before deciding," he said coldly, now beyond exasperated that Entrais had been communicating directly with his father. Why hadn't Entrais just written to *him* and asked personally? Was he ever asked anything? Did anyone ever really give him a choice?

Entrais seemed taken aback, making Louko regret his taut reply.

With a sigh, Louko ran his hand through his-still damp hair. "But I suppose I have nothing better to do," he acquiesced listlessly. Entrais was a king, so Louko got the feeling that this wasn't exactly optional. Besides, he didn't feel like fighting. He would just have to settle with being distant and irritable. Such a shame.

"Thank you. I'm sorry. I thought you knew." Entrais' sincere words made Louko again wonder what was really going on. And for some reason, all Louko could think of was the possibility of an arranged marriage between him and Astra.

Few things could be worse than that, and it didn't help that Louko knew for a fact that his father had on occasion attempted to force someone into the terrible fate of marrying him.

But for now, Louko just waved his hand and bit his tongue from saying something he would regret. He'd talked himself into trouble enough for one night, and as panicked as he now felt....they *were* in public. He needed to pretend to behave.

"What are you two gossiping about?" Soletuph's voice, rare as it was to hear, took a moment to register. He had come from behind Louko to stand near Ent.

"About you, of course," Louko so easily slipped back into the banter he and Soletuph had developed during The War. They had a friendly sort of hate for each other. It worked well to distract him from his thousand fears.

Soletuph grunted. "I suppose I'm more interesting than you, at the very least."

Rolling his eyes, the prince replied, "So true. No one *ever* talks about me when I'm not around." He noted how Entrais' face turned a strange shade of red.

Astra, on the other hand, seemed to miss the implication. She had positioned herself carefully between Entrais and Soletuph and didn't appear to be paying much attention to the conversation. She looked more a prisoner than a guest, and an absent one at that.

"So, Astra." *Idiot.* "I hear we are to be stuck together for the unbearable future." Louko was sure Astra needed to be brought out of whatever world she was hiding in...and yet, he was definitely not the one for the job.

Astra's gaze flicked towards him, then up at her brother. There was a hesitation before she answered dryly. "So it would seem."

Well done, idiot. Well done. If you're going to be stuck with her, you might try and behave at least a little.

"If you're trying to make Ent feel guilty, Louko, you're doing an excellent job," Soletuph droned.

Entrais' hesitant laugh only made everything more uncomfortable.

And, of course, Louko felt the need to try and deflate the situation. Or inflate...whichever. "See, this is why I wanted to stay in Litash." He kept his voice purposely monotone. "...such lively conversation."

"Not to mention all the lovely people," Astra grumbled.

"Yes, that too." Louko's reply came out much more sincere than he had meant, so he quickly added, "And it's not like half the flora are trying to kill you or anything," referencing the *lovely* habit Litash had of housing man-eating flowers, creatures, and just...general unpleasant things.

Out of all of them, Soletuph reacted the most—and all he did was snort, contrasting against Astra and Ent's weak, distracted smiles.

"As I said, lively conversation." Louko raised an eyebrow. "Here I was thinking good company and food would improve the mood. My mistake."

Astra looked sidelong at Soletuph and gave the closest thing to a smirk Louko had seen since before...well... "Good company, eh?"

"Oh, my bad. Should I go?" Louko pretended to be innocently offended.

"Don't be so rude, Louko. Just because you can't handle Astra's manners doesn't mean you can leave us to deal with them alone." Soletuph's monotone always made it hard to tell when he was joking. Nonetheless Louko had learned it was usually implied—a stark contrast to his sister Jade, who had always been sincere and earnest, going hand in hand with Entrais.

"Oh, my bad," Louko said again as he just stared at Astra, unimpressed. Then he turned to Entrais, realizing something he had not even thought of before. "Where's Jade?"

He wasn't very good at conversations, but he had been there at the wedding and coronation, and they'd been inseparable. Jade had not been well, but she'd been improving, so Louko had thought. It was odd she was not here now, and he started noticing the dark circles under the Litashian king's eyes. Usually Louko kept a rather close eye on politics, but being back in Merimeethia had become more like living under a rock than a life—not surprising, after the stunt he had pulled.

"Oh, um," Ent stumbled, pressing his lips together. "She was needed in the capitol and couldn't spare the time to travel out here."

Clearly that was an avoidance tactic, and Louko didn't buy it. But Astra went very still, eyes fixed on some distant object. Apparently

34

Louko's talent of picking tactful subjects had struck again.

He wasn't, however, desperate enough to be thankful when another guest and her husband appeared. Both gave over-flourished bows, and Louko barely kept himself from rolling his eyes.

Nonetheless, he took that as his cue to make himself scarce, deciding it was best not to intrude any longer. Instead, he would chance the dangerous journey to get a drink, knowing full well he probably would *never* make it.

Surprisingly, Louko had gotten rather close to his target, when he heard a birdlike voice behind him. "Prince Louko?" It was a genuine surprise mixed with a hint of disdain. Louko's favorite.

He readied himself and turned, putting on a polite smile, though dismay was hidden beneath."Miss—"

"Havlir. *Lady* Havlir," The parrot lifted her chin—or was it beak? —and looked down at him. The scent of a very strong tropical flower embedded itself in Louko's nostrils, and he felt like he'd just been poisoned.

"Lady Havlir, have we met?" He asked, putting on a mask of politeness.

"Everyone is acquainted with you, Prince Louko—or at least, your reputation. I'm afraid your charms will not win over anyone here— except, perhaps, Princess Astra." She took a sip from the glass she held in her hand, seeming quite pleased. "The two of you seem to have a great deal in common...perhaps too much."

Louko had three complaints. First, he was wondering what idiot had spread lies about his charms, because last time he'd checked, his were severely lacking. Second, there was no point to this conversation

35

other than the lady poisoning Louko with some deadly flower.
Third….no no no. Was the lady hinting at them plotting something, or at
a marriage?

All that being said, Louko did not want to spend a moment
longer in the poisonous parrot's company, and so shoved down his
fears and simply said, "I'm so glad you have been warned of me. If you
get the time, perhaps put a reminder out about that stench-ridden
venom you're wearing. Now if you'll excuse me, I am quite thirsty and
could use a drink. And I do believe your perfume is trying to kill me." He
nodded and walked away, making it to the table with refreshments and
pouring himself some punch. One sip and he decided that the punch
was put to better use as decor than as a refreshment.

Fortunately, no one else seemed to see him as he kept his head
down and made his way to a nice little corner where he could observe
others without being too noticeable himself. He could see Entrais in the
distance, but not Soletuph or Astra. Astra, of course, was too short to
spot in such a crowd. Soletuph, on the other hand… Louko scanned the
crowd and found the blonde head making its way across the room.
Every now and then, he got a glimpse of Astra's red hair alongside.

But then he saw two ladies heading for Astra, and he recognized
that vulture-like look in their eyes.

Why can't you just walk away, idiot? Leave it alone. It's not your
problem to deal with. Of course, Louko convinced himself he was
stepping in only to stop Soletuph from getting involved—as the shape-
shifter hated gossips, trivialities, and was likely to use less than socially
acceptable force. Why had Entrais and Astra brought him again?

With that lovely though in mind, Louko walked right into it just before the ladies landed on their prey.

Astra looked immensely uncomfortable. Ironic that someone so fearless in battle should cower before these silk-stuffed gossips. Of course, Louko couldn't exactly say he was comfortable himself; all he could think of was the echoes of Lady Havlir's comment, and Louko wondered what exactly he was missing as he dove headfirst into the fray.

"Princess Astra! So nice to see you out and about!" The first lady set upon her without hesitation, and Louko wasn't sure if vulture, or puffed peacock was a better description.

Astra's smile was brittle. "It's been a while," was all she said.

"What have you been doing, dear? It must be dreadfully boring in that castle of yours, and I do find that being away from society tends to make one imagine all sorts of dreadful things... don't you?" The lady shared a smirk with her vulturous companion.

The other silk-stuffed gossip cleared her throat. "But I hear you're planning a trip? I do understand you don't really know your way about the social circles yet, but perhaps a better choice of companion? I wouldn't want you to soil your already...interesting name." She smiled and cooed like a peacock alright, but feeding on the dying or wounded was *definitely* what this lady was doing. "Of course, maybe even Prince Louko's reputation would be an improvement to yours."

What did *that* mean? Louko decided to say *something,* anything. "I could say the same about you, Lady Izla. I heard something about your husband remaining neutral during The War. I do hope you explained that to your king. Or his sister, while you're here already." He gave a grating smile, finally glad that Mariah's gossip at the table paid off for something. And yet he had still missed whatever was going on with Astra…

Astra's gaze flicked towards him, then back towards the lady. Louko noticed that the princess' fake smile was much reduced.

Lady Izla's companion tried to take the offensive. "But what family housed the two princes during their exile? Certainly no Litashian family…"

Though he had fully been expecting this, something in Louko still snapped and his face hardened. "Well, who accused a man and banished him simply because he was related? It could be said you created The War, you know. But why must we argue about technicalities?" He hid the regret he instantly felt. Ugh. He had said too much. *Idiot.* Why did he have such knee-jerk reactions??

A chilly silence fell over the two ladies, but it was Astra who looked shocked.

"Well," she breathed. "I believe I could use a bit of fresh air. If you ladies would please excuse me." Astra nodded more than curtsied, then slipped away. Only Soletuph followed her.

"The truth comes out," Lady Izla cooed in triumph, smiling to Louko as she repeated, "the truth comes out….good evening, *Prince Louko.*" They both bowed and walked off, leaving Louko wishing more than anything he had stayed home.

He shouldn't have brought *him* up in front of Astra, not after what Tyron had done to her. What an idiot Louko had been. He knew he never should have gotten involved—it would have been better if she had had to deal with them herself. No. It would have been best if Louko had never come at all… and now he was going to have to be stuck with her for weeks at the least...or rather, *she* would be stuck with *him*.

Louko felt as if the room was pressing in around him, having brought up his own worst topic. He needed some air as well, so he headed for the door—but the one in the opposite direction of where Astra had fled.

<u>Astra:</u>

Astra found a balcony that opened out from one of the rooms and over a small garden She was thankful the rain has subsided. From out here, she could still hear the jumble of chatter and laughter, but it was distant and indistinct. Astra leaned against the rail and looked up at the night sky as she tried not to think of her ever-present guard. While she knew Soletuph well, and while he was much more discreet than eight soldiers in full regalia, she hated the feeling of being watched. Knowing her actions had earned it did nothing to help.

Her attention drifted from her guard in the shadows to the stars in the sky. They were faded in contrast to the brilliance of the moons. Both were out in full, swirling with color and undeterred by the stray wisps of cloud that wafted by. They seemed to be watching the whole world. Could they see Tyron?

That was at least some good that could come from her exile. She would have the chance to track him down without drawing attention to any of her family. And, as the ladies inside had reminded her, the fallen princes *had* once lived in Merimeethia; surely they'd left some information behind.

That also called into question Louko's comment: did he believe they had been innocent? The thought disturbed Astra. She recalled that, though Louko had fought wholeheartedly against Euracia, he had never been involved against the brother. Had Louko known them? Was he old enough to remember the time they had spent in his home?

Astra had never considered this before. It cast her almost-friend in a different light, one she did not like. Yet, it was hard to tell what Louko thought, much less what side he was on. He was secretive, cynical, and mocking—not a winning combination for anyone trying to make friends.

"You look worse than Louko." Soletuph's voice cut through her thoughts.

Astra knew Soletuph well enough to know that he was asking if she was alright. "I'll pretend that's a compliment," was her sarcastic response.

"So you are going to look for him?" The change in tone was abrupt, even for Soletuph.

It told Astra that he was not referring to Louko, but to Tyron. It was understandable. As Captain of the Guard, Soletuph surely knew what Astra had said in the Proceedings Hall—and as Tyron's nephew, Soletuph likely had his own opinions on the matter.

"I suppose I'll have nothing better to do up there." Astra shrugged.

Soletuph sighed. "Jade says we should let the dead lie…" There was a long pause before he added tartly, "I say we should kill the ghosts, too. I only wish I could come with you to help."

Astra did not know how to reply. She felt one hand go to the cuff around her wrist. "I think Jade needs you more than I will," she finally said.

Soletuph said nothing. He didn't even have to for Astra to know how much he worried for his sister.

Minutes of silence slid by, and Astra decided she had taken up enough of Soletuph's time for one evening. So she picked up her head and squared her shoulders, nodded to Soletuph, then went back inside. She was more careful to steer clear of conversation this time; having Soletuph glaring from behind her probably helped. Fortunately Ent wasn't hard to find, being a head taller than any in the room and wearing a highly polished crown.

Astra found Entrais finishing up a conversation with some noble. When the nobleman bowed and began to turn away, Astra took it as her cue to approach. Her brother looked strained, and that was putting it mildly. She wished she didn't add so much to his already heavy burdens. Or was she the brunt of it?

"Are you alright? You look pale." Ent's eyes surveyed her carefully, the stormy grey always full of worry.

"Just tired," Astra lied with some semblance of a smile. Then more quietly, she asked, "Do you think it is late enough for me to leave yet?" Ent knew these sort of things much better than she did.

"Yes." Ent looked tense. "By all means, please."

Please? Astra tried not to wince.

"Are you alright?" His brow furrowed.

"You already asked that." Astra gave him a dry look to cover her tracks. "I think I should be asking you."

Soletuph's sigh emanated from behind her. "You two are the worst."

41

"Thank you for your input." Ent sounded so tired. He returned his attention to Astra and said, "You just winced…"

"And you just…" Astra gave a loose gesture up and down towards her brother. "...concern me," she finished, only partially in sarcasm.

Ent didn't smile. He never did anymore—and Astra wasn't sure if he just didn't get the joke...or if he felt as bad as he looked.

Astra swallowed hard and searched for something else to say. She used to make an art out of coaxing out Ent's laugh. Apparently, she'd lost her touch.

"I think I will retire for the night," Astra said, noting the host making his way towards Entrais. "Could you pass on my regards?" If they were wanted, that was…

"Of course." He nodded, still watching her carefully, "Get some rest."

"Thank you," Astra murmured. Then, even more softly, added a, "Goodnight."

"Goodnight, Slip," he echoed.

With that, Astra turned and walked away. She wrapped her hand around her wrist, wishing she could have wrapped her arms around him instead.

CHAPTER III

Astra:

"You already sent my horse?!"

Ent shifted uncomfortably under her stare, his boots scraping on the wooden pier that led out to the Sea of Triscri.

Astra didn't mean to sound so angry, but it felt better than crying. She knew that it wasn't Ent sending Dannsair first that made her so upset. It was only one more thing on top of everything else: the weight of exile, the fear of her untameable Gifting, the separation from Ent, the fact that her parents hadn't even so much as written a letter to say goodbye…

She turned away, hands tightening around the little satchel full of red bronze cuffs her brother had given her. Just in case she broke another one.

"Sorry," she murmured as she turned back, accidentally saying it at the same time as Ent. She gave a half smile. Ent never changed.

"I can still leave alone, it's really alright by me." The annoying tenor of Louko's voice broke through.

"It's bad enough I'm abandoning you in Merimeethia." Ent's voice was soft as he switched to some other language.

Astra's mind switched for her. **"You're not abandoning me,"** she murmured in reply. **"I know you are doing this to help."**

The look he gave her was tortured, as if he wanted to say something else, but only said, **"I'm sorry. I'll get this figured out."**

"You have nothing to be sorry for," Astra insisted stubbornly.

43

If this was anyone's fault, it was hers. **"And I know you will find a way. I trust you."**

The hug that followed was sudden and unexpected, full of force and emotion. **"I will get you back. I will,"** he whispered.

Astra let herself give in and hug him back as tightly as she could, but she swallowed the childish wish that would have her pleading for some other way. She didn't want to go. She didn't want to leave him. Even in the palace, where she so rarely saw him, at least she knew he was near.

"Wow. This is awkward." Louko's voice shattered the touching moment.

Astra wished Louko would leave without her. Reluctantly, she let go of Ent and shouldered her satchel, turning towards the boat that waited at the end of the pier.

"We could have gone by Dragon if it wasn't for you," she pointed out.

Louko huffed. "That thing nearly ate me last time!"

"Only because you have no idea how to keep your mouth shut."

"Not my fault it had no sense of humor." The grumpy prince turned to go up the gangplank.

Raising her eyebrow, Astra stopped to look at Ent and give some attempt at humor. "Thank you for condemning me to that for the next two weeks." She reminded herself that she was lucky she didn't have any guards coming, too.

Ent hesitated, returning to Litashian as he said, "Uh…my bad… good luck." He put both hands on her shoulders so that she was looking him squarely in the eye. "I'll get you back, don't worry—write every

44

month. I don't care where you are. Just please write," he whispered.

Trying to swallow her whirling emotions, Astra nodded.

"But I *will* get you back. You're exiled, not banished. There is a big difference in Litashian law—apparently. So don't worry. I'll get it all sorted out." He tried to put on a hopeful expression, but worry seeped through.

Astra hesitated, partially to stall for any spare second she could, and partially to make sure her voice would not crack when she asked, **"Could you say goodbye to Mother and Father for me?"** Any betrayal she had felt from their absence was overcome by the desperate need for some kind of closure.

"Of course." The reply was strangled.

"Thank you." Her voice cut off without her permission. She wanted to say goodbye, but the word lodged in her throat and refused to budge. She had never had to say it to Ent like this before.

"It's alright," he said softly, sweeping a stray strand of her red hair out of her face and tucking it behind her ear. **"I know. Just go."**

So she did. Slowly, Astra turned away and followed after Louko as he boarded the ship.

As the two reached the deck, the prince readjusted the travel sack slung over his shoulder. "Alright. Now you stay on one side, and I'll stay on the other. No one will have to know we're even on the same boat," he muttered darkly.

Before Astra could give any kind of sarcastic response, their widely grinning captain interrupted them, calloused hands on his hips as he said, "Now, yew par o' luv birds, I'll 'ave to ask yew ta go below decks whilst we cast off."

Astra and Louko gave each other a skeptical glance and headed for the ladder. Astra let Louko go first, just so she could have a moment of fresh air before being stuck with him for the rest of the day. Well, for the next three days. The sea would take two days to cross and then they would have another day of fighting their way upstream towards the village of Getwyn. With one last look at the stretched out Sea of Triscri, she climbed down into the hold.

"Cozy," observed Louko sarcastically. His witticisms were already wearing on her, but looking around at the low roof, the dim lighting, and the grimy floor, Astra decided the musty quarters were rather deserving of such disparagement.

In truth, Astra couldn't help the way her stomach knotted at being trapped in this small space. What if her Gifting went out of control while on the boat? She tried to banish the thought.

"I call top bunk." Astra said, pulling herself onto the upper bed. She never did like the feeling of being underneath someone else while sleeping. It was more vulnerable.

Louko just groaned and said, "And here I thought I'd be spending time away from annoying siblings…"

Astra did not envy the prince his two siblings, Keeshiff and Mariah. "Surely I'm not *that* bad…"

Louko just rolled his eyes and plopped himself on the bottom bunk. "I suppose it depends on the day, really…"

"On my day, or Keeshiff's?"

A sigh emanated from the below her. "I don't care."

Astra took that as Louko saying—in his most polite way—"please shut up".

The ship began to move then, giving a slight lurch before steadying itself as they pulled away from the dock. Thankfully, the boat ride wasn't a long one. After spending so much time in various prisons, Astra did not like being confined to the indoors. Ships, with their smell and stale food and lack of sunlight, were only that much worse.

Especially if her only cellmate was Louko.

***

All of Astra's premonitions were proven false. The days on the ship were actually far worse than she thought they'd be. Poor weather led to them being confined below decks while the small ship bobbed violently on the waves. Louko didn't seem to take this well, becoming more and more irritable over the course of their journey. It didn't help that half the sailors seemed to think that they were eloping to Merimeethia. The last straw came when one poor sailor brought it up on the second day. The prince had turned a peculiar shade of red and started off on a half-comical tirade.

"No! Astra and I are *not* eloping! I was dragged into escorting her like I'm some sort of maid, when I thought usually *I* was the one in need of escorts and guards and all that nonsense. I mean, really, why in the world would *anyone* think that?? Do I have to throw her—wait a minute...that wouldn't work... I amend my statement—Does *she* have to throw *me* overboard to make the point clear??"

As tempting as the idea was, Astra had kept her mouth shut. Louko had certainly given enough defense for the both of them. However, it did make her realize that the prince might not know about

47

the letter that Ent had received nearly a month before the Court incident. Signed in Louko and Omath's—Louko's father—names.

So Astra brought it up.

They were both lying on their bunks after supper. Louko was pretending to read—it was far too dark to actually read—and Astra was fiddling with her new leather coat. Ent had given it to her to protect against the Merimeethian rain.

"So, Louko..."

"I'm reading." The interruption came quickly.

Astra felt like she was dealing with a toddler. She probably was. "We both know it's too dark for you to see anything."

He huffed. "You don't have to be an Elf to have good eyesight."

"And you don't have to be very good at discerning lies to know you're fibbing."

Louko sounded worried. "...really?"

Half of her wondered what else Louko was hiding. The other half commented as if addressing a child, "There's one lantern in the entire hold and it's nowhere near your bunk."

"Oh."

"Can I talk now?"

"You seem to be doing just fine as is." Louko remained as charming as ever.

"As I was trying to ask," Astra proceeded. "Do you recall the letter you and your father sent Entrais?"

There was an abrupt silence, and a second later Louko's head popped out from under the bunk, looking very, very dismayed, "Um..." He laughed nervously. "What letter?"

Astra leaned out and looked at him. "It had your signature on it."

He blinked at her.

"Well, uh, I think it might be the source of our sailors' misconceptions about our...relationship." Realizing he had probably never seen the letter, Astra suddenly didn't quite know how to say this.

"What??" Louko's face paled. "Please tell me that is *not* why you are coming to Merimeethia?"

Astra nearly fell off her bunk and screamed the word no. Instead, in her boredom, she thought better of it. This could be mildly amusing. "Ent didn't tell you?"

Louko's silence was actually blissful and his face more blank than she'd ever seen it. "Um...." She watched as the words passed over and over in his brain, trying to register this possible horror.

For the sake of her own dignity, Astra did not continue the joke. "Relax. I am not going to Merimeethia to marry you," she said, loudly enough for any eavesdroppers.

Louko's face melted in a relief which was promptly burned off by fury.

Before he could say anything, Astra went on. "But your father did send a rather, uh, flattering letter. To which Ent gave a courteous, negative reply."

"Why you little liar, I could throw you off the ship right now!" He made as if to get up, but reason—if not just pure embarrassment—kept him from fulfilling his threat. That, and perhaps the knowledge that—as he had so eagerly explained to the sailor earlier—she would be more likely to throw *him* off.

Astra didn't bother to move. "I'm not lying. There truly was a letter."

It took a few awkward minutes of silence, but Louko finally settled back out of view and seemed to calm down. "So... what did it say about me?" There was an odd twist to the voice, a childish sort of curiosity that was different from Louko's usual sarcasm.

Astra laid back on her bed. "It talked all about your exploits in battle and how brave you were. It even praised your *great* political mind." Ent had had great fun reading the letter.

Louko sounded sort of wistful as he replied, "Well, will wonders never cease." Then he added almost too quickly, "I was never told I had any mind at all!"

Somehow, the joke seemed forced.

"Well, don't let it go to your head. The letter also said Keeshiff was available, if Ent would not accept you."

"You know, you could always marry him, kill him, and take the throne of Merimeethia for yourself. Then when your brother gets annoying, you can wallop him," he replied very matter-of-factly, before adding, "Or kill him, too."

It took a moment to register that Louko wasn't serious. "As always, I am inspired by the depths of your familial love."

"Aren't we an inspiration, though? I am so glad our high standards of love and respect give you and Ent something to look up to," he said, with his annoying laugh.

"I can't say I'm sad that he and I don't meet those standards."

"Me either." Louko's voice, unusually soft, came from the bottom bunk.

They both paused.

"Uh…Goodnight," Louko announced abruptly.

With nothing else she could say, Astra echoed his response. "Goodnight."

Louko:

Fresh air and life greeted Louko as he went above deck. It was a beautiful day to be setting ashore, and he would almost enjoy the remaining ride home. Suddenly the whole feeling soured. Ugh… he was almost home. He touched his sword and again thought of who had given it to him. Almost home...and with Astra. If only it was *anyone* but Astra! Except Ent… or Soletuph… or...

"The 'orses are waitin' ashore." The captain informed Astra as she emerged behind Louko. "I've bin told they arrived yesterday, an' 'ave bin given feed an waterin' an a full day's rest."

Perhaps Louko did prefer being misconceived as Astra's fiance; at least then he wasn't invisible. Though he still was relieved that such a thought was indeed a misconception.

"Thank you, sir." Astra said.

What? No snobby remark? Louko had half expected Astra to change when the Elves had given her the title of princess. But then again, Louko was used to his sister, Mariah.

"Well, shall we?" Irritable sarcasm dripped unpleasantly from his voice, and Louko sort of wished that he had tried to put on a better face. But if this was going to be a disaster, than it might as well be his own stupid fault. He pretended it wasn't really because he didn't want to get his hopes up.

Oh, what are you even doing, anymore, idiot?

With that question haunting his thoughts, Louko led the way down the gangplank as he ignored the captain's icy glare.

At the bottom of the plank, a couple men had Dannsair—who did not look happy—and Louko's borrowed horse. Dannsair was Astra's mare, and *not* the most friendly thing in the world, as Louko still had the sore spots to prove. Louko tried not to think of old times as he noted how the *evil* mare wore the old, specialized tack that Astra always used during The War: a simple pad in place of a saddle, with several attachment points for all of the princess' gear.

Entrais had given it to her.

"How many men did you lose trying to keep that one down?" Louko asked, with an overdose of annoying cheeriness.

The men didn't find this amusing. Or maybe it was just him?

Before Louko could say anything else, Astra rescued the moment by taking her very perturbed horse and speaking softly to it, allowing the other men to quietly flee. Louko chuckled a little, knowing he would have once been just as quick to get out of the mare's way. Now, he wasn't sure if he was more comfortable around Dannsair, or just didn't care anymore.

"You know, I think your horse is just spoiled." His grin widened when Dannsair gave him a more rotten look than her owner. It still unnerved Louko at how... intelligent Astra's horse was. He still didn't understand how the animal managed to make such expressions. Perhaps she watched Astra very carefully.

"I mean, really," Louko continued as he mounted his bay steed, "look at that glare she's giving me. It has *"Spoiled Rotten"* written all over that painted mug of hers!" His further argument was only evolving Dannsair's body language further and further into hostile territory. He would have been more guarded against the horse, if Astra hadn't just mounted. Dannsair wouldn't risk hurting Astra to get to him… right?

"No. It's your manners. I'm afraid she finds you terribly grating." Astra managed a small playful smile.

Rolling his eyes, Louko just sighed dramatically, "Well, it's not my fault she's not used to the polish of Merimeethian conduct." And before Astra could respond, Louko nudged his horse into a trot and entered the small village of Getwyn.

Louko was, of course, fascinated with the place. It was small and rather rugged looking, the people in it bearing the marks of war even as politics seemed to have moved on around them: A man without a leg. A woman with one eye and a scar that clearly showed it was no infection that had taken it. Even the village itself held marks, the houses looking made from whatever had been around at the time. Nonetheless, it still seemed to thrive more than some of the places in Merimeethia. Maybe the rest of the country was done in by the swamps and the mud and the rain….Or maybe it was just the people.

Litash had always had such a fighting spirit, and as Louko rode quietly through with Astra by his side, he thought of the differences even between the two of them. Yes, Merimeethians did not seem to have much going for them. Even in this small place, there was bustle and trade and laughter. Perhaps it was just Louko, but he couldn't really say the same of anywhere in Merimeethia.

***

OF SHADE AND SHADOW

Every day that they travelled northwards into the Forest of Riddles, Louko felt colder. The forest that straddled the border between Litash and its surrounding countries was thick, almost otherworldly in its unnatural quiet. But even the twilight woods could not hide the shift in the air. He always forgot how much milder Litash was, and how soggy and unpleasantly cloudy Merimeethia was. Even when the sun shined there it was cold and unforgiving. Yes, Merimeethia was definitely home. It mirrored Louko perfectly.

The mysteriousness of Litash and its many beasts began fading the closer they came to the border. While the Forest of Riddles stretched into Merimeethia, the wonder seemed to diminish outside of Litash. Louko found himself even missing the Shadow faeries—who seemed even more annoying than himself. Most people hated Litash for it's mystical beasts and powerful Gifting; but Louko rather liked it. Even if it meant the occasional life or death appearance of a strange creature, Litash and the sword he carried reminded him of the adventures they'd had, and the glimpse of free—*snap out of it! Idiot. What an insufferable little daydreamer you are.*

That being said.... Each day brought them closer; each day made Louko more irritable and no doubt unbearable. They'd reach the border today, and with every step they took, Louko's urge to just turn around and run grew deeper and deeper. He was being so childish, so idiotic. He would just have to get used to the fact that life wasn't all fairy tales and amazing happy endings. Sometimes you had to go home and live out your terribly boring, pathetic existence. It was apparently all he was really good at doing.

"Louko?" Astra's voice rang through Louko's wishful brain, jerking him out of his reverie. "Why did you stop?"

Louko twisted around and saw the barest etching of worry on her face. Oops. She thought he'd heard something, probably.

"Just enjoying the familiar scenery. We're just about at the border," he said, noting winter-like gloom coming through the trees more and more as up ahead the foliage was thinning. Louko had stopped to get one last gulp of the freedom he'd once had here in the forest without even registering it.

"Yes. Such beauty," Astra said dryly, again breaking the dreary spell hanging over Louko.

They continued on, and just as Louko had said, in just a little under twenty minutes they found themselves where the trees changed. Giant darkwoods hung with moss and vines gave way abruptly to the entwined greybarks and the wet foliage they guarded—a shift too sudden to be purely natural. One more pace, and they would be in Merimeethia.

"Well, then," Louko said, not willing to spur his horse on. He didn't have the courage anymore. "Ladies first." He turned to face her and smirked, but she didn't seem amused.

Astra looked oddly grim, hesitating before finally urging Dannsair forward and out onto the rain-soaked turf of Merimeethia. It occurred to Louko that the princess had likely never traveled so far without Entrais there to protect her. Was that what was going through her head? Louko felt slightly guilty for having his silly problems feel more important. Then again, he always was quite the selfish one, wasn't he? At least he was living up to the rumors.

"Well. At least it isn't raining…" Louko murmured as he also spurred his horse forward into the misty afternoon. "But who knows if that will keep. We still have a good four day journey to my father's palace." He looked up at the sky, peering at it suspiciously as if it could hear him. Rain was about the only good thing about Merimeethia…. But it had too much of it, so as much as the sandy country of Pershizar envied that, Louko really would rather live in their desert. But perhaps the truth of it was that he would rather be any place on Eatris than headed back home. Home meant…. Well, never mind what it meant. Louko kicked his horse into a longer stride, and wished his thoughts would be left in the mud. Oh, the drama.

It was a little later than usual when they stopped for the night, Louko not really wanting to press their luck with the weather. The boat had been enough trouble already. Of course, it could have just felt later, due to Merimeethia having fewer daylight hours than Litash—a little oddity Louko had noticed in his several travels between the countries. Not that he cared much. He only seemed to observe the useless things, now, didn't he?

Without so much as a word, Astra got firewood, and they spent the night in pleasantly awkward silence. Louko didn't want to talk and it appeared that neither did Astra. The fire was a pathetic warmth against the Merimeethian air, leaving both of them sitting there shivering. He'd almost offered her his coat or something stupid like that, but was afraid of disrupting the silence, and he really didn't feel like carrying on a conversation. The closer they got to his father's palace, the more and more out of sorts he was beginning to feel. Emotions were such annoying things; only home seemed more annoying.

Louko tried to make it look like he was doing something—anything... So he began scanning the skies for clouds that might hold rain. Merimeethians had a knack for telling the difference, and Louko had rubbed that in Ent's face a couple more times than necessary back in the good old days.

To his surprise, he actually saw two brave little stars peaking out with the dim moons, shining obstinately and warding off the stray clouds that hung around them, shrouding the rest of their kind in shade and shadow. Then a cloud passed over, and the two stars disappeared into the night. Hm. Louko took in some of the cold air, letting the aimless train of thought go along with the puff of foggy breath. He'd enjoy this peace while it lasted.

They were both awoken in the early morning by the soft drizzling of rain, which Louko sighed and murmured at. Of course. Naturally. He'd been too distracted with the pathetic little stars to *actually* take a close look and read the clouds before drifting off. They hadn't put the oil tarp over the tent and now they were all soggy *and* still had to ride in the rain.

"How pleasant." Astra muttered as she rolled up her bed and pulled her cloak on over her coat.

Louko rolled his eyes, "Home sweet home. Have to love it." Or hate it. Personal preference. Louko was feeling the latter at the moment.

With only complaints about the rain, the two mounted their horses and were off. Louko hoped that by getting an early start, they would get out of the rain sooner. Not that such a hope was realistic.

The sweet smell of fresh rain was probably refreshing to Astra—

as unpleasant as the rain itself was—and Louko wondered what she thought of Merimeethia. Did she find it as dreary and full of gloom and despair as he did? Or was it just his experience in the country? Or his own knack for drama? He did like to play things up, as he was so often reminded by those around him. However, Astra's opinion of his home was nonetheless an intriguing thought, and Louko spent the rest of the day's journey trying to view the land through a stranger's eyes. It was amusing, but more importantly, distracting. Viewing it as a stranger made him feel like a visitor and less like an intruder. How did that even make sense?

The rain let up about noon, to their relief, and all was quiet for the rest of the day. Louko stopped them a little earlier, only because they did need to get dry and warm after the hard day's travel. Besides, Louko was familiar with this little hollow. He'd spent a night in it when he'd first run away from home, and he couldn't help his ridiculous sentimentality at the memory. *Such good times...*

After the fire had been built and the tent had been set up, the two sat finishing their small dinner. Louko had forgotten how nothing ever tasted as good when it was all soggy with rain. Maybe it was disinterest in the meal that prompted him to speak. Maybe it was boredom. Either way, he wasn't sure what possessed him to say:

"You know, if I ever was on the run, I think I would hide here." Well. On the run *again*. But that would never happen.

....idiot.

Astra blinked at him, chewing her mouthful slowly and then swallowing. The poor girl tried hard to make his awkward statement into something conversable. Glancing around the hollow, she commented,

"It seems to be well-sheltered. Definitely small enough to be missed from the outside."

"It's not far from some old ruins—a duke used to live there about seventy-something years ago, I think. Tried to overthrow my great-grandfather and ended up dead instead...but it makes a great spot to make a camp." *Wow. What a conversation, idiot.*

"Oh." Another slow reply. "I suppose it wouldn't take long for a manor to fall to ruins in this climate."

"Nope..." Louko, not willing to make himself into any more of a fool in one evening, just nodded and finished the last bite of his food.

But now Astra seemed intent on carrying on some sort of conversation, for she turned the subject and asked, "Are you glad to be going home after so long?"

It was so abrupt, and so unexpected, that Louko's first reaction was that of apprehension. He stiffened, but at the very same instant caught himself and flashed his most *charming* smile, replying, "Oh yes, I miss Keeshiff *so* much." And rolled his eyes in emphasis. If only that were the extent of things...

Astra only shrugged off his response. "What about your sister?"

And here Louko had thought bringing up sore topics was his thing. But really he was a little too surprised by Astra's pressing. "How did you know I have a sister?"

"I've been to your home before." Astra said, looking at him oddly. Then she seemed to recall something. "I guess you weren't there at the time. It was right before we met you."

"Oh. Right," was all Louko said. "I see." He didn't like where these questions were leading, so with a fake yawn, he stretched and

59

settled himself in his bedroll. "Well, I'm tired. With any grace it will rain on us tonight…" he added optimistically.

Astra looked at him a moment, making him uncomfortable. *Please, no more questions.*

"Alright. Goodnight," she said, but got up from her bedroll instead of laying down.

Louko sat up, "What are you doing?" he asked, confused.

"I haven't tended to Dannsair," replied Astra quietly.

Louko's eyes narrowed, but he said nothing. If she went away, there would be no questions, so that was a good thing… right? With a strange reluctance, he settled back into the bed roll, trying to keep his mind off of what going home was going to entail.

CHAPTER IV

Astra:

The weather wasn't much better for the remainder of the journey. Astra was just wondering if it was possible for the rain to get any worse when the thin remnants of forest they were riding through gave way to open fields. They were strange spaces, so full of rocks that it seemed they grew stone instead of crops. The mouldering stubble of long-harvested grains only added to the misery of the view. Then, in the distance, she saw the parapets of distant city walls through the gloom. It was hard to tell if she was imagining it on account of the sheer amount of water dripping off her hood.

"Are we here?" she asked Louko.

All she got was a nod from the prince, who was hunched over his horse.

Throughout the entire day, Louko had acted more like he was going to the gallows than home. Now, it was hard to tell what he was thinking. Both of them had wrapped their cloaks tightly around themselves to try and escape the rain. Astra wondered if he was as soaked as she was.

The two entered the city of Melye, and Astra was glad when the mud roads slowly morphed into cobblestone streets. The clay terrain that they had struggled through for the last few days was very slippery for the horses and she worried about the strain on their tendons.

It hadn't been raining so torrentially last time Astra had been to the city, and yet, there were just as many people out. In Litash, such a storm would have driven everybody to their homes for refuge. Here, the market square was still bustling. That's when Astra realized that she was no longer getting wet; though the thunder of rain could still be heard, there was no rain to be seen. Amazed, she looked up to find a giant, beautiful glass ceiling—or something similarly transparent. Astra had not noticed it the last time—of course, last time she had entered the city, it had been under different circumstances, and she *had* been blindfolded…

Astra and Louko navigated the crowds and streets alike to get to the castle gates. There was no glass cover there, and both travelers struggled to get their hoods up. A guard came out of the gatehouse, a long coat protecting him and his metal armor.

Louko dismounted stiffly and went up to speak quietly with the man, almost as though hoping Astra wouldn't be able to hear them.

"Is my father waiting?"

"Yes. You're late. He was expecting you a day ago."

Astra watched Louko shift his weight from one foot to the other. "The rain delayed us."

"Well, get in then, before it kills me, too."

And with that, they were let in. Louko never remounted his horse, only leading it slowly by the reins.

Astra didn't like any of this. The guard's out-of-place response added to the foreboding of previous experience. Last time she was here, she'd been imprisoned, along with her mother— and this time, there would be no Ent to help her. Though Astra trusted Louko a fair bit, it seemed like he was more worried than she was. But the worst part, she decided, was knowing she was following in… *his* footsteps. Tyron had come here when exiled, and now Astra was doing the same. A bitter taste filled her mouth as she dismounted and followed Louko.

Once more, Astra found herself out of the rain. It appeared they had entered an indoor courtyard of sorts. There was a ceiling high above them, slanting at an angle to allow the rain to run off, yet made of a material transparent enough that the rare bit of sun could still be allowed to enter. This was definitely nothing like the glimpses Astra had seen when last in Merimeethia. This made the rain look…beautiful.

A stone's throw ahead of them lay great marble steps that climbed up to the doors of the palace. Not for the first time, Astra hoped desperately that no one here had heard of that day when she'd lost control.

But she had no time to dwell on it. The double doors swung outwards, and a small entourage emerged. Among them, Astra immediately recognized the auburn-haired Keeshiff, his darker-complexioned sister, Mariah, and the stern, broad shouldered form of King Omath. He looked even less pleased than usual as he reached the bottom of the stairs, stopping right in front of his son and guest.

"You're late," he stated, voice hard as he addressed Louko.

"My apologies, Sire." Astra was the one that answered. "It was my joining him that delayed him."

Omath's countenance softened as he turned to Astra, seeming to remember his civility and hospitality. "But of course. And there was also the rain. I apologize on behalf of my country for the unforgiving climate."

Astra could not help all the unflattering thoughts that rose in response to this man who, apparently, thought himself sovereign over even the weather.

"But you must be exhausted, Princess Astra, and I'm sure Louko is not the easiest company in the world. I have tried to break him of that tongue, but I'm sure you are fully aware of his unyielding stubbornness." Omath's last sentence did not even seem aimed at her at all. "Louko will take your horse to the stables, so that you may warm yourself inside."

Astra was almost too stunned to reply, taken off-guard by the callous comments. Hearing a man speak so harshly of his own son to strangers—in front of the son, no less—was simply wrong. But to reply rudely would reflect poorly on Ent, who currently needed all the help he could get.

So Astra set her teeth and forced a smile. "Oh, the journey was not bad at all. I am not too tired. Thank you for your courtesy," she said. "However, it might be best for me to take my mare to the stable. She is often unruly when being handled by unfamiliar people."

She heard some sort of nervous sound escape from where Louko was standing. She'd never heard him utter anything like it before. "Really, Astra, I insist. It would be my pleasure."

Omath glared at him, "Louko. Don't be rude to our guest. If she doesn't wish to have someone take her horse, then we will not force her. And address her properly. Have you no manners at all?" His tone was even harsher than the storm outside. He turned to Astra then and completely changed, an apologetic smile overtaking his face. "I'm so sorry, Princess Astra." He shot another dark look at his son.

"My apologies, Princess Astra." Louko said quietly.

This was wrong. Astra glanced at Louko a moment, trying to rein in her confusion. Why didn't he defend himself? "No need to apologize," she said, turning back to Omath. "Louko was given permission to use my first name."

Hopefully, that would spare Louko a tongue lashing. Astra realized that maybe taking Dannsair to the stable was a way for Louko to escape all this, so she held out the reins.

"If you are sure you don't mind, I think Dannsair trusts you enough for you to take her to the stables."

Louko stared at the reins for a moment, then at Dannsair. Astra saw suspicion in his eyes as he sized up the horse. True, in reality, Dannsair didn't much care for the prince, but Astra knew her mare would make an exception. Just in case, she whispered a few words in Litashian, telling the horse to be good.

Louko took the reins and nodded. "Of course. No problem at all, Princess Astra."

The title stung.

As the prince led Dannsair away, Astra turned back to Omath and the rest of his entourage.

"Why don't we go inside, Princess? But first, I don't believe you have met my chief advisor and aide, Kaeden."

A lean figure of a man stepped forward and bowed to Astra, his neatly trimmed blond hair contrasting greatly to his jade green eyes.

Green eyes.

Astra could barely breathe. Nightmares mixed with memory and she fought the urge to run. Even as she forced a smile and courteous nod, her own heartbeat filled her ears and she couldn't hear anything Kaeden said.

Astra snapped out of it sharply.

"I said, are you well, Princess?" Kaeden asked, apparently again. He was visibly concerned.

She was quick to answer with, "Oh, yes. Perhaps more tired from the journey than I first thought."

Thankfully, Mariah intruded then, saying in an immaculate purr of a voice, "Oh, I'm sure Princess Astra is dead tired and would like to get to her chambers. Don't talk her up and down, Kaeden." She gave a playful laugh. "We want her alive for supper." This was followed with a wink at Astra. "Leyda will show you to your room."

A young maid stepped forth then, auburn hair tucked back in a neat bun with not a strand out of place. She gave a carefully rehearsed curtsy to Astra. "Princess…. Please follow me." Her voice was mouse-like in its timidity.

Astra thanked Omath and those with him, shouldered her bag, and followed the maid.

After offering to take Astra's bag—and being politely turned down—the maid led Astra up several flights of stairs and through several hallways before arriving at the room.

"Here is where you'll be staying" she said, opening the door. "This is in the guest wing of the castle, and since we have few other guests, you'll have plenty of privacy."

Good. Astra stepped inside.

By her standards, the room was huge— as big as the house she'd once lived in. Yet, it was cozy compared to the rooms at the Ethian Palace. The walls were of the same stone as the rest of the castle, but hung with tapestries to try and keep out the pervading dampness and cold. At one end, a fire had already been built and was crackling merrily in the hearth. A large bed stood not far away. At the other end was a table and chair, with ink and quill atop the desk. Two large windows with thick glass panes let in the dim light from outside, wavering as it was from the pattering rain.

Astra set her bag on the end of the bed. "Thank you."

The maid curtsied again, then pointed to a bell pull on one of the walls. "If you need anything, just ring. Dinner is in two hours."

"Oh, thank you." Astra felt awkward. Even after nearly a year at the Ethian Palace, she was not used to being waited on, and did not enjoy the feeling. "Where do I go for that?"

"Someone will come fetch you, no need to worry, Princess. One could easily get lost in this palace. Even with directions." The maid smiled gently.

The smile set Astra at a little more ease. "Okay. Thank you." She tried to breathe more deeply. "Your name is Leyda, right?"

"Yes ma'am."

"You can just call me Astra, if you'd like."

Leyda smiled again. "Alright, Astra."

Astra was glad that the other girl wasn't set on formality. The princess wasn't accustomed to it, nor did she wish to be.

"I suppose I will just get settled," Astra said. "Thank you for showing me my room."

Leyda nodded in genial acknowledgement and exited quietly, leaving Astra completely to herself.

Astra sat down heavily on the bed, looking around. Each moment only made her long for her family more. She thought of her parents and wondered how they were. Were the Elves any more cooperative than they used to be? She hoped that things were at least calm enough for her parents to visit Ent. Maybe, when she wrote her monthly letter to Ent, she could put a little note in for them. Just to say goodbye for herself.

She rubbed her red bronze cuff, reminding herself of the danger she was to them; she couldn't go back. Still, Merimeethia only held more sorrows. Astra recalled the way Omath had treated Louko—was that normal? Was Louko's father always like that to him? It would explain why he'd run away. Actually, it would explain a lot of things.

Then there was Kaeden. Astra shuddered. She knew having green eyes did not mean it was *Tyron*—Jade and Soletuph had green eyes, too. But it didn't change that consuming terror which sprung up so readily. Knowing her enemy had once lived here did not soothe Astra's deep-rooted fears. The princess chided herself for her paranoia, yet couldn't get that old lesson from Ent out of her head.

"Always remember, Slip, shapeshifters may change everything about themselves except their eyes. The eyes are windows to the soul, and even while a shifter changes their skin, their soul remains the same."

With that grim thought in mind, Astra began to unpack her bag. It would take the full two hours to steel herself for dinner with Louko's family. It would also take a while to convince herself she had to wear a dress as uncomfortable as the one that awaited her. Perhaps she just wouldn't tighten her kirtle...

Astra had started pacing by the time she heard someone knocking on the door. With one last tug at her long sleeves, she bade them enter.

In walked Louko.

Astra had not been expecting this. Apparently, neither had Louko, for he looked very annoyed.

"Um...Dinner," he said abruptly, turning around and walking out the door without even waiting to see if Astra would follow.

Astra had to keep from grumbling under her breath as she followed, hiking up the skirt of her dress in order to catch up. Out of self-consciousness, she had asked Ent for dresses that didn't adhere to Litash's typical knee-length fashion. He'd given her several along with a ridiculous collared coat—what had he called it? A houppelande?—that was meant to go over top. While the heavy thing was floor-length and successfully hid all of her unsightly scars, it also happened to be perfect for tripping. What was the point of even having such long sleeves?

"Stupid dresses," she muttered. The only benefit was that they could conceal much larger knives than breeches ever could.

Louko halted his determined stride and turned around, giving her a quick look up and down. "Sorry, what?"

Wait—Louko, saying sorry? Though taken aback, Astra remembered the encounter with his father earlier that day and bit back her comment. He was acting so oddly...

"I was just talking to myself," she said awkwardly. "About, um, how stupid dresses are." Her voice trailed off. She coughed slightly and tugged again at one trailing sleeve.

His brow furrowed. "I... wouldn't... know," he said with raised eyebrow, before turning around, apparently determined to keep moving.

Astra struggled again to keep up with the pace. "Well, if you're ever curious..." she said. It came out as more of a threat than she had intended. All the same, it would be amusing to see how Louko dealt with a bodice as tight as this one.

Once again, the prince stopped and turned around. "Um. Not particularly...Is you wearing a dress somehow my fault? If so, I'd dearly like to know." A hint of his usual sarcasm crept back into his voice.

This time, Astra walked past him. "Well, I suppose you could have just let me die," she said, as if it were a logical option. "You had a few opportunities."

"Oh. Sorry... I'll keep that in mind upon the next occasion."

For the first time in a while, Astra just laughed.

Louko:

So... Louko wasn't quite sure *how* he got her to laugh, or whether it was a good thing... and he really didn't want to find out right now. He still wasn't quite sure why he insisted on escorting her, especially after his father's scolding, but he supposed he'd had some sort of idiotic notion that he could gauge her reaction to his father's comments. Or perhaps maybe he wanted to be on semi-genial terms at least one last time before this disastrous dinner. Whatever it was, Louko just wanted to get everything over with now. He would have faked illness, but that was too old a trick to play on his father. Perhaps Kaeden would be able to help... Louko had actually almost given in and tried to look presentable tonight, but he had sworn long ago that if he was going to be a disgrace, he might as well be one on purpose.

"So...tadah." He stepped aside as they arrived at the dining room doors.

The servant at the door nodded to Louko, whispering "Good luck," as he opened one of the doors.

Walking in, Louko was horrified to find everybody already seated. How did he always manage to be late? *Idiot.* What lovely punctuality he had. What a spot on sense of time! How he set such high standards for everyone else. Truly, he was the highest example of a fine son...

"How nice of you to finally join us, Louko", his father said irritably.

Louko bowed his head, "My apologies, Sir, I got lost." Louko had run out of good excuses about five years ago.

"Don't bother," Omath growled.

Louko felt ready to leave already, but dared not try anything yet. He'd be far more likely to be able to be excused at least halfway through dinner. So instead he chanced a desperate glance at Kaeden before stepping aside and allowing Astra to enter. *Oh, the drama.*

"Ah, Princess Astra, how beautiful you look," Louko's father said as he stood for her, tone polar opposite of just moments before. The other men at the table stood as well.

Louko felt about ready to run and hide. He despised it. It was a feeling of weakness, and he was already too much a coward. All he knew was that he was about to lose the closest thing he had to a...a friend. And that had already happened before, so really, why was he complaining? Anyone would think he was *Mariah* if they knew what was going on in his head!

Speaking of Mariah...

Louko's sister motioned for Astra. "Princess Astra, my father set aside a place for you over here," she announced in her sweetest voice. Of course he had... Louko resisted the urge to cringe.

Perhaps he imagined the perturbed look Astra gave him, but it quickly disappeared. She gave a small smile and took her seat by Mariah.

"I must thank you again for letting me visit with you," Astra said, addressing Omath.

His father gave one of those perfect smiles, and Louko tried to look away and ignore everything. *Idiot.* Just pretend nothing is happening...

"Our doors are always open, Princess Astra."

Louko forced himself to cross the treacherous open space to his seat at the opposite end of the table, coincidentally right across from Astra. How lovely.

Dinner began with a small course, which Louko could barely touch. Seeing that Rhumir—a servant close to his age and fiery to the point of recklessness—was involved in the serving didn't help. If the night exploded into too much chaos, the servant could lose his patience with the king. However, this anxiety was distracted as Louko noticed Astra was strategically moving the food around on her plate to make it look like she'd eaten some. He wondered why she was so uncomfortable. Maybe it was the dress.

"So, Princess Astra, I can't help but marvel at your lovely little mare. Wherever did you get her? Do you ride much?" Mariah always seemed to know what to say.

Louko looked down at his food. Why did stupid Entrais have to make Astra come with him?

Astra's smile looked like it took effort. "She's a cross of an Elvish breed with the Alarunian mountain horse," she explained. "I ride quite often just for ease of travel, but I do enjoy it. Do you ride?"

Oh dear, that was the wrong answer. In Merimeethia, riding was only ever a sport for those in high society—to treat as a means of transportation inferred that you couldn't afford a carriage. Louko felt a twinge of sympathy for Astra. Did she still not understand all the stupid social talk? Of course not, because Astra was an actual *person.*

Fortunately, Mariah was still polite, and gave a smile as she replied, "How lovely. Perhaps you and I can take a ride together while you are visiting."

"How was your journey here, Princess Astra? You didn't cause her too much trouble, did you, Louko?" His father immediately turned the conversation to Louko. Really? It wasn't even the main course yet!

Louko looked over at his father and tried to think of something to say. Should he try to aimlessly avoid getting into trouble, or just dive in, as Astra's opinion of him was bound to suffer by the end of the night either way.

"Oh, the journey was actually rather pleasant," Astra said before he could even decide how best his social death would be accomplished. "I haven't been this way in quite a while."

Face ever so slightly red, Louko's father remained silent for a moment. Astra had referenced the fact that she'd been held prisoner here during The War. Clever princess. Louko heard Kaeden laugh at the hidden meaning in her comment, and couldn't resist a quick smile himself.

Especially when Kaeden hid his laugh by commenting, "It has

been a long time since I've heard any Litashian say they enjoyed a proper Merimeethian deluge."

Astra smiled again, though not directly at Kaeden. "I say so only thanks to my warm cloak."

Everyone at the table chuckled a little as the tense situation deflated. Everyone except Louko, who didn't dare do anything more risky than smile.

He noticed Keeshiff was also being terribly quiet, and almost hoped he'd be more genial tonight. But one never knew with Keeshiff, and besides, the more guilty or uncomfortable he felt about something, the more he tended to lash out. Louko dared not look to him for support. Just a few more courses… then he'd pretend the food had gotten to him or something. Somehow, feigning sickness didn't seem such a poor decision anymore. How'd that happen?

"Ah! And here is dinner," his father announced broadly as the servants brought in the main course.

"Lovely." Louko accidentally let the thought escape.

Kaeden spoke up then, covering up his blunder. "I must admit, Princess Astra, you are quite a legend in Merimeethia. I imagine you are rather famous in your own country as well," he said pleasantly. Louko was thankful for a conversation he could stay out of. "Is it true you rallied even Dragons to your brother's cause?"

Astra was starting to look a little ill. "I suppose you could say that, though I cannot claim to have planned it."

Louko wondered what could be the matter… and why she was avoiding eye contact with Kaeden. What was it? What was he missing? Louko almost wished he had the guts to ask. But he didn't, and so continued to play with his food like a perfect little toddler.

"Louko," Omath snapped, interrupting the conversation. "Stop making a mess of your plate."

Louko could feel his face whiten in embarrassment, and set his silverware down. His father treated him like a child just to spite him, but Louko did deserve it, he supposed. Of all the hopeless idiots, Louko was definitely the worst. There had been a time where he hadn't believed that, but Tyron had taken that hope with him the day he'd left.

"What was that?" His father raised an eyebrow in expectancy.

Swallowing any pathetic attempt at pride Louko had possessed in Astra's presence, he managed, "Sorry, Sir, it will not happen again."

"I should apologize as well," Astra said humorously. Did Louko imagine the edge in her tone? "It must be my boring table conversation driving the poor prince off the edge."

Omath scoffed. Louko looked down. Maybe this would be a disaster after all.

"Perhaps a new topic," Astra proposed undeterred. "I hear, King Omath, that you are currently rebuilding the City of Light?"

Everyone stared at Astra in confusion. "City of Light?" Omath repeated slowly.

Louko suddenly jerked to attention as Astra looked embarrassed. It dawned upon him that the others didn't realize this was a common Elvish problem, accidentally translating old terms into modern ones. Ent and Astra both had mixed words up many times before in Louko's presence.

"Oh, um, sorry," Astra stuttered, looking flustered. "It's, uh, my Elvish…"

Without thinking, Louko jumped in to save Astra from her apparent embarrassment. "You see, part of Elves' Gifting is naturally switching to the language being spoken around them, but since the city's name Anahli is an old Merimeethian word for light, she hears no difference. It really is quite a common thing. We've just been so isolated from them for so long we're not used to it."

Now everyone was staring at *him.* It would seem Louko had accidentally insulted his father's political acumen… again… oh dear.

"Well then, I'm so glad you feel the need to point that out." His father's voice was hard.

By now Louko was so completely mortified with himself that without even a second thought he slumped forward and buried his head in his hands.

"Sit up straight!" Omath all but bellowed.

Louko, not seeing a point in trying to avoid worse trouble, did nothing, only muttered, "I'm sorry, I don't seem to be feeling very well. If you'll excuse me," and made a very abrupt departure, not waiting for his father to allow him. That was a bad move, but he had made plenty of those this evening as it was.

Still, he didn't have the guts to leave *entirely*, and secretly stole back into the servants' corridor, where he could listen to the conversation, yet not be seen. But regardless, whether from paranoia or his hopeless curiosity, Louko couldn't leave well enough alone.

"Princess Astra, I must apologize for my *son's* lack of manners." Omath finally broke the silence.

"Oh, there is no need to apologize." Louko recognized the flush of anger in her voice. "I am not offended by *his* actions."

The conversation changed directions from there, and to Louko's surprise it was fairly light and harmless. But then, that could be just as bad a thing.

"What are you doing?" The voice startled Louko half to death, and he spun around to find Rhumir holding a platter of dirty dishes. He had to have entered through another passage, otherwise Louko would have seen him first.

"Um, just, you know," Louko sputtered, trying to find an answer that would not incur the wrath of the short-tempered servant. The last thing he needed was for Rhumir to get dismissed from service....again. The only reason he'd gotten his job back last time was because his father was the chamberlain. If it happened again, not even Julyn would be able to get him rehired.

"What did he say?" The voice was deadly already, and Louko would have been annoyed if he wasn't already so stressed out by the fact that Astra was now eating dinner with his father, and he was too busy trying to calm down Rhumir to see Astra's reaction. Brilliant.

"Now now, Rhumir, let's not do something stupid." Louko put his hands in front of him as Rhumir's teeth grit. "What would your father say?"

"It's *your* father that's the problem."

Louko barely caught the tray in time as Rhumir just let go of it. The servants had a...less than favorable opinion of Omath, but sometimes it did more harm than good when they didn't keep it to themselves.

Like Rhumir.

"Why don't we take care of these dishes?" Louko's voice had an edge to it, as he was being torn away from his spying...which was probably a good thing...but nonetheless undesirable. Before Rhumir had a chance to contemplate spilling something on the king in front of guests, Louko steered him away to the kitchen, the prince holding the tray and the servant bickering like a discontented housewife.

The kitchen was busy, as always, with people running back and forth preparing the few courses that were left in the meal as well as cleaning the things that returned. They appeared to be behind in the last task, a gaping hole where it was clear a servant should be.

Rhumir was definitely the worst servant in the entire country...

"Rhumir! Where have you *been*?" It was Graece, hollering from where she was preparing dessert.

Louko closed his eyes and took a deep breath as Rhumir launched into another rant. While the servant monologued about the injustices of the king and the monarchy as a whole, Louko started washing dishes.

"At it again," Pela—a young girl who was doing dishes beside Louko—murmured. "You don't have to help us, Louko. Graece can box his ears."

"But I like it. The soggy feeling between my fingers is..." Louko trailed off with a raised eyebrow. "Really relaxing."

"What we need is a good old Merimeethian usurpation!" Rhumir's voice rang through the soap filling Louko's ears.

"Rhumir, stop it before someone thinks you're serious and reports you to your brother," Louko called over his shoulder, scrubbing the less than pleasant grits on the silver platter. Oh wait. This was his half eaten plate...how fitting.

"But I *am* serious!" Louko didn't have to see Rhumir to know he was waving his arms dramatically. As much as he denied it, Rhumir was much too like his brother. Louko couldn't help but feel bad for Julyn.

"Would you please stop trying to get yourself executed?" It was Graece now, stepping in. "You will do nothing but get us all expelled from the king's services. And I don't want to be a martyr to your idiotic rants."

Rhumir was subdued at this, but nonetheless got out of doing the dishes. Which was fine, because it was something to keep Louko busy—something to keep him from thinking about what his father could even now be saying to Astra.

Astra:

Astra forced herself to stop gripping her fork so hard only because the metal had started to bend. She couldn't *believe* how Louko's own family was treating him! She had to physically bite her tongue and think of Ent just to keep her mouth shut. This was *wrong*.

She wasn't exactly sure how she made it through the rest of the meal. She remembered taking bites of food each time anyone looked her way. No one had seemed terribly interested in anything besides small talk anyway. It wasn't until after the meal began to close that Astra saw King Omath watching her. Her apprehension grew…and when everyone stood to leave, her fears were confirmed.

"Princess Astra, might I speak to you for a moment?" Omath asked courteously.

Astra, still biting her tongue, managed a nod.

OF SHADE AND SHADOW

The king waited until the others had bowed and left. Then his amiable expression turned grave. "I take no pleasure in warning you against my own son. I know to you it may appear a heartless thing to do, the way we are treating him, but let me shed some light upon the subject." There was a pause, Omath looking uncharacteristically burdened as he spoke. "It's no secret Tyron was exiled here. Louko was young when he arrived. I was just getting over the...the death of my wife." He stuttered a moment. "And then Tyron arrived offering help in Louko's education. I didn't know who he *really* was, or that he'd been exiled. Tyron took him under his wing—groomed him, some could say. I allowed it, thinking he was giving the boy an education..."

Astra felt like she couldn't breathe. *What?*

His brow furrowed, "But then Euracia arrived, and the two brothers' true plot to use my family as a path to their war became clear. Tyron used Louko to force me to obey him and his brother. He threatened the life of my family." There was a long pause. "But the problem was, he did more than that...he turned Louko's head—made himself an idol in my own son's mind. I tried to explain what Tyron was, but all he did was grow more erratic. Louko would defend Tyron at social events...soiled the names of my other children and myself. Then, just like that, he left for the very man that I had been trying to protect my family from. You met him on his way to Tyron—when you and your brother found him during The War, that is. He was going to Alarune."

Astra was too stunned to reply. At first, her mind was completely blank; then it was overcome by a flood of thoughts she could not wrangle into any kind of sense.

"If you'll excuse me," she heard herself say as she turned and rushed out of the room.

But she didn't even make it halfway down the hall before her escape was halted by a kind voice. "Princess, if I may..."

Astra made the mistake of looking up. The sight of Kaeden's bright green eyes made it nearly impossible to breathe.

Kaeden seemed not to notice. "While I admire your attempts to defend Louko, you've only made the next few weeks into misery for him."

"I...I..." Astra's voice faltered.

"The best way is not to rebuff the king's anger, but to redirect it." Kaeden explained quietly, glancing up and down the hall as if looking for eavesdroppers. "Change the conversation. Distract him. Lead him away from Louko."

Astra tried to keep her breath from coming in gasps.

"I mean no harm," Kaeden spoke again. "I say this for Louko's sake."

All Astra could get out was a cracked, "Thank you."

And then she fled from the hall.

OF SHADE AND SHADOW

CHAPTER V

Astra:

Astra slammed the door of her room behind her and leaned back against it. She closed her eyes, but all she could see were those eyes. Tyron's vivid, green, sadistic eyes.

She threw up.

And then Leyda walked in. She took one look at Astra, one look at the floor, and said, with concern etched on her face, "Went that bad, huh?"

Hand at her mouth, Astra whispered, "I'm so sorry."

Leyda's smile was gentle and sad. "It's alright. Not the first time it's happened. I'll get a bucket. Would you like help getting cleaned up? Your hair…"

"I'm fine, thank you." Astra shook her head. "I don't think I got anything in it."

Leyda disappeared for a bit, and Astra used the opportunity to get changed out of her dress. The maid returned with a bucket of soapy water and a rag.

"Please, let me help," Astra said.

Leyda looked skeptical. "Um. How about you rest, Astra. Better not to aggravate your stomach anymore. If you argue, I'll be forced to get Graece. And trust me, no one argues with her. Not even Louko."

Astra felt awful for making her clean up the mess. "Really, I am alright. It wasn't the food. My stomach is fine."

"I'm getting Graece," Leyda threatened.

Astra backed away then, unable to stand being around any more people. So while Leyda cleaned up the mess, the redhead sat on the window seat, pushing the pane open and sticking her hand out to feel the rain. The city lights of Melye shimmered through the raindrops and gave her one more tangible thing to latch onto. She still felt sick. All of her old scars itched and burned as if remembering how they had come to be there.

Was it true what Omath said? The very idea was horrifying. Astra knew that Tyron and Euracia had come here when exiled, but it had been so long ago. She hadn't quite realized that Louko was old enough to remember. But taught by him? *Raised by* him? Memories came unbidden, then, of all the times Louko had kept quiet when they laid the siege plans for Tyron's castle. Or the times when Louko had even defended him, such as that evening at the Triscri ball. She withdrew her hand from the icy rain, staring at it and yet not seeing it. What if… what if Louko still…

Then her mind caught on what Omath had said about Louko's running away: that he was planning to join Tyron in Alarune. But Astra and Ent had stumbled upon him nearly half a day's journey into the Forest of Riddles. Louko never would have risked the Forest to go into Litash—especially not when he would have to risk it again to cross into Alarune. Louko was smart. He would have gone straight to the coast, hitched a ride on a ship, and made it to Alarune within a week. Omath had to have lied.

The discovery was a relief beyond imagination. It let Astra breathe more deeply, think more clearly, and remember the other side of things. Louko had still fought on that night when they had taken

Tyron's castle. He'd been in the party breaching the lower yards, yes, but he had still fought. Louko and Soletuph had rescued her and Ent from Tyron. Louko had saved her from Tyron's assassin. He'd helped train all of the troops before the attack on the castle. If Omath was even telling the truth about Tyron training Louko, then maybe he had even been teaching them Tyron's techniques, and saved lives by doing so.

There was too much good to outweigh the bad. And, if Omath had treated his son like this even when he was younger, who could blame Louko for turning to anyone that would accept him? Even the Ethians—yes, even Soletuph—had once considered Tyron their favorite uncle. It would have been around the same period of time. Maybe it had been an act, maybe Tyron had changed, but either way, Astra knew one thing: she could not condemn Louko. He had proven his character too many times for her to dismiss it all in a single evening.

Now, his personality, on the other hand…

"There. All clean." Leyda's voice broke through, startling Astra. She'd quite forgotten she wasn't alone.

"Oh. Thank you," Astra said. "And sorry."

Leyda began blowing out the lamps. "Now get some sleep," she ordered mildly before leaving, not giving Astra a chance to keep blubbering out thanks and apologies.

Astra tried to do as Leyda said, but found the bed too soft. She was used to sleeping outside; even in Litash, she had slept on a few blankets rather than a mattress. So Astra took the cover from the bed and curled up back in the window seat. The cool air washing over her was soothing, but her thoughts were still restless. Now she thought of Kaeden's words. Had she really caused Louko so much harm? How he must loathe her. No wonder he had been so reluctant for her to come.

Next time, she would do better.

***

"Oh my! What in Eatris are you doing on the cold floor!"

Astra woke with a start, sitting up instantly with a knife at the ready. She was greeted by the sight of a shocked and startled maid.

"Oh, sorry, um..." Astra didn't actually know how to explain herself. Why was she on the floor? She must have slipped from the window seat. She made her trembling hand lower the dagger. "Sorry." She sheathed the little blade as she stood, trying to shake off the effects of last night's nightmare. She wracked her mind for the maid's name.

"No need to explain. I was just going to see if you were up. Since you are, I shall go get your breakfast," the maid replied with an oddly amused smile.

Leyda! That was her name.

Astra shook her head. "No need to bring it all the way up, Leyda. I can walk down with you."

Leyda raised an eyebrow doubtfully, but did not refuse. "Alright."

As Leyda restocked the fire in the hearth, Astra returned her blanket to the bed. Then the maid waited in the servants' passage so Astra could change. It didn't take the princess long to pull on breeches and a fresh tunic, although, as she tied the laces of her overshirt, she couldn't help but wonder if females wore breeches in Merimeethia. All of the women she'd seen so far had worn skirts or dresses. Since Astra didn't have any of those besides her formal attire, she decided breeches would have to do. The girl buckled on her sword as always, and joined Leyda in the servants' passage.

Astra had not seen these corridors. She followed Leyda through them, fascinated to see the hidden—and rather extensive—maze of tunnels that appeared to run through the entire castle. They were broad enough for two to walk side by side, and yet Astra had never noticed the missing space while walking through the main halls.

After several long passages, stairways, twists and turns, they emerged in the kitchen. It was the very picture of organized chaos: Busy cooks stirred broths and mashes in great steaming pots, barely noticing as other kitchen hands ladled the food into gleaming dishes. The food was then carried on a precarious course, past glowing ovens, piles of produce, and hanging herbs, all to be delivered to a perfectly prepared tray. When the tray was full, some servant or maid would rush it away. It was incredible how none of them ever collided despite the many moving bodies.

Astra stood for a moment, taking in the sight and all of the tantalizing smells that went with it. Her stomach growled as if to remind her how empty it was after last night. She was glad when Leyda pointed her to a small table by the wall; but to her surprise, the table already had one occupant—Louko. She stopped short, looking at him. Astra had not expected to see him so soon.

But, she had decided to trust him. So.

Astra walked towards the table, staying by the wall to keep out of everyone's way. "Good morning," she said.

As she sat down, Louko opened his mouth, a strange look on his face. Then he snapped it shut again. After another moment, there came a, "Morning." He quickly averted his eyes to the commotion around them.

They sat in uncomfortable silence until Louko suddenly looked back over, his demeanor still uncomfortable as he started off a strange, stilted type of conversation. "You know, since it's still raining out, you really should see the gardens. The architects that built this palace were able to get a hold of some of Pershizar's prized Red Sand. When you melt it into glass, it has a strange property for magnifying the sun's light just enough to really make plants grow… But anyway, it allows the plants to grow that would usually stay very small and unblossomed. It's quite a sight…" His voice trailed off, as if realizing he had just been the one who had said all that.

He gave a shrug and was distracted as one of the servants came over and set a tray in front of Astra. The girl thanked the servant quietly, but only proceeded to toy with her food. Astra's appetite had begun to dwindle as the awkwardness of the situation had grown. She still didn't understand the reason for Louko's spontaneous chatter… which was still going on…

"And then there's the Spying Glass. It's not actually a spying glass… it's a tower. You can see for miles, including below you. I'm surprised you didn't see it when we arrived…but maybe you did. Big tower, made of a strong glass that probably also came from Pershizar. Though it's quite a sight…and after last night… Sorry about that, it seems nobody warned you that Merimeethian food can be terribly heavy."

Astra was caught off guard by the last comment. She blinked in surprise, then turned away in blushing embarrassment. Apparently, the prince was very close to his servants; Astra would have to be more careful in future.

"Um. Well…" It would seem Louko had not actually meant to say that, as now he was blushing and stammering, "You see—I wasn't checking up on you—-no purposefully—I mean not in a stalker way—I mean, wasn't being nosy. I just came down, and they said—I swear I didn't ask." He finished with some form of exasperated sigh, "Shutting up now. Sorry."

"Um," Astra had meant to follow that up with some assurance that he was alright, but couldn't find anything. There was another uncomfortable silence, both of them poking at their food. Astra had rather lost her taste for her breakfast. Then one of the servants broke through the moment.

"Louko?" The elegant lady, wearing a flour-dusted apron, spoke his name like a mother.

Louko got up and gave a weird half smile. "Yes, Graece?" The smile faded, "Oh… Right. I'll be off then." He immediately got up from his seat, straightening his ruffled shirt as if self-conscious.

Astra looked in confusion from Louko to the one he'd called Graece. "Is everything alright?" she dared to ask.

Louko rolled his eyes. "Of course everything's alright. I just forgot to make my bed, and Graece will give me a scolding if I don't go do it now," he answered, with a bitter sort of sarcasm.

"Louko…" Graece's low warning sounded odd.

Astra winced slightly at Louko's tone. She remembered how commonplace such biting sarcasm had been when they first met the prince. Truly, he had warmed up over the years. Only now, with such vivid comparison, did Astra see how much he had changed.

"Sorry," Louko said in a rush, leaving before anyone could utter another word.

Graece sighed.

Astra turned to the weary cook. "What's wrong?"

Graece looked hesitant, biting her lip and peering around the busy kitchen. "His father just wants to see him."

Oh. Even after just one day in Melye, Astra had come to see that this was a bad thing. She began fiddling with the red bronze cuff on her wrist. "Is there anything we can do?" Even as she hated to think of what Louko was going to face—what he had probably faced all his childhood —the princess remembered Kaeden's warning, and had no wish to make things worse.

Graece let out a deep breath, eyeing Astra as if to size her up. For a long while she didn't say a word, doubt and hope fighting in those eyes which seemed to hold centuries. Finally, wiping the flour from her hands, she said, "The throne room is in the main hall, one floor down. You can't miss the large doors. If you want to talk to him afterwards." And with that, she disappeared into the hubbub of the kitchen.

Astra hesitated. Would it be best to try and speak with him afterwards? What could she even say? Her worries about his affiliation with Tyron seeped in again, but this time she banished them completely. Louko needed her help—not her mistrust. The least she could do was wait outside for him.

Decision made, she followed Graece's directions and, after some wandering, found herself in front of ornate double doors. This had to be the throne room. Feeling out of place, Astra stood on one side of the hall until she noticed the stone benches. Then she sat, feet together and hands on her lap, waiting. It felt like a long time; without any windows, there was no sure way to tell. The only sign that time was even passing was given by the slow shrinking candles in their elaborately wrought stands. Astra was just wondering if she was in the wrong place when one of the doors creaked slightly, and she jumped to her feet.

Out slipped Louko. He stopped the instant he saw her, staring at her for an awkwardly long while. "Um…" He rubbed his cheek, eyes riveted on her in an almost suspicious manner, like a cornered animal. "Are you lost?" he asked, side stepping away from the door he had just exited.

Astra suddenly felt clumsy, and wondered if she should not have come. "No, Graece told me how to get here. I thought that, um, maybe…." The random urge to explain herself welled up. "I just… yeah." Her attempt drifted off lamely.

He didn't say anything for a long moment, instead settling for looking really confused. Finally, he asked, "Did you…need something?"

She shook her head. "No. I simply wanted to make sure you were alright." she finally said outright.

Louko stared at her with a mystified expression. "Oh." He blinked. "Why in Eatris would you do a thing like that?"

It was Astra's turn to stare. "Um, I thought…" She looked away, doubting herself. Maybe they weren't such friends? Or maybe…

Louko looked suddenly curious, standing up straighter and peering at her. "Thought what?" he asked with that same quirky smile.

Astra felt vulnerable now. She crossed her arms almost

defensively. "You know, that we had each other's backs." She stumbled a little over the words, uncertain of herself.

The expression Louko's face turned to something akin to a fascination, and after a moment he asked abruptly, "Well, you know, you did come here for research, right? Isn't it about time someone showed you the library? It's just a little way from here. If you know where you're going, that is."

His tone was nearly bright, cheerful even, though Astra thought she caught a slight self-consciousness to it. It was very different from his usual sarcasm. But she didn't spend too much time wondering, since Louko's mention of her research reminded her of Tyron and her duty.

"Alright," was all she came up with in reply.

Louko led her down the long hall, stride definitely slower than last night's. He was a little more talkative, too. Almost, *too* talkative…

"So, have you ever seen our library—oh, of course not…. Last time you were here. Well, anyway. It's rather large. But it's organized, so you shouldn't need help finding things. She was always very good at keeping things that way—the library keeper, I mean. Er—what are you looking for again?"

Astra wondered if she ought to tell him. If he really had been close to Tyron… even if he was no longer loyal to him, it still might be unkind to bring up the topic. "Records. Mostly within the last fifteen years." It seemed the safest thing to say.

Louko stiffened ever so slightly. "I see. Well, we are loaded with those. Not much on Litash, I suppose. But probably more than your sorry little library has at the moment. How *is* that project coming? I really can't see Ent as much of a reader… but he does seem set on getting the records back. Was that your idea?"

Astra had nearly forgotten that Louko didn't know she was exiled. She had to remind herself of the story Ent had invented to keep that fact secret. "Somewhat," she answered, trying to keep the discomfort from her voice. "When Ent took the throne, he found himself in political messes we had no record of. Euracia certainly did some rewriting during his reign, and much of the records we have are useless for Ent's cause."

"I see. Well, I hope you find something. Ent wasn't much for politics to begin with. Still not quite sure how he ended up as king…" Louko trailed off, leaving the sore topic open.

"Me neither," Astra murmured. Selfishly, she wished again that Ent was not king. Or at least, not such a busy one.

Louko stopped so abruptly that she almost ran into him. "Aha! Here we are." His annoying tone of voice had returned, and overly broad gestures with it. "Princess Astra, I welcome you to the library. Try not to drool; the floor was just polished…" And with that, he opened the deceptively simple looking door, leading them into quite possibly the largest room Astra had seen in her whole life.

It had three open stories, stairs and balconies giving access to the endless numbers of books which flowed down the wall like a petrified waterfall of knowledge. Everything in the room was grand, yet simple and elegant, not overdone. The books themselves were grand enough.

Astra's first thought was that she rather liked this room. Her second thought was that finding the records she needed was going to take an eternity.

She decided to focus on her first thought. "It's lovely in here," she said simply. At least she wouldn't feel so useless here.

Louko cleared his throat. "Really? I find it rather stuffy. They should have put in more windows, really. Well. Anyway. Records are on the second floor, chronological order. It has countries listed on the woodwork. Have fun." He turned to leave.

Oh. "Thank you for showing me," Astra called after him.

Louko looked back long enough to roll his eyes. "Nothing better to do." He shrugged and gave what Astra now suspected was a very fake smile.

"Thank you all the same."

With a raised eyebrow, and not another word, the prince left Astra alone with shelf upon shelf of books.

Time to get to work.

Louko:

Louko hadn't been able to stand being in there in the library any longer. Not today. Not now. The unquenchable fear that perhaps something had happened at dinner last night was always persistent, outweighed only by the fact that—even if nothing *had* happened—she would be here for days...weeks... And she *would* find out eventually.

Her comment about having each other's backs had only made it worse. He wanted it to be true so badly, but he knew that it could only end in disaster, like all the other times someone had been foolish enough to befriend him. Even if *he* didn't ruin it, his father would. And yet it was so very hard not to want to try. His father had already let him have it for his behavior at dinner last night. Escorting Astra had already been a break in etiquette, but there had been plenty of other missteps aftwards to warrant punishment. He shouldn't have left early. He shouldn't have been so careless with his words. And Astra shouldn't have defended him.

Idiot. What are you doing?

He felt physically and emotionally spent, and as Louko wandered down the lonely halls towards the gardens, he tried not to rub his cheek, used to the occasional blows from his father and yet feeling a sting that was worse than physical. He was so tired of this.

He took his hand away from his face and found himself fingering the sword that always lay sheathed by his side, the ornate patterns on the hilt twisting and curving under his fingertips. There was the sudden urge to throw the Elvish sword across the room, not deserving it or wanting the constant memory anymore. The sword Entrais and Astra had given him had once been a glimmer of hope; a reminder that things could be better. But it was a lie: things would never be better, and he didn't deserve it to be so.

Compose yourself, idiot. What exactly would that accomplish? Nothing, just like every other silly thing you think up. Throw the sword...it's better than any other sword on this side of the Macridean Sea! Louko shook his head, clearing his mind from the morning's mistakes and his father's irate words.

Regardless of them, he was actually looking forward to the rest of the day. Kaeden had asked him to meet in the garden, and showing Astra to the library had made him late as it was. Not that Kaeden would mind. Kaeden seemed to be just about the only person in all of Eatris that didn't care if Louko was late, didn't care if he wasn't socially acceptable, didn't care who he was. Astra and Entrais didn't count. They didn't know who Louko really was, not really. They were too perfect. Kaeden knew, and still he'd stuck it out. That still didn't stop those irrational fears that one day Kaeden would change his mind... would leave like Tyron...but he shut those out. Best enjoy it while it lasted. He'd regret *that* decision later, however, he was sure.

"Ah, there you are, Louko," Kaeden greeted him warmly.

Louko looked up at the clear glass ceiling high above them, watching the rain pattering against the glass as it begged to be let in. He knew the feeling.

Then he remembered Kaeden. "Yes, sorry. Was a little detained."

Kaeden waved the issue away. "Oh, no matter," he said. "I'm glad to see you safe, all the same."

Louko rolled his eyes. "Sentimental this morning, I see. So, what are we doing?" He glanced over at the sparring equipment in the center courtyard of the large garden, not far from where they were now.

"That is up to you," Kaeden said. "Consider it your welcome home present." He grinned. "Still, you will have to tell me of all your adventures at one time or another. Don't think you'll get away from me this time, lad."

Oh. Louko had hoped Kaeden had forgotten about that. Months had passed with Louko managing to avoid his experiences during The War—The War he was never supposed to be part of in the first place...but he'd thought maybe he could help...or even see, well...see Tyron. Louko still had so many doubts and wrestlings over his time with

Astra and Entrais that he was even afraid to bring it up to Kaeden. But perhaps it was time.

Resigned to his fate, he replied, "Well, seeing as sparring is not really something one can carry on a conversation while doing, why don't we stick with TetraChess? One tends to be less out of breath doing that." Inwardly, Louko sort of wished he had chosen sparring instead. Was he really ready to tell Kaeden about... about Tyron?

"Shall we go over to the table then?" Kaeden suggested, gesturing over to their usual spot, right under the towering, gnarled vito tree. They sat at the elegant glass table where Kaeden had already set up the three-tiered boards.

"Well then, and here I thought I got to choose what we were doing today," Louko said with a raised eyebrow.

Kaeden almost looked smug—an odd expression for a usually austere royal aide. "You did. I just happened to know what you would choose."

Louko's face was all seriousness as he pretended to stare down the man. "Should I be worried?"

"My ability to predict what you'll do is unfortunately lesser when applied to chess," Kaeden said, shaking his head as if in regret. "You have little to fear."

"I'm still sure you just let me win," Louko said with a wry chuckle, making his first move.

Kaeden made his own move. "For the sake of my own vanity, I shall pretend you are right."

"One would think you were taking lessons from Mariah." Louko regretted his own words, and his smile faded slightly.

Kaeden raised his eyebrows. "If you are implying that I use cosmetics, I must argue—I doubt even I could use them and still look this ill-favored." He gestured towards his admittedly plain face.

"Your move, when you have time, Your Majesty." Louko said with a distracted attempt at a jest.

The older man moved a pawn and both fell quiet as they were absorbed by the game.

Kaeden was the first to break the silence. "Now, tell me about Litash," he said, simultaneously taking out one of Louko's rooks.

With a slightly uncomfortable shift in his seat, Louko replied, "You're just trying to distract me from the game," but with a huff, he gave in. "It was... tense."

Kaeden regarded him a moment. "Go on."

"Well..." Louko was really hesitant now. "Um. It was a lot of fighting." He wasn't sure why he was bothering to be vague.

"Were you ever wounded?" Kaeden prodded, concern edging his features.

Louko's look was incredulous. "Hardly." His face darkened slightly. "But there were plenty who were, and plenty who died. And others who had it even worse."

Kaeden's brow furrowed. Then understanding dawned in his expression, mixed with pity and abhorrence. "I am most sorry to hear that."

"I just don't understand *why*," Louko said nearly breathlessly.

"What do you mean?"

Ugh. Louko had sort of had hoped Kaeden would actually understand. Then there would be no need to explain. No need to say it.

98

"Why did he do it?"

Kaeden was visibly struggling to make sense of the question. "I'm sorry—I still don't understand."

Louko sighed in exasperation. He was really going to make him say it, wasn't he. "*Tyron* was the one that did all those things, Kaeden. How could he? How could he do such a thing?" Indignance rose in Louko's voice, and he slammed the pawn down on the next spot, almost knocking the pieces on the top tier over.

Kaeden's face went blank. "Tyron?" His voice held his disbelief. "You are sure about this?"

Louko slammed his fist against his leg, only thinking to redirect the blow away from the table at the last second. "Yes, Tyron!" The memory of Tyron mourning Rhioa came fresh, and with it the way he had always set that aside to keep Louko from despair. How could that man be the culprit of the horrors Louko had seen? How?

Now Kaeden looked deeply troubled. He leaned back in his chair, rubbing his forehead. "How could one fall so far?" He murmured, more to himself than to Louko. Then he looked up. "Did you see him?"

"No, I was afraid of what I would do." Louko couldn't stand this conversation. He wanted to change it. Louko still wasn't sure what that statement meant. Would he have throttled Tyron...Or understood him? The prince was afraid that, somehow, it would have been the latter.

Kaeden looked distracted. "I suppose that's for the better, all things considered." He let out a long breath. "I'm sorry. I did not mean to trouble you so." He straightened his shoulders. "Let's change the subject—tell me about other things. Did you see any fabled animals? Or meet any shape-shifters? Did you find any friends?"

Louko rolled his eyes. *"Friends."* He was tempted to take refuge in sarcasm, but decided to play fair. "They were all a very close troupe."

"They?" Kaeden caught on right away. But of course he would; Kaeden was such a stubborn, intuitive person. Sometimes Louko hated it...

"We," He corrected.

Kaeden raised an eyebrow, seemingly unconvinced. He used his rook to take out one of Louko's knights. "The princess seems to like you well enough," he commented.

"Does she really?" Louko raised an eyebrow, too amused with Kaeden...or perhaps too determined to be, and thus dismiss his comments as a joke.

Kaeden's face betrayed no humor. "She defended you, after all," he said quietly.

Louko flashed his false grin. "She's the type that defends everything. Too loyal for her own good." It was about time he reminded himself of these things.

"I believe you," Kaeden said. "But I don't trust that fake smile of yours. I don't think the princess does, either."

Louko would have smiled, but apparently that 'wasn't trustworthy', so he rolled his eyes. "Oh, grand."

"Make your move," Kaeden reminded, but didn't stop the conversation. "What do you think of her?"

Louko took Kaeden's rook. "She's a good person." Too good, perhaps? Louko didn't know how to say it.

"And her brother?" The advisor took a pawn.

Louko moved his king. "They're a good family," he replied

plainly.

Kaeden's queen moved and blocked a bishop. "Did they treat you well?"

Hitting on the sore spots today, wasn't he? Why did he feel the need to ask that? "Of course they did." Idiocy and all. Louko didn't have the heart to break it to Kaeden the lengths he had gone to in order to make sure he would not grow any attachments in the troupe. And yet, here he was, still afraid of what Astra thought of him...and still wishing he could just give up and stop fighting her friendship. But he could never have such thing as *true* friendship, anyway—why couldn't he seem to remember that?

"Good." Kaeden's sincere response scattered the thundercloud train of thought.

Louko didn't say anything in response, only taking Kaeden's bishop and a pawn. Kaeden's queen doubled back, only in time to allow Louko to skirt it.

Of course, he was letting him win, the vain...vain...oh dear, Louko was so irritated he had run out of witty comebacks...

Louko made his last move, saying, "Checkmate."

Kaeden gave a sigh and tipped over the king.

"Your sigh is falser than my smile," Louko said darkly.

The accusation was rewarded with nothing more than a laugh from Kaeden. "Then I'd say we're both done for."

Louko rolled his eyes, beginning to put the pieces away. "I suppose so," he said.

Kaeden started collecting the boards. "I'm assuming you don't plan to stay here," Kaeden said, ever the patient one. "Will you try to reach your uncle again?"

Right. That. Louko hadn't had the guts to tell Kaeden yet...but he knew it was now or never.

"I already wrote to him." Louko forced the answer out. How he wished sometimes Kaeden would leave him alone. Really, that's all Louko wanted: to be left alone. "And informed him I will not be going to Nythril." He'd had his chance, and like a perfect little idiot, he'd thrown it out the window to go galavanting.

The advisor's hands froze. Then he set the last board down in its box. "Louko." His voice was soft. "Think about what you are doing. You *can't* stay here. Would you live under your father forever?"

Louko shrugged. "He's gotten better," he flat-out lied. It didn't really matter that much. "Besides. I had my chance. He's very forgiving, really. He was about ready to have me under watch all hours of the day for fear I'd run off again." Louko put on his act and said all this completely calm, not portraying the price he had paid for the small freedoms he had now.

The expression on Kaeden's face told Louko that his lies had not been bought. The muscle in Kaeden's jaw had tightened like it did whenever the man was angry and was gritting his teeth. "What did you do?" he asked, voice low. "What did you tell him to stay his wrath?"

Louko gave an exaggerated sigh and stood up. "You're so dramatic, Kaeden," he said, still playing this off as if it were some light conversation. "But really, my stupidity is my own concern. You needn't get so worried over it—you nosy fool." He forced out the insult.

"I am not so easily put off by your little jabs." The words sounded sour. Kaeden's green eyes pierced Louko's. "What did you do?"

Shoulders sagged, but still he did not want to tell the advisor. "You are a terrible worrywart," he said, false bravado gone, only leaving behind the tiredness he suddenly felt. The tiredness he had so successfully been hiding all these months—the weariness that had been hidden by wit and fake smiles and meaningless, idiotic chatter. *Idiot. Can't keep up the act, you pathetic coward?* Louko sighed. Well, this was going well, clearly.

"And you are honorable to a fault," Kaeden said, insistent. "You always feel obligated to make up for everything, whether it's your fault or not. Now tell me what you've done."

The reminder of what he *had* done made him feel like a captive again. Running his hand through his hair, Louko finally gave in. He knew he couldn't argue with Kaeden forever. "I just promised I wouldn't run off like some stupid coward again." He made a pathetic attempt at sounding casual. A very, *very* pathetic attempt.

Kaeden stood up so abruptly that Louko jumped back in surprise. "What in the entire planet of Eatris were you thinking?!?"

The anger was expected, though still catching Louko by surprise with its strength and suddenness. But he had encountered it on several occasions, and swiftly hid his surprise. "I don't know. I was going to be a prisoner either way. I might as well be a willing one." Louko turned away, unable to face him and wishing he didn't have to face the truth of his promise. "Besides. Now he won't have to worry about me running off or doing something stupid. I'm not *always* confined here, anyway. He allowed me to go to the coronation—and the ball, though now I suspect it was because of the letter he had sent Entrais." Louko tried to reason away and make everything sound as if it was alright, even though he knew Kaeden would not buy it.

"You had a chance! A real *chance*, Louko!" The anger in Kaeden's voice was now off balance, revealing sorrow. But then both emotions receded as his tone grew quiet and forced. "You cannot hold to what you promised. Just let him think you will stay until he believes it."

Louko laughed bitterly, "No, Kaeden. It's over. It's time you leave it be," he said with a heavy resignation. "I never should have run away in the first place. It was a selfish thing to do."

Kaeden scoffed. "Selfish? Escaping your father's tyranny? Do enlighten me."

Rolling his eyes, Louko retorted, "Enlightenment was never my strong point."

Kaeden only ever thought kindly of him. The one person close enough to Louko to know him and still had yet to change their mind. Sometimes Kaeden could almost get Louko to think his father was mistaken, but only for brief moments. And today was not one of those days.

"This is *wrong*." Kaeden leaned into the last word. "Your father has no right to hold you to such a vow."

"And here we were having such a lovely time," Louko murmured dryly, trying to guilt Kaeden into being quiet. He despised himself for it, but he couldn't listen any longer. It hurt too much to remind himself he couldn't leave—that this would be his life forever—the pathetic shred of a life it was, anyway.

When there was no reply, Louko looked up at the elder man. He was nearly frightened by the fire that burned in Kaeden's eyes.

"One day—" The advisor's hands formed fists. "—your father will have to give account for everything he's done. And then there will be no escape for him."

Louko stiffened and shook his head violently. "Please, Kaeden, stop."

The man said nothing, sitting back down in his chair and resuming the cleanup of the chess pieces. Tension and deep anger were evident in each brisk movement Kaeden made.

Having nothing more to say, Louko helped him in silence.

Then the chamberlain, Julyn, came up from a servants' passage in the courtyard wall, looking very official. His greying hair was combed neatly back and his servant's uniform, as always, was the picture of perfection. Unlike either of his sons. Julyn gave a genial smile to Louko, then turned to Kaeden. Louko liked the servants, but was always careful not to get too close. He had learned long ago that, to his father, servants were easily replaced.

"Sir, the King requests your presence," he announced.

Kaeden gave a short, sharp nod. "Thank you," he said, voice suddenly calm. "I will be there shortly."

Julyn gave a half bow and left.

Kaeden let out a long breath before standing. "It would seem I have to leave you to the cleanup, then." He said to Louko, voice heavy.

The prince only nodded.

With one last long look, Kaeden left.

Louko's mind began to drift now that there was no one to distract it. He didn't let himself think of that last conversation. Instead, his thoughts turned slowly to Astra, still tucked away in the library. His good

—ish—conscience begged him not to go and disturb her, but Louko was just ever so slightly curious about what she was looking for. He tried to pretend he wasn't a little dismayed as well. She *was* after all, looking at the records. Those held some pretty nasty secrets. And as much as Louko wanted to stay far away from the library today...

That was it; he would go check on her. She was probably in dire need of his assistance anyway. A foreigner in his family's library could get very overwhelmed... or so Louko liked to think. He packed up the last of the chess pieces and snapped the case shut. He left it on the table, knowing Kaeden would retrieve it later.

Louko was nearly out of the gardens when he heard an all too familiar voice. He only just skittered behind some of the large gythian bushes before his sister passed by. The shrubs were usually no bigger than a hare, but with the Pershizarian glass overhead to filter the daylight, they were bigger than Louko. Lucky him.

"I've heard her brother is so stuck up as well." Mariah's socially acceptable whine buzzed through, talking to her servant, Meitha, as usual. Louko knew for a fact that Meitha hated these... chats. "Never saying a word at social gatherings, as if he was better than everyone else. And as if she isn't bad enough with her little comments about 'oh, I ride my horse everywhere'. So uncouth."

Louko had the good sense for once not to purposefully eavesdrop. He didn't want to hear anymore, if only to keep from running the risk of yelling at her and getting himself into trouble. She didn't know them, so how did she have the right to judge? She had no right to talk of them like that—no right at all. But Louko was getting unnecessarily emotional...

So as soon as the pair passed by, Louko hurried out of the garden and into a servants' corridor, weaving through the intricate maze of inner passages with the skill of familiarity Within minutes he arrived at the door that led to the library. Well, the servants' door. He much preferred to sneak around unobserved. So much easier to get things done.

Of course, after he opened the hidden little door, he wished he'd used the main one after all, because who else did he startle to death than…

"Oh. Well, hello, Astra," was all he could manage as he stared at the sword pointed very calmly at his throat. Whoops.

OF SHADE AND SHADOW

CHAPTER VI

Astra:

Astra kept an even grip on the blade, struggling with the instinct that told her she had to kill or be killed. With a deep breath, she lowered it slowly, then put it away. She turned away from the prince and tried to speak above the sound of her own pulse pounding in her ears.

"Sorry about that," Astra said. She didn't want him to see how much being startled affected her.

She watched him warily as he straightened his rumpled coat.

"Right, well, lesson learned. Use the actual door. Feel free to kill me next time if I don't get the point. Always was a slow learner," he replied almost too seriously, dry smile the only hint of his joke.

Astra raised an eyebrow, trying to return the smile. "Ah, yes, so slow. So slow that, back in The War, you had to start teaching Ent's captains swordsmanship instead of them teaching you."

His expression turned more roguish. "Oh, I'm useful." With that, he sidestepped and closed the small bookcase door that Astra had unknowingly been standing near.

Astra looked back at the pile of scrolls and books that covered the table she'd been working at. Useful? She wished she could say the same of herself. She turned back towards the table, trying to think of what she was missing.

"You find anything?" Louko's voice came from behind her; apparently he'd followed her.

"Not as much as I'd hoped," she admitted, wondering at his

sudden interest. "But there are plenty more places to look in here, I suppose." Too many places, perhaps.

"So serious," he murmured. "Would you like some assistance? I am a little more acquainted with the interior of the library, and would be more than happy to help," he added in that assumed annoying voice.

The offer caught Astra by surprise. "Um…" Suspicion crept in, and she tried not to think of Omath's warning. She reminded herself instead of her decision to trust Louko.

"Don't have any subjects in the 'um' territory, but I can give it a go."

The reply was so normal for him that Astra relaxed. "In that case, why don't we try some other areas? For starters, any royal records from around fourteen years ago."

Louko was halfway across the balcony even before she managed to get all the words out. "Which country? Alarune, Litash?"

"Let's start with Litash."

She watched as he kept walking, wondering if perhaps he hadn't heard her. But then he stopped near the end of the bookshelves and tugged on a dangling rope. A ladder slowly slid down, and the prince climbed it with what appeared to be years of familiarity. She watched in curious fascination as his fingers glided along the higher books, not even reading the covers, it appeared. Astra's Elvish ears could hear him murmuring numbers, as if he was counting books. His hand stopped abruptly, and he pulled out a thickly bound leather volume. Not bothering to climb, he slid to the bottom of the ladder and walked over to Astra.

"Start with this. I'll keep grabbing things, if you like. Probably more helpful than the others you found. This one has a terribly misleading title, I know."

Astra took '*The Years of Decline*', raising an eyebrow at the title, and opened it, but she was still distracted by how oddly at-home Louko seemed in this library. He had never mentioned books or learning in all the years she'd known him. Of course, Louko was clearly too intelligent to have foregone formal education as a prince. Astra thought again of what Omath had said. Had Tyron really been Louko's tutor? Had they studied here?

Astra corralled her thoughts; she needed to get back to work. She began thumbing through the large volume, trying to make sense of the scattered pieces of the timeline that she already knew. She stopped when she saw Omath's name written on the page. His accounts started off with his coronation, moved into negotiations with Nythril, brushed over some accounts of rebuilding projects and taking on a new advisor named Tuloi, then finally came to what Astra had been looking for:

In the second Month of Koven of the year One Thousand and Eighteen—Second Prince Euracia and Lower Prince (widower) Tyron arrive in Melye.

Astra's attention was caught by the titles. She had known Euracia was the Second Prince, and Tyron the Lower, but Tyron was a widower? She noted the date—at least two years after Tyron had been exiled, but not long before he had captured her father.

That's when she realized Louko was looking over her shoulder, "Anything more I can do to help? I found a few more books. Not sure if you'll find what you're looking for. Do you have a specific part of history in mind?"

"Uh," Astra was again put off by his genuinely helpful attitude. "Any time during Judican's reign."

"Early reign, or after he meddled with the Miadoris—I'm assuming the latter? The early reign is a bit boring if you ask me. He didn't really accomplish much. Not that he accomplished much otherwise. A little bit of the typical entitled royal. Thought he could solve everyone's problems with a click of his fingers. I suppose he did at least try to bring the Elves and humans into a more peaceful relationship, however. Oh. But anyway. Which part?" Louko bit his lip a little and began to rock back and forth on his feet, hands fiddling by his side.

Well, then. Louko seemed to have some rather clear, and perhaps, rather unflattering opinions in regards to politics. Not that Astra could blame him. Still, Louko had always shunned political conversation, so it struck Astra oddly that he would seem so informed now. She wondered again about his relationship with Tyron.

"The latter part."

"Right," he said awkwardly. "I shall return, then." And with that, he turned on his heels, heading to the stairs that led to the next terrace up.

Astra watched him. She hadn't realized how much tension Louko normally carried around. Turning back to the table, she scribbled down her findings about Tyron's marital status and time of arrival, making sure to use a language no one in Melye was likely to know. Then she returned to the books before her and kept scanning them.

Unfortunately, there was nothing more on Tyron's late wife.

Astra closed the book in frustration, knowing she needed more Litashian-based histories. This one only focused on Merimeethia. She wished that she could have used the record room of Litash. Of course, Euracia had burned any literature that did not align with his views, meaning that there was likely very little there of use. Not that it mattered —Astra couldn't go to Litash anyway.

Just then, Louko returned with three books. He held out one particularly worn volume. "This one is actually from Litash. I figured you could use it. The lady who had the library made was a lover of literature. Loved getting books from other countries. It's in Litashian, so it will be a little easier for you to naturally read." Well, Louko seemed to be falling into the habit of just… talking.

"Thank you," Astra said, taking and opening the book.

She flipped through the pages for several minutes, scanning for any key words. The girl did not get far before getting caught up on a paragraph about Dragons. She read it with interest, surprised to find that Dragons had once been a major political factor, along with a race called Drogans. Was that just a misspelling of the word Dragon? How odd. Without thinking, she asked Louko about it.

"Oh. Those." He sat down across the table from her. "No, it's not a misspelling. Drogans were like Bandilarians, except they could only shift from Dragon form to human. Very cunning. Their history is a little vague the farther back you go, but they had a reputation for being very manipulative. In most of the stories about Drogans, people say they were prone to twisting words and getting leaders to do what they wanted. I was always curious about that, though. If you have the reputation for being manipulative, how can you successfully be so? I imagine Gifting had a part in it, or something… But besides being manipulative, those that kept in their Dragon form too long could become savage like the beast. They'd start to think like an animal, even go insane—Drogan Madness, they called it." He paused, brow furrowed. "Though, come to think of it, I've met a Dragon and it was nothing like that."

True. It had been quite civil and not eaten Louko after he insulted it.

"Maybe they're blaming the wrong side of the Drogan," Louko shrugged, regathering himself as he seemed to realize just how long he'd gone on. "But why do you ask? What does that have to do with King Judican?"

Astra blushed. "Oh, um, nothing," she stammered. "Got distracted. Never heard of Drogans. Sorry." Louko was even more the walking book than Astra had previously thought.

He leaned on his elbows, idly opening one of the other books he'd brought. "Ah. They aren't really well known anymore. So, not surprised."

"Then how do you know so much about them?" Astra asked, then shook herself. She needed to focus. She began skimming the page again.

He fidgeted with the cover of his book. "Heard some of the problems they caused out west and… just read about it, I suppose. Boredom can do that." Looking down, he pretended to continue reading.

"Oh." She tried to stick to her task, but now she was curious. Louko seemed to know quite a lot. She reminded herself that even with Omath's awful treatment of his son, the king had allowed him an education. Astra was nearly envious of him for that; her childhood had been too scattered to allow for such things. *No time for self-pity, especially if you're comparing yourself to Louko. Besides, do you really envy him his tutor?*

Astra continued flipping through the book, but it wasn't until near the back that she started seeing pieces of history she recognized. The last entry was about Judican's coronation. Astra closed the book with a slight frown. Tyron hadn't made his move until after Judican was king. *Or had he?* Astra opened it again.

This time, she turned to a little before that last entry and began reading. She read all the way to the end and found no mention of Tyron whatsoever. Strange. Not even his birth was noted. Astra looked up from the book, thinking, and started when she realized Louko was staring at her.

"Er. Sorry. You look… confused. My first instinct would be that I grabbed the wrong translation, but…" He stared at her with a serious expression.

Astra was slightly bewildered, then embarrassed when his hesitant joke took her so long to grasp. "Oh. Yes. Haha. Sorry."

She fumbled for her wrapped-charcoal pencil and jotted down the book's title down on her sheet of parchment. With it, she noted her odd findings. Well, lack of findings. She set the book off to the side with a dull thud and a cloud of dust.

"Which one's next?" she asked.

Louko made a face, peering intently at her. "Why don't you take a break?"

Astra realized some time to process might not be a bad idea. "To do what?" she asked.

Louko:

Louko had been so busy this morning that he had hardly eaten anything for dinner last night...and neglected to really eat much of his breakfast. Now...he was all too aware of his growling stomach. "How about lunch? Do you eat that sort of thing?" He gave her a sarcastic look.

"Um…" Astra's hesitation made Louko wonder if she really didn't. The princess glanced down at the books on the table before answering, "Alright."

Yeah...she definitely didn't. "Well!" He clapped his hands, getting up and stretching for a moment. "Let's away to the kitchen, then."

Astra gave no response, but rose from her seat to follow.

Now...to use the back tunnels, or the main entrance… Louko decided against the servants' passages and headed for the *normal* exit. So boring… But then again, Louko was so prone to boredom.

Neither said a word as they headed down the halls, and Louko was glad for it. He was currently busy straining for any sound of people. His father had a few other guests at the castle, but running into a member of his family was his main concern. Especially Mariah.

How loving you are… really, Louko, no wonder your family adores you….

A couple of turns, stairways, and corridors later, and they were safely in the servants' section of the castle. Louko relaxed, but only

116

slightly.

As they continued down the small, unimpressive hall, the clatter of dishes filtered down and echoed off the walls. Above the growing noise, Louko could hear Graece's brisk orders being shouted to sluggish and diligent servants alike. The prince allowed a small, wry smile. "Well. Graece sounds in fine spirits this afternoon."

"She sounds like Salah," came the murmured response.

Oh, yes. Salah had been the cook in Entrais' camp, during The War. She had been an...odd sort. The lady had never allowed anyone to compliment her food. In fact, insults had always been encouraged. Not that such a thing had been difficult for Louko....

"Yes...Well, don't insult her food. Graece is not *that* weird," he finally replied.

As they stepped into the kitchen, Astra said, "I'll keep that in mind."

"Louko! Good, I was just about to come throttle you." Graece's boisterous voice turned on him the moment they entered. He could tell, however, she was scanning him for signs of abuse from his father.

"Don't look her in the eye, Astra, she's dangerous when she's like this." Louko remained monotone, showing how unimpressed he was by Graece's threat.

"Wouldn't think of it," Astra replied in turn.

They made their way through the hurried clutter of people and various counters towards the little table in the corner. Louko hesitated for a moment before motioning for Astra to sit in the chair across from him. It was stupid of him to be so attached to that empty chair, but it had always been where he and... well...Tyron had sat to eat. It was both stupid and incredibly insensitive of Louko, and yet even after having seen what Tyron had done in The War, he still could not help longing to see him again.

He wasn't sure if she noticed the hesitation, or was distracted by the bustling surroundings, but either way, the princess was slow to take her seat.

It only took a few moments before Rhumir came up to the table looking very annoyed, as usual.

"Cheery as always, I see." Louko gave him an unimpressed expression.

Rhumir pretty much dropped the tray of food onto the table. "Who's this?" he asked, head tipping towards Astra.

Rolling his eyes, Louko replied, "Someone who's pleasanter than you, that's for sure." The servant disliked people even more than Louko.

From behind Rhumir, Astra raised her eyebrows.

"That's not much of a recommendation," came Rhumir's retort.

True. Louko turned back to the food he had dropped, taking one of the bowls of soup. Stirring it a moment, he then tore off a piece of the long loaf of bread and dipped it in the soup. "I suppose it isn't," he at last replied to Rhumir, "but seeing you and your brother….anything is an improvement." With that, he took a bite of the bread, looking over at Astra and explaining, "They're terrors. Trust me," through a mouthful of food.

"Am I supposed to be surprised?" Astra asked, quiet even in her sarcasm. She pulled her bowl closer and began to stir.

In response Louko simply shrugged, giving Rhumir another

cynical expression.

"What are you doing? You lazy boy!" Graece yelled from her spot across the kitchen, "Get back here before I fetch Julyn!" She would have sounded fiercer if there hadn't been an edging of a smile on her face. One could see it even from across the room.

"Why can't they just kick me out already?" Rhumir grumbled. Then he gave his most forced smile and joked, "Enjoy the feast." With that, he took the empty tray and walked away, ducking a swat from Graece as he did so.

"As you can see...we have lovely service here," Louko commented unconvincingly as he took another bite of his bread.

Astra tore a piece from hers, though not eating it yet. "Charming," she confirmed, then paused. "Is he a friend of yours?"

Louko caught himself before he could let a wince escape. "He is...an interesting acquaintance," he replied instead. Friends. Not a desirable term. Not one Louko let slip nowadays. Especially regarding Rhumir; the more that boy knew, the more likely a violent outburst could ensue...and Louko didn't want to witness an execution.

Nodding in understanding, Astra dipped her bread in her soup and swirled it around.

Louko watched, wondering if she would *actually* eat or not. She must be starving; she had thrown up last night, and barely eaten anything this morning.

Just when Astra seemed resigned, something caught her attention and she set the bread down. That something turned out to be Graece.

"Oh, good," the cook said, one hand on her hip and the other holding a spoon. "That miscreant actually brought you food."

Not that Astra was eating it. Louko hid that thought and turned to Graece. "Yes. Miracles happen, I suppose."

At this, Graece gave a scoffing noise, but Louko again could catch her watchful eyes surveying him like a concerned hen. It annoyed him to no end, and he was thankful again that there was no bruise.

At least Graece no longer asked about it in front of everyone.

Apparently having finished her evaluation, the cook turned on Astra. Her tone was gentler as she asked, "Is there something the matter with your food?"

Astra reddened and shook her head quickly. "Oh, no, sorry. Just letting it cool."

Louko knew it was indeed hot—but that was, after all, why he had been dunking his bread in instead. That should have been the solution for Astra as well. He wondered if she still had eating problems from The War; he still remembered the way Entrais always had to coax her into nourishment.

"Oh. Let me go get some ice, then. It's a common thing to do here in Merimeethia—of course Louko hates it." She gave him another eye.

"There's really no need for such bother." Astra seemed only further flustered. "It's almost there."

"Alright." Graece conceded, but did not move. Louko was unsure which was worse. Graece pressing Astra to eat... or giving Astra the option not to.

"I do believe Rhumir ran off to change the sugar and salt again, Graece. You had better check." He gave a pointed glance over to where everyone was bustling about preparing for dinner. Rhumir wouldn't mind getting thrown in the line of fire, probably. Seeing as he was always throwing himself into it...

Graece looked over her shoulders and her eyes narrowed suddenly. She murmured something along the lines of 'that rascal' and was gone with no more than a hurried goodbye.

"Good thing we didn't need salt," Louko announced without breaking his serious expression.

"Now to hope no else does," Astra said with a shake of her head.

"Yes...." The response was slow as Louko idly watched the bustle of the room, "Rhumir has been trying to get fired for a while now..." then, clearing his throat, went on, "Anyway. Once you're done we can get back to the library." He again thought of where Astra was sitting, but was fortunately now more concerned with her behavior. He wished there was some way to help, but he wasn't sure how.

Astra took a quick bite of bread and got to her feet. "Ready when you are."

Why did he feel so disappointed? Then—as usual—Louko did the most idiotic thing he could think of and said, "Oh. I'm not done yet." And with that dove his spoon into what was left of his soup.

Astra blushed red enough to match her hair. "Oh. Sorry." She sat back down and returned to stirring her soup. Then, as if reluctantly, she took a bite.

Louko tried to be preoccupied, so as not to draw attention to her. It must have worked, since Astra actually finished the entire bowl and all of the bread.

Relieved and ready to get out of the noise, Louko got up, making

121

a motion with his head to ask if she was ready.

He received a nod as Astra practically jumped to her feet.

***

They were sitting in the library; the second day Astra had been conducting the research on whatever she was looking for. In that time, Louko had thoroughly evaluated that she needed a distraction. Her mood had been so withdrawn and consumed that he worried. If only Entrais were here, he'd know what to do...But since he wasn't, this pathetic attempt at a substitute had to do something.

"You look like you could use another break." He didn't bother to lead into that any better, deciding just to pounce on the problem, no matter how weird.

Astra:

Astra looked up from her book, "What do you suggest?" she asked slowly.

Running his hand through his hair, the prince gave an over dramatic sigh. "I do know one game. Probably pretty boring." He rolled his eyes.

Astra cocked her head. "What sort of game?"

"Like a board game. Strategy, you know?"

Shaking her head, Astra said, "Not really. I've heard of board games, but never played any."

It was almost comical to watch the transformation of Louko's

122

face. First, it was full of confusion; brows knit and eyes searching her, waiting as if for her to laugh and claim the joke. Then, a slow, wide grin spread itself across his face, and he got up, fingers drumming the table. "Oh, you're dead serious. How wonderful. I suppose we will just have to teach you, Princess Astra. Excuse me while I fetch the object for our lesson." Without so much as waiting for a reply, he disappeared to the lower level of the library.

Astra, feeling ignorant, embarrassed, and awkward, thumbed through a few books as she waited.

It was only a few minutes before the prince returned, carrying a fairly bulky case with a handle on it. It looked like one of those trunks Astra had seen the Pershizarian peddlers store their items in.

The prince's grin had tapered down to one of his more characteristic expressions, and he looked dangerously mischievous as he set the small trunk down on the table. He opened the dark wooden case with a click. Curious, Astra ever so slightly leaned forward to see if she could catch a glimpse at what was inside. It brought little success, as the cover obscured her view.

However, she did not have to wait long to see. One by one, Louko set out the contents. It was a strange set of objects.

The first thing he set on the table was a funny, square-shaped wooden board. It took a moment for Astra to realize it was in fact three thin boards of different sizes, all connected by a foldable wooden frame. Next out of the box there came numerous figurines, all beautifully carved marble—some white, some black. Astra noted the various shapes, including majestic horse heads, the tall tower-like statues, and then the many little turrets with round orbs on the tops of each.

"This is what we call TetraChess. Very popular for bored royals like us," he said with yet another dramatic sigh, taking out the wooden frame and unfolding it so that it held the rectangular boards up in a three-tiered formation. "I hear some people play it with only one tier, but that seems a pretty dull and amateur way of playing it. No strategy in it at all."

Now that the boards were set up, Astra could see that each was checkered with tiny painted squares of different colors. She also realized the boards were different sizes—the largest at the bottom and the smallest at the top.

Everything set out, Louko sat down. "So. It's almost like a war," he began, "and each piece represents someone or something. An asset. Soldier, friend, whatever you like to think of. They can each do certain things. For instance," He picked up the horse. "Dannsair is only good for looking moody." He smirked. "Or, more practically, transporting you places easier than your feet can. She is not someone you send to spy on someone or anything like that. In much the same way, each piece has a role. These—" he picked up two tall pieces, one black with a white circlet crowning the top, and the other white with a black circlet— "are the kings. Each side gets one. If it is taken—killed—the game is over." He set those down and picked up a small, castle-looking piece. "These are almost like an Ethian Guard," he explained, referencing the Ethian Council's personal guards—the best and most gifted Bandilarians, who served the crown and its council. "They can attack, but are also very important in the defense of the king. If you are careful in how you use them, then they can do more types of maneuvers. But use them too soon and they become permanent warriors."

Astra's curiosity was definitely piqued now.

"These are like spies." He lifted up two funny, domed pieces, each one in its respective color. "They can only move diagonally—at an angle. Never straight forward. Cunning." Putting those down, he took up two other pieces that looked much like the kings he had just shown. The only difference was the crown: it was smaller, and in its own color. "These are the most powerful pieces in the game, many say. The queens. They can move like any of your other pieces—except for your knights." He motioned to the horse pieces. "They are often very overused. If they get taken, it is very hard for your king survive. Just like real queens," he said, mouth twisting. He set the pieces down abruptly, and reached for the last type of piece—the small ones with the orbs on top. There were several of these, so he just picked the two nearest. "And these are my favorites," he announced. "They can move very little, and are not much use for taking other pieces, but they can become anything if you get them to the right spot." He tossed one carelessly into the air and caught it. "It's also very important, because this is a piece that often takes the fall for the others. They're like the common soldier. Important, but not given much credit." Explanation done, Louko set the two pieces down and put his elbows on the table, resting his chin on his folded hands. "So, any questions? Ask now, or die a slow and painful death."

It was a lot to take in in just a few minutes. "Slow and painful, eh?" Astra raised an eyebrow, bemused. "Is there no mercy for the beginner?"

He winked. "Never—but for your sake, I suppose we shall omit a few of the advantages. We'll start with basic rules. Was that your only question?"

"So far," Astra's reply was slow as she tried to decipher why Louko would be winking at her. Even taking the prince's difficult background into account, his odd habits and mood swings were hard to follow.

Louko set up the pieces, placing them on the different boards. "Each board affects one another. Let's start with the simplest version. It's not quite accurate to how it is supposed to be played, but I don't want to dispose of your sanity too quickly." He took a breath before continuing, attention entirely set on the game, "So let's say that each board represents a certain rank. The top is royalty—so just your kings and queens. The second is the nobles, meaning everything but the pawns. And then the pawns, the common soldiers, are the bottom board. Does it make sense so far?" He demonstrated the principle as he explained.

Astra nodded, not taking her eyes from the boards.

"Now, just like in real life, each rank has certain rules they have to follow. Take our royalty, for example." He gestured to the kings and queens on the top tier. "They aren't allowed to kill each other directly. However, they can manipulate each other's movements."

How could the pieces be taken, then? Astra didn't get a chance to ask before Louko went on.

"You see, whatever square the queen is using on this board—" he pointed to the top— "can't be used by the opponent on *this* board." Louko then pointed to the middle board, tracing an invisible line between the two. "What's more is that the queen is never allowed to be next to the opponent's king. So, if you are using your queen to block one of my pieces on the middle board—" Louko set up a quick demonstration. "—I can use my king to sort of shove your queen somewhere else."

They had only gone over one board, and yet it already seemed complicated.

Louko picked up his explanation on the middle tier. "Nobility lives by different rules. They can kill each other in battle, but doing so affects the troops they lead. That's why in TetraChess, if you lose a 'noble' piece, you lose any pawns that are in the space directly underneath as well as the space before and behind."

Astra nodded to show she understood.

"Now, our last board—the common soldiers—has the least amount of etiquette." Louko seemed to find this amusing. Astra, having known plenty of soldiers, saw why. "Their orders are pretty straightforward: kill as many enemy pawns as possible. They are only allowed to move forward, no side-to-side or questioning of orders." Louko demonstrated again. "However, if one should make it all the way across the board, it advances in the ranks." He moved the little white pawn up to the middle tier. "Then its goal is to reach the enemy king or queen by landing in the space directly beneath one of them." He moved the piece beneath the black queen and then promoted it to the very top tier. "Here is what the whole game comes to: the pawn trying to kill the king, the king trying to escape the pawn, and the opposing queens trying to either protect or kill the pawn."

Astra watched as Louko went through a few turns. It was fascinating to watch, though massively complicated and strategic beyond what Astra thought herself capable of. Finally, Louko let the black queen topple the white pawn.

"Now..." He looked at her. "Ready to play?"

"Please tell me that was a hypothetical question," Astra responded dryly.

Louko just rolled his eyes. "Fine. Before we have a go, let's review everything one more time. Tell me what you remember?"

Carefully, Astra repeated everything back to him.

"Good. Now, let's try it." Louko pointed to the side that held the white pieces. "Those are your pieces. I get the first move. Don't be so set on the king or queen that you forget about all the other players, though. Feel free to ask questions as we go." As he spoke, he moved a pawn on the bottom tier.

And so began their game. The two played several rounds, Louko explaining more rules with each one. The longer they went on, the longer the games went on. Astra was fairly sure that it had more to do with the new rules than it did her improving skill. She won only two of the matches—and those she was sure Louko allowed her to win. She had lost count of her losses by the time the prince said, "I think that's enough for one day." Louko began to pack up the pieces.

"Did we at least get through all of the rules?" asked Astra, helping.

He laughed. "Oh, we barely even got to half of them."

"You compared this to a war, but I am beginning to think actual war is simpler," Astra groaned.

Louko just shrugged. "Depends on the war, I suppose."

***

After that, Astra and Louko stayed in the library, him pulling out book after book and her digging through them. Occasionally, Astra would allow herself a small break, but for the most part she was too deeply absorbed. Eventually, Louko announced he had to leave to meet someone, and so left Astra alone. It was some time afterwards that the servants came to prepare her for dinner.

The girl left reluctantly, not wanting to give up her work when she had made no progress to show for all her time. To add to it, dinner meant getting into another gown. It wasn't that Astra disliked pretty things. No, even though they made her look even plainer than she knew she was, she did like them. Perhaps it was simply the fact that she did not get to choose what things she wore. Thus, she ended up with uncomfortable dresses and a bracelet that had the same function as a manacle. This particular case was no better: Astra would not only have to dress like a princess, but also hold her tongue like one while Louko's family tore him to shreds. Yes, Astra definitely would have preferred the library. Nonetheless, she arrived promptly to dinner, dressed as her title demanded she be.

As the king motioned for everyone to sit, Astra tried to ignore the sickening feeling settling in her stomach. Louko wasn't here. Was that good? Was he excused for the evening? Or was he late? She didn't want a repeat of the other night. Perhaps she should follow Kaeden's advice…

"Ah, Princess Astra, how are you this evening?" King Omath greeted her cordially.

Astra's gracious smile was probably as fake as the king's

warmth. "Very well, thanks to your generosity."

"Ever at your service."

Astra thought to herself that Omath wouldn't say that if he knew she was exiled.

With that, dinner began... but Louko still wasn't there. Astra watched nervously as the king began giving pointed looks at the empty chair.

Then a side door opened and Louko entered, never lifting his gaze from his feet. Astra saw Omath's frown deepen, and jumped in before a scolding could ensue.

"So, Prince Keeshiff, how goes your training?" Astra acted as if she was interested enough to not even see Louko enter. Hopefully, the attention to his oldest son would delay the scolding to the younger.

Keeshiff looked to his father ever so slightly and, even though he seemed to get a hint something was off, was either dumb enough to keep going or smart enough to play it off. "Grueling. I am afraid these new trainers are not much good at their trade. Father should definitely look into getting them replaced."

Omath seemed somewhat put out by the remark, but it was enough to draw his focus from Louko sliding into his chair. Keeshiff was evidently very uncomfortable, and the way he had made the comment seemed forced. Keeshiff wasn't... helping, was he? Astra didn't take too much time with the thought.

"Oh, that's a shame," she said, shaking her head. She addressed Omath directly, this time. "Perhaps, if you'd allow me, Sire, I would like to test these trainers for myself."

The king nodded. "If you desire." And thankfully, he let Louko slide. For now.

Astra didn't let the conversation stop yet, just in case. Feigning innocence, she turned to Mariah. "You must excuse my ignorance, for I am not well versed in these things. Is it common for the females of the royal household to also train in the fighting arts?"

Mariah gave a pretty smile. "Not generally; however, I know a little myself. Father was always so afraid something was going to happen to me." She rolled her eyes and gave a mock-annoyed glance at her father.

"I suppose it certainly can't hurt," Astra said in what was hopefully a pleasant tone.

This time, she let the conversation close, and everyone turned to their food. Across the table, Astra met Kaeden's disturbing green eyes and he gave a nearly imperceptible nod. She looked away, but was somewhat glad of their unspoken agreement to shield Louko.

And then Louko spoke up. "Astra, what did you think of the library?"

Omath sat up even stiffer in his chair. "What did you say, Louko? Two offenses in a day?"

Louko sighed and gave Astra an almost invisibly irritated smile. "*Princess* Astra. My apologies."

"Oh, there is no slight, Sire. I gave Louko permission to use my name," Astra explained again, in the most patient voice she could find. She hadn't, but fighting alongside her for several years had earned him the right.

Omath cleared his throat. "With all due respect, Princess Astra, may I please discipline my children as I seem fit?" Now his voice was cool.

Astra knew she could not argue this time, but the silence tasted bitter in her mouth. This was not fair. She repressed the childish urge to slam her silverware onto the polished wood of the table. Or throw it at Omath.

The quiet didn't last too long. "So, Astra," Mariah began. "I visited the stables the other day and got a look at your pony. She is simply gorgeous," she commented, all grace and glamour.

It took all Astra's self control not to glare at the princess. Of course, Omath didn't correct *her.* Trying not to grind her teeth. "Why thank you, *princess.*" Astra said. Let Omath know she was displeased— she didn't care. Then Astra stopped herself. She couldn't let her temper ruin Ent's reputation. She attempted to sound kinder. "I hope my mare didn't charge at all. She does get feisty around strangers."

"Oh she was a little feisty, but I don't blame her. In a strange place, all alone. It can be quite a shock. Hopefully she calms, though. I was thinking perhaps we could go for a ride tomorrow?"

Astra had the uncomfortable feeling that Mariah was mocking her. "That would be very pleasant." As pleasant as being buried alive, anyway.

"Perfect! I look forward to it, Astra." Mariah clapped her hands together and gave a huge grin.

At the use of her name, Astra froze. She glanced sideways at Omath. Still nothing? Really? Surely Mariah was doing it on purpose.

"Princess," Astra murmured, her grip tightening on her fork in her growing anger.

Mariah cocked her head and looked confused, "I'm sorry?"

"Princess," Astra said, anger making her bolder. "With all due respect, the king has made it clear that he desires us to retain formal titles." Her smile was brittle.

Mariah's jaw tightened, but she gave a polite bow of her head. "Oh. Of course, Princess."

Astra knew she needed to calm down. She stole a glance at Louko and saw his lips drawn back in a very tense smile. The sting that left on Astra's conscience was enough to soothe her temper after that.

"Riding is just wonderful though, don't you think?" Mariah addressed Astra, surprisingly on the same topic, and apparently refusing to acknowledge the lost fight by using neither title *nor* name. "The stables were actually redone by Father, right?" She turned to Omath at that. He did not seem pleased with her topic choice. "Didn't you make them for Mother?"

"Mariah." The reply was simple, but an odd mix of warning and gentle.

Mariah made a very good impression of being penitent. "I'm sorry, Father. I just wanted to hold onto the memories." At that, she turned her gaze on Louko, but addressed Astra. "I have so few memories, so I hang on to the good ones, you know, *princess*? Mother also added the library. Do you enjoy it?"

Astra tried to find words that would not offend everyone in the room. She knew how touchy a death in the family was. "Yes. It is lovely. It has been a great help to me."

Mariah smiled, "I'm so glad you came and were able to enjoy it. It's finally gotten some good use."

Astra smiled again and just nodded. Anything to let the

conversation move on.

CHAPTER VII

Louko:

Louko was in a sour mood. He was in the library, leafing through one of the books that had his mother's personal signature in it—marking her favorite—and feeling selfishly miserable. Dinner last night had, for him, gone worse than the night before. He'd lost track of time *again*— apparently a newly-formed habit he had avoided until now—and the lapse of self-control in the middle of dinner had been unforgivable. His father had made that much very clear this morning when he'd called for him... What in Eatris had he been thinking, asking Astra *in the middle of dinner* how she liked the library?

Don't try to make sense of idiocy.

But even worse, Louko hated when his mother was brought up, and yet, he didn't have a right to tell Mariah to stop talking about it. Seeing the pain on his father's face...

He needed to clear his head. So with a quiet thump, he closed the book, stretching his stiff limbs as he decided to wander over to the domed section of the library. His hands soothingly brushed the bookshelves as he made his way over, taking deep breaths and beginning to get ahold of himself again. Until he saw Astra. She was sitting at a table, four or five thick books stacked up in front of her. Worse, she was buried in another one of his mother's favorites. He had tried to keep her away from those.

"Oh. You're here early," he said as he walked up to her table, not being able to help the small pinch of hurt as well as confusion that

135

began rubbing inside him.

Astra started, and looked up. "Um, sorry," she said quickly. "Wasn't sleeping, so I thought I might as well get to work. I didn't think it would be a problem if I came alone, and I didn't want to wake you for nothing."

"Did I do something wrong?" The lapse in his self-control led to the question burning within him. Had it been from dinner last night? Could he have embarrassed her by addressing directly and without her title?

Astra blinked at him. "What?"

"I'm sorry, I didn't mean to embarrass you last night. I just have this thing where I don't shut up, I guess...I'm sorry. I can leave, if you want." *Would he shut up??* Louko felt rather emotionally unhinged this morning and now he was putting it all on Astra, sitting here trying to apologize instead of just sucking it up and walking away to leave her alone in peace. But he didn't want to. He really, *really* didn't want to, and the acknowledgement of that was frightening.

"I'm sorry," Astra looked nearly flustered. "Are you talking about last night? I don't really remember anything embarrassing. Except, for, um," her cheeks flushed red. "Would you rather I not use the library?" Her expression was earnest as she looked back up. "I realize now that it holds a very personal value to you, and I have no wish to intrude."

Idiot! Look what you did. "Oh, no, you're fine. It's nothing personal at all. Just had it basically to myself all these years. Have to get used to sharing." Louko ran his hand through his hair. "I just, didn't want to intrude if you didn't want me. I guess I sort of assumed and didn't think I could be...getting on your nerves," The last bit was a pitiful attempt at a joke. Well, an attempt to mask it as such.

Astra gave no initial reaction. "You...you realize that I am the guest, right? *I* would be the one intruding. And besides, how would you be getting on my nerves? All you've done is help."

Oh. Louko was both embarrassed and oddly touched at the same moment. Slowly his shoulders relaxed as he allowed himself to believe this, even for just a little while. "Really? You're sure? Not a bother? I'm not...talking your ear off?" He winced even as he gave a sheepish smile.

Astra's head tilted and bafflement showed on her face. "Ears...off?"

"It's...an expression..." He realized that again interpretation might have been lost on the half-Elf. "It's stupid, don't worry about it." Tension further dissipated, and Louko felt he could again breathe. That being said, now that he was a little less absorbed in his stupid insecurity, he realized just how exhausted Astra looked. "Though speaking of phrases you might not understand, your eyes look like they're about to fall out of your head from reading so long. Maybe a break would be wise. I mean...I suppose you could just stay in your little corner and keep reading and I could just go find a corner of my own...somewhere..." He looked over his shoulder for dramatic effect.

Astra also relaxed and a smile tugged at her lips. "I suppose I've never been one for corners," she said. "What would you suggest doing instead?"

"How about a tour? Somehow, Mariah giving you one no longer sounds so appealing... more of a death sentence for you, I suppose." He forced amusement, secretly relieved that the tension had been so easily resolved. Astra now seemed much more relaxed.

The girl arched one brow. "Indeed. I rather think I've fallen from her good graces. Though I don't think I mind." Astra glanced once around the library, then nodded. "I think a tour would be lovely."

"Good. Then follow me." Louko motioned, instantly taking off.

Astra:

Astra followed Louko down the winding maze of corridors, glad she was with him and not his sister. Mariah had sent a note right after breakfast asking to cancel their planned excursion. While the other princess had claimed a headache, Astra had the feeling it had more to do with the way the conversation had turned last night at dinner. Not that she minded. Mariah's excuse had meant that Astra didn't have to come up with one.

Louko led them onwards, explaining each room they passed. "We'll come back to these later. The Duchess and Duke of some Ilnorian city are visiting—arrived yesterday. Don't think you would care to have a three-hour conversation with them."

It was fascinating how well he could navigate the seemingly identical stone passageways, though Astra also noted at how adept it made him at avoiding others. It took no genius to see the correlation.

"They should be in the art gallery right now, so we'll visit it after. How about the Spyglass Tower first? The weather is actually tolerable...so might as well while it lasts." Louko ducked around another corner.

Astra followed. "Alright," she replied, honestly somewhat

distracted. She puzzled again over how the Merimeethians had managed to keep such big tunnels from being obvious. For all the castle's drafty, damp, plainness, there was cleverness in the architecture.

"Aha. Here we are." He stopped in front of a door and opening it, revealing the light of day ahead. "After you," he said, gesturing.

Astra stepped out, finding herself very disoriented. They were...in one of the gardens. Strange. She must have lost her sense of direction in the library. Or perhaps the halls were even cleverer than she thought. The girl turned to her guide, waiting for his explanation.

"We could have just gone farther down to get to the tunnel, but I figured a detour to outside—well, the closest thing Merimeethians *get* to outside—would be nice," Louko explained, taking the lead once again and guiding her through a section.

The garden was beautiful and very well kept. Yet, there was something about the neatly trimmed orderliness of it that felt out of place, as if the things that grew here were meant to grow beyond the little patches they were confined to. Astra told herself that she was being melodramatic, and tried to redirect her thoughts by finding anything she recognized. They were halfway through when she spotted some flowers that seemed to resemble ones on the northern edge of Litash—however, not deadly or poisonous or... Yes, perhaps Astra was not the best judge of agricultural beauty.

They reached the other side of the garden and reentered using a main entrance instead of one of the hidden passages. Louko walked more slowly, often glancing from side to side. Astra was inwardly debating whether or not to ask him what he was on guard for when he stopped. The prince raised one finger to his lips to signal the need for silence, then motioned her over to one of the doors. He lifted the latch and pushed it open with a speed and soundlessness that caught Astra by surprise—but after years of such wartime maneuvers, she followed without a thought.

Louko closed the door behind them, then put one ear to it. With her advanced hearing, Astra had no need to copy him in order to hear the voices outside. It was a small group, talking leisurely and loudly. Definitely not servants.

Then the footsteps stilled, and the voices came to rest right outside the door.

"To be frank, I found her dress to be simply hideous." A high-pitch voiced leaked through the wooden door. "I can't even think what would have possessed her to put those two colors together."

Louko rolled his eyes, shaking his head and mouthing something along the lines of "How rude". He stepped away from the hall entrance, and ushered Astra to follow. The prince led her to another door in the back of the room that let out into a smaller back corridor. They walked four doors down, took a right, and came out further along in the main hallway that they'd started in. Astra could hear voices echoing from around the corner.

"Almost there," Louko commented in a hushed voice, only turning around long enough to make sure she'd heard him.

It was strange to see the comparison between this Louko—the one who loved books and sparring and clever tunnels—and the one who kept his eyes down at the dinner table where his family was. It filled Astra with sorrow to see how little anyone really knew him. Even she had misjudged him; during The War, he had seemed brash, grating, arrogant and puffed up till no one could stand him. But now…

They came to yet another door, and once more Louko opened it and stepped aside. "I like to think this would be impressive even to a Litashian, but then again I don't get around much," he said, an almost genuine-looking smile on his face. Almost.

Astra walked through to a small room, where another door awaited. Granted, not impressive.

"Well, I suppose I forgot to mention there was another door…" Louko brushed past and opened the other one. In another moment he was leading her up through the dark tower, climbing the cold stone stairs. Then, suddenly, there was light. Not from the lanterns, but sunlight—real sunlight from above them. Another couple steps, and the stone walls gave way to glass. All around, Astra could see the castle right below their feet. Staring up, she realized there were still quite a few stories to climb, the glass barely visible against the bright grey skies.

"Come on, this part's boring." Louko urged her on, continuing up those heavenward stairs which carved up through the clouds.

As much as Astra would have liked to stay and look, she obeyed and followed him until the stairs came to a stop. Louko was already ascending a ladder that led to a marble ceiling. Deftly, he opened the trapdoor and disappeared through the hole.

His head reappeared. "Are you coming or not?"

The prince's adventurous mood had now caught, and Astra did not hesitate in climbing up after him.

The view was breathtaking. They were high above the castle now, faraway hills and forests creating a patchwork of green and brown along the horizon. It was as though they were standing in a hall made of the sky itself, with the glass roofing creating its own mosaic around them. With the movement of the mist below, it looked as though the glass was alive.

Astra could not hide her smile. She slowly turned full circle in the room before going to its edge. There, she pressed one hand to the icy pane and looked down. Yes, she had ridden Dragons at steep heights many times, but this was different. One never got to stop and stare when moving at such high speeds.

"Well?" Louko's voice echoed about the glass dome.

"It is beautiful," Astra managed no more than the simple reply, now gazing out across the forests which rose and fell beneath the fog. How could words describe this?

There was a long pause, and then a, "Yes. Yes it is," as he too admired their perspective from the other side of the tower.

Astra wasn't sure how long they stayed there; she was shivering with cold by the time Louko broke the silence again. "Ready to see some more?" he asked.

He'd led them well thus far. "Lead the way," Astra replied with a nod.

Still, she was slow in descending the ladder and the steps that led back down to the world below. Only when the walls of stone returned did she match Louko's pace.

"Well. The Duchess and Duke's tour should be past the art gallery by now. Why don't we go there next?" Louko said with a flourish, diving with energy down the hall they had gone from before.

The mention of people suddenly made Astra realize that the

visiting nobles were the only other guests she had seen at Melye. Curiously, she asked, "Are there usually so few people here?" Ent's palace had always been so busy. Not that she had left her room when she could help it.

Louko let out a short laugh, "Well, between the *lovely* climate, it's seclusion from the rest of the Macridean Seaboard, and the even *lovelier* company, there isn't much reason to come out. Especially not all the way out to our capitol. The City of Light is prettier and more accessible, so most people just go there. Melye used to have some Nythrilian nobility who would visit, but with tensions being so high between them and Merimeethia, there haven't been any here in many years."

It made sense. Astra wouldn't want to trek all the way through the mud and rain to visit Omath, either.

They retraced their steps, sometimes walking through the actual halls until they heard someone coming; then they would dive back into the tunnels, and Louko would listen for a moment before hurrying her on. Soon they emerged into another hall, and Louko's voice echoed grandly as he announced, "This is the art gallery." And then, "the only good view here, I'm afraid is the painted portraits of dead people... I suppose it's less inviting when you say it that way..." He clapped his hands together and said cheerily, "Oh well, where shall we start?"

Astra found more and more that she was never sure how seriously she ought to take Louko. She gave a diplomatic answer: "We can start at this end and work down to the next, I suppose."

"Excellent. Follow." His footsteps echoed as he took off, appearing quite at ease. Astra, however, could see the fleeting glances he would chance around him, as if to make sure there would be no sudden visitors.

They stopped in front of the first picture, a grizzled, weather-beaten man with what must have been a crown on his head. "This, is my father's father's....et cetera...cousin. Ceryn. He is dead, obviously. But he was the one that built this place. Quite paranoid—hence the maze of secret passages."

That made sense. Astra nodded to show she was listening, and followed him down to the next portrait. She couldn't help but think that her brother and parents looked much better in their paintings.

"Queen Enda, his niece. Reigned very briefly while his son was exiled. Then he came back and killed her." Louko's voice was very deadpan as they stood before the blond, elegant—albeit arrogant—looking lady.

"Charming," Astra said dryly, before she could stop herself.

"Yes. Very." Louko mimicked her tone. "But that's only the beginning. Just wait." And with that, the very interesting tour of the art gallery continued. Astra did not realize so many people could be usurped, disinherited, *re*inherited, and murdered. The paintings, of course, were beautiful... but Louko's explanations seemed very, well, blunt. There were only a couple he gave flattering epithets to. Finally, they came near the end to the last couple.

"This is my father's father, Belayr. He was pretty alright. Died young of pneumonia. Common problem here." He moved on to the next picture, a flaxen haired, ornately adorned lady. "This is Lady Dyla, my father's first wife. Died in a riding accident."

Astra paid more attention to this lady; she had not realized that

King Omath had married twice. This woman certainly shared strong characteristics with Keeshiff... but Louko looked nothing like her.

However, the smiling lady at the end of the row looked very much like Louko. The brown, almond-shaped eyes, black hair, the little half-smile: This must be Louko's mother.

The prince cleared his throat and looked a little stiff as they moved down to face the lady. "And this is Lady Ravyen, my father's second wife, and my mother. She wasn't from Merimeethia and—er— had trouble adjusting to the climate. Several things piled up and she just died." He added a shrug at the end. "I hear she was nice."

Now Astra's focus was drawn to Louko instead of the painting. In his tension, it was hard to see how he felt. The most notable thing she saw there was regret. Was it because he had never known her? Astra pitied the prince. It only made it worse to think that his mother may have loved him in a way that would have brought the rest of his family around.

Astra searched for words of comfort but found none that would sound sincere. She hoped listening would be enough for now.

"Anyway. What shall we see next? There are more gardens, the stables—though you've probably been—-"

"What, exactly, do you think you're doing??" The indignant voice came from a little way down the hall. Astra saw Louko wince and turn around.

"Oh, Mariah, didn't see you there," he said, sounding suddenly very small.

The way he retreated made Astra step forward. "Your brother was very kindly giving me a tour of the castle," she said, outwardly calm.

"Please. Him? He couldn't give a competent tour if he tried. Why don't I show you around?" Mariah's voice was sweet. The kind of over-sweet that one used to hide a strong poison.

It took effort for Astra to remain gracious. "We're nearing the end of ours. Thank you for the offer, but I think I will finish first. Besides, I wouldn't want to aggravate the headache you had this morning."

Mariah's smile turned coy and she turned to glare at her brother. Louko made some sort of sad excuse for a smile, and looked as if he was about to say something.

"Don't bother." His sister cut him off, spinning around and flouncing away until she was gone from view.

There was a moment of silence before Louko asked weakly, "Well, shall we continue?"

Astra turned from the now empty hall. "Lead the way."

CHAPTER VIII

Louko:

Louko stood before the large doors, wondering what horrible death awaited him this time…

Well, aren't you being a little toddler?

Regardless of his leanings towards drama, this didn't alleviate the stress Louko felt as he stood there, wishing he did not have to go in.

But he knew better. Not going in would be even worse.

Nonetheless, he still delayed. Still he waited, and wished he didn't have to go in. Mariah must have told his father about him showing Astra around. He tried not to feel even more apprehensive; Omath had always been very clear that he didn't want Louko fraternizing with guests….

"Shall I announce you are waiting? Or are you going to gawk all day?" asked one of the guards standing nearby.

Snap to it, idiot, Louko thought to himself, forcing focus to return. "Yes, thank you," he managed to reply.

The guard nodded and disappeared behind the side entrance to the throne room, giving Louko only a moment more to stew. *Just get past this. It will be over in a few minutes, and whatever punishment it is this time, it can't be any worse than being stuck in this place. Besides, you told Astra you'd meet her in the library later. That will lighten whatever is about to come.* And so he tried to convince himself.

It didn't help.

The guard door opened, and the man soon appeared, opening

the official door and ushering Louko in. The prince chanced one more quick breath.

"Ah, there you are, you pitiful excuse for a son," Omath's voice boomed across the empty room. As always, there was no audience. Louko couldn't say he minded.

Knowing it would only anger his father, yet having nothing else he could possibly do, Louko bowed in respect.

This only got him a biting, "Oh, get up."

Louko obeyed, not looking up at his father. He wouldn't be able to stand the hate in his eyes—the hate he had put there. The hate that perhaps his mother would have been able to stop. Louko wondered, as he had a hundred times, what his father would have been like if...

"Now, boy, do you know why you are here *this* time?" Omath's voice was colder than usual, and dread only grew.

"No, Sir," Louko replied.

This received a snort from his father. "Oh, please, don't claim ignorance. You constantly claim not to have any interest in politics, but at every moment seek to ruin my credibility."

Louko's heart sank—he was definitely talking about Astra. Louko didn't like where this was going—more so than usual—and in his beginning stages of panic, made a fatal mistake and looked up, allowing his confusion to show for a moment. "What? I w—"

Smack!

Louko didn't bother to wince as the hand came into contact with his face, bitterly used to the unpleasant occurrence. It was his own fault for the lapse in discipline and letting his emotions rule him. *Idiot.*

"Getting a little fresh, are we?" Omath growled, bringing his hand back and threatening another strike, "I thought you knew better than to talk back to your betters—but I suppose this only proves my point." His voice held resignation, and Louko's fists clenched by his side in anxiety as he realized that he had just made whatever it was even worse for himself.

Classic Louko…

Omath lowered his hand. "So why don't we just get to the point then, before you dig an even bigger hole for your idiotic self, hm?" There was a pause, and then, "You are meddling with my guests, *Louko,* and I thought you knew better." The way his father said his name always sounded more like he was spitting out a deadly poison. Louko supposed that wasn't too far from the truth, considering their history…

But that thought was drowned out by his father's words.

"You are trying to wheedle your way in and usurp me, and that will not be tolerated. My guests are *mine,* and not yours to play with. Leave them alone." The last sentence was firm.

Swallowing hard, Louko gave a quiet, "Sir, I meant no—"

Idiot.

That was the only word he had time to think of as he received another blow, this one nearly knocking him backwards.

"Dare you argue with me?? *Again?* Indeed, you are still not much broken of your habits from your little escapade. This will hopefully fix some of that disrespect." His tone held the usual cold disappointment.

Louko only waited in silence, *finally.* Again, he had only made things worse for himself. His father was right. He never should have left in the first place.

Then Omath spoke, the words that followed proving Louko had not been worried enough, "So, to start with, you can stop idling with my guests. Princess Astra has much more important things to do than put up with you, I am sure, and you distract her and irritate her. If I see you with her again, you will wish you hadn't been so eager to stay here."

Louko felt like another part of him was dying as his father's words sunk in. Stay away from Astra? He had—-against his better judgement—rather begun not to mind her company. He had thought she didn't seem to mind it, either. But his father's words brought forth the usual fears he had managed to shut out. Was he irritating her? Probably. Still…. Not see Astra…at all? The despair he had gotten so good at keeping at bay returned full force. With it, the panic at being so alone again returned, and he found words coming out even though he knew to be silent. "Please, Sir, I won't be trouble, I pro—"

"Silence!" his father shouted, grabbing Louko by his shirt collar and bringing him closer. "Perhaps I did not make myself clear enough, *Louko*. Since you have made my life a living hell, I can make yours quite the same. I've been quite civil up to this point, and as long as you mind your own business and show some respect, I will continue to do so—but don't. Test. Me," he said through grit teeth. His face was hard.

Idiot.

Louko felt numb. He heard the words, "Yes, Sir," come out of his mouth, but it sounded as if someone else had put them there. All the same, they held little conviction. Perhaps his father was right; he was getting out of hand. But Astra was offering him a small piece of the freedom he'd had during The War and Louko was loath to turn it away. Even for his father.

Omath glowered at him "Is that the nice way to say you're lying?" Louko didn't say a word, looking down at the floor.

The next words shattered any hope Louko had tried to piece together. "Because I *informed* the princess this morning of your affiliation with Tyron. I have to say, she looked rather ill...barely excused herself in time to hide her disgust and shock. So if you won't obey me, would you please leave the *poor girl* alone in some semblance of peace."

"Yes, Sir." His voice was the ghost of a whisper. Louko's face drained of the little color it had, and he couldn't face the reality of this. How Astra had to despise him now...knowing...knowing that...

Louko recalled hearing his father dismissing him, but did not remember leaving the room. His thoughts were a mangled mess.

As he slowly made his way down the hall, sensation returned— but only the utter depression and loneliness. He just... he didn't think he could be alone. Not again. "Oh please, not again." He didn't realize he'd said the words out loud, but when they broke the silence, they only weighed down further upon him.

Besides, Louko, he's probably right. Astra's just bearing you for politeness' sake. She will be happier without your distractions. Right? The thought hurt, but all the same he wished it to be true. It would be easier, he supposed, than the worse truth that she had indeed enjoyed his company, and now wouldn't even be able to stand his presence. Oh, why had he allowed himself to get close to her? Idiot! How many times had he warned himself—-tried to convince himself to pull away while he still could! Now...now it would hurt. Now he almost had a, well, now he *had* almost had one. A friend. But of course, Louko could never keep one before; why would it be any different now?

"Oh, Louko, there you are." Astra's voice startled Louko right out of his skin, sending his heart to the pit of his stomach in dread. She stood before him, brow furrowed as she looked him over.

Please. Please no. He found himself begging with, well, himself, pleading to find some answer in Astra's eyes and to believe his father was wrong for once.

But he knew he didn't deserve it.

"Are you alright?" she asked.

Clearing his throat, Louko began backing away, "Yes, I'm fine. I just—um—well, I have to go. Sorry, I don't think I'll be able to help you in the library later. Things to do, obviously. Can't spend all that time in a dusty place like that. Could catch some plague or something like that." As he spoke, he got farther away, forcing his obnoxious, stupid smile and thinking of the closest servants' passage he could slip into so she couldn't follow. There was one right around the corner.

Astra's expression was hesitant, closed off. All she gave was a simple, "Oh. Okay."

"Well, bye then." Louko practically darted around the corner before she could say another word, reaching the discreet side door before Astra was able to round the corner. Though it hadn't sounded like she was *going* to say another word. He barely had time to process this as in an instant he was behind it, closing the door with the utmost care and darting down the dark passage and into the maze of corridors, wishing he could lose himself instead of Astra. This time, it was his own fault... his own, stupid fault.

Louko wandered the passages for a little while before coming to a familiar exit. The heavy load of loneliness was unbearable, and he kept wishing to go back and ignore reality and see if maybe his father was wrong. Maybe the emotions Louko had seen on Astra's face were wrong. But he couldn't...he wouldn't. Because he *knew*. Astra could never forgive someone who was so deeply involved with Tyron. Oh, why was he such a *stupid* idiot?

With a sigh, he slumped down before the door, putting his head in his hands. The crack of light flitted through the bottom of the door, and for a while he just stared at it. He felt trapped in the dark, with only the illusion of light on the other side. All he ever got was a glimpse, and now he began once more to think it was all he ever would get. If only...if only Tyron had taken him with him, perhaps things would have been different. Louko had dreamed of rescue for so long, but now he supposed he had finally accepted the fact that he would never get one; nor did he really deserve it. What had Astra ever done to deserve this?

A sigh escaped the burdened prince, and slowly he got to his feet. He needed to stop thinking. Opening the door, he walked out into the large, elegant art halls, where elaborate paintings of each predecessor of Merimeethia were perfectly placed between tapestries of their victories, adventures, and battles. Louko kept walking. He always found himself here, in this hall. The closer he got to the end, the slower his step, already dreading the last painting. The kind, gentle eyes. The thick black hair. The smile. The life cut short. He stopped before her, staring as he always did as if it were the first time he'd seen her.

"I'm sorry." Louko's murmur echoed around the abandoned hall, coming back to haunt him. He wished those words meant something to someone, anyone. He wished she was here for at least a moment to know how sorry he really was. He couldn't replace her, he couldn't be a worthy son, and now he had just ruined it again. Every time he thought he was getting better.... But even Tyron had realized he was better off without Louko.

Astra:

Astra sat at the table in her room, staring down at the letter she had written. She drummed her fingers as she reviewed her words one by one. Then she picked up the parchment, crumpled it up, and tossed it in the corner with the other rejects. She sighed to herself as she picked up the quill again, picking up a fresh sheet of parchment and starting anew. *Now you're just being wasteful.*

When Louko had so abruptly canceled their meeting in the library, Astra had not taken it to heart. Her guess was that something had happened between him and a member of his family, and that the prince needed some time to himself. But when Astra had tried to find Louko that evening to check up on him, he was nowhere to be found. One day turned into many. The prince never returned to the library, never came to escort her to meals, nothing. He made no eye contact whenever they both sat at dinner. When Astra asked where Louko was, servants misled her. It didn't take long for her to realize that she was being very purposefully avoided.

But why? What had she done? She didn't understand. Had she said something wrong? Was it that day in the library? Or something at dinner? Or... the thought had chilled Astra when it occurred to her: had they learned of her exile? That had to be it.

It explained the sudden decrease in cordiality from the royal family as well as the fewer invites to dinner. Perhaps Astra was paranoid, but it seemed even the guards watched her more closely. She had to get away. Omath would use it against her otherwise. The only question was: why hadn't he done so already? Was he biding his time? Waiting for the best moment to strike?

It didn't matter. Whether he knew or not, Astra would leave. Why should she stay? Even Louko didn't want her around anymore. And yet, she didn't want to leave him alone to face his family, not when they were so cruel. He ought to know that he did not have to be alone.

So here Astra was, trying to decide what to write to him. But what in Eatris was she supposed to say? She didn't even know what to apologize for. "Sorry for not telling you how unpopular I am. I thought you knew"? "Sorry for not being politically acceptable"? "I didn't mean to make your life worse"? Astra frowned to herself. She didn't entirely know what she had done to cause Louko to suddenly ignore her. Yes, he had clearly learned of her exile, but political scorn had never seemed to faze Louko before.

It didn't help that Louko had been avoiding her. Not that Astra blamed him, of course. Yet, it somehow hurt to know that he was hiding from her the same way he hid from his family. Not being able to do anything to even try to resolve the problem was just as bad. As much as Astra had pleaded with the servants, and as sympathetic as they were, they would not help her. But she could not afford to wait even a day, now that Omath knew of her exile. He could turn on her in an instant.

So, this was her last idea: writing a letter for Louko and asking the servants to deliver it. While they might refuse to do so, she saw no other option. Louko didn't want to see her.

With another little sigh, Astra began again. The quill scratched softly, quickly, leaving words in its wake. Finally, Astra set it back in its holder and surveyed her work. This was the best she could do. The girl folded the parchment and sealed it with wax, standing up from her seat.

As if on cue, Leyda entered the room.

"Oh, Leyda," Astra greeted her.

The maid's guarded look said that she thought Astra was going to pester her about Louko again.

"No need to worry," Astra said, "I just wondered if you would be able to give this to Louko after I leave."

Leyda's expression relaxed, through confusion and curiosity arose. "You're leaving?"

"Yes." Astra nodded. "Matters have come up that have called me away unexpectedly. I leave as soon as I am packed."

"So soon?" Leyda looked crestfallen. "Oh. Then I suppose a letter could do no harm."

"Thank you," Astra said, relieved. She held out the letter which the maid took carefully.

Then Astra realized that she did not want word of her leaving to spread lest they try to stop her. "Leyda, if you would, don't mention this to anyone 'til I have already left. I have no time for formal goodbyes, if you understand me."

"Of course." Leyda seemed to accept this. Then she visibly thought of something else. "Would you like me to bring you the afternoon meal before you go?"

Astra was hoping to be gone by afternoon. "Would it be any trouble to have the meal packed instead?"

Leyda shook her head. "None at all. I'll see that it's brought up for you."

Now Astra was the one who shook her head. "Don't trouble yourself. I can pass through the kitchen as I leave and save you the trip. As long as Louko won't be there eating."

With a blush in response to the last comment, Leyda said, "I will ask." With that, the maid ducked out of the room.

Astra turned her attention to her next letter. This one would be equally short and sincere, since she knew how busy her brother was. Ent had more important things to do than read letters. Besides, this letter would have to be encoded, each word in a different language to discourage anyone who might intercept it. The cipher was effective, but time consuming.

Astra made no mention of her being found out, saying only that she was moving on from Merimeethia, and would write when she stopped again. She assured him that she was well. She knew that her brother had plenty of worries without adding herself to the list. However, she could not help herself from adding one small request: that he would pass on her love to their parents. Astra wished again that she had gotten to say goodbye—but now was no time for wishes. The girl swallowed the aching feeling of longing, and started to fold the parchment.

Then an idea came to her. Quickly now, she dipped her quill in ink and started a new line. In it, she asked Ent to come up with some excuse to bring Louko to Litash. Whether it was to employ him as a swordmaster, or as a foreign scholar, it didn't matter. As long as it got Louko away from Melye.

Satisfied, Astra signed, folded, and sealed the letter. She would ask Leyda to send it out. Astra turned to packing her things. She didn't have much, just what Dannsair could carry with ease. Her saddlebags were packed within half an hour. Then the girl sat back down and scribbled down a note of apology and excuse for Omath to soothe any overly ruffled feathers. No one would miss her here, only the opportunity to exploit her position—and Astra couldn't allow that to happen.

The door creaked, announcing Leyda's return, and Astra looked up in time to see the maid enter the room.

"You can exit through the kitchen," Leyda said, folded hands and red cheeks showing her embarrassment. "Graece will have provisions already waiting for you."

Astra stood. "Thank you," she replied sincerely.

Leyda only nodded. Then she noticed the letters. "More?"

"Yes," Astra affirmed. "One for the king, one for my brother. Could you see them out?"

"Of course."

Astra left both letters on the desk. Then she shouldered her bags, took one last look at the room, and left through the servants' passage so that no one would see her go. She hoped Louko fared better than herself.

Louko:

For the first few days after the meeting with Omath, Louko

employed his years of skill and knowledge of the castle to avoid Astra. It was sadly easy, though he knew she didn't have a chance; he'd done this for far too long with his father and siblings, so a stranger in this castle was as good as lost. Every time she asked a servant for directions, they would let Louko know. The poor nosy servants kept trying to get him to see her, but he refused, giving them no explanation. That would only make them try harder, and Omath had fired servants before for trying such things. He figured Astra would give up soon, but she didn't. Still, he told the servants to keep him updated on where she was, and make sure to lead her astray. It hurt, and Louko couldn't forgive himself for not giving an explanation or warning…but he couldn't face her. What a coward he was…but he couldn't face her. Knowing Astra, she was trying to find out both sides of the story—but both sides were the same. He couldn't look her in the eyes and tell her.

"Louko?" Leyda broke into his pensive mood, and he got up from the bench he was sitting on. The pleasant scent of the exotic flowers in the garden were lost on him as he faced the disturbed servant.

Louko took in a breath of the outdoor air. "Yes, Leyda?"

She shifted uncomfortably and fiddled with the hem of her apron. "Princess Astra is asking where you are, again."

A sigh escaped him. The servants had shown their reluctance to cooperate, but had not openly argued. "Tell her I'm in the West Wing, if you must," he said at last. It was easy to have them lie to his family, but he felt absolutely cruel to do it to Astra. But he could do nothing else.

Astra stopped asking after that day, or so Louko gathered, as the servants stopped mentioning her. He had known she would eventually give up, but all the same, it only made it worse. Perhaps it meant she'd finally really come to terms with it. Oh, what must she think of him?

The days turned to a week, then two, and Louko could almost forget Astra was still in the palace. At least, that's what he told himself. It was a little nice when he did remember, he supposed. He felt less alone. Once, he did see her through a window, and in a moment of weakness began mulling over the idea of disobeying his father completely, and just going over and explaining what happened—pretending he would have a different answer... But his father had already scolded him twice for being caught near Astra's location, and he knew better than to push any further. So instead, he had made sure to go in the opposite direction of Astra.

The memory played in Louko's disorganized brain as he sat once more on the bench in his mother's little section of the palace garden. None of his family went here anymore, so it was a little sanctuary. Sometimes. Sometimes, it felt more haunted than safe. Louko sighed and let his shoulders settle heavily down.

From behind him came the sound of someone clearing their throat, and Louko turned to see Leyda standing at the entrance to the garden.

"May I come in?" she asked quietly.

Louko rolled his eyes and forced that ridiculous smirk on his miserable mug. "I suppose. What's the matter?" he asked, already getting up.

The young girl entered without a word, pulling a letter from inside her apron and holding it out to him.

"What is this?" Louko asked, brow furrowed.

"Astra asked me to give it to you," she replied.

Slowly, Louko took it, turning it over and over in his hand. Not having the spirit to open it yet, he asked, "What is it for?"

"I don't know the specifics," Leyda replied. "But she didn't want it given until after she'd left."

This caused him to stare at the letter. She'd left? Louko quickly opened the letter.

"Louko:

I realize that you do not wish to see me. You will not have to worry anymore about avoiding me, for by the time you read this, I will be gone. I admit that I do not know what I have done to cause this, but I am sincerely sorry for whatever it may be. I intended no harm nor hurt towards you.

I hope that all goes well with you. Should you need my help, you need only find me.

-Astra

Your father is wrong about you."

He stared at the paper, frozen. What had he made her think? But then again, what in Eatris had he expected?? Astra was too nice a person to think it was anyone's fault but hers— He had to find her. Find her and make this right. Idiot! Selfish, spineless idiot! But the letter said she was gone....

He hadn't thought she would think that *she* had done something —but Astra was so caring, so of course she had! What had he done now? Louko's whole body went rigid, and he ran out of the little garden area. Already gone??

He made his way to the bottom level, past the main garden entrance, past Mariah—who gave a yelp in indignation—past everything. With desperate swiftness he made his way to the Spying Glass, running up the stone spiral stairs and not even looking out through the glass as he ascended. He didn't stop until he made it to the top, finally keeling over, breathless. After only a moment he went to the far edge, looking over into the foggy rain of the afternoon, where the city gave way to the wild lands. He wished—he hoped—no, he desperately *needed* to catch a glimpse of Astra, somehow. He needed to see where she was going. Maybe he would go after her, maybe he would break his promise and—his heart fell. He kept staring out into the fog, but still nothing. He resorted to looking in all directions, but still, nothing but fog and gloom and nothingness. Nothing but the same thing he had seen and felt for nineteen years. He truly was too late. Just like the day Tryon left. The memory came flooding back, still raw and painful despite the intervening years.

Little Louko ran faster, afraid Tyron might leave without him. The child skidded into the courtyard just as his teacher was starting to mount. Wait! No! Why was Tyron going to leave without saying goodbye? But then Tyron handed his reins to a servant and crossed the courtyard to Louko. He knelt so that he was at eye level with him, placing his hands on the child's shoulders.

"I will miss you, Louko," Tyron said quietly. Louko could see the way his eyes glistened with tears. "You are a good boy that will grow to be a great man; never listen to anyone who tells you otherwise." He gave Louko a sudden and tight hug, which Louko returned with a fierceness—as if that might be enough to keep his only friend from leaving.

"I will come back for you," his teacher whispered. Then someone cleared their throat and Tyron shook himself, getting to his feet. "You are never as alone as you may feel." Tyron took his steed's reins and in one motion, mounted. "Farewell," he said and rode to join his brother.

Louko watched them numbly as they made their way to the gate, a solitary tear running down his cheek as the only person in the whole world who had ever cared for him rode away.

Louko shut out the memory, guilt overwhelming any idiotic self-pity he felt this time. This time was different. Tyron had been wrong. Louko was not a good man—he couldn't even be a good friend. Yes. Astra was also wrong...for Louko's father *was* right about him. He wasn't much good for anything, and in trying to spare Astra, he had instead *hurt* her.

With a defeated sigh, Louko slumped to the cream marble floor. He couldn't live like this anymore. He couldn't pretend; he couldn't bow to his father; he couldn't run from everyone and keep hurting them. He wouldn't. Something had to change, and really, he didn't care how.

OF SHADE AND SHADOW

***

When I enter the library, Omath is standing at a table, frowning at the abandoned pile of books. He turns when he hears me enter. His frown deepens as his annoyance rises.

"I suppose you have some idea why she left?"

I walk towards him, letting my shoulders rise and fall in a nonchalant shrug. "Perhaps she realized the true nature of everyone here, and was smart enough to run."

Omath's face goes blank with confusion, unable to comprehend that I would dare to say such a thing.

But I have more than words for Omath.

Before he can even move, my dagger drives through his chest and protrudes from his back. His eyes go wide and his lips part in a gasp.

I hold his shoulder to keep him upright, wanting him to hear my words before he dies. "Oh, don't act so surprised. Did you really think I could bear you and your domineering forever?" I twist the blade, enjoying his pain. "You have only received your dues. But you won't be alone long—Keeshiff will be next in line."

I pull my dagger and let him fall lifeless to the floor. I wipe the blood carefully from the blade, then drop the cloth on to Omath's now reddening chest.

"The time of reckoning has come."

CHAPTER IX

Astra:

Astra was weary. She had been riding for several days, and her thoughts were still stuck on Louko. What a fool she had been to think she was his friend. It seemed she managed to make a mess of everything. First her Gifting had been too much for the Elves to train, and her parents had sent her off to Ent. Then she had managed to lose control entirely, and Ent had had to send her off here. But this time? This time it almost felt worse. Because she could no longer blame her Gifting: the problem had simply been her.

She sighed, pulling Dannsair to a stop at the top of another rain-soaked ridge. Down in the valley, she could barely make out a small town. Smoke floated up from chimneys, mingling with the fog and rain. The scent promised warmth and dry shelter, and Astra was in no mood to resist. Besides, she had no better place to go. She didn't even have a plan to go off of. All she knew was that she was travelling away from Melye.

So the princess and her mare carefully descended to the valley floor. Just as she could almost taste the warm bread she smelled baking, the guards at the town gate stopped her.

"State your name and where you come from." A tall, pale guard crossed his spear in front of Dannsair, an unwise decision.

The black and white mare snapped at the shaft, and Astra barely pulled her back in time. "TaReev, of Belayr" she lied flatly.

"What direction do you come from?" The guard looked her up

165

and down skeptically, but stepped back slightly, apparently in fear of Dannsair. Smart.

"South," she said with growing impatience. "And if this is the welcome in all you northernly towns, I'm of a mind to go right back down there."

"I'm sorry, ma'am. But as you know the country is in an uproar, and we are still looking for the assassins," the man said severely. "What was the last city or town you were in?"

Now Astra was genuinely confused. "Assassins? What assassins?"

The other guard stepped in, repeating the question. "What was the last city or town you crossed?"

"Cheyd," Astra answered truthfully. It was a small village that was not in between here and the capitol. "Now, what assassins?"

The guards gave each other knowing glances, and they both relaxed slightly. The pale one spoke first. "Prince Keeshiff and Prince Louko, miss. You must have left right before the news reached Cheyd, it being out of the way and all. The king's been murdered," he said grimly.

Shock settled slowly over Astra. She was suddenly aware her mouth was open and she snapped it shut. But... how? Who? Surely not the princes! It must have happened right after she'd left.

"I had not heard," she murmured. "Thank you for the news." Then she came to her senses. "Then perhaps I should return home."

"Where are you from again, miss?" The other man asked.

"Belayr," she repeated. "It is to the east. But perhaps I could get a little closer before the sun sets." Astra wanted to escape without suspicion.

Both men seemed uneasy, "It can be terribly dangerous after dark. There's bandits in these parts, and with the murderers on the loose... Steward Kaeden is doing all he can to keep order. But still, dark is dangerous, Miss."

Steward Kaeden? Astra suppressed a shudder at the memory of green eyes. Suspicion immediately blossomed, but she set it aside to think of later.

"Perhaps you are right," Astra said slowly. "Thank you for your advice." Then she spurred Dannsair forward and into the town. She didn't need suspicious guards following her.

Escaping the town was easy enough. She simply rode through to another gate and told the guards she was going to visit relatives at a nearby farm. Truly, the most difficult part was resisting the scents of food which had drawn her to the town in the first place. As soon as she was out of sight of the walls, she pressed Dannsair into a gallop due south. Astra had promised Louko her help in that final letter she'd written; she intended to fulfill that promise.

***

Astra picked her way through the thick trees, Dannsair close behind. She hoped she was right about this—it was her only guess. But even though she remembered Louko going on about the ruins and how it was the perfect hiding place, she wasn't certain that she remembered how to get there—or even the hollow where he'd talked about it. She had been searching the same region since late morning, and now the light was beginning to fade. Astra, being experienced in the woods, knew patience was needed, but this was becoming frustrating. What if she was wrong? Or in the wrong place? Or what if they'd already moved on?

Astra refocused on scanning for footprints. She didn't have enough daylight left to risk wasting it on idle worrying. At least in this soggy place, any footsteps or hoofprints would be easy to find.

That's when Astra noticed that the sound of hoofsteps behind her had stopped. She turned around to find Dannsair sniffing the breeze, ears forward. Then the painted mare turned sharply off course and began walking. They'd been through enough together that Astra knew what to do next: she followed.

And Astra's trust was rewarded. She hadn't gone on more than a few minutes when the two came to a thick swath of churned up mud. This worried Astra. It would have taken more than six horses to create such a slough… Had Louko been followed by a patrol? The girl took only long enough to determine which direction they'd gone before mounting back up and following the tracks.

It was nearly too dim to see when Astra finally heard anything. Voices, high and loud, apparently arguing. Astra dismounted, signing for Dannsair to stay. She crept forward, noticing that this was indeed the ruins Louko had once described, and came up to where the trees gave way to a crumbling stone wall. She stayed low and quiet and tried to get a better look at the group.

"Oh, come on, just leave him, Keeshiff!"

Keeshiff?

"He'll be found in a day or so—then he can pay for what he did and your name can be cleared." It was hard to mistake Mariah's voice.

"Oh yes, let's leave the poor boy tied to a decrepit stone column and just assume he killed the king." This voice was older, one Astra didn't recognize, "Do you really think just leaving him here would clear your name, Keeshiff? I mean, you were *both* accused "

"Let's just set this straight. I didn't say to tie him up, and I didn't say to leave him behind, but with you all going at it I am finding it hard to think." This had to be Keeshiff.

Astra had heard enough. She didn't have to be able to read minds to know that they were all talking about Louko. And the fact that anyone was *actually* considering leaving him behind—to be caught and executed, no less—made her angry.

Anger always made her little bolder than she ought to be.

She stood up and stepped out of the shadows. "Agreed. Your little row also makes you incredibly easy to find."

She would have been slightly impressed by the group's reflexes had she not been so furious.

About nine people stood in what had once been a large hall or room. Most of the current occupants—surprisingly—were Merimeethian knights, the rest comprising Keeshiff and Mariah. All were pointing some form of weapon in Astra's direction.

Then Keeshiff's eyes widened as he recognized her, "Astra! How did you find us?"

Before she could open her mouth to demand where Louko was, she heard someone indirectly answer that for her, as from behind the group Louko himself spoke up, "Oh, great. Now maybe you all won't get yourselves killed." The comment was bitter and humorless.

Astra only barely thought better of announcing that she hadn't been looking for them, but rather for Louko. "I knew where to start and your tracks showed me where to end," she replied a little more tautly than intended. "Now, please explain what happened."

"Yes. Because then maybe you will untie me... which would be nice...seeing as I can no longer feel my feet..." Louko sounded all too calm.

Astra drew her sword and walked forward. Whether out of fear of her or concern for Louko, the knights stepped back and let her through. Louko was just beyond them. Indeed, he was tied to what was left of some decorative column that must have once been part of the manor hall. He was pale and tired-looking, a fake smirk still stuck on his face in a way that showed how worn thin he really was. Astra undid the rope with one swipe of her blade and then held out a hand to help him up.

He stared at it a long while, rubbing life back into his discolored hands. Just when Astra thought he wouldn't take her hand, he did suddenly, allowing her to help him unsteadily to his feet.

"Thanks," he murmured.

With a sharp nod, Astra turned back to the group. "Now. Explain."

'He killed Father!" Mariah pointed an accusing finger towards her younger brother.

There were already disgruntled sounds from the knights, but Keeshiff interjected. "*Someone* killed him, and my men and I were on patrol a few days ago when Louko showed up and said Kaeden had killed the king and was coming to kill me as well."

Kaeden. This was too much to be coincidental.

"By the time we found the nearest village, I'd already been

blamed for the murder along with Louko," Keeshiff went on. "Mariah only showed up this morning."

"To stop this traitor from getting you in trouble!" she interrupted.

"If you cannot give proof or facts, please keep silent," Astra said, with a glare at the other princess. She looked back at Keeshiff. "Did anyone see what happened? Does *anyone* have any evidence?" Her earlier doubts about Kaeden were turning into fears.

"No." Keeshiff shook his head and sighed.

Astra scanned the knights, but no one said anything. She turned to Louko. His eyes were averted, and he was still rubbing at his hands. She wanted to ask him about what he had seen, but she was too afraid to do so.

"But we don't have any evidence *for* him either, and everyone knows he wanted Father dead." Mariah was becoming extremely grating.

"Mariah. I understand your concern, but Astra is right. We are going to get caught if we stay here arguing. It's better if we talk this through in safety." Keeshiff didn't sound extremely confident in this, but he locked eyes with a few of his knights as if daring anyone to say otherwise. No one did. Not even Mariah, as Astra noted with some satisfaction. But the eerie quiet held tension, as if everyone knew that it was only a matter of time before someone started another argument.

Then, with a show of at least *some* common sense, Keeshiff began assigning tasks to people: preparing food, gathering wood and starting a fire, watering and feeding horses, and other menial tasks. But it was not a permanent solution, as soon it only left everyone sitting and standing idly in a rather ragged sort of circle around a pathetic looking fire built on what remained of the manor's foundation. Astra noted Louko —who had been the only one not given a task—standing nearby but outside, still quietly rubbing life into his undoubtedly sore limbs.

Astra took the moment of tentative peace to go back to where she had left Dannsair outside of the ruins. The semi-obedient mare had stayed put for once. Astra gathered the reins and led her to a quiet spot in the clearing where no tents had yet been set up. That's when Astra realized how many tents there were, and all in good shape. It would seem that Keeshiff and his knights had not been on the road long. Good. That meant they would have plenty of supplies.

A younger knight—closer to Louko's age, perhaps—started the next conversation. "So what exactly is our next step?"

Astra drew closer to the little group, but didn't speak.

"We have to go somewhere they won't expect to look for us— just until someone gets this cleared up," Keeshiff looked nervous, rubbing his face with his hands. Astra thought of all he must have been through. "This can't last long. Everyone knows I would never even think of killing my father, certainly."

"I'm afraid that that may not be the case," the man who had spoken in Louko's defense earlier chimed in. "Merimeethia doesn't exactly have a history of being very loyal to its leaders. And the way you were said to 'fraternize' with the commoners wouldn't help your case."

"But Kaeden surely will find out the truth…" Keeshiff spoke with less surety.

"That doesn't mean he'll reveal it to everyone else," Lucian scoffed. "He has a pretty clear path to the throne as it is."

"He couldn't have cared less for the throne." Keeshiff shook his head. Astra was surprised how quickly he came to Kaeden's defense. "He was never ambitious."

"And somehow I was?" Louko's voice rang with an unexpected, only half-hidden, hurt.

Astra saw Keeshiff's jaw go taut as his gaze dropped away from his younger brother.

Mariah was the one to respond. "You had plenty of other reasons, of course. Vengeance, jealousy...Who knows, maybe you were even just bored." She glared at the younger prince, who did nothing but return her gaze, face like stone.

Astra wanted so badly to lash out in Louko's defense. Mariah's accusation was so low, so baseless... But Astra knew better than to reply and so validate it. Instead, she said, "I thought we had agreed to make it to safety before discussing who did what. So I suggest we return to the topic at hand: where can we go that is least likely to be searched?"

Another knight—dressed in forestry clothes and chainmail rather than full armor—quickly took up the topic. "They will expect us to try and stay near where the available supplies are. Wooded areas where game is plentiful. They will also think we won't go to the north, as the weather is worse up there. But I don't know if we want to travel further inland. If they *do* catch wind, we'd be easily surrounded before we could make our way back south. However, if we head south for the outskirts of the Forest of Riddles, many still avoid it out of superstition—even though The War dissolved much of the threats such a place holds." The level-headed reply was refreshing.

Keeshiff let out a tense breath and looked at the fellow to his left.

"If we forage as we go, will rations hold, Delnor?"

The knight, apparently Delnor, frowned in thought. "I think we'd do alright. There should be enough game for us."

"And is the Forest indeed relatively safe to travel?" Keeshiff asked Astra.

Astra had never had as many bad experiences with the Forest as her brother had. Indeed, he had always commented that crossings were easier with her. "With such a large group, we should be safe."

"Good." Keeshiff turned back to everyone, "Does anyone have anything against Bandon's idea?"

Some looked disgruntled—especially Delnor—but none protested.

None but Mariah.

"Really? Go further away from civilization in the company of a *murderer?* Have you all gone mad?"

"Would you *please* stop?" Lucian stood up, clearly fed up with the princess, "You don't think we aren't *all* uncomfortable with it? But we don't know for sure who did it, and the information won't help if we're all dead."

"What do you mean we don't know?" Mariah was practically throwing a fit now. "He *killed* him! He took Mother away, and now Father too. He's nothing but a no good, murdering traitor, and you've let him deceive you, too!"

"Deceive you?" Louko's voice was again startling in its force. "Mariah, what in Eatris would I be deceiving you *for?* All I want is to be left alone—but again and again you all drag me out and claim I want some form of attention." His expression was hard to see in the dark, but

Astra could hear the emotion in his tone. "If I'd really killed him, no one would know, and Keeshiff would be king right now—not Kaeden."

There was an unsettling weight on the last part.

"Oh please, you wanted him dead more than anyone! And after he wouldn't let you out of his sight because you ran coward, you were angry. You killed him *like an animal.* He's dead because of you. You killed my father, you rotten murderer!"

"He's not even your real father!" The reply was almost a shout. Astra had never heard Louko say anything out of anger, and the force of the words was like a blow to the chest even though they weren't directed at her.

And then came the slap as the princess' hand went right across Louko's face. He barely even flinched. "How *dare* you," Mariah seethed. "At least he *loved* me."

Enough. *Enough.* Astra stepped forward, catching Mariah by the wrist as she prepared to strike Louko again. "Touch him again, and you will regret it," she hissed through clenched teeth.

Mariah's eyes were both full of hate and shock at Astra's interference, and she relaxed as if to show she would not. "Fine," she muttered.

"Now, I would suggest you walk away before you make any more enemies." Astra's voice was acidic. "After all, you may be stuck with us for a long, *long* time, and keeping your mouth shut may be your best chance at making it through this."

Mariah opened her mouth as if to speak, but nothing came out. Instead, it clamped shut and, without a word, she marched off.

Astra ignored the open stares of all the knights as she turned around in search of Louko. He had vanished. He must have made his escape during her intervention. The knights began to filter out of the firelit circle, but Astra remained, still at a loss for what to do. The heat of her anger swirled with that regret-stained sorrow, tying her stomach in knots and constricting her chest. The memory of Louko's face when Mariah had said those awful words played over and over in her head. He had looked so...so... The emotion had been so strong, as if built up over long years and then breaking out all at once: Agony. That had been the look in his eyes.

At first, Astra went in search of Louko. She didn't know what she would do if she found him; all she knew was that she couldn't do nothing. But Astra was still shaking. Since Mariah's first accusation, the humming in the back of her mind had grown louder and louder. Mariah slapping Louko had only made it more deafening. By the time Astra had reined in her temper, she realized it was too late.

The best she could do was get away from others. And so she had, putting herself beyond hearing and seeing distance from the camp, hiding away in a little hollow. One hand worked in ceaseless anxiety around the cuff on her wrist. If only she could trust it to help. Astra didn't even remember sitting down, but she found herself leaning back against a tree with her knees drawn up tightly, and her hands clapped over her ears.

She had never wanted any of this—why couldn't it just go away? As if in response to her useless wish, the humming grew more deafening. It felt as if Astra was trying to hold back a river by herself, and was only going to get washed away. She fought it, pushing it back and trying to suppress it. The more she worked and the closer she came to success, the harder it became. It was as if her Gifting was angered by her attempts.

Just when Astra thought she was nearly safe, something shifted. The surge of power hit her like a tidal wave. Amidst the roaring in her ears, the girl heard a metallic crack, and saw her cuff begin to rend. It burst into pieces before she could even move a hand to stop it.

Silence reigned. The total lack of sound made Astra's ears ring almost as loudly as the humming had. Slowly, she lowered her hands from where they had been clasped around her ears and opened her eyes. Had it passed? Had it only been fighting the bronze?

Then it exploded. Caught off guard, Astra was helpless to do anything as massive surges of blue leveled the nearby trees. The girl curled up instinctively, as if making herself smaller might lessen the damage. *Please, oh please stop.* No begging, no demanding, no pleading made any difference. All she could do was wait.

Astra didn't know how long her Gifting raged. Even with her eyes squeezed shut and her hands pressed against her ears, she couldn't escape the blinding blue light or the horrible sound of splintering wood that accompanied it. It felt like hours before the storm of Gifting finally subsided. When it did, she was totally and utterly exhausted, barely able to push herself up to her feet. Then the sight of what she had done left her motionless.

Everything around her had been destroyed. Not just knocked over or broken, no, completely annihilated. Where once was a hollow full of thick, tangled woods was a circle of ash with Astra at its center.

The very air was hot and thick, making it hard to breathe. Nothing in the hollow was alive but her.

Was this all Astra was capable of? Was this all her power could do? The girl became aware of her dry mouth and trembling hands. What if she had lost control in the camp? Or back in her brother's palace? They had been right to send her away—yet now she was endangering others. She couldn't understand why anyone called this Gifting: it was nothing but a curse.

Tears burned in her eyes and she blinked them away. What would crying help?! As her mind cleared and her thoughts were no longer buried by humming, Astra realized she needed to move. Surely all that had not gone unnoticed; if she remained, she could be found. However, try as she might, she no longer remembered which direction the camp was.

Astra leaned down and scooped up the shattered remains of her cuff off the ground. Blowing off flakes of ash, she stared at the dull metal. It didn't feel so reassuring anymore. Still, just from holding it, the humming diminished and Astra was able to recall which way she had entered the hollow. She dragged herself up the now-bare hillside, and into the shelter of the trees. It was easier to breathe outside that circle of death.

In her state of exhaustion, the hike back was arduous. Her panic had made the way to the hollow seem so quick earlier, while now Astra could barely climb over fallen logs. Anxiety pricked as she wondered if she was even going the right way. There was no way to see the stars under the combined canopy of trees and clouds; what if she got lost?

The girl stumbled through the dark for over half an hour before she saw light through the entwining trees. Cautiously, she approached. From the edge of the ruins, she could just make out Louko, sitting by the fire with his head in his hands. Astra suddenly recalled all of Mariah's cruel words to him, and pity swelled in her heart. Louko had gone through so much for his siblings, and all she had given him in return was hate.

Before she had even thought through what she was doing, Astra approached and sat down across from him.

***

I smile to myself, not letting anyone else see it. Astra is starting to slip. It won't be much longer before she falls entirely. All I have to do now is wait.

CHAPTER X

Louko:

Nine Years ago:

Louko burst into his room slamming the door shut behind him. He clenched his fists, leaving his knuckles white. His posture writhed with fury and pain flared unhidden in his eyes, the scene playing over and over in the young boy's mind. His sister's face when his father told Mariah. It hurt, but Louko let it.

He had tried to deceive himself—tried to believe he could love and be loved. FOOL! Walking slowly over to the mirror, the young prince gave himself a good, long stare. How dare he! He had no right, no right at all!

In an overwhelming burst of emotion, Louko swept his fist right into the glass, shattering his image into a million warped shards.

Pain shot through his hand; glancing at his fist, the boy saw glistening red.

He briefly wiped the beat-up knuckles on his breeches, wincing only a bit. It didn't hurt nearly as much as his shattered heart. Putting that back together was as impossible as piecing back together the mirror.

Everytime Louko had gotten close to someone, it had ended in disaster. His selfish attempts to ignore the guilt, the trouble he caused, the tears he forced others to shed…

It was HIS own fault, trying to pretend he was worth something.

Stupid emotions.

Now, forced into realization, Louko felt a single tear slide down his cheek.

NO!

Fiercely, the boy rubbed away the droplet from his face, gritting his teeth in determination. He would never cry—never let himself feel. If he did? He would make sure to push the pain of feeling down, down where he could feel it without showing it. He'd gotten the message; he wasn't worth loving.

Sinking to the floor, he numbly picked a large shard of mirror from the floor, holding it up to his face.

Two empty, lonely eyes stared out at him, red rimmed with suppressed tears. The eyes hardened, and they sparked once more with anger.

Anger at himself. His stupid, weak self. Why was he so selfish? Why had he so cruelly led Mariah on, only to break her heart?! His father had said she wouldn't love him if she knew...Why had he even tried? Why....why had he made his family suffer…

The glass slipped from Louko's slackened grasp and the sound of it crashing to the floor echoed across the room, much like the whispered loneliness echoing in Louko's empty heart. His head dropped hopelessly and the small boy felt as if a huge, unbearable burden had been placed upon his shoulders.

His hand throbbed as it bled—knuckles most likely broken—and Louko felt drained.

But nothing...Nothing hurt as much as the knowledge of what he could never have. The knowledge that no matter how hard he tried, he would never be worth anyone's love.

***

Louko's very breath had been stolen away, and as soon as eyes were off him, he disappeared out of the decaying ruins and into the night. It had served him right, saying such an awful thing to Mariah...and yet her reply still hurt. His knuckles were white from clenching too tightly and his muscles ached with the force he was contracting them with, but he didn't bother relaxing. For once in his pathetic life, he was going to let himself be miserable.

Or not. He couldn't afford to for long; too much was at stake. But Mariah's words were ringing too clearly in his head, and the events of the past year were catching up. The seclusion, the hopelessness, the stress...No wonder Keeshiff believed Louko was capable of murder—look how weak he was, and how quick to lash out. Louko found a quiet place right outside the long-forgotten manor and sat down against a tree, letting his head rest against it. Everything was just so hard, and he was so tired of fighting. Tired of trying to convince his own brother that he'd not murdered his father; tired of his sister's senseless berating because she liked to believe things that would allow her to be a victim; tired of staying quiet. But it was even worse to speak, as tonight had shown so clearly.

And so he sat there, trying not to think and instead letting the cold night breeze refresh him. Louko had yearned for so long to be free of Melye and his father, and yet Omath was gone and he was *still* a prisoner. He couldn't just leave Keeshiff and Mariah to face Kaeden on their own, and yet he wanted more than anything to run off into the dark and never have to come back. But he couldn't, and he wouldn't. There wasn't any point, anyway. What would he do if he left? Why bother?

Louko didn't know how long he'd sat there, but when he returned to camp everyone except Gavin—who was quietly standing guard—was asleep, and so with a sigh Louko sat down by the low fire on a small makeshift seat—which was in reality just a piece of wet log—and rubbed life back into his hands. It was quiet, other than the normal animal noises and the pleasant crackle of the fire. Soothing, even. Louko let in a deep breath and stared at the tongues of flame, remembering sadly how everyone had been happier before Omath's death. Too late to change things now. Too late to go back... always too late. Another burdened sigh escaped the prince, and he rested his head in his hands. What was he supposed to do?

There was a slight noise and Louko jerked his head up in time to see Astra on the other side of the fire. She looked disheveled: hair messier, mud on her breeches, even a scratch on her cheek. There was a strange light in her already unnervingly blue eyes, something he didn't dare try to put a name to.

"Are you alright?" He somehow managed to speak, not realizing until after the words left his mouth that Astra had also asked the same thing at the same exact time. "Don't do that again...that was creepy," he half mumbled, feeling quite uncomfortable.

Astra's lips pressed together as if she was going to say something, but she never did. She gave a stiff shrug and sat down across the fire from him.

"*Are* you alright?" he asked again, relieved when it was only his voice that asked this time.

"Um…" Even though Louko had asked the question before, she didn't seem entirely prepared for it. "I'm alright. But, I mean," her words were unusually stilted. "Are you?"

Louko looked at the fire, staring deep into the embers, a humorless smile on his lips. "Oh yes, fine as always."

Movement drew his attention upwards, and he saw that Astra's head was bowed, her shoulders drooped. "I am sorry." The soft words were hard to make out over the crackling of the burning wood.

"'Sorry'?" Louko echoed, lost. "Sorry for what?"

Astra did not look up. "For, for…" Her hand went to her wrist, and she grit her teeth. "For all the things you father did, for what your sister said, and what your brother won't do. No one should have to live with what you do." Astra's voice was bitter. "I wish…" She stopped herself, shaking her head and letting the sentence drift away.

Louko cocked his head, staring at her strangely. "Well, first off, it's not your fault. It's not like you did any of it." That didn't come out right, but he couldn't take it back, "And wishing gets no one anywhere except stuck in a fantasy." And….that *definitely* wasn't the right thing to say. *Idiot.*

"I will grant you your last point," Astra's posture seemed taut and strained. "But as for the first, while I have not caused these things, I could have helped stop them." Again, she stopped herself. "I guess it doesn't matter. This is not about me. I wanted to see how *you* were doing."

"Why?" The question was almost desperate. Why did she care? Why had she come back? He knew very well she now knew about his relationship with Tyron, and she had every right to hate him—more right than most. So why was she bothering?

Astra finally looked up, meeting his gaze. Her brow furrowed. "Why wouldn't I?"

"You know why." He hadn't quite expected that sort of reply. "I mean, come on Astra, I know my father told you."

Confusion lingered for moments more, then suddenly vanished. "Oh, you mean in regards to Tyron?"

The lack of ceremony with which she asked only made Louko more confused. And Tyron's name being said aloud only made the feeling worse. "Yes, what else would I be talking about, Astra?" He had seen what Tyron had done to Astra, and yet still he defended the man. Knowing she knew had been one of the only reasons he'd so willingly bent to his father's order to keep away from her. How could she be *surprised* at it?

Astra's confusion returned. "I am not sure what this has to do with anything," was her slow response.

What did that *mean*?

Running his hand through his hair, Louko said, "The better question is what *doesn't* it have to do with? Tyron was like a father to me, do you understand? He practically raised me. Why else do you think I avoided you after my father told me he'd informed you? I was there with Soletuph when he rescued you and Ent from that castle. I saw what Tyron did to you—you should be disgusted with me. Astra, why do you have to be so—so—so unbearably polite?" So good and kind and always putting on a brave face. Louko could only imagine the memories this all stirred up. What was he doing? *Selfish, blabbering idiot!*

Astra's face was pale and drawn, with lips parted. "So... you avoided me because your father told you that." Her hand went to her mouth and she fell quiet. Then she took a deep breath and let her hand return to her wrist. "Louko, your father told me all that the very first night I was there."

It took him a moment to process what Astra had just said. "What?" No. He didn't want to hear that. No no no. That would mean...

Astra nodded. "He told me that evening after you had left dinner early," she explained.

"Why didn't you *say* anything?" was all he managed, aghast. He had done *all that*...avoided her, made himself miserable... for nothing??

"What was there to say?" Astra returned with a shrug. She took in his horrified expression, and seemed to feel the need to explain further. "I mean, how old were you when Tyron came?"

"I don't know, five perhaps," Louko answered, more instinctually than sensibly as he tried to calm his stupid self. He was such a fool...such an ignorant fool.

"And did your father treat you so badly then, too?"

"No, not really. Astra, I was five, I don't remember." Louko threw up his hands in uselessness. "Does it matter?"

Astra's shoulders straightened, and her tone became firmer. "Yes, it does. Because how would you expect me to blame a little *child* for seeking love from the only person apparently willing to give it?"

Louko went deathly quiet. He didn't know what to say, or how to say it. He was tired of trying to find the words, and confused by Astra's stubborn refusal to condemn him. Worse, he began to wonder what she

187

must have thought for his sudden avoidance in Melye. And yet, here Astra was, still trying to help. Who was helping her?

"Whatever he is now, I cannot hold it against you for being close to him then," Astra went on, eyes lit almost feverishly. "You have always proven yourself loyal to Ent and me." Then her posture sagged again. "I am only sorry that I did not do better at seeking you out back in Melye. I had no idea that your father told you such things. I just thought…" She let out a long breath in a sort of sigh.

"Thought what?" Louko urged, brow furrowed.

Her delay was nervous. Her hand twisted around her unusually bare wrist as she fought some unseen battle. Astra looked from side to side as if scanning for eavesdroppers before letting her gaze drop down to the ground beneath her feet. "I thought you avoided me because of my political status. I should have known better."

"Political status?" Louko couldn't help but add, "What political status? And since when have I cared about that?" He slowly began to recall the odd behavior at the ball, and the stares Astra had received.

Astra winced slightly. "My apologies. I should have known better," she repeated. Then her voice dropped to a whisper as she admitted, "I have been exiled from Litash."

Louko just stared at her. "*What*?!" Exiled? She had to be joking. She *had* to be, because her brother was king. But her face was clear; it was no joke. "How—why—-but Entrais?" Was the only words he could form into an incohesive question.

"It was my own fault." The reply was small and Astra seemed to shrink before his very eyes. "Ent did it to protect me."

"Protect you from what?" Louko didn't understand.

"The Court," Astra answered. "They, they wanted to lock me up. Or experiment on me."

The look on Louko's face was one of horror, "Why?"

Astra's disquiet only made it worse. "I...I..." Her expression crumbled into distress and she looked away. When she looked back, it was a blank facade once more. "I made a mistake. I couldn't control my Gifting and I nearly killed everyone in the Court."

His eyes widened, and it took a while before he could find words to say, "Well, then..." He perhaps would have been impressed, if Astra was not so clearly torn up by whatever had happened. "Is it the Miadoris?" he asked at last, remembering the encounter she'd had with it during The War. But at that time, it hadn't manifested so... forcefully. And while he'd assumed—her being Elvish and all—that she had Gifting, she'd never seemed to have a large amount. But again, he'd only seen her during The War. Perhaps Entrais just hadn't had a chance to teach her until after it had ended.

Biting her lip, she nodded. Her clenched hands were white.

"Are you alright?" He didn't even know what exactly he was asking for, but he asked anyway. He could only imagine how she felt; banished by her own brother, cast out from her country. Alone. He wished he'd tried harder for her.

The way Astra looked up so sharply told Louko that he'd caught her off guard. "Yes, sorry, I didn't mean to take over the conversation," she murmured hastily.

"You didn't," Louko reassured, though confused at the apology. "I didn't realize you'd been exiled..." He trailed off a moment before adding, "I suppose we're both alone."

"I suppose so," Astra echoed hollowly. She regathered herself before saying, "Ent has kept things quiet, so I suppose you not knowing means he has been successful. If you wouldn't mind, I would rather the others not be told."

"Of course," Louko said, hoping Astra knew she didn't have to ask. "Well, I'm going to try and convince Keeshiff to go to my uncle's in Nythril. I'm sure you'd be welcome to stay with him too... if you wanted, of course."

She looked him right in the face, as if searching him inside and out. As if evaluating his sincerity. When she spoke, it was soft and nearly raspy. "Thank you."

"Heh, that's what friends are for." He froze after saying the words, not really sure how they had come out of his mouth.

Maybe it was just his paranoia, but Astra's face seemed suddenly inscrutable. That was, until her whole posture softened and hope flickered to life. "Friends?"

But for once in Louko's life, he didn't back down. "Yes. Friends." He swallowed his doubt.

Something like a smile crossed her lips. "I like that," was all she said.

The following silence was warm as they both tried to comprehend all that the little word meant.

"So," Astra spoke first. "If we are friends," she sounded as hesitant as Louko felt. "Can I now ask how you are? How you *really* are?"

Louko laughed an actual, genuine laugh, and replied, "I suppose that's fair."

The laugh visibly let her relax further. "Good. Then how are you?"

His face fell. "I don't know," he admitted, with no small amount of effort. "It's my own fault, though. I played into her...provoked her. Shouldn't have opened my mouth." Then he sighed. "I don't know how I am, or how I should be, or how I ever will be.... I am alive at least, and that I am thankful for. But I am *tired*. Just tired. It's always the same, and nothing changes or ever will, and if I think about it, it would just get worse." Louko's shoulders dropped a little with the sudden and honest outburst.

He had never seen Astra look so sad. She sat completely still, not even wringing her hands. The pause was long before he barely heard her say, "I am so sorry." Her shoulders dropped, too, and it was another pause before she added, "But please, don't give up hope. Things *can* change. Perhaps it is terrible of me to say, but you are now free of your father. And if you get to Nythril, no one will have any say over you. You do not have to stay this way." She was so wonderfully earnest.

Louko had been trying not to think too much about it, actually. "But that's the problem Astra...." He sounded almost as desperate as he felt. "I have no more left in me to hope. If it happens then that will be wonderful, but I don't have the courage to hope anymore. I've done it too many times already, and been disappointed... But perhaps you are right. It would be nice." He ran his hand through his hair, not really comprehending that he was saying any of this out loud. To a person. To Astra.

It didn't help that Astra didn't reply. She sat there looking as

191

agitated as he felt. Then she got up, walked around the fire, and sat on the same soggy log Louko was on. At first, she kept her eyes down. "I suppose it's not much, but it is all I have: I will do what I can to help you." She looked up, expression serious. "Because I think you are already much more than you realize. And you do not have to keep living like this. If we can get to Nythril, maybe then you can see the way out."

Louko let a sigh escape, and his brow furrowed as he tried to comprehend her. "Thank you." The words were nearly inaudible, and yet sincere as he spoke them. She had risked herself for him so many times, and he didn't have the right to just turn her away again. He didn't want to...and he did so want her to be right.

Astra nodded, lips pressed tightly together as if debating with herself. She must have reached some sort of decision, for she said, "You are not what your father told you you were. You are not even what he tried to make you. I hope one day you are able to see that."

There was a small, wry smile on his lips as he said, "And you are good to a fault, Astra. You see the good in people until it's hard to argue with you."

Her expression lightened and she arched one brow. "If that is so, I will consider it my best trait," she said dryly.

With a mock annoyed frown, Louko replied with, "I don't know about that. I haven't decided yet."

"Haven't decided? My best trait?" Astra tried valiantly to hide her amusement.

"Well, that too. So many to choose from." He rolled his eyes.

Now Astra smiled and shook her head. "Now I know you're making fun of me," she said, surprising him by elbowing him slightly. "I was serious, though."

Louko honestly couldn't remember what she was serious about, and really, he didn't care. He hadn't even flinched when she'd elbowed him, and she had acted so normal that it was almost like they really *were* friends. And looking at her, Louko let himself believe that that was exactly what they were.

Friends.

Astra:

Morning came, as cold and grey as it always did in Merimeethia. As Astra rolled up her bedroll, she found herself missing Litash simply because one didn't start the day with damp clothing there. The feeling only grew as she pulled on her leather coat and felt all the moisture trapped within it. It was going to be a long day. Astra allowed herself a soft sigh before exiting her tent.

A quick scan of the camp told her that no one had yet stirred. Only Louko sat awake, keeping watch near the dying fire. Astra had no time to give anything more than the slightest of waves before one of the knights came out of a tent. It was the one they called Rufio. He nearly tripped over the decrepit remains of a stone wall, causing him to drop his sword as he recovered his balance. He picked it up with much grumbling and buckled it on. This, combined with the noise of a flock of birds somewhere in the trees, proved enough to stir the others.

The slow emergence of the knights set Astra and Louko in motion. The two went to work in silent agreement, both used to how Ent had run his camp and both eager to get this one moving. Fortunately, there wasn't too much to pack, and these men were used to being on the road. Astra was glad to see that they were well supplied. Each man had a mount, sturdy and sure-footed, with thick coats to keep out the rain. The knight who cared for the horses, Ivinon, also led a pack mount. Additionally, each knight had a tent of oiled canvas, a wool blanket, a waterskin, and a leather pack. The only ones lacking were Louko and Mariah. So, some of the knights had volunteered to bunk together to make up the space.

Apparently noticing Louko and Astra's example, the knights— even one they called Coryn, who had insisted on shaving—caught on and the whole clearing dissolved into a slow effort to pack up. What inefficiency. Astra thought of all the times Ent had gotten a group of fifty men to not only pack up, but effectively hide an entire campsite in half an hour without making any noise. These men were not trained for the haste that being on the run required.

But Astra could not be the one to hurry them up. Not unless Keeshiff publicly gave her the authority to do so. If she did otherwise, it would only undermine whatever hold the prince had over his men—and without that, there was nothing to hold the band together at all.

Mariah was even slower than the rest, coming out of her tent with a groggy, agitated expression. "What is going on?" she demanded in a perfect little act of innocence. It was maddening to Astra that one could act so selfishly in a crisis like this.

Nonetheless, Astra kept her voice even. "We are packing up the camp to move," she explained. "It is not safe to stay here. Any of us may have been followed."

Mariah groaned and returned to her tent. How helpful. Some of the knights must have seen, for several wore frowns.

So Astra knocked sharply on the tent pole. "Might you need any help with your packing, princess?"

"What?" came the squeak from inside the tent.

Astra sounded far more patient than she felt. "Your brother has given orders that we ride out immediately after breakfast. You'll need to make sure you are packed before we eat." Again, Astra made her offer. "If you need any help, I would be happy to assist you."

"I can do it myself, thank you!" came the snobby, defensive response.

Hiding a sigh of relief, Astra replied, "Very well. Then I shall see you in twenty minutes."

Astra then went to check on breakfast, which no one had thought to make. There was no time to cook anything now, so Astra spoke quickly with Delnor, the knight in charge of food rations, and he distributed a bit of bread and fruit to each person. Astra took her own ration as well as Mariah's and went to check on the other princess.

Mariah's tent was still up. Well. Not her tent—the one Farian had given up for her.

Knocking again on the tentpole, Astra called, "Your breakfast is ready. Are you?"

"No, I'm not. This isn't enough time for *any* human being to pack!" Her irritated voice came, followed by a soft *thud.* Probably Mariah kicking something in the tent. A perfect completion to her whiny temper tantrum.

"It was enough time for every other knight in the camp," Astra replied. "Assuming you want to go with them when they leave, I suggest you come out and eat, and allow me to disassemble your tent."

There was a muffled commotion from inside, and a very disheveled Mariah came forth, mouth set in a pouty line of annoyance. If Astra had not already known Mariah's age, she would have easily put her years younger than Louko. Her attitude was that of a three-year-old at best.

"Fine." She snatched both of the rations from Astra and flounced off.

Astra didn't try to reclaim her breakfast; the last thing she wanted was for Mariah to come back. She ducked inside the tent, and found nothing packed at all. Really? This was a special sort of childishness. Astra quickly rolled up the bedroll and threw it in a bag along with the few other things Mariah had. Then she took the tent down. Folding the canvas and poles, Astra suddenly wondered if Mariah was trying to slow them down on purpose.

The girl tried to brush off the disturbing thought. What reason would Mariah have to do so? Surely Mariah was too flighty to be of use to Tyron. Astra finished attaching the tent and saddlebag to Mariah's saddle, and went to find the other princess.

"Here you are." Astra handed Mariah the reins of her horse, and tried to walk away as fast as she could.

"Riding *again*?" Mariah sounded as tired as Astra felt. "But I don't think I can ride another minute after the last few days."

Slowly, Astra explained again, "We have no choice. To stay here puts everyone in danger—including you and Keeshiff. We must move."

Mariah made a face, but seemed defeated...for now.

The other knights had all finished packing, and were already mounting up on their horses.

"Do you think you could stay up front with Keeshiff? Seeing as your hearing and sight might be able to better find any traps we could fall into," Louko murmured from his position next to Astra.

"Ent is the one with better vision," Astra corrected quietly, feeling a pang at the thought of her brother. "I have better hearing. But I suppose even that could still help." She did not relish the thought of riding near Mariah. "I will see what Keeshiff wants."

"Right," Louko acquiesced. "Thank you."

Astra mounted up on Dannsair, collecting her reins even as the mare pawed the soft ground. Then she nudged her up to where Keeshiff was helping his sister mount up. It looked like a rather exasperating process. Astra waited until they were done to address the prince.

"Where would you prefer I ride in the group? My hearing is better than most thanks to my heritage, and I was not sure if it would be useful in any specific area."

"Why would Astra ride with us?" Mariah interjected before her brother could even speak.

Astra stayed quiet, knowing Keeshiff ought to reply for himself.

"To report what she sees and hears." Keeshiff's voice was taut, but uncertain.

Mariah scoffed. "Bandon is the best scout in Merimeethia." Her voice turned matter-of- fact. "And he is a grown man. Why not send Astra to the back to watch Louko? She seemed capable of that before, at least."

Astra watched Keeshiff's turmoil play out on his face. With the chaos and trauma of the past week, Astra could not blame him for being emotionally unstable and easily swayed. He gave Astra a look that confirmed he had given into Mariah. "Perhaps if you stayed in the back...to make sure no one is following us."

"As you wish," was all Astra said. She wheeled Dannsair around and rode to the back of the small group as they began to move out.

Louko was just plodding along, appearing to be talking to his horse or himself. Astra couldn't decide which was more odd. It would have been more so had he not noticed her, but fortunately both for her sake and his pride, he did. "Oh. Back so soon, eh?" he said with that knowing look.

"Can't complain." Astra shrugged, falling in line alongside the youngest prince.

"You know it's bad when you hate someone so much, you let them steal your food." The slightest hint of a wry smile touched his lips.

An answering half-smile slipped across Astra's face. "If I protested, she might have come back," she reasoned.

"Very true. The risks we take." He seemed a little sober at that last remark, but quickly rallied. "So, I apologize that you are to be stuck with my company. But is there anything that might amuse the great Astra Verzaer?"

Realizing that Louko did not intend for that to hurt, Astra gave no retort. "Now that you mention it," she said, "I recall you knowing quite a bit of history. Perhaps you could make an effort to educate me." She knew better than to ask of Kaeden or Tyron.

Louko rolled his eyes. "What in Eatris could I know to outdo a Litashian's education?" It took Astra a moment to realize he was serious.

She tried to think of how to explain Louko's error. 'Well, fortunately for you, you don't have to," Astra said. "I never had one."

The look of shock on his face would have been comical if Astra didn't feel so embarrassed.

"I wasn't raised in Litash," she said with a shrug.

"Ooooh." Louko looked completely uncomfortable now. "Right." Then came an awkward cough. "Well… In that case, where would you like to start?"

Astra shrugged. "I guess there's not much of a beginning. Start wherever you'd like."

"Well. Anything from the library pique your interest?"

Trying to think back, Astra immediately thought of Tyron. She shivered. It would not do to speak of him with the knights so close by.

"How about Drogans?"

"Well. That is a funny one. Their early history doesn't really make sense. But for starters, they were like Shape-Shifters, but could only turn into Dragons. I think I told you that already, though…" He got an official air about him as he seemed to gather his thoughts, then went on, "At one point they seemed to be the counselors of, well, all of Eatris. They ruled during the time when Elves were actually not confined to one city."

Astra wanted to ask about that, but he didn't give her time.

"But the Drogans did not last very long as a favored power. With the Drogan Madness, they became very disliked and were hunted and driven out for the most part. There are some still today, but they almost all disappeared around the time that Euracia made war upon Litash. Anything specific about them you wanted to know?"

"Where do they live now?" Astra asked.

He shrugged, "Some live in Dragon country—Beclian, some call it. It is said the rest have scattered and hidden amongst other races. But more likely they were killed off by Drogan hunters. There are many of those in Nythril and the West."

"Why?" Astra blushed after realizing she sounded like a toddler. Self conscious, she adjusted her reins.

"Nythril hates Dragons, and thus Drogans by default. It goes way back to when the two countries split, but Dragon hunting was a rather popular sport among nobility for a long while. I think it still is actually...along with Drogan hunting. To be able to track down and kill a Drogan became quite an honor."

Astra did not keep the disgust from her expression. "No wonder they all left." She thought of the Dragons she had met and now understood why they had spoken so poorly of humans.

"Indeed," Louko murmured, "I suppose Nytrhilians just didn't like the fact that the Dragons had taken up colonizing the West in an attempt to get away from the chaos of Beclian."

"What happened in Beclian?"

Louko shifted in his saddle, adjusting his reins as he said, "The texts are very old—and therefore very vague—on what started it, but it was something to do with a king called Malnimar. And something about a gift from the Drogans that he used for ill some thousands of years ago. Apparently he used it to take over some place called Baeno and much of the East."

Astra would have been ashamed of her questions if Louko hadn't seemed to be enjoying answering them so much. She soaked in the new information. "I have been to the East," she commented. "Though not as far as Beclian."

He looked at her longingly, "Have you? What was it like?"

Astra thought back to the time when she traveled with Ent. "Which country? We visited several."

"Did you see the Cadbir Isles?"

"Yes." Astra nodded. "For a few days." She tried to recall what the Isles were like; at the time, she had been young and scared and on the run. "It was hot. Very hot. But not so dry and thirsty like Pershizar. Everything was wet and saturated. It would rain every day, but not all day—it would go from bright sun, to a downpour, and back to sun within the span of an hour." The forest around her reminded her of the jungles on the Isles. "The trees were strange. Inland, they were thick and entwined—impossible to get a horse through. Near the water, they were tall and skinny, with leaves only growing in big strands at the top." She shrugged. "Maybe it was because of the sand. Their coasts are covered with sand instead of stone." Astra tried to think of any other detail Louko would want to know of. "The people all had an accent that made their speaking sound soft. It was as though they weren't used to consonants and would slide over them into the vowels. Most of them had darker skin as if they'd spent too much time in the sun." She recalled the markets, thick with scents of spices and animals. She had wondered then how so many people could afford the bright clothing and jewelry in the quantities she'd seen. "They wore many colors and carved beads—even the men."

"Hm. That sounds intriguing," Louko said softly, with a faraway expression. For several minutes, the only sound was that of squelching mud under the horses' hooves Then Louko came back to reality and asked suddenly, "So what else would you like to know?"

"What do you know of the Miadoris?" Astra was curious about the power that had latched onto her.

His brow furrowed, "Not very much, really. It's the source of all Gifting. That's about it. You probably know more than I do...How does that work, anyway?"

How to explain? "No one really knows for certain," she started off slowly. "Some think it is the source of Gifting, others think it embodies every creature's Gifting, and still others say that Gifting is life itself, and that specific Gifts are merely a manifestation of it." Astra paused, thinking back to the time when the Miadoris had taken her over completely. "Whether it is the source of life or whether it draws from it, I do not know. But I can tell you with certainty that it is connected to every living thing." She stopped, wondering if she was talking too much.

"Huh." came the prince's simple, yet seemingly thoughtful reply. After another moment, he asked, "How are you so certain...I mean, what exactly happened—or, no. That's not how I wanted it to come out..." He trailed off with the usual muttered, *"idiot"*.

"It's alright," Astra assured quickly, not wanting to make him feel awkward. She loosened Dannsair's reins as she started to speak, switching to Litashian in the hopes that the knights riding in front couldn't speak the language. **"I came into contact with it when I was very little. I don't remember it at all, but it still had repercussions."** One hand rubbed her new red bronze cuff self-consciously. She was glad Ent had given her several spares. **"Euracia theorized that because I survived that small amount, I had an immunity and so** could be used to contain and weaponize the entire Essence. He captured me and tested it." Astra remembered all too well the nightmarish ordeal that had followed. "The problem was that I also absorbed each personality that the Miadoris was linked to. I switched back and forth so rapidly between them all that I became unstable and dangerous—luckily too much so to be of any use to Euracia."

"Well. That sounds...horrible," Louko commented nonchalantly.

The response made Astra suppress a smile, though she didn't entirely know why. "I wouldn't recommend the experience," she replied dryly. "It is a once in a lifetime occurrence, if you understand me. I'm only here because Ent found a way to extract it in time." Her thoughts drifted towards the way it still plagued her, and her humorous mood died.

"Good thing you didn't die or anything. I'm pretty sure your horse would be on a murderous rampage by now otherwise," Louko said with something approaching a laugh.

Dannsair snorted as if in confirmation. Between that and Louko's laugh, Astra was pulled from her sour thoughts, and back to the conversation. She smiled and searched out another topic. "What in history interests you most?" she asked, returning to Merimeethian. Probably best to let the knights overhear so that no one accused her and Louko of conspiring.

It took the prince a moment to answer. "Such hard questions." He gave her a sarcastic smile. "But if I must choose, Merimeethia is the best. It has just the right touch of self-pity."

That certainly did sound like several Merimeethians Astra knew. "Do tell."

"Merimeethia was a Dragon country long ago. Then when they invited humans, there were Dragon riders. That, and the sun used to exist here." He added an exaggerated shocked expression at that last bit.

Astra rolled her eyes, but pushed past on. "A Dragon country? Are any here now?"

"No. The rain and gloom came, and they decided they liked Beclian and the Eastern Lands much better. Can't say I do anything but envy them."

Astra shrugged. "Unless you really like the beach, I don't know if you'd like Cadbir."

"What's it like?" he asked suddenly, getting that whimsical sound to his voice again.

"Um," Astra was fairly sure she had just told him about Cadbir... "Like I said, Cadbir is—"

"No, no. I mean the beach. The ocean. The water... you know. The big great lake?" He smirked at her in what seemed an attempt to hide embarrassment at his own lack of knowledge.

Astra looked over at him curiously. "You've not seen it?"

The prince shook his head.

"You're not missing very much," Astra said. "It's empty and flat, like an endless blue plain. When it moves, it comes with horrid storms. But it was the sea serpents I particularly disliked." She could still remember the serpent pulling her down beneath the water. The scar on her leg was still there.

Astra realized Louko was staring at her. "I may be a little biased…" She shifted, feeling awkward.

"Sounds…wonderful." He seemed to be fighting an amused smile.

"What did I say?"

"Well," He gave that bored expression of his. "Everyone always goes on and on about it, so I suppose I was not expecting…sea serpents…"

Astra was unsympathetic. "When one is trying to drown and eat you, you might remember it, too."

"You know, I didn't feel that way about Dragons even after one tried to eat me. But then again, perhaps that's not something to be proud of…"

"Dragons are different," Astra stated. "Much more reasonable creatures."

"With no sense of humor. And scales. And teeth. And very…very…long… tongues… I'm not seeing the difference," Louko said.

"The difference is that you insulted the only Dragon you ever met."

"Yes. Yes I did." He seemed almost proud of himself. Then his face turned solemn as he looked up to the front. "Perhaps you should check up on the front…just to make sure Mariah isn't…" He trailed off meaningfully.

The transition from past to present was sudden and unpleasant. "Good idea," Astra said, subdued.

She nudged Dannsair to a trot and went up to the front of the line. "How fares our path?" Astra called out to Keeshiff.

"Just fine." he said with full sarcasm. How did Astra have more social graces than such a highly educated prince? Maybe that was the problem...

"Where do you plan to stop for nightfall?" Astra pressed, undeterred.

Keeshiff looked like he might actually have an intelligent answer... but then Mariah gave a squeak.

"Wait. We aren't stopping until nightfall??"

Astra resisted the urge to roll her eyes at Mariah's interjection. She settled for ignoring the other princess, and waiting for Keeshiff's reply.

"Well. The men seem to be getting tired." He seemed uncertain now.

"Better tired than dead." Astra regretted the bluntness of her words before they even left her lips. For such a little person, she had an awfully big mouth.

"Dead?" cried Mariah.

"Um," said Keeshiff.

"Nicely done," came Asher's murmur from behind Astra.

Astra was beginning to understand some of how Louko felt. "What I meant was that it is not safe to stop quite yet."

"Actually, Your Highness, I think she meant exactly what she said." Asher stepped in. "I couldn't have said it better myself."

Asher seemed to actually pay attention to things. Astra wondered if any of the other knights did... She hoped so. Still, the physician was not helping Astra out of the hole she had just dug herself into.

"Fine. We'll keep moving for a while. But it looks like rain."

"It always looks like rain. So I think the fact that it still is only *looking* is a pretty good sign." Now it was Gavin who spoke up, humor touching the edge of his voice.

Keeshiff was probably too upset to do anything else other than continue. To say the least, his face was the color of his auburn hair.

Astra knew better than to force herself into the decision any further. "Perhaps one of your men knows the area. Maybe you could ask them where a good stopping place would be."

"When Bandon returns from scouting ahead, I will ask him," Keeshiff managed to say.

"As you say," Astra said.

She turned Dannsair again to return to the back, ignoring Mariah's glare. Louko seemed to be amused as Astra rode up with a dark expression.

"*Sooo*...how did it go?" he asked.

"I'm beginning to understand how you feel," Astra huffed.

With an annoying grin, Louko replied, "Ah! So it went swimmingly, then?"

***

I open the book, skimming till I find the right spot. It's hard to find amidst all these records. But I know what I'm looking for, and soon I have everything I need. It won't take me long to find the location now.

I close the book and return it respectfully to its proper shelf. To think that Astra spent all that time in here, and still missed what I came for. I shake my head, chuckling as I leave the library.

CHAPTER XI

Astra:

"What!?" Keeshiff's response was drastic, as expected. "You are absolutely mad. Aelor Ven *hates* my father—and he hates me!" He clenched his fists and stared at both of them; mostly, however, at his brother.

It had been two or three days of travel, but they were finally far enough into the Forest of Riddles to feel some sense of security. That was when Louko had approached Keeshiff about hiding in Nythril. Louko had warned Astra that Keeshiff wouldn't like the idea; it appeared he had been right.

"Then where do you suggest we go?" Astra questioned now.

"Not to Nythril, that's for sure. Nythrilians are to be trusted with nothing except the dark in which they hide—especially Aelor Ven."

"Funny how grudges are so mutual," Astra heard Louko mutter under his breath.

Making an educated guess, Astra took a risk and asked, "Not even if they are Mariah's kin?" Mariah resembled Louko far more than Keeshiff with her dark hair and almond-shaped eyes. Astra had noticed it even more since the princess had been without any cosmetics to hide her darker skin and less pronounced facial features. And there was, of course, Louko's comment on the day the two had argued in the ruins. Hopefully Astra was right about this...

Keeshiff's anger wavered slightly, but he held firm in his folly. "She does not associate herself with them."

"She won't associate with anybody if we all get killed," Astra pointed out. "We can't stay here. It's not a permanent solution, and it's not looking like anyone is going to help you anytime soon. Not from Merimeethia, anyway."

A long silence followed. Astra could practically see Keeshiff's pride warring with what sense he had. In the end, he would need to realize that if he wanted to stay alive, he had to stop worrying about always being right and instead start listening so he could do what was right.

"Why not go to Litash? It would be far more welcoming, and trustworthy. Why must it be Nythril?" Keeshiff questioned stubbornly.

Astra couldn't tell him of her exile or her brother's weakened power. He could use it against her. "Because the country is too unstable to offer us any help," she said. "Inducing a war between Merimeethia and Litash could very well lead to another Great War." Theoretically, Keeshiff would know better than to try the coast. They would never make it through any of the coastal cities with such a large, recognizable group—much less onto a boat.

Keeshiff's deepening frown told Astra she had won her point. "Fine. Nythril is our best option, it would seem. You win." He stared at Louko as he spoke.

Astra merely nodded. "When do we leave?"

"Now," Keeshiff answered, clearly not pleased with the decision. "After the rest have eaten, I will order camp to be broken."

"Alright." With that, Astra left, Louko close behind.

Outside the tent, Astra turned to Louko. "I would say that went fairly well, all things considered."

"I do believe I must agree. For a child he seemed very well behaved today," Louko said dryly, an insincere smile flashing quickly. "Though, I don't blame him...Uncle Ven has been very clear about who he tolerates and who he doesn't..." He ran a hand through his hair, eyes flitting away as his attention was drawn elsewhere.

"You have to leave the fire going," Coryn argued, razor still in hand from this morning's shave. "Otherwise you'll offend the Shadow Faeries."

Judging by Lucian's expression, the latter knight had no respect for such superstitions. "You've been listening to too many of Grandfather's bedtime stories," came his cynical reply.

"But Shadow Faeries are real," Farian interjected from beyond the campfire.

"Yeah," Lucian snorted. "A real annoyance."

Astra had to agree with Lucian. Shadow Faeries were pesky things, and had a habit of making off with one's shinier belongings. Fortunately, they were so small that they couldn't lift anything smaller than a coin or two—not that that stopped them from their little tricks.

Delnor, who seemed to be attempting to mediate the whole affair, spotted Astra and asked, "Princess, what do you think?"

This was probably the first time any of the men had asked her opinion on anything. Though, considering the subject in question, she did not count herself as flattered. "I think it doesn't matter," she replied. "For we are not deep enough into the Forest to encounter any Faeries."

With a smirk, Lucian made eye contact with Coryn and poured out the rainwater that had collected in the stewpot. The dying coals sizzled and died.

Coryn, somewhat undignified in defeat, grunted and walked off, leaving Lucian to bury the evidence of the fire.

"And here I thought we were all adults…" Louko murmured, a hint of amusement in his voice.

To which Astra's only reply was: "Blame the Shadow Faeries."

Louko:

It was actually not raining, such a rare occurrence that Louko was in a rather good mood. Of course, the lack of rain was most likely due to being on the fringes of the Forest of Riddles, and that didn't exactly ease Louko's nerves. Certainly, he had run into no serious problems on the journey to Litash just a month or so ago, nor on the way back to Merimeethia, but that didn't mean he hadn't been uneasy. The Forest had a knack for never behaving when it should, and when he'd journeyed before, he'd used the road. Here, they were in uncharted territory, and would remain so as they followed the forest west all the way to Nythril. It meant plunging into the wild in the hopes of emerging in one piece.

Louko's less-than-confident opinion of the forest reminded him of his uncle, and of the less-than-favorable opinion he held of Litashians. Hopefully he wouldn't mind Astra... Louko was sure he could convince Uncle Ven not to kill her or anything drastic like that. Then again, seeing as he had once tried to start a war over custody of Mariah...

"We should probably stop for the night, Keeshiff," Bandon announced.

"Yes, *please*." Mariah, of course, was all too willing to stop. Her almond eyes were red with weariness, and her hair snarled to the point of abandon. She'd been trying to keep up her appearance, but she'd learned there was only so far one could really take that while on the run for their lives.

They made a quick camp and a small fire was built to provide a little warmth. Louko hoped it would keep any animals away as well. So far, they'd been lucky enough to avoid anything. But then again...The Forest never behaved the same way twice. Granted, since The War it was much better, but he still had suspicions. It did, at least, look like a normal forest now.

Louko, however, had learned looks could be deceiving.

Everyone settled down for the evening without argument, and only Gavin (who was standing guard), Louko, and Astra were left awake. Louko was too on edge to sleep, and he guessed by Astra's appearance that she fared no better. When they'd both gone up to Merimeethia together, neither had been terribly concerned. Funny how circumstances changed one's outlook on things.

As the night wore on, the weariness of the day's ride began to catch up and win out over all of Louko's worrying. Exhaustion made his eyelids feel heavy and he couldn't remember a good reason to stay awake. But just as he was ready to give in, Louko saw Astra sit up. The motion was quick, deliberate, and yet she didn't get to her feet. He saw her turn her head just slightly as if looking for something. What had she heard?

"Gavin," she said in a calm, quiet voice. "Don't move."

The knight, though his expression was questioning, went still.

Astra looked to Louko next, but he had already done the same.

He knew better than to ask. Now fully awake, he strained to hear whatever it was that had set Astra on guard.

It was quiet at first. The soft snuffling sounds, the padded footsteps, the muted thud of something knocked over into the wet leaves. Then Louko saw it. The lumbering black outline near the tent that held the supplies. It lifted its head and looked towards the fire, illuminating a pair of nearly lamp-like eyes. Louko didn't so much as breathe. Whatever it was blinked a few times, then returned to its snuffling.

The sudden movement of someone coming out of a tent was startling. "I can take over now, Gavin," Coryn said with a yawn, still pulling on an overshirt.

The tense mood was shattered into a thousand pieces of panic as the creature reared itself to face Coryn, growling. Louko's hand inched closer to his blade. He saw Astra out of the corner of his eye, and waited to see what she would do; Louko was unfamiliar with this creature, and Astra had more experience in this.

But the beast looked like it was now preparing a charge, scraping its claws against the earth and letting out a resounding groan.

It was interrupted by the shrill clanging of metal. It was Astra, clashing her sword and dagger together. She went back and forth between this and waving her arms in wide circles. Whether it was the sound or the light reflecting off the blades, this seemed to disconcert the monster.

"Copy me," Astra called. "They are skittish by nature."

Everyone began copying, and the creature's moans turned to more of an unpleasant shriek as it began backing away.

Unfortunately, the grating noise had also woken up the rest of the knights—and Mariah—and everyone came rushing out into the night, confused clamor melding with the clash of metal.

"Do not attack it!" Astra shouted over all the noise. She had been slowly taking ground and so getting the beast to leave, but now there were too many people for her to do so.

Keeshiff—thankfully—appeared to immediately understand and started making noise as well. Others followed suit and Louko was glad to see the creature slowly giving ground and edging back to the dark.

And then there was another moaning cry—this one aggressive. Louko swiveled around just in time to see Farian grappling with another one of the hulking animals, which had apparently just charged him. Rufio was nearby, and Louko saw the blood glimmer on the tip of his sword.

Not good.

The appearance of the second one seemed to rile the first. The beast let out a nearly deafening roar, scraping the ground again before barreling towards its wounded mate. Several knights dove out of the way to avoid being crushed.

Not thinking—as usual—Louko swung his sword out, nicking the thing's leg as it ran past him. They couldn't afford both in one place, and Farian would be dinner in a moment. The creature shrieked again and tossed his head, swerving off to one side. An arrow protruded from one side of its dark muzzle.

Astra.

Louko moved around one side so that he and Astra both faced the beast in a strategic position to herd it out of the camp and keep it from the other beast, which the other knights were pulling off of Farian. These things were huge, and Louko wondered how much it would take to kill it if they had to. Too much, he guessed. But if they got them out, then they would likely be too scared to return. Soon Lucian and Delnor joined Louko and Astra as the rest drove the second creature away back into the woods.

With the second one gone, the first was much easier to deter. It swiped at Lucian, growled and moaned a moment more, then spun away and loped off in search of its mate.

"Is everyone okay?" Keeshiff asked, loud enough for everyone to hear.

Louko looked for Farian and spotted him just outside the ring of tents. Rufio was helping him to his feet. His face looked scraped up, but he gave a curt nod.

"I think the bigger question is are the supplies alright." Delnor's voice held apprehension. "Because those things really had at it…"

Everyone's eyes were drawn to the tattered ruins of the supply tent.

Great. Just great.

***

After the incident with the Nodroits—or so Astra called the beasts that ruined most of their supplies—it was quickly agreed that they should move further out of the Forest of Riddles. Not so far as to stumble upon outlying villages, yet also not so close as to have any more run-ins with monsters. Hopefully, this area of compromise would have enough forestation to hide them, and enough game to boost their currently slim rations.

The decrease of food, the increase of rain and mud, the ever-present threat of being found, and of course the attack of the Nordroits, meant everyone was in an unusually sour mood. That's why Louko was thankful when no one argued after Bandon suggested settling down a little early that day. However, when the prince tried to *help* Keeshiff and the knights set up, he quickly gave up; everyone was too grumpy for that.

Instead, he went over to see if Astra wanted any assistance.

"We need food," she commented as she brushed down Dannsair. "I will go hunt after everything is settled."

Louko wondered how much of her desire to hunt was for the food, and how much of it was for the solace. He chanced a quick glance over to where his siblings were, and saw Keeshiff carefully helping Mariah with her tent. Maybe some solace wouldn't be so bad...

Louko hesitantly asked, "Would you like some help?"

Astra paused her brushing to look at him. After only a moment, she nodded and then stowed the brush back in her packs. "Sure. What do you know how to do?" She asked.

"Um..." Louko looked slightly embarrassed. "Perhaps challenging the rabbit to a duel?" *Idiot.* He felt like such a useless prince...not actually knowing how to do much else besides forage for edible plants and berries. But no one had bothered to teach him how to hunt.

But rather than reject him, Astra grinned. "I've never employed such a method, but I would be glad to see a demonstration." Chuckling softly to herself, the girl gave Dannsair one more pat, then picked up her bow where she had left it leaning against a tree. "Follow me."

Louko obeyed, glad to see the grin he had managed to put on Astra's face.

"And where do you think *you're* going?" It was Rufio...who had apparently noticed them preparing to leave.

"Hunting," Astra answered, before Louko could speak. "Unless you would rather eat grass with the horses."

Rufio eyed Louko, but appeared less hostile. "Do you need help, then?" he asked.

Astra's tone was kinder this time. "Yes, actually. If you wouldn't mind building a fire, it will be down to coals for cooking by the time we return."

The knight looked up at the sky skeptically, then looked back at Astra, "I'll do what I can."

The princess thanked him, then turned back to Louko. She didn't have to say anything out loud to tell him to hurry; he followed her into the woods before anyone else could stop them.

Astra led them a little way from the camp, then stopped. She took stock of their surroundings, then quietly asked, "Do you know what plants are good to eat here?"

"Yes. That, at least, I am acquainted with." He had learned that before his escape attempt all those years ago—in case he'd run out of supplies.

"Good. Then after we catch something, we can gather whatever forage we can find before we go back." Astra drew an arrow from the quiver on her back and placed it in the hand that already held her bow.

"Now, hunting should come somewhat naturally for you. You

already have some experience with tracking and maneuvering the woods quietly. You only have to learn how to apply that to animals." Her head tilted slightly. "And how to shoot," she added. "We have no time to set traps."

Louko nodded, just listening.

"How do you think we should start when looking for an animal?" asked Astra.

"Finding its source of food?" Louko made what he felt was a very bad guess.

Astra seemed to consider this. "It is a good start: keeping an eye out for food or water and then following the tracks," she said. "We have a limited range since we cannot get too far from the camp. Unless we come across something obvious, our best bet is simply to walk the perimeter until we find any signs of what we're looking for."

Louko nodded. "Alright." He was rather intrigued about how to do this—especially shooting a bow. That would be most interesting.

The two walked in complete silence, scanning their surroundings for any signs. They did not move quickly, but their pace was steady. Less than an hour had passed before Astra raised one hand to stop them. Louko promptly obeyed, wondering what Astra had found.

He didn't have to wonder long. The princess waved him over and pointed to a patch of mud. The footprints of some large bird remained clearly in the ooze. Now Astra gestured for Louko to lead.

Oh, joy.

How had he survived a whole war without hunting? True, Entrais' camp had been very organized. Everyone had their role and Louko's had *not* been in the kitchen.

Hoping he knew what he was doing, Louko continued on, trying to remind himself it wasn't much different from tracking an enemy or spy —and since Astra and Entrais had been the ones to teach him those skills, theoretically he had been taught right. Now, whether he'd *retained* the training correctly.... He hadn't led for long when Astra stopped him again. Had he already led them astray? But when Louko turned to her, she had one hand cupped to her ear, as if she heard something.

Elvish hearing. He resisted the urge to make a face. Instead, he looked around, trying to see if he could spot anything. Nothing. Only when Astra moved on did he start to hear the chattering of birds. Flawkey birds. They would make a good meal.

The two got quite close to the flock without startling any of them. The birds were gathered in a small clearing, busily rooting around in the grass and mud for any bugs they could eat. Louko felt something nudging his arm and turned his head. Astra was holding out her bow to him.

He mouthed, "I have never shot one before".

Astra's little smile was mischievous as she continued holding out the bow.

Louko hoped the birds were deaf...

Awkwardly, he took the bow, hoping he picked the right side to be the top as he held it and waited for Astra to either give him an arrow, or...not...

The princess set the arrow to the string for him, then demonstrated what kind of grip Louko should use to pull the string back.

Louko copied it, but waited for her to nod before pulling the string back. He did not expect this part to be so hard, but it took him a moment to get it set. He nearly ruined it by dropping the bow, for once he settled, the bow changed shape in his very hand. It grew a little longer and the handle grew thicker. It no longer took so much strength to hold the string in place.

Well. That was... not natural.

Louko did his best attempt at aiming, copying the stance Astra modeled for him, and then shot. Of course, it missed, and the birds sputtered and squawked in an explosion of feathers before disappearing into the air. Louko smiled slightly. "Guess I really *should* have challenged them to a duel instead."

Astra laughed. "Perhaps you should have," she replied. "Luckily for you, my brother has taught me a few other tricks." She stepped out of their hiding place, and into the clearing. On the closest edge, one of the Flawkey birds lay motionless on the ground, Astra's knife protruding from the base of its neck.

Louko made a face, pretending to be indignant. "I feel used," he said with a dramatic gasp.

"Don't bother," Astra said, smiling once more. "If you had hit, we would have had two birds and we could have gone a few days on the meat. Now you'll just get more practice sooner. Besides, I'm not skilled with knives—my own kill was a lucky hit."

She pulled the knife from the bird, wiping off the blood with a leaf before returning it to its sheath. Then the princess picked up the large bird by its feet, and looked to Louko. "If you would kindly retrieve my arrow, we can work in your area of expertise and pick some things to eat."

Louko made a flourishing bow before obeying, soon returning

with the errant shaft. "Now. Shall we admire the shrubs?" he asked.

Amusement lighting her face, Astra slipped the arrow back in her quiver. "We shall," she replied in an equally formal voice.

They walked back through the thick woods until they reached a patch they had walked through earlier. Louko had noted several edible plants there.

"Now it is your turn to teach me again," Astra said as she tied the Flawkey to a branch and rejoined Louko.

He knelt down, plucking a couple dark berries from their patch—Geltum. "These are edible. Look for the four leaves, though. There is one with a broadleaf that is actually quite unpleasant. Doesn't kill you, but don't expect to do anything for two days," he explained.

With raised brows, Astra nodded and began to pick some, depositing each berry into the little sack she had brought with her.

They went on, Louko showing her the various edible and inedible things she could and couldn't pick. After a while, she was sufficiently educated, and they were laden with plenty of things to go with the bird. "Well. That's probably enough," Louko announced.

Astra agreed, shouldering her sack before untying the bird.

Together, they hiked back towards the camp, fighting the undergrowth and their growing sense of foreboding.

They entered the camp, finding Rufio and Bandon tending a good fire in the center. The tents were actually all set up, and there was some semblance of order. Farian was in the corner with his brother Ivinon, brushing down the horses.

But Louko's eyes wandered to Keeshiff and Mariah, who were sitting side by side on a log by the fire and talking quietly, as if they were best friends. They had always been close. Poisonously so.

It was Astra's voice that cut through his thoughts. "Would you like to help me dress the bird?"

"Sure," Louko replied, turning back to her.

"I see you were successful, Astra," Keeshiff piped up from his spot. "Do you need any assistance?"

Louko caught the princess' short glance at him before she turned to Keeshiff. "If you wouldn't mind, then yes," she replied. "Louko showed me what plants are edible, so I'm going to show him how to prepare a bird for cooking. If you would slice up the roots we gathered, we can have a good stew going quickly."

Keeshiff nodded and got up, and as always, Mariah did as well. "I'll help you, Keeshiff," she said with that purring tone.

Louko resisted a sigh. If only she was always so eager to help. Some of the knights exchanged glances that seemed to agree.

Astra didn't say anything outright, but her good mood from earlier had dissipated back into her usual serious expression. She gave her sack of roots and berries to Keeshiff, then turned back to Louko. "Have you ever done anything like this before?" she asked as she tied the flawkey to a branch by its feet.

Louko shrugged. "I've helped in the kitchen before."

There was a poorly hidden snort from Mariah.

Now Astra's lips formed a firm line. But she pressed on. "Alright. That will help." She used the heel of her boot to make a hole in the damp soil beneath the bird. "That will catch everything we take off," she explained. "First, we will need to borrow some of that water Rufio has boiling."

And so it went. Astra showed Louko how to clean, pluck, and gut the bird so that it resembled something that actually belonged in a kitchen. Then they cut and pulled until it was in manageable pieces that they dropped into the pot. With the messy part done, they buried all the entrails and feathers in the hole Astra had made.

"Now to clean ourselves up," Astra said, looking down at her blood-smeared hands.

Louko raised an eyebrow, about to comment on how they looked like they'd just murdered someone. Then he looked around at the knights and his siblings, and thought better of it. Such a comment from him would *probably* not go over very well, so he simply nodded instead.

After cleaning up, Louko returned to find Mariah and Keeshiff's job done, and the former standing by the pot with Asher. She talked casually, asking a couple questions about the cooking process. Keeshiff sat nearby with Gavin, who had apparently found some greens to contribute to the stew. The other knights were not far off. In short... everyone was really quite hungry.

Only Astra could appear disinterested. Louko watched her as she stayed outside the circle, checking on Dannsair, cleaning her knife, checking the used arrows—anything, it would seem, to be busy and far away from the nearly finished dinner. She picked up her bow and pulled back the string. It changed again back to the perfect size for her, and without ceremony she relaxed the string without letting go.

Louko was just determining to go over and try and figure out what was the matter when Asher announced, "Dinner is ready," dishing out the first bowl and out of respect giving it to Mariah. Then all the other knights crowded around, but Astra gave no sign of having heard.

After everyone else had gotten food, Louko went up and got two bowls. Gingerly, he made his way over to Astra, not really sure how to broach the subject. Of course, typical Louko, he decided just to completely jump into the fire, and proceeded to give an awkward cough, extending one of the bowls to her without a word. Last time he had tried to make her eat, it had been rather awkward...but of course, the idiot he was, he would try again.

The girl looked up at him, eyes showing her uneasiness. But she set down her bow and took the bowl.

"Thank you," she said quietly.

This eased Louko only a little bit, and he raised his own bowl in a sort of toast. "Anytime. I did, after all, contribute...in missing the bird," he said, taking a mouthful of the stew to stop from appearing any more awkward.

Astra's lips turned upwards just slightly, only to fade as she looked back down at her own bowl. She stirred it slowly with the crudely carved spoon. Then, delicately, she took a bite.

"We had just enough supplies that it wasn't crucial for you to hit it," she said, returning to her stirring. "We have time; we can always work on your archery skills."

"Probably a good idea. I don't want to go skewering anybody by accident," Louko replied matter-of-factly, though watching her movements carefully. He didn't have the guts to press her more, but he did worry about the fact that she did not seem to want to eat. Was it an Elf thing, maybe? Louko remembered Entrais often having to press her during The War. In fact, he remembered that pressing to be mutual.

"Mm. Yes. Save the skewering for when you do it on purpose,"

Astra replied wryly.

Louko wagged his spoon at her. "When I can do that, you should be very afraid."

***

The days of travel that followed were not much better than the beginning of their journey west towards the border. The weather was dreadful, of course. Astra was the only thing that made it bearable, as her constant questions kept Louko distracted. Of course, it appeared he wasn't alone. Louko had carefully watched as some of the knights would slow their horses, pick up the pace, and lean forward or back in order to hear them. Not in the spying or distrustful sort of way, but in a curious one. Well, at least, if nothing else, Louko was educational.

Glad to be of service… finally.

It did not stop Louko from remembering *who* had given him his education. He wondered if they would be so eager to listen to Louko if they knew…

Today was particularly miserable. The air was unusually and oppressively warm, and the rain unrelenting, the combination of which turned their path into a muddy slough. The only fortune they had was that they were currently going up a gentle rise. The water drained fairly well and the footing was manageable, but still, a bad footing was ever imminent as the water slowly trickled downhill.

The knights in front of Louko suddenly pulled their horses to a stop.

"This doesn't look good," Louko heard Ivinon mutter ahead of him.

It would appear they had just come to the ridge of the Se-Ednian Valley, and it was raining so hard one could hardly see beyond the mist and rain. Not good.

"We need to try and make it down the ridge before nightfall!" Keeshiff called above the roar of rain.

"No!" Louko scarcely realized he had said the word, let alone *shouted* it. *Idiot!* Too late to go back now. "Keeshiff, that is madness. You must know this valley's reputation. We should go around it. It's too dangerous to try and descend. The mud would come loose."

Rufio glared at him. "Not if we go through the village. They have shored up the roads and made them safe."

"I see. Let's walk right up with a big sign that says 'take me now'!" Ack. Louko shouldn't have said it that way, but he was feeling a sense of near panic at the thought of them trying to go down there. "We've come close enough to patrols as it is."

"Enough already!" Mariah yelled over the arguing knights and the sound of the rain. "Why would we wait in this miserable weather? Let's just get to the bottom."

"If we start now, we should get to the bottom before the rain makes the ridge unstable," Keeshiff said.

Louko was at the end of his rope. "Keeshiff, you can't be seri—"

"If we keep arguing about it, then we'll be nowhere. Astra said we needed speed and stealth. The other ways will not be so. Now we must go."

Wonderful. The one time Louko *didn't* want Keeshiff to be assertive… He sighed. This was not going to be good. Louko had read enough history books to know that this valley was often associated with *bad* events. Like The Battle of the Thundering Valley, or The Drowning, or The Great Flood of Se-Ednian…

Louko fell to the back of the line, hoping to be able to keep an eye on the slope as they descended. Hopefully they would not be too late… but even once they made it down, they would be in great peril until they made it to the other side. If nothing disastrous happened…They should make it. Probably. Maybe. How long had it been raining again? Louko tried to remember back to when it had only been cloudy, and was distressed to find it was longer than he'd hoped.

Oh dear.

"What's wrong?" Astra asked as he returned to the back of the line. She was trying to adjust her hood to better protect herself from the rain.

"This valley… you may notice it isn't inhabited on this side at all. Well, that's because it floods. Even if we escape a mudslide on the way down, we'll still only have a couple days—at best—to escape before we are all drowned," he answered grimly. The squelching of hooves in the mire made Louko shiver; all he could think of was the sound they would hear before being covered in mud… Suffocation did not sound like a pleasant end.

The footing was precarious at best, and the horses were constantly slipping and sliding, each one threatening to cause the whole group to fall to their doom. The rain grew ever heavier, making it hard for Louko to keep watch for any signs of slides. "Can you hear or see anything, Astra?" he called back to her. Perhaps her Elvish senses could catch something.

"No," she shouted over the rain. Then after a pause, "Wait…"

There was a panicked whinny from the front of the group, and then Mariah's scream wrenched the air. Louko watched in horror as her horse reared, sending his sister flying off at an angle. She landed on her back, winded…. And then she began to slide.

Keeshiff tried to get off his horse, but Mariah's panicked steed stood between them, and the other knights' horses had spooked too much. Mariah was slipping down towards the edge of the path…to the cliff.

Louko tried to dismount hurriedly, but his horse had caught the nervousness. Mariah was screaming again, clutching at the unforgiving mud as she slid faster and faster to her death.

"Astra!" was all Louko could think to shout—her horse being the only one not spooked.

There was a blur as Dannsair galloped past him in a mad rush, Astra urging her on. When the two reached the edge, Astra undid her cloak as she swung herself off the mare and onto the muddy slope. Louko couldn't risk dismounting and causing his horse to go crazy, and so he was helpless, left instead to strain to see Astra's movements. Instead of trying to slow her fall, she was pulling on objects to go faster and to steer her fall towards Mariah. Astra reached his sister, and Louko heard shouts. He could barely make out Mariah taking her hand. But they were both still sliding rapidly towards the edge. He pulled his horse up closer to get a better look.

Astra pulled out her dagger and stabbed it into the clay. They went a few feet, still sliding, before the blade caught. The jerk caused Mariah's weight to suddenly catch on Astra's arm. Astra's face contorted in pain and Louko's breath stuck in his throat even as he instinctively lurched forward—though much too far away to actually help.

By some miracle, Astra did not let go of Mariah.

"Please!" Astra cried up to the ledge. "A rope! Quickly!"

Mariah's legs dangled off the edge of the cliff.

Someone threw a rope to Asher, who was nearest to where the two were precariously dangling. Asher quickly handed the end to Lucian and tossed the remainder down to Astra.

"Mariah, take it!" Astra called down. "They will pull you up."

Louko watched as Mariah grasped wildly for the rope with her free hand. He felt useless, but knew there was nothing he could do. The rope went taut as she finally caught hold, and Louko held in a breath of hesitant relief as Lucian backed his horse to pull her up, the rope tied about the horn.

Asher had been finally able to dismount his horse, and grabbed hold of the muddied Mariah as she got back on solid ground.

"Throw it back down for Astra. Hurry!" Louko heard himself shout. He could already see the blade slipping.

The rope snaked down next to her, but Astra didn't grab it. Louko realized that the force of Mariah's weight on Astra's arm must have dislocated it, leaving her unable to use her free hand.

The blade began to tilt towards the cliff. Millions of emotions rattled through Louko's empty head, but all that would come out was a blank, "Wonderful." He was about to lose his only friend in the world— and what was he doing? Sitting idly on a horse watching it all!!

Louko had just been about to dismount and recklessly try and go to help when, with a sudden motion, Astra released the dagger and tried to grab the rope. Her hand was around it, but she was still sliding. It was as if she couldn't get enough grip. Her hands must be too muddy! As her legs began to slide over the edge of the cliff, the line went taut and Astra jolted to a stop. The sound of ringing metal echoed as her dagger fell to the rocks below.

Louko felt dizzy. It had taken all of his will to keep from making a desperate run for the rope to help. But Astra was hauled up, and Delnor grabbed hold of her, helping her back to safety.

Both of the princesses were shivering, but Louko knew that if they stopped now, there would only be worse to come. Everyone else seemed to get the gist as well, and after helping the princesses back onto their horses, the group went on, a foreboding air settling with the foggy rain.

Louko reached Astra and looked her over. Her right shoulder hung oddly at her side, and Louko's stomach clenched. It was definitely dislocated. "Are you alright?" What a stupid question. Idiot. Even now he could see the blood that had mixed in with the mud on her clothes where the rocks had torn at her.

Face white and strained, Astra only nodded. She tried to put on her cloak and wrap it around herself with her free hand. Louko grit his teeth. She was going to get herself permanently hurt.

It took them almost another hour to reach the bottom—an excruciating, unbearable hour. The rain had lessened only slightly, and already the small valley was becoming a bog, the ground squelching unpleasantly beneath the horses' hooves.

This was *beyond* a bad situation.

"We can't stop now, Keeshiff." It was Gavin who spoke this time.

"This valley is going to turn into a drowning pit if we don't get out of here. Give the princesses some blankets to warm themselves as best as possible, but we must go on."

No one argued.

Louko was closest to Astra, and instantly took his water-resistant blanket out of his pack, riding up to her and wrapping it around her so she didn't use her arm. "You should really set that," he said simply, hiding the worry edging closer and closer to panic.

Astra murmured her thanks before replying, "I will ask Asher to set it once we stop." She pulled the blanket closer, and Louko could see her shiver beneath it.

There was the slopping sound of a horse coming back towards them, and Louko turned to see Asher, who had apparently somehow heard Louko. "Let me see your arm," he ordered, dismounting. He had that look that warned against anyone trying to argue with him. Louko backed away.

Astra paused, looking at Louko and then back towards the physician. Reluctantly, she let the blanket fall from her already swollen shoulder and then slid off of Dannsair..

Asher took her arm gently and moved it slightly. Astra winced and he moved it back, touching the socket. His face was grim. "I'm sorry. This, I'm afraid, will not be pleasant."

Astra nodded shortly. "Such is life." Her lips were drawn tight. "Just spare me the countdown, would you?"

Asher's smile was disarming. "Oh don't worry. That old thing is so overused. All that nonsense about people tensing on one, relaxing on two, I think that's such a stupid—" Without warning he yanked on her arm, a sickening pop synchronized with Astra's silent grimace.

"Idea," Asher finished.

"Thank you." Astra's voice sounded more like a gasp. Louko saw her slowly uncurl her clenched fingers and try to relax her arm.

"Don't go using it. I am sure you would not desire a repeat procedure," Asher replied matter-of-factly as he mounted his horse and returned to his spot ahead of them.

Louko wanted to ask if she was alright, but it seemed a stupid thing to ask again. Instead, he watched as Dannsair knelt down to allow her master to remount easily. Then he fell in alongside her as the journey wore on.

***

The next day, the deluge had returned full force, and it was all they could do to keep moving. As they rode, the rain grew more intense and the bogs began to turn into ponds. Drowning was beginning to seem a more and more probable death by the moment. It made Louko shiver even to think of it—or was that the rain? But even when they got to the other side...what if it was too muddy to climb? What if they had been caught in the worst trap of all?

The princesses had it even harder. Both were scraped up and bruised from the day before. It didn't help that there was no change of dry clothes to be found for either, leaving them constantly soaked and shivering. Mariah looked shell-shocked. Astra could barely use her arm. But they had to keep riding. Louko wished more than anything that they could stop and rest, but the water was beginning to scare him now.

***

Two days. Mariah looked barely conscious, and Louko had a feeling only Astra's Elvish blood was keeping her with it. Even Louko was beginning to feel out of sorts—and he could only imagine how everyone was feeling—let alone the two who were covered in mud.

The hill to the valley was so close, now. All they had to do was manage to get up it...

The rain had lightened again, but the path up the valley was in shambles. They constantly had to stop and drag branches off the road, hoping their horses wouldn't spook and knock them off the edge to the quickly flooding valley. It took them hour upon agonizing hour, and with each moment Louko grew more aware of Astra and Mariah getting weaker and weaker. They had to get out of here. Anger welled inside. *Keeshiff, you idiot!*

It seemed forever before they reached the top. Even then, they didn't dare stop. They rode on another two hours to be clear of the valley before making camp. Louko had never seen the knights so organized in setting up camp; all seemed to sense the dire need for shelter. Funny how the weather brought people together.

Asher's tent was put up first, and Louko went over to Mariah's horse to help her down. She was so sick that she didn't even protest. In fact, she clung to him like a lost child, groaning softly. Louko could feel her laboring to breathe. Gently, he carried her inside the dry tent, and laid her on the blankets that Asher had set out on the floor. Astra entered behind them, breathing sounding just as haggard. Louko looked at her, brow furrowed. What a mess.

"I can help her," Astra said. "I can use Gifting."

Asher shook his head. "I know enough about Gifting to know you need rest first. She is in danger, yes. But I can care for her at least until you get a good night's sleep."

Louko agreed, but said nothing as he tried to stop shivering, himself. He looked down on Mariah's pale face, and then to Astra. Again he thought, *What. A. Mess.*

"My Gifting is different," Astra stated simply. "It will not tax me, but waiting will cost her." She looked at Mariah.

"Alright." That seemed enough to convince Asher, but it was Astra's stubbornness alone that stopped Louko from arguing. Astra was weak...what if this put *her* in danger? What would Entrais do if he found Louko caused Astra's death? What would *Louko* do?

Astra knelt next to Mariah, and Louko saw her slip off the bronze cuff-bracelet-thing she usually wore. The redhead gently felt Mariah's forehead, then the glands on her neck, and then checked the cuts on her arms and stomach. When she was done with the quick examination, Astra took Mariah's hand in hers and closed her eyes.

At first, nothing happened. Then, Mariah's wounds began to change. It was as if time had sped up, the wounds in all stages of healing, but in seconds. Her face remained peaceful, color returning to her cheeks. Louko had been waiting for Mariah to scream, wail, anything. He had seen the work of Elvish Gifting before; it brought the pain of healing on all at once. The result was rarely pretty. But his sister remained peaceful and asleep. Then he saw the look in Astra's eyes. Was she...

Astra put the bronze cuff back on and all the color drained from her face. She staggered to her feet. "Mariah should be alright, now."

Louko didn't think, coming up and catching her as she almost fell forward. "Idiot." He muttered before he could stop himself. Though he wasn't talking to himself, this time. "Now go and rest before *I* kill you."

"Always the gentleman," Astra murmured. But she obeyed, collapsing onto the blankets on the other side of the tent.

"Thank you," Louko said with a roguish smile hiding his frantic and helpless feelings. He went over by Asher, who had been watching the exchange with quiet amusement.

Without a word, Louko passed the field surgeon and went for the exit. The others would still need help setting up tents, and all of them were really in not much better condition.

"Wait." Asher's voice was firm, and he grabbed Louko's arm before the prince could leave the tent.

"I need to go help," Louko said, wrenching his arm away to hide the jump of startlement from the physician's touch.

"Forgive my caution, but you have your mother's health," was all Asher said, tone quiet as with his other hand he handed a small bottle to Louko. "Take a good swig of that," he ordered.

Louko's lips were pressed together in a hard line as he took the medicine, barely able to force them apart in order to obey instructions. Without a word, he gave the thing back to Asher and left the tent, forcing his thoughts away from the selfish anguish Asher's words had brought and focusing instead on how selflessly Astra had put her life on the line for Mariah. He couldn't help but feel a little ashamed when he knew in his heart that had the roles been reversed, Mariah might not have done the same for Astra.

***

Even Louko is doing his part well. Albeit perhaps a little unconventionally, but that has always been his way. I'm sure he will deliver in the end.

OF SHADE AND SHADOW

CHAPTER XII

Astra:

Astra couldn't tell whether or not she was awake. Everything was distorted, but chillingly real: the man with green eyes leering over her, inescapable pain cutting through her, the taste of blood, her brother's screams echoing in the stone cell...

The girl's eyes opened suddenly and all the horrible sensations melted away and back into far off memory. But now Astra couldn't remember where she was or what had happened. All she knew was that she couldn't feel her shoulder. Then she sat up and *wished* she couldn't feel it. It was swollen and hot, tender to the touch and too stiff to move. The rest of her fared little better. The girl laid back a moment, trying to remember all that had happened. Her mind was still irritatingly blank. All she knew was that she was alone in a tent that was not hers. And for once, it actually wasn't raining.

"Oh good, you're awake."

Astra jumped about three inches as Asher spoke. Apparently she *wasn't* alone in the tent.

"Careful," the physician said gently. "Your shoulder is still very swollen."

"So I see." Astra tried not to sound so sarcastic. Then she asked, "What happened? How long have I been asleep?"

"A day and a half. How do you feel, Princess?" Asher asked as he moved about the tent, rummaging around in his half-unpacked supplies.

Astra sat back up, alarmed. "A day and a half?" She tried to stand. "We should not remain in one place so long!"

"The other knights are too weak. Louko advised Keeshiff to wait. We should be able to move out tomorrow. The flooded valley, however, now stands between us and any other threats. It was the best place to rest," Asher reasoned, once more showing his level head.

Astra hesitated, uncertain. She tried to think it through, but her thoughts were frazzled and her mind tired. She sank back down onto the blankets.

"What happened?" she asked again.

"You and Mariah fell ill after the incident. We somehow made it out of the valley. You healed Mariah, but were still very ill. Sleeping seemed to allow your Gifting to work its healing on you."

Allowed her Gifting to work? Astra suddenly comprehended the words and felt at her wrist. The cuff was gone. Too scared to pretend otherwise, she immediately demanded, "Give me my bracelet back." Then, as an afterthought, "Please."

Asher motioned to the side of her bed, where the cuff was laying neatly on a little folded piece of cloth. Astra snatched it up and put it on. The cut off from the energy immediately weakened her, but let her feel safer. She pulled her sleeves down to cover both the cuff and the scars on her wrists.

Astra realized she had acted very oddly. *Um.* She tried to think of something to say to hide her blunder. "Did you say I healed Mariah?"

Asher raised an eyebrow. "Yes."

She had *healed* someone? What was she thinking?! But wait. Asher had said "healed" as if it had been a successful venture. Which would mean that she had actually used Gifting without causing harm. She had *healed*. Hope stirred anew, and Astra allowed it. True, perhaps she could only do it when she was rather ill herself. At the very least, she wouldn't have tried it if she was well enough to think things through. But either way, this was progress.

"Oh good. You're awake." Astra looked up to see Louko standing in the doorway, looking uncomfortable as he commented verbatim what Asher had said only moments ago.

Astra nodded. "How is Mariah?" she asked, still excited about this healing.

"Complaining—I mean, better. Much better. How... are you?" he added, seeming very amused and almost comically suspicious about something.

"Uh, I'm fine," Astra replied, slipping the hand with the red bronze beneath the blankets. Was he suspicious over her using Gifting? She had sort of told him it was beyond her control, after all....

"Well. That's good," he said with a small smile. "Up for something to ea—wait. Er. Asher, is Astra alright to eat something?"

"It's not like her stomach was punctured." The physician gave Louko a nearly amused look. Was that... a joke? It was hard to tell.

"This time. Anyway, I was actually allowed to cook dinner. So it's poisoned, I promise." Louko seemed to realize Asher's sudden rigidness. "Um... What I *meant* was..."

"—that Salah wouldn't approve, but everyone else will still like it," Astra finished for him. The old cook at Ent's camp during The War had accused everyone besides herself of poisoning the food.

"Ah," was all the very confused Asher said, looking from Astra to

Louko, and then Astra again.

"Now that *that* whole life story has been given, I'll go get you dinner," Louko said with a wink, looking ever so slightly embarrassed as he disappeared.

Astra had hoped she would be allowed to leave the tent, but apparently not. She sat in silence with Asher until he started asking medical questions.

"How does your shoulder feel?" Asher came over to where she was and seemed ready to inspect her.

"Swollen, but not outside the normal range for having been dislocated," Astra said truthfully. She would rather be honest than have Asher doubt and start touching her.

He seemed to believe her, since he continued with other questions. "How hard is it to breath? I suspect you have broken a rib, or bruised it, but it is hard to tell without you being conscious enough to tell me."

Astra took a careful but deep breath, feeling gingerly around her ribcage. "None broken, I think. Just well bruised."

"Good," Asher said simply, not really having much chance to say anything else before Louko returned, carrying two bowls of food. He handed one to Astra, and the other to a slightly surprised Asher.

Astra thanked Louko and began to eat. She tried to take it slow, not having eaten in a while. It felt good to be full again. The food actually tasted pretty good, too. Who knew Louko could cook?

When both Asher and Astra were done, Louko took their bowls and left. Asher began to pack some of his supplies.

Partly out of suspicion and partly out of curiosity, Astra asked,

"No more prodding or questions?"

Asher seemed hesitant, looking over her again and giving a long, drawn out sigh before saying, "I suppose you've spent enough time in clinics for me to trust you to know what you can and can't do."

Astra was taken aback. How would Asher know? Then she realized a possible answer. "Were you in the clinics during The Great War?"

An almost sly smile crept onto the physician's face.

Relaxing, Astra said, "In my defense, I spent very little time there."

"I believe the only reason for that was because your brother tended to you personally, am I right?" Asher resumed meddling with his supplies, a calm amusement in his tone and movements.

Astra reddened, suddenly conscious of all the scars she bore. She did not know how much Asher had seen. "Better him than the Elves," she mumbled.

He shuddered, disgust evident in his voice. "Oh. Elves. Handy at healing, but really, their manners…Not something of legend. I remember this one—" he turned around— "Maybe you know him? Very tall—I mean, most Elves seem to be reddish blond, had a sort of turned up nose…or maybe I just envisioned him with one…always threatening to dispose of my human patients. I wasn't quite sure what side he was on half the time. He only showed up near the end of The War as it was, and only to tend to the Elves. Made where he stood on human existence *very* clear." He raised both eyebrows and sighed. "I do think I hate Elves—you and your family excluded, of course."

There was an awkward pause as Astra tried to figure out a

tactful way to respond; if she was correct, the particular Elf that Asher was referring to was her uncle, Tallaman. She decided not to mention it. "That's alright. I believe most Litashians would agree with you." *Especially* in regards to Tallaman. Even Ent couldn't stand him.

And then Louko reentered. "Well. I can tell Astra's social charms are wearing off on Asher," he said dryly, seeming to grasp the situation.

Astra only grumbled, "Does this mean I can leave now?"

***

"Are you sure you're alright?" Louko asked…again. They were tacking up their horses, the cold Merimeethian wind making everyone duly miserable. But, naturally, Louko seemed in a good enough mood to try and make conversation.

"Yes," Astra replied in monotone. She was preoccupied by thoughts of her brother. It had been over two weeks since she had written her last letter. She would have to start looking for a place to send out her next one.

"So…If I poke you, it won't hurt?" he asked mischievously, letting go of his horse's half-secured tack to pretend to poke a finger at Astra's shoulder.

Smack.

"Ow!" Louko withdrew his hand and began to rub it, clearly playing up the dramatics.

Astra tried to hide her smile. "Aw, are you sure *you're* alright? Maybe you need to rest more."

He glared at her and began to mutter, using his 'uninjured' hand

244

to finish tightening the girth on his horse's saddle. "Survived a whole war without a single scratch. Not one scratch. Nothing. Now maimed… by a stuffy, spoiled princess."

"Don't talk about your sister that way. It's rather rude," Astra said before she could catch herself. "Er. Um…" She opened her mouth to apologize.

"Oh, rubbish," Louko scoffed without missing a beat. "I was talking about Keeshiff." His smile was at once sly and smug.

Astra laughed. "Well, in that case, by all means continue."

Louko rolled his eyes dramatically and sighed, leaning against his horse… who sighed as well. "Oh, you know. Always so stubborn. Must be the red hair. The nerve. Just because one has royal blood, they think they have wonderful taste in men's fashion. But I mean…I don't think mud counts as an accessory." But was he *really* talking about Keeshiff?

"Um…are you two…ready…." Poor Ivinon had walked up to see what the holdup was… just in time to catch the last bit of Louko's sentence, or so it seemed by his stricken expression.

Astra and Louko looked at each other, then at Ivinon, and nodded. They both withheld snickers for as long as they could as the knight stiffly turned and walked away.

Then Louko grinned. "Maybe we should poke him to see if *he's* okay."

It was on that note that everyone fell in line and began moving.

They hadn't gone very long before Mariah's voice pierced through, apparently having listened in on their earlier jests. "Speaking of appearance…You *all* look atrocious. I know fashion has little to do with anything in this situation, but shouldn't you at least cut your hair? Someone's going to get lice or mildew and get sick!"

As trifling as most of Mariah's complaints were, Astra could understand this one. Everyone had shaggy, overgrown hair and beards —except Louko, who appeared unable to grow facial hair—and smelled of every day they had spent on the road. A bath sounded wonderful. There was still mud caked in her hair from the mudslide, not to mention the dried blood that mixed with it on her clothes. Though, if Astra could choose anything, it would be to be dry for a few hours. Maybe then she wouldn't have to deal with the constant smell of mold and mildew. Even her spare tunic, which used to be white, now sported green patches.

There was a murmur of chuckles from the knights, and then Coryn said, "Why, Rufio is excellent at cutting hair—aren't you, Rufio?"

"You say that like I'm supposed to be embarrassed," Rufio growled back.

"Oh, but it's nothing to be ashamed of. It's not like you embroider or anything," Ivinon added with a snicker.

"Hey, you'd be surprised how much money you can make off of embroidery and sewing," Gavin said with the imitation of a haughty air. "I think you're just jealous because I was patient enough for Graece to teach me."

"Well, *I* think Mariah is right. Someone is bound to get sick if we don't try and keep at least a little sanitary," Keeshiff cut in, tone serious. At least, serious until he added, "So I think you should all wait until *after* Rudio cuts your hair to insult him. He will, after all, have a knife very close to your face."

Astra couldn't remember ever seeing Rufio grin so widely. "Well, when you put it that way," he said, drawing a dagger, "I think Coryn should go first."

As the knights all laughed at Coryn's vanishing smile, Rufio sheathed the blade.

The rest of the day was actually rather relaxed, with the banter giving it a good start. Astra never thought she would be able to say anything positive about Mariah's presence... but it did seem to have accomplished *something* for the good of everyone.

After a successful day of travel, Keeshiff was the one who announced, "Why don't we set up early so Rufio can exact revenge upon you all."

There was a groan amongst the knights, but Astra still felt it was all in good fun, and stayed silent. She knew they couldn't afford to cut a day's journey early...but as Mariah *had* pointed out, they couldn't afford anyone getting sick, either.

After setting up camp, Rufio once more took out his knife, playing with it and asking casually, "So, who's first?"

"On second thought, I think I'd rather not..." Gavin said, pushing Coryn in front. The latter knight gave a defensive, "Hey!".

Lucian chuckled and raised an eyebrow at Gavin. "You had a *first* thought?" he taunted, helping shove Coryn nonetheless. "But I agree, let Pretty Boy go first."

"Oh come on, guys. Just because I have the decency to shave, you have to sacrifice me to the hair-cutting warlord over there with a broadsword??" Coryn pointed an accusing finger at Rufio, whose usual scowl had relaxed into an amused grin.

"A lady who demands you shave everyday——*even when fleeing*

for your life—isn't good news," Ivinon chimed in. "Now, stop being a princess and go over to your fate."

So *that's* why Coryn shaved every day? Astra had always wondered. But really? For a lady? Whom he wouldn't even be seeing in the near future?

"Yes. Let's get on with this," Rufio urged. "I have almost ten others to do. Er, and Coryn, you don't need two ears now, do you?" he added wickedly.

Coryn's face drained of color, and he looked to his other comrades in vain for help.

"I'm joking! My father would die of shame if he ever saw me miss-aim. Or, for that matter, using a knife to cut hair." Rufio turned to Asher. "Would you lend me your scissors, Grandfather?"

"Don't cut yourself," Asher said in reply, searching in his nearby saddlebag before producing a pair and handing them to Rufio.

"I hate you," Coryn muttered, as he was directed by Rufio to a nearby seat on a stump.

Rufio simply continued to look very pleased with himself. "Oh, wait until *after* I'm done with you, please." Astra noted it was the first time she had seen Rufio relax.

In fact, Keeshiff himself appeared to be enjoying this as well, calling out, "Make sure to get his eyebrows, Rufio."

This comment brought on another round of chuckles from the group, Mariah's among them—the Merimeethian Princess was sitting nearby, watching with interest.

And so the poor knight's torture began, amidst the guffaws and jeers of his audience. By the time Rufio was done with him, Coryn had

—surprisingly—both eyebrows intact, and an actually half decent head of hair, cut in the typical short Merimeethian style. The same style that Astra noticed Louko had always chosen to ignore.

"I need a mirror, does someone have a mirror?" Coryn asked, practically jumping out of his spot to get away from Rufio. He scratched his head, glaring at everyone like a wounded ligrean.

Astra smiled, but kept quiet and far away from Rufio's scissors.

"Usually I do, but I'm afraid I didn't think to pack it before running for my life," Mariah added to the commotion from where she sat by Keeshiff. It vaguely sounded like she, too, was trying to joke.

"So. Who's next?" Rufio asked with a demonstrative click of his shears.

Now it was Coryn who was pleased. "Oh, Ivinon is clearly eager. He's had such bad luck with love, maybe a new haircut would do him good."

"Ha ha," Ivinon replied unenthusiastically.

"He's not wrong, you know." Rufio clicked the scissors again. "Now sit." He pointed to the stump.

Ivinon was not pleased, but obeyed—albeit very slowly.

Rufio gave an evil lift of his eyebrows, and began snipping at the knight's nearly chin length hair.

Astra looked over to Louko, who also stayed on the fringe. She very specifically eyed his messy hair before making eye contact. He didn't look excited about this.

The haircuts continued, and soon Keeshiff was in the chair, unfazed. "Now if you do mine wrong, Rufio, I will have to kill you. After all, I actually had some faith in your abilities."

"But of course, Your Majesty." Rufio gave a dramatic bow before beginning his work.

With the prince done, all who remained were Astra, Mariah, and Louko.

Rufio turned first to Mariah with a slight, bowing tilt of his head. "Would you like a trim, Princess?"

Mariah shifted nervously. "Um, I'm fine, really. Unlike you, I actually tried to keep a handle on my hair."

"Oh come on, Mariah, Rufio won't bite." Keeshiff came up to her, smiling and giving her a hand up. "...hard."

Mariah laughed, but it didn't sound like a comfortable one. All the same, she nodded, a cornered look in her eye as she sat on the stump. Astra even saw her wince as Rufio's shears cut the first lock of her black hair.

But even her haircut was soon over and deemed satisfactory by the royal herself. Astra noticed Louko was now the edgy one— especially when Ivinon visibly noticed him.

"I found your next victim, Rufio."

Louko took another step back, giving an uncomfortable laugh. "I don't see what the fuss is about. It's not even warm enough in Merimeethia for fleas."

"Oh come on, you big baby, sit in the chair," Keeshiff said, still sounding fairly light hearted.

Louko's smile was very, very forced. "Pardon my skepticism, but I do recall my life being threatened the other day."

At Louko's comment, however, Farian chimed in happily, "And we'll threaten again if it helps."

"How about I just do it myself, it's not like I'll care what I look like...I just want both ears." Louko's hands fiddled at his side, and Astra realized Louko was legitimately apprehensive.

But now Lucian walked over with Coryn, with the obvious intention of dragging the prince up. "Come on, Louko," Lucian coaxed. "Do your time."

Louko laughed again and obeyed, but Astra caught the subtle tension. She wondered if she should intervene, though she found no way to do it.

Rufio took the wooden comb he'd been using and set it to Louko's hair. He tugged once. Only once. Because then the comb he was borrowing from Mariah was thoroughly stuck. With a frown and several jerks, Rufio freed the tool.

"Do you have hair or a rat's nest on your head?" he asked, tone still full of jest.

"How'd you guess?" Louko said with a half-smile to hide his wince at the tugging.

"Someone fetch some water," the knight called. "Maybe that'll loosen it."

Delnor obliged, dumping it unceremoniously over Louko's head.

The grumpy, wet prince appeared to give up on any attempt at arguing. He sat there, glaring at everyone from the stump. Rufio, still with his determined frown, tugged and pulled and combed Louko's hair until it held some semblance of neatness. Astra noted it was much longer when not tangled and tousled.

After that, Louko was quickly shorn. He leapt up from his seat the very second he was allowed, eliciting much sympathetic laughter from the audience.

"I think I trust your brother more," Louko mumbled sourly as he brushed himself off.

The comment provoked a red face from Rufio. Before the knight could reply, however, Farian turned to Astra and said, "I do believe it's your turn, isn't it?"

Astra felt every eye in the camp turn towards her. "Um, I do believe that there is far too much mud left in my hair for it to be touched, much less cut," she said. "I'll have to wait 'til after I can wash it well enough." She wondered if they would believe her if she said she would lose her power if it was cut. Most of them held enough foolish ideas about Gifting to make it possible.

"Oh come on, everyone else did it. Surely you wouldn't let us all down?" Mariah wheedled.

Astra nodded. "I will indeed," she replied. "At least until I get cleaned up."

"Delnor! Get another bucket for the lady, will you?" Ivinon called out to the other knight.

"Uh…" Astra's eyes went wide and she backed up. This was getting out of hand. "I think I would prefer some soap and privacy."

"Well, I expect you back in time for your trim." Rufio twirled his scissors.

Astra had no intention of such. She took care of her tent and Dannsair, then decided to actually clean herself up. The creek, though cold, sufficed to wash the dirt and dust from her hair. It was longer than she remembered; nearly waist-length when not put up in her usual fashion. It would have to be left down to dry.

For the rest of her, Astra brought water back to her tent and cleaned up in there. She changed into her spare set of clothes and cleaned the other set as best as she could. It wasn't much, but she felt better.

Emerging from her tent, Astra tried to stay in the background whilst making sure everything had been set up properly.

"Perfect! Come sit, Princess Astra. I still have my scissors handy!" Rufio called out from where he was.

"Those are *my* scissors, actually," Asher corrected, "and careful, it would be a pity if you fell on them."

Astra really had no desire to be so near to anyone. Physicians and Ent were the only people she had had physical contact with in years. "I really have no need of a trim," she said, knowing that it mattered little to anyone.

"Oh come on, it will take only a minute," Gavin said.

"Only a minute?" Astra echoed nervously. She knew that, at this point, refusing would build a wall between her and the others. They would think she thought herself superior. She had seen groups build resentment over lesser things.

"Absolutely. If they let me live, I'm sure you'll be alright." Louko's voice came from somewhere in the shadow of the trees.

Why did that not assure her? This whole matter was simply silly. She had no need for a haircut, but no real need to refuse. It was just... as silly as it was... she did not like scissors.

Telling herself over and over that it wouldn't be long and that they wouldn't even touch her, Astra sat down on the stump. She suppressed a flinch at each snip of the shears.

It did not feel like only a minute, but finally Rufio announced that she was released. Astra wasted no time in getting out of the chair.

"There. Everyone's done," Rufio announced, surveying his work and seeming very satisfied with everyone's significantly less gnarled hair.

"Wait. Who's going to do yours?" It was Farian who piped up.

Astra stayed at the edge of camp, rebraiding her hair and calming herself.

"I can do it," Asher volunteered. "My scissors, after all. It's only fair."

Now Rufio blanched. But too late: the men would have their revenge. Even Keeshiff, whom Rufio called to for help, just laughed. And so it was that at the end of the day, Rufio had to be held in place for his haircut—which ended up being the worst of anyone's in the camp.

Astra decided that he deserved it.

Louko:

Louko leaned against a tree, glad the clamor had finally died down. Most everyone had now settled down for the evening, and a fire had been lit. What a miracle...the sopping firewood had somehow taken. Yeah, Louko really hated Merimeethia.

Absently, the prince ran a hand through his hair...and then realized it was very easy. *This is what happens when you actually take care of it, you idiot.* Yes...yes it was, and Louko did not like it in the least.

His attention turned to Astra, who was sitting by the fire, looking into it as if it held the very mysteries of life. He may have been amused, if he perhaps did not know so well why the haircut had bothered her. It was only a guess, of course, but he had seen the state she had been in after her encounter with Tyron so long ago. He knew what must have happened then.

Well. That's dramatic, he thought to himself, rolling his eyes. Yes, very dramatic... Especially since "so long ago" was only a year or so. Louko remembered the wounds Astra and Entrais had come back with after he and Soletuph had rescued them. Still, he couldn't say he believed it to be by Tyron's hand.

All the same, Louko wondered if the scissors and close contact had somehow brought up that memory. So, like the brilliant idiot he was, he determined to not let her mope...somehow...

Somehow, he got the feeling it would involve talking.

Oh, well. They were friends, right?

With that, Louko straightened and walked over to the fire, absently fiddling with his Elvish blade as he did so. Aha. An idea came to him.

"You look bored," he commented abruptly as he came up to Astra. Actually, she looked *awful*, but somehow saying that didn't quite seem helpful. *Not that it's ever stopped you,* he thought.

"Oh." Astra straightened suddenly, as if she hadn't seen him. "Sorry. Just lost in thought. What is it?"

"To be honest, I'm the one that's bored." He wasn't *lying*. "And then I realized I haven't sparred since—for a while." Wait. What an idiot he was! Here he had thought he'd get her mind off of the horrors of The War...and what had he just asked Astra to do? Swordfight. **With**

swords! *Well done, you imbecile.*

Astra's head tipped to the side in thought. Then she stood, brushing herself off. "That is a good idea."

No! It's a terrible idea! And yet...Louko did not have the guts to say such. At least, not out *loud*. So, withholding a sigh, he made an airy gesture for her to lead the way.

Astra did so. Louko followed her to a small space on the edge of the camp that was just level enough to use for sparring. Yes, it was muddy, but welcome to Merimeethia: everything here was wet.

"So..." Louko was such an idiot. "I suppose our choices are using soggy sticks instead, or just being really careful and trusting each other not to accidently impale the other." *Or...well, just let her impale you. Put you out of your idiocy.*

There was a pause before Astra asked, "Your blade is Elvish, correct?"

"Yes..." Louko replied slowly, trying to figure out what this was leading to. He decided to just say his bumbling theories out loud. Perhaps it would deter Astra from fighting as well as pull her out of her dark thoughts. "Can they not kill Elves? That seems somewhat useless. And what about you? Would it just kill half of you? What does that even mean? Does it mean you die, or just become completely Elvish? Which is worse? I'm sorry...that was probably the most idiotic thing you have ever had to endure hearing."

There was a chorus of snickers, and Louko became all too aware that they were being observed by everyone else.

Louko rolled his eyes and turned briefly to face where they were sitting by the fire. "We haven't even *started* yet. Wait until she beats me, please."

"Sure," Keeshiff huffed almost under his breath. There was, however, the elusive small smirk that Louko had almost never seen.

"Don't say that." Astra's voice was quieter, though she did look more relaxed. "I have the feeling that it won't end up that way, and I hate not to measure up to their expectations. Now here." She stepped forward. "Let me see your blade."

His secret possessiveness of his sword nearly caused Louko to reject her request. But as that would be stupid...he reluctantly handed it over. He was far too protective of the gift.

"Elvish weapons adapt to their master," she explained. "Meaning that you can will it to change depending on your need." Louko watched as the shining, sharp edge of his blade dulled to a rounded point. Astra held it out to him. "See? If you ever have to sharpen it, you need only will it to do so."

"Aha." Louko raised an eyebrow skeptically, taking his sword back and inspecting it. He was also thinking of all the hours he had spent on cleaning and sharpening it...

Astra stepped back and drew her own blade. She took a moment to dull it before taking a stance. "Ready?"

Assuming a relaxed stance, Louko shrugged. "Why not?" he replied, hoping this was not a terrible idea.

At first, neither moved. Not until Louko motioned for Astra to begin did she give a cautious, evaluating swipe.

Louko blocked it, and just like that, the dance began. Any tension left in either of the players' shoulders evaporated as they both became fully immersed into the match. It was strange, this flowing connection, this back and forth. It was so quickly established, even though it was certainly not practiced. Louko decided that this felt so much better than dancing with Astra.

Then, before he could even register it, he found Astra's sword locked firmly in his and a second later he had disarmed her. Astra did not try to hold on to it, letting Louko pull it from her hands. She remained still until Louko had plucked it from the ground.

That's when he noticed the Keeshiff and the knights; Keeshiff, he noted, was not surprised, but the other knights definitely were.

"What?" he asked innocently, handing Astra her sword without taking his eyes from the group.

"Where did you learn a move like *that*?" Farian broke the silence, awe in his voice.

Louko shrugged. They wouldn't like it if they knew. "I have my secrets." He held out Astra's sword to her, hilt first.

She took it with quiet thanks.

There was a chuckle from Asher. "All I know is, you all are squires compared to those two!"

This elicited a ruckus of response from amongst the knights. Only Lucian and Coryn, the eldest two, seemed to find it amusing—though Coryn certainly mumbled under his breath.

"You're one to talk," Rufio shot back at Asher

"Yes, I am," the physician smiled. "After all, my specialty is not the sword, but rather putting you back together when your skill fails."

"That is, if you have skill. Which some don't." Ivinon's joke was not very appreciated by Rufio.

Louko's attention was drawn back to Astra, who said in

Litashian, **"Perhaps we ought to continue before they begin a brawl."**

Louko smirked. **"Sounds like a splendid idea."** He gave an experimental swing of his sword, watching Astra carefully to see if the sparring had improved her state or made it worse. She at least looked very focused. He wondered if Astra was embarrassed at all to be beaten in front of so large a crowd...

Astra parried and used her momentum to swing back around. *Idiot!*

Now came the dilemma... was he supposed to let her win? Louko again watched her, trying to figure out how to get away with such a thing. Because if she knew he'd done it... knowing Astra, she would feel even worse for it. But Louko did have years of experience faking a loss. A deeper instinct took in before he could fully weigh options, and Louko allowed Astra to get past his guard. Her sword stopped inches in front of his throat.

There was a moment of silence, then the knights all offered clamorous opinions on various moves.

Astra withdrew her sword and walked back to her starting point. Her lips pressed together and her eyes were sharp. **"Please do not throw the match for the sake of my pride,"** she said in Litashian. **"I would much prefer to lose and thus learn."**

Louko ran his hand through his short hair, feeling ashamed. In response, he took the offensive.

Astra kept up, giving quick defense with a series of upwards parries. **"I did not mean to embarrass you,"** she said, following with a crescent cut. **"I just..."**

Louko wasn't sure if her sentence faded because she had no more, or if she was simply too focused on swiping away his thrust towards her left side. Louko made a quick counter and once again got past her guard, but did not end the match. He let it go on, still unable to bring himself to beat her after she showed it annoyed her so. But now if he threw the match, she would be even more annoyed. *Idiot! Get out of your head. Or don't. Maybe get distracted and she'll win fair and square.*

That's when he realized he hadn't yet replied. Dodging another offensive blow, he replied in Litashian, **"You did not."** If anything, *he'd* embarrassed *her.*

Astra followed one blow with another. **"What's wrong?"** she asked.

Clearly, he was not good at this. *Drama Queen....*

"Oh, nothing, sorry." He forced himself to get past her guard again, his sword stopping at her chest.

"You guys are making this weird. Are you plotting to kill us or something?" Gavin sounded only half in jest as he addressed the language change.

Astra studied Louko for a long moment before looking at Gavin. "Why? Are you afraid you wouldn't be able to defend yourself?" Louko wasn't sure if her tone was playful or simply sarcastic.

"Please. *I* could kill you, Gavin." Lucian murmured dryly.

Louko decided the tactic had not helped Astra at all, and decided to stop before it got worse. With a stretch, he sheathed his sword. "Well, I think I will let you two battle it out, then."

Was it just him, or was Astra's expression that of disappointment? She worked hard to swallow it as she mimicked him and put her sword away. "Alright," was all she said.

Louko was ready to scream. Why was Astra so complicated! Or was it just him being once more completely inept at knowing how to help? But he said nothing, only going by and taking a spot at the far end of the fire.

A few of the knights decided to try their hand at sparring with each other. It was a boisterous affair, full of bets and laughter being tossed back and forth. Louko noticed Astra took no part of it. She somehow extracted herself and became part of the background. At one point, she paused, looking towards the fire and Louko in indecision. Then she sighed and turned towards Dannsair.

He sighed. In his attempt to help her, he had made things worse. Now he knew he should try and do something, but he was uncertain to the point of hurting her even more. So he stayed sitting, as indecisive as any idiot could be.

He idled there a while, poking at the fire with various sticks as he tried to figure out what to do. Just as he decided he should go find her, Astra seemed to appear from nowhere by the fireside. She sat down across from Louko, glancing up only at intervals. Her cheeks were red as she toyed with her cuff. "Sorry for earlier," she said.

Again the cuff. If he had not been so confused by her apology, he would have thought more of the odd piece of jewelry, but the sorry was distracting. "We are doing it again, aren't we…" he mumbled. "This seems to be a nasty habit of ours." He would do something, and then she would apologize, thinking it was her fault.

Astra's head dipped, and she rested it on one hand. "It would seem so." She sighed, and began to apologize again only to cut herself off halfway.

Louko decided that since things had already gone bad, he might as well try something drastic, and asked, "So what is bothering you?"

"I didn't mean to be so rude about the match," Astra said, voice dull. "You are not so petty as to throw it just to patronize me. I shouldn't have been so sharp with my words."

Louko did not recall her words being sharp. "There is no need to apologize, Astra. Really. Besides. I shouldn't have pressed you to do a match. I did not think everyone would be watching. Not that it helps us *now*," he added with a roll of his eyes.

Astra looked up, expression somewhat hopeful, even if doubt was still evident. She glanced towards the knights' ongoing matches and shrugged. "I enjoyed it," she said simply. "Besides, it's been awhile since I've been able to practice." She looked back to him with sincerity. "You didn't pressure me at all."

Louko was certain she was just saying that, but decided he had pressed her enough for one day… week… month… that. "Alright," he said.

"So what is bothering you, then?" The question was abrupt.

"Oh, that. Nothing." Louko lied easily.

Those intense blue eyes searched his. "Nothing?" Astra echoed softly. It was clear she didn't believe him.

Louko sighed, leaning back and saying half-heartedly, "Sadly, my brain is a little empty. My apologies."

Astra's head still rested on her hands, though her mouth pulled down slightly at the corners. "Are you sure nothing is bothering you? You seem tense."

Louko stared at the fire, giving a pathetic excuse for a chuckle. "I'm never sure."

"What is it?" Astra prompted again. Then, more hesitantly, she added, "We are friends, aren't we?"

A sigh escaped his lips, and for a moment he couldn't speak. She was right—of course she was—but years of training had turned his survival tactics to instinct, and it was a horrible thing to even consider talking about anything. But they *were* friends... they had each other's backs. And he couldn't expect her to open up to him if he never even tried to do the same. "I suppose I am not very good at helping," Louko's answer was honest. "Perhaps when this mess gets sorted out, I will figure it out," he added, voice faraway.

Astra's brow furrowed. "What do you mean, not good at helping?"

Louko couldn't stop the words from regurgitating forth. "I was trying to help and get your mind off of the, um, scissors—but then I got caught up in my own idiotic issues and thought too much and couldn't figure out if throwing the match or beating you would be better, and then...um...right. Yes..." The sentence came to a skittering halt.

"Oh." Astra mouthed the word more than said it. It was so hard to tell what she was thinking. At first, she seemed to withdraw in what might have been embarrassment, breaking eye contact and looking down at her feet. Then she looked back up, looking almost...touched? Was that the right word? "I did not realize that you did that for me," she admitted, voice quiet and sincere to the utmost. "Thank you."

"I'm sorry?" His brow furrowed in the deepest of confusion.

"I hadn't realized that you proposed a match in order to keep my

263

mind busy," Astra tried to explain. "That was very kind of you."

He couldn't help it, he just stared at her. When he realized he really ought to say something, he somehow got out a, "You're welcome." He was baffled. And somehow...not stressed.

Astra's shoulders rose and fell as she looked down again. "I did not realize, that, um..." Another pause. "...that you knew. And would do something about it." She took a deep breath, as if she had forgotten to breathe till then.

"Oh. Well. I mean. It just seemed like you, er... yup." Again, he came to an abrupt stop.

Astra, still not looking up, nodded slowly. Then she gathered herself and looked him in the eye again. "So don't worry—you aren't bad at helping."

There was an odd release of tension as she said those words. "Well...that's good." The thought of actually having helped her was rather...nice. Because that's all he wanted to be able to do. Help.

Louko was rewarded with a glimpse of one of Astra's soft, genuine smiles.

They both sat a moment in contented silence before Louko at last decided to— very ineloquently—switch subjects. "So, are you sure I can just will the sword to be sharp again? If it's stuck like this forever, I may be a little bit annoyed."

With a nod, Astra answered, "Yes, it will go back. Think of my bow and how it adjusted to you, but went back to size for me." She gave a look to the sword. "Try it."

Narrowing his eyes, Louko unsheathed the sword and... well... stared at it. This was stupid. He made himself think about it sharpening, but couldn't help feeling a little idiotic in the meantime. He was not an Elf... and Gifting was not something often bestowed upon humans, so it just felt...wrong. But he still tried.

"Think of its shape," Astra instructed. "Picture it. Then change the picture 'til it looks like what you want it to."

Chiding himself for being stubborn, Louko obeyed and, slowly, so did the sword. He made a face then, testing the edge with his thumb before saying, "Well. You could have told me it could do that when you gave it to me... you know how many times I've sharpened it?" He didn't bother to hide his amusement.

Astra reddened once more, though with a smile this time. "Sorry," she said sheepishly. "I suppose both Ent and I forgot. Though I wasn't accustomed to Elvish things then, either."

"Some excuse." Louko rolled his eyes. "Didn't your parents show you?" Wow. He was being nosy, wasn't he?

There was a pause before Astra shook her head. "I did not grow up with them." She fiddled with the leather wrapping on her bow grip.

Louko did not understand, and had no idea how to reply to this. He stared at her, unblinking, as he tried to figure out how to formulate a question... or reply... or—well—*something* to say.

Apparently, the awkward lack of reply was enough to spur Astra in to further explanation. "Euracia came after me when I was just a toddler," she started quietly. "My parents took me and fled across the Forest into Alarune. Both of them were eventually captured, and I was raised by an Alarunian couple." She gave a little shrug before letting out a long breath. "Poor Ent was training the Ethians at the time. Went home to an empty house and never knew what happened. He assumed we had all been killed." Astra seemed to notice her own fidgeting, and stopped. "I think I was twelve or thirteen when I met him again. I didn't remember anything, so I didn't even know he was my brother. Took us a few months to figure it out." She looked up, apparently noticed his blank stare, and looked down again. "So, yes, I don't know very much about Gifting, or Elvish things, or even just Litash."

Louko's eyes hurt from staring so hard. "Oh." Well, this was awkward. He felt like a jerk, and an intruder for having received all of that... information. He'd apparently arrived on the scene much after Astra and Entrais' revelation of being related. "I see." He supposed it would explain a lot of the strange behavior between her and her mother. "So... how's that going?"

"Um, sorry, what?"

"I'm sorry, *that* was insensitive. Never mind." Louko was probably as stiff as the collar on one of Keeshiff's old dress shirts.

"No, no, I just didn't understand the question," Astra tried to explain.

Louko ran his hand through his hair, wishing he was much better at this. The very word "communication" caused shivers to run down his cowardly spine. "Right. Usually, that's my cue to back out while I can."

Astra raised a brow and mimicked his earlier reply. "I see."

Louko found himself rocking on his heels, wondering the sort of strain Astra must be undergoing in her own family life. "It just must be...stressful... not really having known them."

Astra went back to toying with her bow. "It's not so bad. They are all very kind." Another shrug, this one more tense. "I really haven't seen much of any of them since The War ended, anyway."

Why did that bother Louko so much? "I see," he murmured. "I hope you get a chance to soon." The last bit was awkwardly said. Well...*more* awkwardly said than the rest, anyway.

"Thank you." The words were soft, holding a loneliness that Louko had never heard there before.

"So, did your brother give you your bow, then?" Louko had always for some reason assumed it had been Ameri—Astra's mother—who gave her the bow. It was clearly Elvish—Louko himself having witnessed it change sizes and shapes to fit its wielder—though the strange, gold-inlaid runes were enough to signal its origins.

Astra shook her head, holding up the bow so Louko could see it better. "It used to belong to my mother. She left it with me before she was captured," Astra said. "It's of Elvish make, so it is similar to your sword in that I can adapt it for different uses. If I need quicker, successive shots, I can make the string easier to pull. If I need a longer distance, I can increase it." She looked down at it, running a hand over the wood. "Usually, it just automatically adapts to my strength. For all the years I had it, I never even noticed. But it was how Ent eventually realized who I was."

"I see." Louko was really being quite daring today, wasn't he... "So... what do the runes mean?" The question for the ages: Louko was so hopelessly curious.

"They say, 'To the Daughter of the Stars'. It was my mother's title," Astra explained. "My surrogate parents assumed that was me, and so called me 'Astra'."

"*Oh*," he said in sudden understanding. "So that would explain why your mother kept calling you Kayliene." He had always been confused about that, but had assumed it was some Elvish word for "sweetheart" or something gross like that. "But how did your—er—surrogate parents know how to read the runes? Isn't it Elvish?" Then hastily added, "Sorry... last question and then I'll shut up."

Astra gave a shake of her head. "You're fine," she assured. Then she got up and held out her bow. "See for yourself."

Louko took the bow hesitantly, looking at it like it was some rabid little rubii. His hesitance was replaced by distraction when he noticed how the runes on the bow slowly shifted and curled into different languages—Litashian, Nythrilian, and Merimeethian. His brow furrowed, intrigued but nonetheless confused.

Astra took the cue. "Elves have no true language of their own. If they speak or write in what most call 'Elvish', they will be understood by anyone who hears or sees their words. The inscription on my bow is an example of this."

Louko was now fascinated, watching the language change a couple more times before giving it back to Astra. "So does it just keep shifting between different languages?" he asked.

She took it back, shaking her head. "No. It presents itself in whatever language you can understand. Since you speak more than one, it is probably moving between them."

"Huh. Interesting." Another question that had been forming in the back of his head escaped out before he could stop it. "So... um... I know this is a terrible idea to bring this back up... but why didn't you just go to your people in Cithan instead of here when you... er... left? Aren't your parents there, now?" As odd as her relationship had been with her parents, Louko had still seen the love Astra's parents had held for her.

Surely, as the Elvish city-state was considered a separate entity and not part of Litash, it would have been a suitable place for her exile.

"Um…" He saw the way her grip tightened on her bow, and immediately wished he hadn't said anything. Astra glanced side to side before responding. "If you don't mind, I would rather not speak of that here. I do not mind telling you. But not so near to others who might hear."

Louko realized the knights had begun to settle down and spread out into the camp. Clearly this was a very, *very* sensitive topic, and Louko was not sure he was the right person to hear such things. "It's fine. I was just, well, being nosy. Ignore me." Louko flashed one of his smiles. *You know, for someone who is always saying to keep your mouth shut… you talk a lot.*

"Perhaps it's better that someone knows." Astra returned the smile faintly. "Besides, I trust you." She stood up and set her bow over one shoulder. "I ought to go make sure Dannsair is set for the night. Which one of us is taking first watch?"

Oh dear. Trust. Louko didn't like that. "I'll take it." Louko was rather surprised she even asked. And normally would feel rather triumphant.

"Alright," Astra said. "I'll be back for second." And with that, she walked away.

With that, Louko was left alone to ponder and watch. The night was bitter tonight, and he was thankful for the small fire—even if he didn't like how it could alert patrols to where they were. Hours passed, and with it, Louko turned to the question of what would come after they got to Nythril.

***

She doesn't even realize how close she is to her own demise. It's really rather amusing. Still, all I have to do now is wait. I can do it: I have been patient for this long. The plan must carry itself out before the Game can begin.

CHAPTER XIII

Louko:

"Here. Why don't we review before we get started? It will help you feel more comfortable with shooting," Astra said, handing her bow to Louko.

He took it carefully, nodding. It was her turn to hunt, and she'd agreed to let him tag along again. Louko hoped he could contribute a little more this time.

"This time, even as you start to draw the bow back, center yourself on your target," Astra instructed, handing Louko an arrow.

Louko nodded as he took the arrow and set it to the string. The weapon felt clumsy in his hand, but he tried to obey.

"Think of your arrow as making a direct line from you to your target," Astra went on. "But be careful of your bow grip. If it's tight, the tension will throw off your aim. Your hand should look like this." She held out her arm so that it was parallel to the ground, wrist neutral and relaxed.

Again, Louko tried to follow her example.

"Your hand is better, but your elbow is too straight. Here." Astra put a hand on his arm to help correct it.

The arrow that had been notched went flying haphazardly into a nearby tree as Louko instinctively pulled his arm away from her touch. He turned to see that Astra had also pulled away—likely out of surprise at his reaction—and now had both hands raised as if in defense.

"Sorry," she said immediately. "I should have asked or warned you."

Idiot. Calming himself, he simply rolled his eyes. "You're fine. I suppose I'm still on edge after the haircut." He gave a half-hearted grin, feeling stupid for having reacted so poorly.

"I know how you feel," Astra said, without returning the smile. "Why don't we try again?"

They repeated the steps, this time with Astra demonstrating how he should position his arm rather than trying to touch him.

"Better," she encouraged. "Now, relax the string without firing. We will give your arm a break before you actually try to shoot. The longer you hold, the less accurate you will be because of the strain on your muscles." Astra paused, then launched into another explanation. "The final thing you need is an anchoring point. This is just a point of reference that you will draw your hand back to every time you fire. Otherwise, you will always draw to a different spot and thereby fire at a different angle. My anchor is the back corner of my jaw; it's an easy spot to line my thumb up with. You can decide where you like best so long as you choose a consistent spot."

Louko nodded, deciding that, as he didn't know what he was doing, he would just use the same point Astra had. Seemed safe enough.

The lesson went for a few minutes more, with Louko making several improved shots into their makeshift target; a rotting stump. Then they decided that they had no more time to waste. Collecting the used arrows, they wiped them off and went hunting.

It was a while before they found anything, so Louko was glad when Astra didn't make him shoot this time, especially when their prey turned out to be a large rabbit. It was much quicker than the flawkeys, and there was only one to aim at. Nonetheless, Astra handed him the bow and an arrow on their way back.

"Keep the arrow in hand and be ready to shoot should you see anything worth eating," she said. "One rabbit will only go so far amongst all the knights."

Louko did not disagree, and silently took the bow. They continued walking quietly through the forest, Louko unsure whether or not he wanted a second chance at shooting something.

Astra put a hand out to stop him, pointing up ahead. There, not far ahead, was a marsh deer. The small creature had its head down as it grazed and did not appear to even notice their arrival.

As carefully and quietly as he could, Louko raised the bow, trying to remember everything Astra had said leading up to this point. Anchor, arm, breathe.

There was a twang as the arrow flew from the bow, heading straight for its prey. The deer only had time to look up before Louko's arrow struck it behind the juncture of its front leg. It staggered, then darted away into the woods.

The prince felt Astra take the bow from his hand and watched as another arrow hit the deer in the hind leg. Louko heard, rather than saw, it stumble.

"Hurry. We may get it while it's down," Astra called, already off at a run through the trees. Louko quickly followed her, wishing he had hit better so the poor thing wouldn't have had to suffer.

By the time he caught up to Astra, she had already ended the small deer's misery with a knife. The princess looked up and seemed to read his thoughts.

"Your shot was excellent," she said. "You hit right near the heart, if not the heart directly. But deer are strong. Even with such a hit, it could have gone on a long time. A lesser shot, and it might have gone on for days."

"Well, that's good," Louko said, staring at the dead animal. "I assume field dressing this one will be a bit different than the last?" Gathered from his experience in the kitchen, anyway. Not that that would really be of too much use here.

"A bit," Astra concurred. "Though the goal is the same: separating the inedible from the good meat. We'll see if we can save the skin."

After they had quickly field dressed the deer, Astra had Louko bind its legs together while she found a long enough branch. They threaded it through the tied legs, each taking one end of the branch so that they could carry the deer back to camp. The rabbit was strung along with it.

It did not take long for Louko's arms to grow sore from his half of the weight. It was not particularly large for a deer, but it was large *enough*. Or Louko was a wimp… That was probably it. Almost definitely…

"Would you like to rest a moment?" Astra asked from up front.

Louko was about to make some comment that maybe *she* needed one, but instead sighed and replied, "Yes…If I ever had to carry someone because they were wounded or in dire need of my help…I would have to leave them." *What lovely wit you have….*

With Astra facing away, it was hard to tell if she was laughing or not. "Hopefully you won't be carrying them on a pole," she replied. "Nonetheless, I will keep that in mind."

With that, she found a place where they could rest both sides of their makeshift pole on tree branches, and so keep the deer above the soggy ground. Then both of them sat down to catch their breath.

They hadn't been there for more than a minute when Astra shifted slightly in her seat. "So. You still want to know about Cithan?"

Louko pondered whether it was really a good idea... but if they were going to confide in each other... "Only if you want to." He half-mumbled the reply.

Astra hesitated, glancing at him and then away. She seemed to reach some sort of resolution, for she began with, "I lived in Cithan for the first few months my parents worked there. But I wasn't sent there because of them. I was sent there because of my Gifting." She looked down at her hands. One was toying with her copper-colored bracelet. "As I told you, I, I cannot always control it. Ent hoped that the Elves might be able to help train me, but it..." She winced. "It did not end well. They gave up and sent me back to Ent so that he could decide what to do with me." There was a long pause. "I don't really know why Ent didn't send me there after I was exiled. My guess is that I was not wanted."

"Oh," Louko said very softly. "I'm sorry." He couldn't untangle the various strands of feeling he was experiencing at that moment, but it was some mixture of bitterness, understanding, and confusion. "But... surely your parents wouldn't do something like that?" he asked weakly. They couldn't have just abandoned her. This wasn't like Louko and his father; Astra was good and kind. Her parents had no reason to want her away from them... but why in Eatris had they shipped her here—with *him*, of all people?

Astra gave a shrug, shoulders drooping with the motion. "I didn't think so," was her soft response. "But I simply don't know. They did not visit or even write before I left. There was no chance to say goodbye."

Aha. Louko tapped his fingers on his lap and tried to process it all. She was all alone. *Really* alone, and it made him incredibly sad to think of it. Out of all the people Louko had met, he'd always seen Astra and Entrais as actual "good" people... not motivated by selfishness and deceit like so many others. And yet, here Astra was... alone.

"Sorry." Astra cleared her throat and straightened her shoulders. "Didn't mean to..." Apparently, she didn't know what she didn't mean, because she abandoned the sentence and moved on. "I think you got more than you asked for," she seemed to try and joke.

Louko coughed and shifted, wet leaves sliding under his boots. "Oh. I mean, you weren't obligated to tell me just because I asked. I just asked because, you know...I don't know. I am an idiot." That last part had not meant to be out loud. *Idiot.*

Now Astra's brow furrowed. "I...am not sure how that has any bearing on the conversation."

Running his hand through his hair, Louko replied, "I didn't mean to make you tell me all of that out of obligation. I mean, friends tell each other things, but they only do it if they want, right?—I mean, I am more than happy to listen, I just don't want you to feel you have to... I just..." Louko was ready to scream. "I just haven't really had a friend before. I am not good at this. Sorry."

"There is nothing to apologize for," Astra said in quiet reassurance. "I mean, part of being friends means dealing with the bad things as well as the good." She gave a little shrug. "And you are much better at this than you think; I am glad to be counted as your friend."

"And I yours," Louko wasn't sure if he was relieved, or utterly embarrassed. He gave a hesitant smile. "But I'm still bad at it. Being a friend, that is. I think I have the communicative abilities of a five-year-old. Though I still think a five-year-old would be better at being a friend than I would…"

Astra rolled her eyes, scooping up a handful of leaves and tossing them at him. "If you're five, what does that make me? I'm younger than you."

Louko stiffened, brow furrowed in confusion as he stared at her —ignoring the leaves that fell laughably short of him, "Wait. What? I'm *older* than you?" That couldn't be right…

There was a pause as Astra seemed to realize his confusion was genuine. "…yes… Why? Did you think we were the same age?"

Slowly, he shook his head, "No…I don't think so."

"So you thought I was older than you?"

Come to think of it… "No. Actually…that doesn't sound right either."

"Well, if I can't be younger than you, or older than you, or even the same age," Astra's amusement had returned. "What can I possibly be?"

Louko shrugged, "I don't know. Just…none of those. They don't sound right," He allowed himself a small grin.

It earned him Astra's signature dry expression. "Maybe you really are five. Though I think even five-year-olds have more logic than you just displayed."

His eyebrow raised as he feigned offense. "Logic? I don't know, who threw themselves off a cliff in the middle of a mudslide, again?"

"The person whom *you* called in the middle of a mudslide," Astra shot back.

Folding his hands neatly on his lap, Louko replied calmly, "It's settled then; we're both hypocrites." He struggled to keep a straight face.

"Hypocrites?" Astra cocked her head. "Are you sure? That's a big word for a five-year-old."

"I learned it yesterday. I'm very proud." Assuming a thoughtful expression, he added, "Come to think of it... I think it was you that called me the term..."

"While I am sure that I have indeed used the word to describe you before, I certainly didn't do so yesterday—you must be mistaken." Astra's voice turned superior.

Without missing a beat, Louko replied, "Well, if you weren't such a hyperxelobane, I wouldn't have to be one."

This brought the conversation to a stuttering stop as Astra stared at him in confusion. "Sorry, I believe I missed one of the words there."

This made Louko smug. "Oh, hyperxelobane? Don't you know that one?"

"You are either mispronouncing it, or it doesn't exist." Her reply was unimpressed.

"Oh no, it's quite a real word," Louko insisted, the picture of innocence. "It means one that is overzealous and helpful to the point of killing one's wit. Here. I'll teach it to you as we walk."

The look that Astra gave him was duly skeptical. Still, she got to her feet and shouldered her end of the deer.

Louko did the same. As he walked, he thought of how to get Astra to say the word. "So think hyper like—what do you call those death birds in Litash?—hyperyns. Then you just add a xel as in zealous… and, well. Bane. Hyperxelobane. Tadah." He would have made some flourish, except that he was carrying a dead deer, so…

At first, there was nothing but silence, and Louko began to think Astra had no plans of playing along. Then she let out an elongated sigh. "Hyperynszelbane?"

Louko stopped himself from laughing. "Just the hyper part. Otherwise you pretty much have it," He encouraged, wondering what this must be like for an Elf, and now completely content not to be one.

"Say the first part more slowly." The monotone told him that Astra was giving her best impression of tolerance.

How gracious of her. "H-y-p-er." Louko drew each sound out slowly, realizing he was going through a lot of effort for this when Astra already knew that this was a completely made-up word.

"Hyperzealous—wait, no. Hyperxelobane?"

Louko made a face…and then realized she couldn't see it. "Is this your Elvish, or are you just being difficult?"

Astra stopped to move a branch out of her way. "How different are the two?" she asked in a dry voice. "Now, did I get it right or no?"

The branch returned just in time to smack Louko in the face. After making a very undignified sound, he replied, "You got it right, unfortunately."

Astra did her best to stifle her laugh. "Sorry. But…"

"I know, I know," Louko picked up quickly, "I completely deserve it for making you learn a made-up word."

"Correct." Apparently, it was her turn to be smug.

"But at least now we know Elves can learn made-up words." Louko echoed her tone.

"And to think that I've spent all this time trying to learn real ones."

Louko laughed just as they entered camp.

"Why, someone was busy!" Ivinon exclaimed upon their entry.

Delnor looked up from the fire and relaxed. "Definitely won't be hungry tonight," he added.

From where he was sitting by Delnor, Farian asked, "Either of you need any help? That is significantly bigger than what you usually find." He smiled as he spoke.

Louko allowed Astra to answer the question, both unsure, and in no hurry to spoil everyone's good mood.

"Indeed it is," Astra agreed as she set her end carefully against a tree. "Louko shot it."

"Louko shot it—? Wait, when did you learn to shoot a bow?" Rufio asked incredulously from over by the horses. The other knights seemed equally curious, as they all knew Louko couldn't shoot. Or even, until Astra had started bringing him along, how to hunt.

The prince shrugged, trying to remain casual under all the attention. "She taught me."

Rufio stepped out from among the mounts to eye Louko skeptically. "*She* taught *you*?" He mumbled something about a little girl playing with a bow to Gavin, who stood nearby.

Astra, still working with Louko to hang up the deer, replied calmly, "He was the only one humble enough to listen to a sixteen-year-old."

Louko felt his fingers tighten into fists, but forced himself to look as amused as he usually would by the comment. Narrowing his eyes at Astra, he said, "I can't tell if that's a compliment,or an insult."

Asher and Bandon chuckled.

Even Astra's mouth curved upward. "I like to think of it as open to interpretation," she said, then glanced deviously towards Louko. "Like hyperxelobane."

Rufio looked too confused to be offended. "Hyper what?"

Unable to help himself, Louko let out a short laugh.

***

There was no rain the next morning, but plenty of fog and gloom. Louko didn't like that, as it would mean limited visibility, but what else was one to expect from the charming weather of Merimeethia? Of course, the weather was nothing compared to Mariah's foul mood *at* the weather.

The camp, however, was packed up in a more orderly fashion, and Louko was hopeful that maybe—just maybe—Keeshiff and the knights were getting into a routine. It was that, or they all just wanted to get as far away from Mariah's whines as possible.

Now packed and ready to leave, everyone began mounting up, silent in the wake of Mariah, who was making plenty of noise for the rest of them.

"Why do we have to leave so early? It's too cold for the horses!

And we can't see anything in this fog—what if we stumble upon a patrol?" she argued as she reluctantly mounted her horse.

Louko decided that something had to be done. This was definitely going to get him killed, but if Mariah didn't shut her mouth, they would *all* be killed. Executed, to be exact.

So, leaving his horse with Astra, Louko went over to his brother and said quietly, "Keeshiff, she is going to get us found." It was a dangerous thing to say, true, but somehow Louko got the sense Keeshiff was just as fed up as he was.

Unfortunately, Gavin had been watching Louko carefully, and piped up, "What are you whispering in his ear, now?" He was especially hostile to Louko, having always seen him as the manipulative brother back when Louko had actually tried to linger in Keeshiff's shadow.

Grand. *Perfect*... Louko was beginning to feel like this was less of an escape from death, and more of just a played-out drama. Did they not realize that no matter what Louko's personal opinions might be, he would definitely prefer to be *alive* with them, then *dead* without them??

"Would you both stop? You are not helping," Keeshiff growled irritably, to his friend as well as his brother.

Both backed off, and Louko ran his hand through his unfamiliarly short hair as Mariah zoned in on the small conflict. At least she didn't realize it was over her.

"What is that little traitor saying now?" She looked down at Louko, seeming to enjoy being on top of her horse and so much higher than him.

Louko had only wanted to try and explain they needed to be quiet and get moving, but he had just made this problem so much worse.

Idiot. So much for an orderly start to the day. He should have kept his mouth shut, but, as usual, he couldn't stop himself from making things worse. Classic Louko.

"Keeshiff, we must get moving." Coryn's voice was soft as he spoke up, saving an otherwise suicidal conversation.

"He's right." At least Gavin agreed with *him.*

And then, the worst possible thing happened. An arrow flew out of nowhere and right towards Keeshiff. Gavin barely pushed him to the ground in time. The thing dug itself in the tree behind them, and a dumb silence followed.

And then it was broken by full-throated war cries.

Louko instinctively pulled out his sword, wildly trying to find the source of the arrow as others followed. More arrows began to loose, and Louko was just able to make out a handful of archers hidden in the brush alongside the road. A bigger problem was the mounted soldiers that appeared on the opposite side, yelling as they charged. How had they allowed them to slip past their guard?

Their captain held up his hand a small distance from the party of knights, signaling his men to stop. The men did so despite the pawing and snorting of their horses.

"Surrender now, and you may be dealt with kindly!" the captain called.

Great, grand—Wonderful! They *had* been followed...and now this was a disaster.

"Kindly? Come, Killyan, you know what accusations have been leveled against me. You really think I am going to be treated kindly?"

Keeshiff's voice was gravelly with emotion. Louko knew how well he knew each man in his father's army. And how hard it had to be to confront them.

Keeshiff stepped to the front so that he was in between the patrol and his knights. He turned to his men with a fierce look in his eyes. "What do you think?"

The knights already had weapons drawn. They pulled back into a closed rank with their leader, awaiting his command. Louko slowly began inching towards Mariah.

Keeshiff looked back to the patrolmen and pulled his sword from its scabbard, leaving his arms open. "Please, Killyan, you must know I never would have killed my father," he pleaded.

The captain of the patrol just shook his head and said, "He was an insufferable man, Keeshiff, but that's no excuse for murder. Not for you, or your brother," before cueing his archers.

No arrows came.

That was when Louko realized that Astra was nowhere to be seen.

While the captain shouted at his men to fire, Keeshiff did not waste the opportunity.

"Attack!" he called, and all the knights responded with ear-piercing battle cries.

Louko did not join them. He stayed with Mariah as she screeched in alarm at the violence that exploded around her.

A man came at them with sword drawn, and Louko engaged, quickly getting past the man's guard and tripping him. With another swift movement, Louko knocked him out cold, remembering that these soldiers were no different than Gavin or Asher. Keeshiff would not want casualties if possible, and Louko was just as set against it. Some of these men were like Rufio, and had family still in the service of the king.

Of course, he decided not to ponder the morals of the case too much as he soon found himself driving back another attacker bound for Mariah.

An arrow buzzed not far from Louko's head and he turned to face yet another soldier. But all he saw was Astra, hood pulled low as she gestured past him. He swiveled to find a soldier fighting to pull an arrow from his sword arm.

He gave a quick nod, only to be distracted by another soldier getting the best of Farian. Ivinon must have noticed, too, for he shouted his younger brother's name. But this only distracted Farian long enough for his opponent to slice downwards and across the knight's thigh. Farian fell backwards with a cry.

The soldier might have finished Farian off there if not for Lucian; the older knight barreled through three other attackers to reach Farian's side in time. But that left him surrounded by four men.

Louko was able to make his way to the two, and found himself by Asher and Delnor—who had done the same.

"Stop!!" A voice rang loud even through the fray, and everyone obeyed from pure startlement. As the echoes of steel upon steel died away, Louko looked for the source of the cry.

There, near the outskirts of the group of combatants, was Keeshiff, with his sword to the patrol captain's throat.

"I do not intend on killing *anyone* today. Don't make me, Killyan!" He addressed the captain again. "Tell your men to drop their arms."

The captain said nothing, only struggling against his captor. His men stopped all the same. They looked at him, wary and waiting, with swords at the ready.

"Would you make me kill a fellow Merimeethian?" Keeshiff asked, loud enough for all to hear. "You are my countrymen—I have no quarrel with any of you!"

Louko actually felt rather proud of his brother, but dashed such feelings away for the dire moment. Slowly, he bent down to see Farian's wound, keeping a wary eye on the others and ready at any moment to spring back into the battle.

Farian was trying very stoically to keep quiet, but a soft moan escaped when he tried to move. This seemed to briefly catch Keeshiff's attention, but the elder prince stayed focused on the...*delightful* little situation they'd gotten themselves into.

Louko helped Asher as he also knelt beside the fallen knight, quietly inspecting the wound.

"Well?" Keeshiff's one word rang clear through the silence.

The captain finally stood still. His jaw clenched and unclenched, clearly thinking through his options. Finally, he spoke. "Do as he says, men."

As the soldiers obeyed, the tension was so thick it even seemed to permeate into the soldiers' slow movements as they put down their weapons..

"Gavin, collect the weapons," Keeshiff ordered calmly. "Delnor, search their belongings, and see if there is something we can use to tie them up—they were, after all, prepared to catch us alive."

Gavin and Delnor both jumped to their task. Louko returned his focus to Farian.

"How bad is it?" Ivinon asked Asher.

The physician kept a steady composure. "He'll need some help to get up and get out of here," he replied.

Louko caught sight of Astra, then, still keeping her hood low. Besides her tightly pressed lips, no emotion showed on her face.

"I can help," Louko said, turning back to the conversation. He did not want to draw any attention to Astra, as she seemed very keen on staying invisible.

"Plenty of rope for the lot of em', Keeshiff," Delnor announced as he presented the prince with a good amount of rope.

Keeshiff's voice still held the precariousness of the situation as he replied, "Bandon, go find the horses—everyone else help Gavin and Delnor tie them up."

The order was promptly followed. Louko heard Bandon mutter some apology to one of their attackers, and wondered how many of these soldiers might be friends of the knights. He was only glad no one was killed...so far.

"Will he be alright, Asher?" One of the defeated soldiers called out as Gavin tied him up with the rest.

Asher nodded. "If we can keep it clean and he can keep off of it, he'll be just fine." Weariness laced the man's voice and demeanor.

Keeshiff was hiding his worry well, but Louko caught the way he constantly glanced back at Farian.

That's when Astra approached Asher and said something to him that Louko couldn't make out. The physician patted her once on the shoulder, then turned again to the bound men. "Which one of you took the arrow to the arm?"

Louko remembered Astra shooting the soldier who'd come up behind him.

"I did." The soft response came with a wince from a young man who was not yet tied up with the others.

The whole situation had Louko on edge, but their adversaries were clearly in no mind to fight any longer. Louko noticed that both Keeshiff's knights and the other group actually looked rather torn. Again, he thought of how well they must know each other, and even trained with one another. Even Louko now recognized a face or two.

As Asher attended to the wounded young man, Keeshiff came forward.

"I'm sorry that it came to this," he said quietly. "I meant no harm to anyone and I hold none of this against you. I only hope I see you all again from the same side of a sword, and not at opposite ends." The prince looked to Delnor, who nodded in return. "Your bonds will only hold for a few hours. You'll be free before nightfall."

"Thank you, Your Highness." It was the captain—Killyan—bravado gone.

Keeshiff's expression was hard to read, but Louko knew the conflict inside.

"Don't mention it," Keeshiff replied, turning away from the defeated men with such emotion that Louko was taken aback. "Bandon, are all our horses accounted for?"

"Yes, Your Highness," the tracker called back. "All of Killyan's horses, too. We left them tied to branches."

Keeshiff nodded and turned to face Mariah, who had been

huddled as far from the combat as possible. "Are you alright?" he asked gently.

She was pale, and only managed a shaky sort of nod.

"Good. Then let's get going—Asher, is his arm all dressed?" Keeshiff called as he went over to Bandon and the horses, taking the reins of Farian's steed and walking it over to them.

Asher got up, and after a few kind words to the young man, turned to Keeshiff. "As dressed as I have the supplies for," he replied.

"Then if Farian is fit to travel, why don't we leave before anything else can go wrong?"

Louko could not agree more.

Astra:

Making camp was a silent, gloomy affair. Everyone's minds were fixed on the earlier skirmish and all that would result from it. No fire would be risked tonight—as it was, they'd travelled quickly and much later than usual. Delnor handed out leftover venison and slightly soggy traveler's bread for the evening meal.

Astra found herself no more cheery than the rest. After commending Keeshiff for his decisive action, then checking on Farian, she retreated to the far edge of the camp to sit alone. She noted how all the knights clustered around Farian, clapping him on the back as they talked about his first battle scar.

"Not that I would recommend showing a leg as scrawny as yours to a lady," Coryn said drolly, eliciting a few chuckles.

Ivinon, who sat next to his brother, leaned over and loudly said,

"You'd better listen to Pretty Boy, Farian. He knows *all* about a lady's expectations—like how they make you shave every morning."

It was too dark to tell, but Astra was fairly certain Coryn was now beet red as his comrades laughed.

"At least I can get one, you just sit there and stare at them like a dimwit," Coryn retorted.

Ivinon grumbled something unintelligible, prompting Farian to pipe up. "See! Coryn was right."

This drew a growl from Ivinon. "Shut up and get some rest before you bleed out."

The laughs from the knights, however, were weak and half-hearted. It was clear that the previous events were still very present in everybody's minds.

Astra could not blame them. She doubted she would be the only one awake all night. Swallowing a sigh, the girl turned to her packs in search of paper. She ought to write to Ent and let him know that she was alright; she hadn't managed to write since the last time she was at Melye. Astra dug the parchment out, carefully folded inside its oiled wrappings to protect it from the rain. Now to find a pencil.

This was a more difficult affair, since no fire would be built tonight. Usually Astra just let the tip of a twig go to coal in the flames and used that to write. Ink and quill were too hard to carry. It was unlikely that anyone else had any, either. Dejected, she sat back down, parchment in hand, and tried to think of another solution.

"You looking for something?" Louko's voice came from close by.

Astra turned, looking up as she gestured to the parchment in hand. "I suppose I ought to have brought something to write with," she replied with a little shrug.

"How come?" he asked, "—is something the matter?"

Astra shook her head. "I was just hoping to write to Ent," she explained. "Just to let him know where I'm going and that I'm alright."

How she missed her brother. Sometimes her chest grew tight just at the thought of her family. It always seemed that Ent could wrap his arms around her and everything else wouldn't matter anymore. Of course, now Astra was just being childish.

"Ah. I see…" Louko's voice disappeared into what seemed deep thought. "Perhaps Mariah would have something." Again he trailed off, as if debating whether to venture over to his sister.

"That would be a lot of effort," Astra pointed out, not wanting to make his day any more of a trial. "It will make no difference for me to wait a day—I won't be able to send it for a while yet."

"Mmm. Let me ask her." His eyes wandered to where Keeshiff was talking with Mariah, and he ran his hand through his hair. "She seems too shaken up to cause any sort of commotion." He flicked a brief half smile.

Astra got to her feet. She hadn't meant to guilt him into it. "If that is so, then I ought to be the one asking."

Louko rocked back and forth on his heels. "I can do it. Not a big deal. Besides, I really should congratulate Keeshiff. That was very quick thinking on his part."

"It was." Astra murmured. "Perhaps he has better qualities than we thought."

Louko's answer was quiet. "I always knew he had them." And with that, he headed off in the direction of his siblings.

Astra followed, saddened by the prince's reply. He had such faith in others, even when they would never return it. She felt the small prick of shame for her own brusqueness towards Keeshiff, though she knew her actions would likely change little if she did it all again. Even with his newfound courage as a leader, Astra had witnessed his apathy towards Louko too many times to number.

"Well Keeshiff, I have to say that was nicely done," Louko addressed his brother, once more rocking back and forth on his heels.

Astra stayed silent, noting Keeshiff's raised eyebrows and Mariah's skepticism. At least she kept her mouth shut. The shock must not have worn off yet.

"It was Coryn's idea, mostly," came Keeshiff's stiff reply. "Don't get all excited."

Louko gave a sort of wince, quickly hidden. "A true leader gives credit, so my statement still stands." His tone was sincere.

Now Keeshiff's brow was furrowed and Astra saw his hands were clenched. At first, he said nothing. When he did speak, all he asked was, "Well, what do you want?"

Frustration moving her to action, Astra gave reply. "Actually, it was I who wanted something. I came to see if either you or Mariah possessed anything to write with." She did her best to keep her ungracious feelings from showing. "I wish to write to my brother, but I only have parchment—no quill." Why couldn't Keeshiff see his brother's genuineness? Astra reminded herself that she had been no better all through The War.

Mariah stirred from her silence at this. "I have something you can use, though do be careful with it." She sounded exhausted, and her speech came out as a sigh. Astra, however, caught the subtle look at Louko. "It's in my saddlebag, over there." An idle hand came up from her lap just long enough to gesture towards the supplies.

"Thank you," Astra said, giving a slight bow of her head. "I will be very careful with them."

Unsure of whether Louko would stay or not, she glanced at him before she walked away.

Louko didn't seem so sure either, and hesitated a few moments longer. Astra made her way to the supplies, finding Mariah's bag and getting the quill and small vial of ink out. However, it was not long before Astra heard Louko behind her.

Before she could think her words through, she asked, "Are you alright?" She turned around.

There was some form of laugh, and then, "Quite. Is there enough ink there? Or should we get daring and ask Coryn if he has any?"

Astra nodded, not sure whether to respond to Louko's jest. Coryn, with his reputation for pining after his love, might have been a reasonable person to try if Mariah hadn't had any ink. Though, that begged the question of why she *did* have it.

Astra carried her supplies to the fallen log where she had been sitting earlier. With nothing both solid and dry to write on, she would have to make do with her lap.

Louko wandered off elsewhere, leaving her alone where she sat, and Astra took a deep breath. She wished she didn't have to write these words—as always, she wanted nothing more than to be able to say them to Ent in person. But he was not here. And it was quite possible that he did not want her there.

So Astra thought out her message and began to put it through the code they always used. Most of it was simply translation, as translating the plethora of languages was harder for Astra since she was less experienced. Unless she could think of a word in another language, she couldn't make the switch. This limited her to Litashian, Merimeethian, and the coastal common language spoken in Cadbir. It was Ent who had come up with the solution: when he'd had her red bronze cuffs made, he'd had it inscribed with a word from over fifty different languages. From afar, her bracelet merely looked to be decorated with swirls and patterns. But up close, Astra could read it well enough to encode her letters.

The process was tedious—especially since the translated content still had to be vague—but so far, effective. Astra was able to write that she was safe and on her way to Nythril. She told her brother that Louko had taken care of her as Ent had asked, and that she had no proof yet of Tyron. She left out any mention of mudslides, skirmishes, and suspicions: Ent worried enough without them. For the same reason, she did not add any message for their parents. Ent always did feel guilty, even when things were not his fault.

Finally, Astra finished. It had more to do with the lack of light than it did lack of things to say. Nonetheless, the girl folded the parchment and tucked it safely away in its waterproof wrappings. Then, after she had cleaned the quill and ensured the inkwell was sealed, she went off in search of Mariah.

The princess had already gone to her tent. Astra, deeming that the tent pole was not sturdy enough to risk knocking, opted for calling her name.

"Mariah, I've come to return your ink and quill."

Astra heard the princess stir inside the tent, and a moment later her frazzled hair poked out from the tent flap—followed by her face. "Did you use it all?" she asked, sounding rather recovered from her shock and now foul-tempered.

"No," Astra replied, remaining cool. She held out the supplies and didn't bother with a defense.

"Good." Mariah took the supplies, and without another word, disappeared once more into the tent.

As she wandered back towards her own tent, Astra decided to check again on Dannsair. But even as she gave the mare another brushing, a different question prodded at her mind: why did Mariah have ink and quill? Maybe it was silly. But still, Mariah would have left Melye in a hurry—there would have been no spare time to pack extra things. The few frivolous things she had brought had been dumped long ago to lessen the weight. True, writing supplies took little space, but who would Mariah have to write to? More and more, Astra wondered what the other princess's true intentions were. Surely, they did not bode well for Louko. And if that was so, then the whole group could be at risk.

Astra returned to her seat on the log instead of going to her tent. Her thoughts wandered from Mariah to Melye, and more specifically, to Kaeden. Old fears and suspicions stirred, and she wondered again if it would be possible. Could a shape-shifter hold form for so long? Tyron was of Ethian blood, and therefore amongst the most talented of shifters. If anyone would be able to maintain such a disguise for so long, it would be him.

With a shudder, Astra pulled her coat around her more closely, and pretended it was only the cold that made her shiver. It wasn't raining for once, so she might as well make use of it and take the first watch. Besides, with such pleasant thoughts as hers for company, she had no wish to face the nightmares that sleep would bring.

***

I read the latest note, then crumple it up and toss it into the hearth. It's just as well that Killyan failed. It will be better to wait until the proper time so that the effects are felt in full. For now, I will just have to be content with the torment this will cause them all.

CHAPTER XIV

<u>Louko:</u>

The days that followed were quiet and tense, everyone still paranoid after the run-in with the patrol three days ago. The biggest fear Louko had was not that they were being tracked, but that they didn't need to be: surely it had been guessed that they were heading west towards the Merym Pass. He wondered what would happen the next time they ran into a patrol... would they be so lucky as to get away with no deaths? The thought was not a pleasant one, and so Louko forced his thoughts to his uncle, and what would happen next.

What were they supposed to do once in Nythril? Somehow Louko had a feeling Keeshiff would not be keen on staying an outlaw... but Louko couldn't help but wonder; was Kaeden as a ruler *so* terrible? It was a deplorable thing to even consider, but in all Louko's years of knowing the advisor, Kaeden had shown potential as a leader. But he was also a murderer, so that did rather complicate things... besides, Louko did still believe, given the right chance, Keeshiff could become equally great. Yet what exactly was the right chance?

Such were Louko's thoughts as he sat on this almost-warm night, keeping watch. Actually... he wasn't really, but Ivinon had fallen asleep, and Astra was sleeping for *once,* so he felt it prudent to take up the guard. Not that it would be such a bad thing if someone came and took Mariah in the night... at least, if Astra hadn't just gone through so much trouble to save her.

Louko looked over again at the sleeping Astra. It had been warm and dry enough that no one had bothered with tents. He still just couldn't wrap his head around the fact that she was really sleeping. Amazing what a fight could do to a person... he thought another moment. No, it was amazing how good Asher was at sneaking things into people's food to make them drowsy. Louko would need to keep that in mind— Keeshiff might enlist Asher to poison him or something.

Louko's attention was caught by a movement beyond the campfire; Astra seemed to be stirring. Oh. What a shame, she was waking up already. But after a few more minutes, Astra still hadn't gotten up. Instead, she started thrashing more, and Louko could hear murmurings of "no... please, no."

Was she alright? Louko wasn't really sure what to do. He remembered she'd had some nightmares during The War, but he'd only ever seen it happen once or twice. So...

Very unsure of himself, Louko walked cautiously over to her and knelt down. Now what? Maybe it would just go away if he left her alone. What was worse? Nightmares, or her waking up with him standing over her?

Then she started screaming.

Yup. He was going to wake her up.

So, keeping his face as far away from her hands as possible in case she lashed out, Louko began gently shaking the writhing Astra. Aaaaaaand, she got worse. He sighed. He was going to have to call her name...He vaguely remembered seeing Ent hugging her comfortingly until she woke, but all Louko could say to that was no. Just, no.

"Astra, wake up." He tried to sound soothing, but how did one do that? "Come on, you idiot." Ugh, that wasn't it. "Sorry, er, please? It's just a dream…Maybe…probably…But the question is, are you dreaming, or am I?"

That was right about when Astra woke and Louko was certain he was not dreaming; if he had been, her kicking him in the face would not have hurt nearly so much. As his vision went black, all he could do was think that Astra hit remarkably harder than Mariah.

Next thing he knew, *he* was the one being shaken awake.

"Louko? Louko?" Louko heard Astra's voice distantly calling his name, followed by some other gibberish he couldn't make out.

He opened his eyes slowly, acutely aware of his head throbbing madly. *Ow…* Astra was hovering over him, eyes wide as she shook his shoulders. She seemed to be saying, well, something. Honestly, Louko wasn't sure if she was stuck in another language, or if his concussion was worse than his original estimate.

"I am in awe of your wisdom." He tried to sound sarcastic, but only winced as he sat up. His head was going to explode. "Now, in Merimeethian, please?"

"Oh," Astra stuttered to a stop before trying again. "I am so *so* sorry! I didn't realize, I mean, I thought, that, uh, I… I am so sorry." She tried to help him sit up, but her hands were shaking too much. "Let me heal you."

She'd thought he was Tyron. Yup, Louko could see that. But as to her offer… "No, no." He put his hands in front to try and stop her, only, he couldn't tell which one of her he should stop. Astra was a triplet? "I'm—I'm fine." Louko was not a fan of Elvish healing. Besides, last time she'd healed someone, she'd fainted. "You hit like a little kid, anyway."

Astra's expression went blank with confusion. She backed off a little bit, which Louko was glad of. "Sorry."

Then something dawned on him. "You know what? I just realized…" He took a moment to pop his jaw. "No one woke up."

Astra glanced side to side, as if only now realizing he was correct.

"You screamed, I got my face removed…And everyone is still asleep." He sighed. "That's just pathetic." In truth, he knew it was because everyone was just so exhausted from the ordeal and then a long day of hurried travel. But it was still troubling.

Wringing her hands as if to quiet their trembling, Astra flinched. "Ah. Yes. Sorry about that…" Her voice trailed off. "Is everyone alright? Are *you* alright?"

"No. I killed them all two hours ago. I couldn't take it any longer," he said, the deadpan effect ruined by the fact that he needed both hands on his jaw.

Astra looked startled, but then Ivinon's snore erupted.

"Oops. Missed one." He tried to grin… but that was not well thought through. His jaw throbbed in immediate protest.

After an awkward pause, Astra attempted a smile that looked more like a grimace. She gave up. "Maybe you ought to go sit down by the fire," she said, voice not much above a whisper.

Louko rolled his eyes, "Oh, no need to whisper. If Ivinon hasn't woken by now, I think we are pretty safe." Ow. He should stop talking.

There was no reply this time. Astra took her own advice, going and sitting near the fire.

He, however, stayed sitting, only because he wasn't quite sure if he could get up without his head killing him. So instead—being the idiot he was—he just called over to her. "You know, this was still a much better alternative than hugging you."

"...What?"

"What?" Louko suddenly comprehended what he had just said. "What did you say?"

"Hm? Nothing, my jaw hurts, I need to stop talking." He refrained from an embarrassed bite of the lip, rolling his eyes again instead.

"Oh."

Louko wasn't sure if Astra actually believed him or if she was just trying to get him to shut up. Knowing her Elvish hearing, probably the latter.

She still looked awfully shaken, and it was a little startling how haggard she looked in the firelight. Funny how one could forget she was only sixteen.

Funny how a sixteen year-old could hit harder than his twenty-one year old sister.

Then he wondered if he should go over to her and help her calm down...but...how? Did he *want* to get kicked again? *Well, whatever.*

He got up slowly and walked over to the fire, sitting across from her and ignoring the renewed pulsing in his brain. Now what? She wasn't even making eye contact. Clearly, this was going well.

"Are you alright?" he mumbled. He used the excuse of the jaw, but it had nothing to do with that. Louko didn't do...sympathy...or kindness...or hugs...

Astra looked up with a start. "I think I should be asking you that."

He raised an eyebrow. "Oh, don't worry, you hit the side Mariah always does."

Judging by Astra's stricken expression, that was the wrong thing to say.

Louko would have said something like, "Kidding, it was the other side"... but he felt that wouldn't be wise, either, so he just stared at her awkwardly.

Her eyes returned to the fire and she whispered, "Sorry." Her arms were wrapped tightly around herself now, as if in defense. How did it always come back to her apologizing?

What to do, what to do... Louko settled on asking what he always did: "Are you alright?" He was determined to just keep saying it until she answered. He couldn't be any more annoying than he already was, right?

Astra nodded hurriedly, but said nothing.

"Liar," he said with squinted eyes. Well, that wasn't the right way to go about it.

"You're no better," Astra returned.

He made another face. "No, really. Watch—Ow." He tried to demonstrate by gently hitting his jaw, but that backfired when the following sensation made his vision go blurry.

Astra winced more than he did. "Oh, no, don't do that." She looked like she was going to get up. "Please just let me heal it."

"I'm a wimp. It'll hurt just as much to fix it." He looked suspicious. "But thank you, your sympathy for my stupidity is touching."

"As I remember, it was my fault," Astra pointed out, then tried again. "It doesn't always hurt."

"If you're referring to your little trick with Mariah, I do recall her being unconscious at the time... and unless you want to hit me again..." Wow. This is why Louko stuck to being cynical. Anyone would think he was *trying* to make Astra feel worse. He really wasn't. Really.

Teeth gritted, Astra said, "As tempting as your offer is, there is no need for you to be unconscious."

His eyes narrowed. What did that mean? He tried to think how Elvish healing worked. Usually it just accelerated the healing, so the pain was briefly intense because of that. Thinking of it now, Mariah really should have woken. Right? She really wasn't someone to suffer through any sort of discomfort. Really, a hair out of place on her head was enough to stir her from a coma. So why hadn't she? The pain went somewhere, didn't it? So where did it....oh. Suddenly he realized what Astra had done. Nope. Definitely not letting her heal him now. "I'm good, thank you. With the bruise, Mariah might feel sympathetic and guilty enough not to hit me again tomorrow." Or she would, and it would just hurt a lot more. Oh well.

"Alright," Astra said, giving in far more easily than Louko had ever seen her do.

Should he be relieved? Or horrified?

After a while of awkwardness, he thought of trying to go to sleep. There were two problems with that.

One: Astra would be left to guard by herself. In her panicky state, he really didn't think that would be a wise decision.

Two: He couldn't lie down without his jaw being pressed against a hard surface.

"Anything on your mind?" He asked, ignoring the pain. Seeing as they were going to be stuck staying up the rest of the night, he might as well butcher the conversation while he could still talk.

At first, he thought Astra might not have heard him, for she gave no answer. But she finally said, "I, just, uh… sorry. For hurting you. And for waking you. And for the nightmare. And… sorry."

Wow. Alright… so much sorry in one place. Was Astra alri—no, what a stupid question. Clearly she wasn't. But she wasn't insincere, either… So how did he deal with her repeated "sorry"s? He remembered her last apology—from the castle—but avoiding it had not been the right course of action *at all*. So why in Eatris did he think he could get it right a second time? Yeah... no. "It's really alright, Astra." Did that sound cheesy? Comforting? Awkward? Yeah, definitely awkward. "And I was already awake. Ivinon has been snoring all night."

As if on cue, the man let out another curdling snort in his sleep.

"Oh," Astra said slowly. Then, "I can take the watch now if you need to go to sleep."

Oooooooh......uuum… How to say it? "It's really alright… er… I don't feel like sleeping." *Anymore.* "But heh, that's what friends do." The words 'they punch each other' almost came out of his mouth, but he stopped himself. Problem was, he had no words to replace them with. So now he sounded like a doofus. What *do* friends do?

"They...sleep?"

Very, very slowly, he replied. "Yes....?" What else could he possibly say?

Astra stared at him. Then grinned. Then began to laugh to herself. Louko had heard her laugh a total of…two times in his presence, and he found her laughter oddly contagious.

"Stop, it hurts," he said overdramatically as he clutched his jaw, trying to mimic Mariah's whiny tone as he desperately fought the foreign urge to laugh himself. Like, actually laugh.

Suddenly, Louko realized the snoring had stopped.

"What...are you two doing?" Ivinon was staring at them, wide-eyed and groggy. This was becoming a pattern...

The laughter stopped short. Louko and Astra looked at each other, then at Ivinon. Louko couldn't help it...he made an exaggerated snoring sound, and they both broke down in laughter again.

Poor Ivinon.

Astra:

The next day, Astra did not see Louko until after camp had been broken and everyone had fallen into line to march out. Daylight did the prince no favors—the entire side of his jaw was swollen and painted in various shades of blue, purple and black. It was impossible to miss. It also appeared to make it impossible for Louko to speak.

"Good morning." Astra said, now thoroughly embarrassed about the night before. "I, er, see you slept well."

Not seeming able to make any sort of other facial expression, Louko narrowed his eyes.

Astra felt awful. She wasn't sure if she should make a joke of the situation or apologize... again. She decided against the latter.

"Indeed," she said, nodding as if Louko had said something astute. "I also agree that even fools can appear wise when silent."

The prince let out a groan. Not in physical pain...but very

obviously psychological. His whole face screamed "nicely done…".

Astra smiled slightly. "I am beginning to think that it will be a lovely morning," she said with a cheerful voice.

Louko gave her good arm a fake punch. Was he trying to threaten her?

"I believe your aim is a little low," she corrected. "My jaw is up here."

Again the narrowed eyes of death.

"Louko? What… happened?" Asher's voice came from ahead. He slowed his pace so that he was in line next to them.

Louko began making violent hand motions, not really seeming to say anything in particular. It was more as if he was just trying to get the point across that he couldn't talk.

"What happened to your jaw?" Asher was now teeming with worry.

More violent hand gestures.

Simply to keep herself from apologizing profusely, Astra decided to take the liberty of interpreting for the prince. "He says that he was walking through the woods when he saw a flawkling holding a piece of fruit," she said, making up the wildest story that came to mind. "He tried to take it but the flawkling pecked him in the face, leaving him with no fruit and a bruised jaw."

She was very proud of how well her explanation lined up with Louko's terrible attempt at communication.

An ever so slightly amused smile snaked its way onto Asher's face, and the physician said very wisely, "That's what happens when you steal food from children." But Astra could tell there was concern laced in and hidden with the comment, and the physician continued to scan Louko with a keen eye.

Louko was suddenly very still, eyes bulging. He looked from Astra to Asher, and then put his hands up in disbelief.

Up ahead, one of the knights, Rufio, slowed his pace and turned around. "*What* did you just say?" he asked, face scrunched up in confusion.

Astra had planned on giving the true story, but Louko's frantic gestures were simply too easy to twist. The ridiculousness of it was no match to the temptation. "Louko tried to wrestle with a baby flawkling over a piece of fruit, but the flawkling was stronger and rammed him face first into a tree. That's how he got the bruise on his jaw," she said matter-of-factly.

This time Louko gave up any attempt at vindicating himself or denying the story. He only crossed his arms and glared at Astra, sighing at the elaboration of the story.

Rufio grinned widely. "Oh, I see."

Well, it appeared this story was quite popular. After Rufio had gotten his laugh's worth, he rode back up with the others and repeated some of the story. One by one, each knight came back to hear the story from Astra. Each knight got a more embellished tale. By the time the last knight came around, Louko had fallen off his horse, tripped over a spiderweb, punched himself in his sleep, and—most impressively—gotten slapped with a fish when trying to take it from a wolfcat.

Louko was not impressed.

Finally Keeshiff—growing too curious over the hubbub in the back, steered his horse to the back to find out what was going on. His eyes alighted on the bruise, and all he said was, "...What?"

Astra didn't even get a chance to answer before Gavin, who was next to Keeshiff, came up with his own guess.

"I guess Mariah had at him again"

"I did not!" Came a shrill voice from the front of the line.

Keeshiff looked almost guiltily at Louko's bruise. "I see," he said stiffly before turning his horse around to return to the front. "Well, at least we will be spared his incessant talking for a time."

And indeed, they had a little bit of peace after that. Though it had far more to do with Mariah than it did Louko.

After a few minutes, Astra asked, "Are you sure you don't want me to heal you at all? Even just enough for you to open your mouth? I mean, how are you going to eat?"

The thought seemed to actually make him pause, but there was still that weird look of suspicion.

Then Asher entered the scene again. He had been hanging near the back, fishing through a small pouch as he rode. Now he joined them again, and addressed Astra, "Would he like something to help that jaw? Whatever hit him, it would be a pity to have the jaw be broken. I should look at it."

Louko shook his head wildly.

Astra had not actually thought that Louko's jaw could be broken. Now unable to pretend she wasn't worried, she took the physician's side. "Yes, you should."

The prince glared at Asher and made some sort of motions with his hand. Something about drink, and... sleep? Asher seemed to understand, and glared back.

Astra looked to Asher. "What is he fussing about?"

"I don't have the slightest idea," Asher said with a sudden shrug, "I think he's saying your healing will be much better." His lips tugged into an amused smile. "So I shall leave you to it." And without waiting for her to reply, he spurred his horse to take his place ahead of them once again.

Louko did not look pleased.

"I'll wait until we stop to rest," Astra said. "I don't want to mess anything up."

Having a little time to think on what she needed to do would be good. She had only ever healed Mariah, and she wanted to be careful. She'd been tired and ill, then; too weak to be a threat. But now that she was at full strength, she was scared that she might lose control of her Gifting if she tried to use it again.

It was why she hadn't offered to heal Farian when she'd heard his wound was not serious. But if Louko's jaw was truly broken, he wouldn't be able to eat. This was unavoidable. Astra tried to remember how she had done it with Mariah. As long as she didn't use too much Gifting, it should be alright. *Should* be…

It was a few hours later when the small group stopped quickly to eat the midday meal. Louko sighed reluctantly at the food he was holding, and then at Astra. He did not look humble in surrender. Her earlier comment about possibly messing it up probably hadn't helped.

Astra had Louko sit down—just in case—and told him, "Hold still."

She knelt down next to him, trying to be mindful of the soaking wet ground, and slipped off her red bronze cuff. The surge of power was immediate. She tried to recall all of her lessons with her uncle, Tallaman, and all of the times she had seen Ent heal others. Astra used her will to hold the tide of power back, releasing only enough to do what she wanted.

It was a strange feeling to heal another with Gifting. It was almost as if Astra could feel each ruptured vein and bruised tissue in Louko's jaw. She let the outgoing energy gently seal and rebuild the cracked bone, and pulled each nerve's signal of pain from his body into hers so that he would feel nothing.

Once Louko's jaw was mostly healed, Astra pulled back as if putting a lid on her restless powers. Instantly, she put the red bronze bracelet back on, lest her power resist having such limitations.

Louko tested his jaw, slowly working it side to side. He made a face, and looked at Astra. "Er. Thanks," he said.

Surprised, Astra just nodded. She rubbed her own jaw slightly, forgetting for a moment why it was sore. "Sorry that it was necessary in the first place."

His eyes locked on her hand. "Ha. Knew it," he muttered under his breath, apparently a little annoyed. Then seeming to realize he'd said it out loud, added quickly. "No, really, it was fine. Next time, I'll just get to punch you."

Astra wished she hadn't been so obvious about taking his pain while healing him. Nonetheless, she still smiled. "If that means you get the nightmares, then we have a deal."

He looked suddenly guarded. "Wait…can you do the same thing with nightmares…."

"Um, actually, I don't know." Astra had no idea how to try, and didn't really plan to find out.

Louko nodded his head, looking very awkward. "Good to know."
She had a feeling that he was thinking of backing out of their fake deal.

Before Astra could speak, the call was given to mount up. She
swung back up onto Dannsair and fell to the back of the line as usual.

Louko also took his normal spot beside her, not wasting any time
now that he could talk again. "We need to decide how to get through the
Rheritarus Mountains," he said quietly.

Astra nodded in agreement. "Mountains can be dangerous to
those who don't know them."

"These are just dangerous." Louko's voice was grim. "All the rain
in the valley could mean snow there. Avalanches are common enough
in that range as it is." A sigh escaped him. "If we get slowed down, we
may be caught by a patrol. I don't know how we are going to get some
of us to stay quiet." His eyes looked forward, and he ran a hand through
his hair.

Avalanches. Astra shuddered. Growing up in the mountains, she
knew what damage that seemingly harmless snow could do. She had
seen it wipe away entire villages as if they'd never existed. "Tonight, we
should speak with Keeshiff again," she finally said.

He nodded. "Carefully. Maybe we can scare him into thinking
he'll wake the dead Dragons." Louko's normal smirk returned to his
face.

Astra stared at him blankly. "I'm sorry—did you say dead
Dragons?"

The smirk turned into a full-out grin. "Don't you know? Nythril
and Merimeethia used to be one large country. There was a friendship

311

between humans and Dragons, until… well, there wasn't. You know humans, always backstabbing each other." He continued quickly, as if hoping she wouldn't think too long on the comment, "But anyway. A lot of Dragons died in a war between the races, and it's said they made the border of their land from the dead. Well, I mean, they just made graves —and you've seen how big Dragons can get if they have lived long enough. The Rheritarus Mountains became the burial grounds for centuries, supposedly, and that's why the mountains are so high."

No longer sure if the prince was joking or not, Astra just wrinkled her nose slightly. "That's actually a little bit gross."

He grinned. "I think it's fascinating."

"I think you would find it less fascinating if one of those avalanches uncovered a rotting lizard."

"Probably. But at least that one would be less likely to eat me…. *Less.*"

Astra rolled her eyes. "As long as you watch your step and don't end up falling into the stomach."

Louko let loose a dramatic sigh, "I suppose." After a bit of silence his grin faded, "But really, we are going to have to be careful."

***

Odd how confident Astra is becoming. Louko is doing even better than I thought. Perhaps I will not have to wait as long as I first planned. I sit down at my desk and write a quick note of instruction, waiting till the words have melted away before getting up again. Oh, I can't wait for this to begin.

CHAPTER XV

Louko:

Louko couldn't believe how much better his jaw felt. He'd kept testing it all day, moving it, poking it; it was just... better. But why in Eatris was he confused? He'd seen it done many times. Louko supposed because, as much as he'd seen it, he just couldn't believe it actually worked. It just wasn't...natural. But even odder was Astra's strange and humorous outburst. The way she acted was probably the closest behavior to her age he had seen since before she and Entrais had been caught by Tyron during The War. Before that, she used to get into all sorts of trouble, if only to coax out a smile or laugh from her serious brother. Louko had almost forgotten. Seeing her like that was...refreshing.

As evening grew, the beginnings of the Rheritarus Mountains appeared on the horizon. They would arrive at them in just a few days. Hopefully they wouldn't all freeze to death. Hopefully they wouldn't find a dead lizard. If they did, Louko got the feeling Astra would never let him live it down...

A breeze coming from the mountains chilled Louko, and he let out a quick shiver as he untacked his horse. He hadn't been to Nythril in a long time.

Across the way, Astra was rubbing down Dannsair. The same breeze caught her cloak, whipping it around her. She closed her eyes and a wistful smile pulled at her lips. Then she caught her cloak and pulled it around herself tightly, continuing her work.

"And what, if I may be so bold, has our lovely princess's attention this fine evening?" he asked, with an extra overdose of aristocracy. She seemed so...whimsically happy.

Astra shrugged. "As dangerous as they are, it will be good to be close to the mountains again."

He smirked, "Dead Dragons and all?"

Astra made a face and turned back to her mare.

"Doubter," Louko replied, finishing up with his horse before turning to a more serious topic. **"What comes when we get them to Nythril?"** he asked in Litashian. Keeshiff and Mariah would be safe, and Louko was trying to figure out what he would do. He had been entertaining the idea of stealing away to find Kaeden—perhaps he could reason with the man. The motives that had driven Kaeden to kill the king were unfortunately a little too clear for Louko, and he felt responsible for the mess it had caused. He thought again of Kaeden, and the many times he had urged Louko to leave his family.

"Let them get into their own trouble. They've caused enough for you."

"But allowing them would only further my guilt, Kaeden. As sweet as the thought is, I'll pass."

"The guilt is on their own heads, Louko. You cannot fall for them forever."

"Perhaps."

Astra intruded upon Louko's thoughts, answering his question. **"I,"** she faltered, stiffening. **"I don't know,"** the last bit was said quietly.

Louko didn't really know his own plans. All he knew is that he wasn't leaving Astra. **"Good. I'm not the only one."** He didn't know what the best thing for Keeshiff to do was, either.

"Are you not staying with your siblings?"

That lasted long. He should have expected as much out of Astra. **"I'm not sure,"** he replied with a shrug.

"Why?" she asked.

Stupid, nosy Elf. **"Because Keeshiff and Mariah would miss me _so_ much."** He rolled his eyes.

Astra said nothing at first. Then, **"I cannot blame you."**

He made a face. Yes, getting away from them _would_ be nice. But that wasn't exactly what he was doing. **"What is your next move?"**

Again a pause. **"I have work to do that cannot be done in Nythril,"** was all she said.

Louko remembered how she had spent so much time in his mother's library, and paused. **"Is it what you were looking for in the library?"** he found himself asking. He'd never dared broach the subject before, but why did he feel so concerned by it?

Maybe it was because Astra's movements had become so tense. Even Dannsair seemed to notice her master's discomfort, nibbling at the rag Astra was using to rub her down. **"Yes."**

"What is it?" Louko didn't know what gave him the courage to ask. Perhaps it was because he worried that whatever—or whoever— she was looking for, she could be putting herself in danger. But regardless of why, he had asked it, not allowing himself time for the usual self-doubt.

Astra shook her head, trading her rag for a hoof pick. **"It doesn't matter,"** she said. She tried to change the subject. **"What about you? What is your hope after Nythril?"**

Only, Louko wasn't just going to let that go. **"It doesn't matter?"** What did that mean? Why would she think that? Or was she just saying it to get him to stop pressing?

"I mean…" The conflict and frustration was unusually evident on Astra's face. She finished cleaning one hoof and moved to the next. **"That it would not be helpful to speak of,"** she finally finished.

"That's not good enough." He was surprised by his own words.

Apparently, so was Astra. She stopped her work completely and stood to face him. Then, as if ashamed, she looked down at the hoof pick in her hands. **"You really do not want to know,"** she murmured. **"Trust me."**

"I'll have to use that one more often." Louko was almost…angry. Or just, perhaps disappointed she didn't seem to trust *him*. But even more so, he was worried. The fact that Astra wasn't saying anything meant it was dangerous. Terribly dangerous. And now he knew she had no one else to take care of her... and yet, she wouldn't let him. **"Sorry. I shouldn't have pushed,"** he forced the words out soon after his terse remark, knowing the last thing Astra needed was to feel guilty.

Maybe it was too late for that. When she finally looked up, her brow was furrowed and her lips pressed together in hurt and indecision. **"Do not apologize,"** she said quietly. **"You were well within your rights. I am the one being unfair."**

Louko ran his hand through his hair, **"It's alright."** He shouldn't be pushing. But he wasn't going to let her disappear.

"I, I just don't want to put you in a difficult position when

there is no need for it," Astra was nearly pleading, as if hoping he would understand. **"And I do not want you to follow me if I end up having to return to Merimeethia."**

He just stared at her, **"You can't expect me to just be able to turn around and let you go, do you?"** He sounded much more anguished than he'd wanted. *Idiot.* **"No need for it? I have dragged you through all of miserable Merimeethia with my insufferable sister and stubborn brother to get them to safety when I gave you no reason to do so in Melye. And you said we were friends. And if that is true, then you are the only friend I have, Astra. The only one. If you leave, I have nothing—and I can't do that again. I can't just let you go off like you don't matter."**

Astra seemed to have forgotten all about the hoof pick still in her hand. She stood there, lips parted slightly in shock, as if Louko had robbed her of any response. Long seconds slid by before she whispered, **"I'm sorry. I…"** She shook her head and tried again. **"You…you are my only friend as well."** She swallowed hard. **"But Louko…"** Again, she hesitated, looking away and across the camp.

"What?" Louko prompted.

Astra closed her eyes. He could just barely hear her when she said, **"Tyron is still alive."**

Well. He did suppose he hadn't exactly been expecting *that*. The very name of Tyron stole Louko's breath away, as well as the half hope, half fear he had stifled for so long. **"Alright,"** was the only word he could manage to form in his mouth—well, in Litashian, anyway. The statement had been so out of the blue, and yet it only made sense, somehow.

Astra was now watching him very closely, taking in his every reaction, no doubt. **"I didn't want to put you in a place where you felt that you had to choose. This is why—"**

"I'm coming with you," he interrupted, startling himself.

"What?" Astra gaped, horrified. **"No. No, you can't do that. You can't go anywhere near Melye."**

"He's Kaeden, isn't he?" The question was more of a statement. It suddenly made so much sense. The interest in Tyron—the hounding for Louko to run away. The green eyes. *Idiot!* The murder.

"You *cannot* come," was all Astra said, now more vehemently than before.

"So you are going to make me sit back and just wonder what he's doing to you, then? Oh, that's so much better. Thank you, really." The fact that she *still* wasn't giving ground was enough to make Louko scream. He couldn't do this—he couldn't keep watching people and their lives fall apart and go by while he just sat there. Sat there and watched, and got told he couldn't help.

His words seem to catch Astra off guard. Again, she looked away. **"If it came to that, I can assure you that it is worse to have a friend there to watch than to go through it alone."** Her voice was strained. She let out a sharp breath. **"But he has obligations as Kaeden. If I arrive there publicly, he would have a lot of explaining to do if I should suddenly disappear. He is too smart to do that."**

Louko was hardly listening. She'd gotten through about the first sentence and a half when he started shaking his head. He couldn't breathe. No. He was practically pulling his hair out by the roots by the time she was done and, in his emotion, he reverted to Merimeethian,

318

"No… No I can't…I can't do this. I'm sorry, I can't." He turned around with the intent of walking away, the nearest he'd come to tears in nearly ten years. Again. It was happening again, and he couldn't— he'd told himself so many times…and it was happening here, again. With Astra.

"Wait, please, I'm sorry—" Louko turned back to see Astra's hand outstretched as if to stop him. She looked frightened. "I, I just…" She withdrew her hand as if suddenly conscious of it and wrapped her arms around herself. "I don't know what else to do."

Louko was aware of the fact that her call after him had now gained the attention of some of the others, and he struggled to control his panicked emotions and the threatening of childish tears. "I don't know," he whispered. "Sorry— I need some air." He didn't want to leave her like that, but he couldn't just break down right in front of the knights and his siblings. He couldn't argue with Astra anymore, either; they had an audience, and it was clear she wasn't listening. Louko couldn't think anymore, not rationally, so he walked as quickly as he could into the trees to have a moment to breathe—or scream. Either one.

As soon as he was far enough away, he broke down. The stress of the last month—no, year—was too much. Returning to his father after The War; the months of isolation and apprehension; then the murder; trying to coax Keeshiff and avoid Mariah's wrath; and now the sudden realization that Astra was going to try and leave and get herself killed; but most of all, the fact that Tyron was alive.

He knew he was being terribly selfish, but no matter how hard he tried he couldn't keep it in any longer. Astra was leaving—*just* like Tyron had—and what that would mean he couldn't bear to think. He would go

319

after her, of course, but she was leaving. Somehow, he couldn't get past that. After everything, he hadn't been enough; just like he hadn't been enough to keep Tyron from leaving. If he was more useful; if he had Gifting, or could take care of himself and not talk so much, or just...

Louko gave up on thinking. He was being foolish, and he knew it. But for one, selfish moment in his life, perhaps he would just let himself alone.

"Louko?" The soft call was hoarse.

He probably jumped about three and a half feet in the air and spun around to see Astra standing there. She was trying valiantly to hide how badly her hands were shaking, but there was nothing she could do about her red-rimmed eyes. She stood as if unable to meet his gaze, shrinking back when he looked at her.

"I'm sorry. I did not mean to make a scene or to, to, to hurt you like that..." Her voice was still raspy. "I, um, know you need some air, but I wanted to make sure that you were alright. It's getting dark."

Louko pulled through his hair with both hands and took a shaky breath. "No, I'm sorry. This wasn't fair to you." The words took effort to get out of his swollen throat. She looked awful. like the way she had after recovering from her capture. He had forgotten the way she had avoided everyone, staying on the edges of Ent's camp just so no one would see her.

"I still did not act as I should have," Astra said, arms wrapping around herself again. She looked up just enough to scan him as if checking for wounds.

Louko sat back down, unable to say anything and not sure it would help anyway.

It was a long time before Astra confessed, "I don't know what to do." She sat down where she was, still facing him and yet still averting her gaze.

Louko lowered his own eyes to the dirt. "I know," he murmured.

"It's like Ent all over again." Louko had never heard so much despair in her voice. "Why must I always choose between those I am close to and keeping them safe?" He heard her shake her head as if taking back her words. "Sorry, sorry, I... nevermind."

He looked at her, then, watching as her hands fidgeted with the edge of her tunic, "But Astra," he said quietly, "It shouldn't be your choice. It's not. Sometimes...I mean, what would you do if our places were reversed?" His question was earnest, and he was now able to stare at her levelly—even though she didn't look at him. Understanding where she was coming from had lessened his own frantic and violent emotions, and now he felt at least a little more clear-headed.

Her knuckles were white and her lips trembled, even though she pressed them together. "I could ask the same of you." The way Astra said it was not in condemnation, but rather in helplessness as if she saw no way out.

"I'm going back, anyway," he said, knowing that was probably the worst thing he could say, but knowing nothing could really make the situation any better.

Astra's head shot up, horror fixed in her features. "What? Why?"

"Because you not allowing me to come really doesn't mean I can't..." Louko would have been amused if they weren't both just so emotionally distraught. "And Tyron has some answers *I* deserve, too. And we said we had each other's backs. But why do we *have* to go?

321

Isn't there another way of figuring this out?"

Louko had never seen such terror in her eyes before. It seemed a monumental effort for her just to murmur, "Perhaps there is."

"He won't hurt me, Astra." It took great effort to admit this. Doing so out loud made Louko feel like some sort of traitor—perhaps he was—but it was true. If Tyron was Kaeden, then that could only be more evidence for Louko. If it was true, then Tyron helped orchestrate Louko's first escape during The War. If it was true, Tyron killed Omath because Louko refused to run off on his own.

"How can you know that?"

"Because if you're right, and Tyron is Kaeden—" Even though she hadn't said as much out loud, her reaction when he asked had confirmed it— "Then he did all of this for me." Again, it felt awful to recognize it aloud.

Astra took all of this in carefully. She seemed desperate to believe it even as much as it was difficult for her to do so. "You mean, he killed Omath because of his treatment of you?"

Louko nodded. "I... saw him do it—as Kaeden—and heard what he said to my father...but at the time I thought it was Kaeden doing it. I should have seen it—should have known. He'd been going on about it ever since I'd returned." Louko had never said this before, partially because it would only further indict him in the eyes of his brother.

This brought Astra the closest to being calm that she had been since the start of the conversation. When her gaze drifted elsewhere, it was more in thought than it was the fear she'd held before. "If that is true, then I suppose that it is one thing for which I cannot blame him," was her subdued remark.

That comment made Louko even more uncomfortable. "Don't say that... nothing condones murder."

"Nor does anything condone abuse." Astra's reply was surprisingly firm. Only in time for her to immediately mumble an apology. "That was not helpful."

Louko raised both eyebrows, saying, *"Anyway,"* upon realizing just how far from the actual problem they had strayed. "Can we at least just get to Nythril, and then figure it out *together*?"

"Together?" Astra echoed, as if seeking to make sure that he would hold up his side of the bargain.

"Yes. Together," he said firmly, hoping she, too, wouldn't break this deal.

"Alright." Astra gave the word like a promise.

"Good." Louko gave a small half grin, and then realized it was too dark for her to see. "We should probably get back...."

Wet leaves squelched underfoot as Astra stood up. "Good idea," she said, though sounding tired and reluctant.

He followed, glad he hadn't gone too far off when he'd stormed out of camp. "And... we should probably talk to Keeshiff about the mountains," he mumbled once they were just about back to where the others were.

"Oh." Astra's shoulders slumped even further. "Yes. You're right." She adjusted course, and Louko followed her around the outskirts of the camp to reach Keeshiff's tent. She paused just outside of it.

"Probably best if you announce us..." He didn't like bringing that fact up, especially after everything they had just been talking about. He felt exhausted—mentally and physically, and knew she was no doubt in the same position.

Of course, Astra didn't argue. She nodded to show that she'd heard him, set her shoulders, then took a deep breath.

But before she could call out, Keeshiff spoke, apparently sensing their presence from inside the tent. "Oh, come in."

Louko was surprised to find Mariah in already, looking rather perturbed at the intrusion. She looked…odd.

"Yes?" Keeshiff asked, sounding almost... wary, and making Louko feel self-conscious in the process.

Astra gave a sharp look at Mariah. Mariah, in turn, looked down, and Astra faced towards Keeshiff. Slowly, she said, "We thought it might be best to discuss our route through the mountain range."

"Alright." Keeshiff was definitely very taut. Was it Mariah, or Louko and Astra? That was the question...

"What is your plan?" Astra asked simply.

"There's only one pass remotely close to where we are—the Merym Pass. We should reach it by tomorrow evening if we press hard. But there is no need to rush. Kaeden's men could not have come all the way out here already."

Louko was almost too weary to be alarmed. Oh, what was Mariah telling Keeshiff this time... and why was he listening? Louko had almost had a spark of hope with some of Keeshiff's almost responsiveness, but now that was clearly out the window.

"If we are all the way out here, you can be certain that Kaeden's men are," Astra said, voice hardening. "All he has to do is send a fast-riding messenger to the border patrol and we will be in trouble."

"Why are you so sure?" Mariah asked, eyeing Astra like a hawk.

Louko was fighting to keep his mouth shut. If he opened it with Mariah here, it would not bode well for anyone, Astra *or* Keeshiff—he'd opened his mouth enough for one day.

Astra's head snapped towards the other princess. "Because," she spat. "Kaeden is no fool. He will guess that there are only certain places we will go. Has he not lived with you all? Does he not know you all well? He will use all he knows against you. Including the knowledge of your ties to Nythril."

"But that is another problem in itself. Did you ever think that Louko is trying to get you to go to Nythril so that Kaeden would know where to find you?" She pointed an accusing finger at Louko.

Louko bit his lip. That was quite possibly the worst thing Mariah could have thought to say. He forced himself not to bury his face in his hands.

"And where would you suggest, *princess*?" Louko rarely had heard this kind of dripping acidity in Astra's voice.

"Well, *Litash* is apparently out of the question." Mariah gave a gloating, knowing look while bringing up the option... again.

This was all Louko could take. "Oh, I see, so let's just go in the *opposite* direction we are now, add weeks to the journey, and hope we run into everyone who's following. If that's not enough, let's take the advice of an overstuffed, frilly princess who never took the time to so much as look at a map, let alone be able to judge where is safe and where isn't. Last time I checked, Astra was a little more in tune with what was going on, while Mariah has been too busy worrying about the dresses she left behind." He'd had it. Mariah could poke at him as much as her little heart decided, but to twist words at Astra…

325

And that's when Louko realized everyone was staring at him... including Astra.

"That's exactly what a murderer would say," Mariah sputtered out, aghast.

"Would you be quiet?" Louko had not exactly meant to say that out loud... He tried to form an apology, but the word came out as gibberish.

At least Mariah wasn't talking anymore.

Astra turned from Louko to Keeshiff, her voice softer now. "Please. Think this through. Remember the lives that depend on your decision." She glanced sideways at Mariah.

"We will stay our course," Keeshiff said. "But are we prepared for the weather?"

Louko refused to relax his posture, even though relieved—it would only give Mariah ammunition.

"No," Astra said.

"See?" Mariah squeaked.

"Mariah, why don't you go get something to eat?" Keeshiff suggested, sounding almost as fed up with her as Louko was.

She pressed her lips together, but made a small, "Fine," and with that, flounced out of the tent.

"So how do we deal with the cold?" Keeshiff sounded almost... tired. Being with Mariah could do that to a person.

"From the looks of our map, there are a few small villages on our way," Astra said. "Maybe if we stop and buy a few things at each, we will be able to get through."

Louko finally dove back into the conversation. "Do we have

enough money left?"

Keeshiff gave a short nod. "So what should we expect at the mountain?"

"Well, if we want to survive," Louko's said grimly, "we must be prepared to move fast, to move carefully, and to keep quiet. They will be looking for us."

Astra:

The next day, the march to the mountains continued. This time, everything was covered in an icy fog that made their going much harder. Perhaps the pace was alright, considering Farian's still-healing wound, but this did not help to lighten Astra's already dark mood. She had gotten little sleep the night before; when awake, she was haunted by thoughts of Tyron, and when asleep, she could not escape the nightmares of him. How long would it be before he came after her again? She knew that if not her, then it would be her family.

Astra tried to maintain an even temper, hiding her anxiety lest it spread to the others. Besides, it was this same paranoia that had led to her snapping at Louko yesterday. She wished she could take back the whole thing. She had so overreacted. To be honest, she did not remember much of the conversation after he had referenced her being captured. After that, all Astra had been able to see was the memories. And she knew nothing good ever came from those.

"How are you this morning?" Louko burst through Astra's thoughts.

"I'm fine." Astra gave her default answer out of habit more than anything. Feeling bad, but not wishing to truly explain, she pressed on to ask, "How are you?"

"I'm fine," he said with a raised eyebrow, but he appeared hesitant as he looked her over.

Astra managed an unimpressed expression. "That's not very nice."

"Just returning the pleasantries," Louko replied, mimicking her from tone to posture.

Astra bit her tongue and faced forward again. He was right, of course. For someone who was feeling so guilty over her unkind behavior, she wasn't doing very much to change it. "Sorry," she said, keeping quiet so the knights riding ahead of them wouldn't hear.

"You're alright." He reassured quietly. "You just seem... off."

Louko being so nice made her conscience sting even more. "Sorry. I'll be back to normal in a day or two," was the best answer she could think of.

"So, you aren't alright?" The question was still soft—gentle, even.

"No, I meant—" Astra stopped herself before she could grow too flustered. She adjusted her grip on Dannsair's reins, took a deep breath, and said, "I still regret the way I handled things last night."

"I suppose that makes two of us..." Louko trailed off.

Astra didn't want him to feel bad. Not when he had been trying so hard to help. But none of her attempts to show him that he was not to blame had ever worked—not in any conversation. So she tried another tactic. "Then perhaps it is best to put it aside and move on," Astra proposed, unsure of herself. "Let's find something else to speak of."

Louko, thankfully, seemed to like the idea. "Any suggestions?"

"Um," Astra scrambled for one. "Why *exactly* does Nythril hate Merimeethia so much?"

Louko didn't need further prompting, instantly going into his element as he explained. "Well, Like I said before, they were one country a couple thousand years ago. Dragons and humans lived together. There were two in particular that were fast friends—Merym and Nythrian. The records are rather… torn on what happened, but It seems the human Nythrian turned on the Dragons and demonized them—especially Merym. There was much bloodshed, and the countries ended up being created in the split. Nythril still hates Dragons to this day."

Astra found the story sad; so much war over so old a grudge. And since there weren't even any Dragons in Merimeethia anymore, it wasn't even a valid grudge.

"How did you learn all of these things?' Astra asked. Or maybe she was just especially ignorant…

The prince's face flushed. "Um." He ran his hand through his hair and suddenly switched to Litashian, saying very softly. **"Tyron taught me."**

Astra felt her blood run cold. **"Oh."** Was all she said. Somehow, she always forgot. And somehow, she had managed to come to the same bad topic she had brought up yesterday.

But, maybe—just maybe—hearing of what Tyron used to be would help her let go of this crippling fear. At the very least, perhaps it would help her understand him more. So, steeling herself, she took a deep breath and asked, **"What was he like?"**

Louko looked her right in the eyes. **"I don't know that it's a good idea right now..."** He looked kind of sad as he surveyed her.

Right. *Idiot.* She ought to have been thinking of what such a question would do to Louko. **"Sorry."**

"No. You don't have to apologize." Louko's brow furrowed. **"I just don't want to upset you."**

After last night, Astra didn't blame him for worrying about that. She gave a little shrug. **"I don't know. I thought, perhaps, it would be good for me to know."**

For a while, Astra thought he wasn't even going to reply. But then, very hesitantly, Louko spoke. **"He was sad. And very kind."** A slight smile twisted onto his lips, **"And he was willing to put up with me."**

The knowledge of what Louko had faced as a child was beyond horrible. **"I doubt he was the only one. If anything, your father was the odd one out. He simply had the position to prevent others from helping you."**

Louko let out a humorless chuckle. *"Don't think anyone could blame him."*

Now it was Astra's turn to laugh. But hers was a much sharper sound. **"Try me."**

He narrowed his eyes, **"Feeling up for a pitiful sob-story, hm?"**

"Just trying to understand." To understand how someone could hate their own child enough to make his life one misery after another.

Louko just rolled his eyes, shoulders holding more tension than

Astra had seen them wear in a while. **"Well, then. I suppose the journey is boring enough for a story right now…"** He looked terribly uncomfortable. The question of whether he really wanted to speak or not haunted his eyes for a long while. Then he sighed and began. **"So. Not sure if you remember that day in the art gallery… but I may have been, er, selective with the truth. I had said my father had married before, and that Keeshiff's mother died in a riding accident. That part is all true. It's my mother I suppose I wasn't very truthful about… You see, Keeshiff needed a mother, and my father wanted at that time to make peace with Nythril. My mother was a Nythrilian lady whose husband had been killed in battle, leaving her pregnant with Mariah. She met my father in the court, during some of my father's attempts to make peace. It was true love or whatever nonsense you call it. They married, she moved to Merimeethia. Then my mother became pregnant again."** He sighed irritably. **"They didn't need another child. They were perfectly fine already."**

A sick, sinking feeling began to twist in Astra's stomach.

"You see, she got sick. Doctors said that she might not survive. But then she got better, so everything was alright… except it wasn't. But nobody knew that. Not until I was born did they realize she really hadn't recovered. Not enough. She died just minutes after I was born. Poor Keeshiff and Mariah were traded the mother of their dreams for a silly little brother. What a tragedy." The further Louko got into the story, the more dry and bitter his sarcasm became.

Astra still said nothing.

331

"She was a wonderful person, you know. My mother. Avid rider, lover of literature. Keeshiff probably would have been just fine if she'd brought him up. Mariah wouldn't even be so spoiled." He rolled his eyes.

For once, Astra offered no apologies. Saying sorry, having pity, none of it was enough. It would only ring out hollow. Sorrow for Louko's broken childhood mixed with anger at Omath for such abuse—and towards his own child! Keeshiff and Mariah were no better, going along with their father's bullying. All of it was wrong. It was no wonder in the least that the young Louko would have taken to Tyron. Astra was struck by the sad irony that Tyron had been the only one to show Louko kindness.

"It was not your fault," she said quietly.

He laughed again. **"You don't have to say that."**

"But it's true," Astra insisted.

He cocked his head and gave her a funny smirk. **"Depends on the point of view, I suppose. Mariah seemed pretty convinced until Father told her what happened, when I was ten."**

"I am no Mariah," Astra said.

Louko's smirk was a little more genuinely amused now. **"That is very clear."**

"It was wrong of your family to do what they did."

"It wasn't terrible, really. For a while, it actually wasn't bad at all. I remember feeling abandoned... and alone." He was almost mumbling the words. **"And then Tyron turned up."**

Astra's temper fizzled out. **"And he looked after you?"** she prompted quietly.

Louko nodded, **"But... more than that. He somehow got past my father's pride and hurt... he made things better, I think. I was allowed to eat with them, and we almost all... got along."** His face was twisted, looking as if something still bewildered him. **"And then he left..."**

Four simple words, and yet they held every bit of the anguish Astra had witnessed in her friend yesterday. **"And you still don't know why,"** came her guess.

"All I know is his brother showed up. Even though Tyron was practically my father's advisor then, he just up and left with Euracia. And my father got... worse."

Worse. Astra remembered the weeks she had stayed in Melye and felt sick. How could anyone leave Louko to that? Shame swelled to remember that she had done the same, and that the only reason Louko was free of Omath was because of Tyron. **"How long was it until he returned as Kaeden?"**

"A little over three years, I think." Louko replied, **"He didn't really approach me for a while. But I think he arrived back three years later."** There was an awkward pause as he added, **"And then he came back with your father, for a while..."**

Astra swiveled her head to look at him. **"Wait—what did you say?"**

"Kaeden's claimed backstory was that he was an Alarunian pressed into service by Euracia. And your father... Well, as you know, he was apparently captured by Tyron. But Kaeden told me Tyron was trying to undermine his brother. He claimed that, at that moment, the only thing he could do was at least allow Destrin to

see his wife who was kept in my father's dungeon, as it would turn out... That's also how I found out my father was working with Euracia and Tyron. To this day I still don't know why. Some form of duress was clearly a factor."

This new onslaught of information was dizzying. Destrin? Her father? Her father had willingly gone with Tyron? And Tyron had brought him to see her mother? **"But, how can that be?"** She heard herself ask. **"I found my father in the depths of Tyron's castle in Alarune. I can assure you that he was not there by choice."**

"I don't know. But for a while your father would come often. I'm surprised he never said anything when we met during The War... I don't know why he didn't." Louko paused and seemed hesitant about what he was about to say next. **"But he did eventually stop coming."**

Astra didn't know what to think. How had she never known this? Why had her parents never spoken of it? Did they fear Tyron? Or did they, like Louko, know him as someone else entirely?

Hundreds of questions now rattled around in her head, all clamoring to be heard and making it impossible to process any of them. Not that Astra got the chance to ask any of them. Coryn and Lucian, who had been riding just ahead of them, slowed down till they were side by side with Louko and Astra. This way they could pass along the afternoon rations without the whole group stopping.

Astra took hers, barely remembering to thank Lucian in the process. She was too busy trying to figure out all these accounts of Tyron that were so drastically different from any experiences of her own. Her biggest question was: which version was right?

***

I mull over the records again, confirming the location and timing. Precision is crucial if I am to succeed. I close the book and set it on my desk, getting up and examining the chess board near the window. I pick up a bishop and let it cross the board.

We're almost there.

OF SHADE AND SHADOW

CHAPTER XVI

Louko:

Louko…was so confused… Even though he knew she already knew, he had been so ready for Astra to be angry about the whole Tyron matter that, well… he was not expecting what came next. He had taken so many turns of being confused, amused, and worried, that he really wasn't sure what to think of any of it himself. So, yes… Louko was confused. But even more so, there were so many things she seemed not to know about; like her father...

They stopped for the night at the foot of the mountains, only an hour or two from a village. Tomorrow, a couple of them would go to buy supplies before they began the treacherous journey through the mountains. Since they were now so near to the pass, travelers were more commonplace, and therefore more likely to go unnoticed.

As the sun sank out of view, the cold grew more intense, and Louko could not wait until they got some better cloaks. Nythril was very unforgiving.

"It's so cold," Mariah whined pitifully. The knights seemed too busy with their own inner whinings to be annoyed.

"Rufio, start a fire," Keeshiff ordered, coming up and giving his sister a hug to try and warm her.

Bleh. Hugs.

Louko went over to Astra, who had already set up her tent, and asked, "So. Should we ask Keeshiff tonight or tomorrow about who's going to the village for supplies? In other words, while he's still warm, or

337

too cold to argue?" He managed a grin.

Astra did not return the smile, but Louko knew she'd heard him, for she stopped her unpacking. Then she tried to offer some sort of show of amusement. "While he's warm. If it goes badly, we can try again when he's cold," she replied.

Nodding sagely, Louko said, "I like how you think." He looked from his siblings to Astra. "Who's leading? You or I?"

"Perhaps it would be best if you did it," Astra said each word deliberately. "I may not be entirely civil if I speak to your siblings just now."

Louko was not aware she had ever been civil with them... He decided he did not want to know what she was like if *not* civil. "Well, that's settled then. Shall we?" he asked.

She nodded mutely and followed him, and together they made their way over to Keeshiff and Mariah.

"What do you want now?" Mariah stared at both of them, the cold only making her more... charming.

Louko kept wondering if he should have just talked to his siblings without Astra... but she might be the only one who could get Keeshiff to listen. Stealing a glance at the redhead, Louko was glad to see she at least *looked* calm. Calm in a blank, empty-stare kind of way.

"Well, I thought we should figure out who is going into the village tonight, so that way Keeshiff could set up the night watches accordingly," Louko said hesitantly.

"Well, it won't be *you*," Mariah spat.

Louko clenched his fists. "Keeshiff?" His brother needed to speak for himself. Mariah was controlling him. Why did Keeshiff always let others sway him?

Astra seemed to be physically biting her tongue.

What a lovely, riveting conversation.

"Astra is less likely to be noticed. She and Asher will go," Keeshiff replied.

Louko did not like pressing his luck, but... "Will two people be enough?"

Mariah cocked her head. "Why? Does Louko want to go and betray our position?"

"You're one to talk." Astra's low voice was almost a growl.

Louko's brow furrowed, and he looked at Astra in shock, then quickly decided to keep going... especially when he noted Mariah's pale expression. "So... Keeshiff, would a couple more work?"

Keeshiff was staring at Astra, confused at her comment, but trying to go on. "Um... Delnor should go, as he is in charge of rations."

Wow. He was actually kind of thinking this through. Maybe there was hope...

"Perhaps one more?"

Keeshiff sighed, "You're not going, Louko."

"I was not implying that," Louko said, feeling tired.

"Have Ivinon go." Mariah broke in again.

"Fine. Astra, you will take them into the village tomorrow and purchase what is needed. Is that all?" Keeshiff seemed tired, as well.

Astra gave no reply beyond a nod.

Astra was still not talking, even though almost an hour had

passed since their conversation with Louko's siblings. He was tempted to ask if she was alright, but seeing her reaction over the last time he'd asked her... besides, at present she was writing once again— to Ent, Louko suspected. He knew she planned to send all her letters to him while she was in the village. Louko thought over the letter he had given Rhumir to send to his uncle, and once more hoped it had gotten through. Otherwise... that would be awkward.

The other knights were seated around, each absorbed in their *very* delicious dinner... Louko wished they had a better cook.

Rufio was especially displeased. "Who made this?" he grumbled. "This is worse than Louko's slop."

Louko recalled Rufio actually liking his "slop", so he hid a smile.

"Why, Rufio, do you want to learn how to make it?" Delnor asked, amusement and lack of patience seeming to conflict in his voice.

Coryn laughed, which only seemed to increase Rufio's ire.

"I'm just saying that whoever made it should join Louko in whatever punishment he gets after all this," Rufio shot back.

The humor around the campfire died, replaced by an uneasy tension. Louko heard the scratching of Astra's pen stop abruptly, then slowly continue. Rufio had been so good the last few days... but apparently with the closeness of safety returned the accusations...

"Well, I pity the man," Louko decided it was at least best to just control the flames of this conversation, if nothing else.

All of the knights looked up with a start. Apparently, no one had even noticed he was there. Rufio reddened, but gave no apology.

Well, at least they were quiet now...

Asher seemed the only one at ease. He came and sat near

Louko, almost chuckling. "Good thing you're nice," he said.

Louko raised an eyebrow, not *quite* sure what to say to that.

"Aren't they fortunate..." A dry voice came from behind them. Louko realized it was Astra, who was somehow still writing. Talented.

Well, this conversation was getting very awkward, and honestly, Louko almost found it amusing. It would definitely have been, if it had not been so centered around him.

Farian spoke up next. "Well, I don't think Louko did it. He had no reason to. Doesn't make sense."

"Ah, nonsense," Rufio snorted. "He's always had it out for Keeshiff. He just had to get rid of King Omath first."

"Honestly, that's a bad plan. Clearly he would have gotten rid of Keeshiff first." Louko chimed in casually.

"I wouldn't have, if I was trying to dispose of Keeshiff." Gavin said, not even noticing that it was Louko who had spoken.

Louko looked at Asher, very pleased with himself. He liked this game. Especially since they hadn't figured out that he was inserting his own opinion. Sometimes it helped to be ignored...

"But then, why help Keeshiff get away? There were times where he could easily have gotten us turned in," Ivinon chimed in, doubtful.

Louko felt the need to try his luck and interject again, "Yes, but perhaps he was waiting for the right moment?"

"Exactly!" Rufio interjected. "That's what I've been saying all—" He stopped suddenly, staring at Louko as if he just realized it had been Louko talking. Because... he had.

Asher burst out in deep laughter. He was joined by Ivinon, Farin, and Lucian. The rest shifted in their seats, embarrassed. Rufio just muttered under his breath and stomped off. The knight was as bad as his brother, Rhumir.

Louko smiled ever so slightly and said, "Temper, temper." He shook his head, as if a disappointed mother. Then he turned to see Astra's reaction. Even she was smiling somewhat as she folded her letter and sealed it.

Everyone stayed fairly quiet after that, and one by one they began wandering off to their tents. Louko stayed by the fire to keep it going as long as he could. Astra sat on the opposite side of the fire once again. He wasn't sure whether to engage or not... She was just looking out into nothing, one hand toying with the red cuff she always wore.

"So. Hope everything goes well tomorrow." Louko was trying not to think of it. As childish as it sounded... it would be the first time Astra would not be with him since Keeshiff tied him to a tree. Most of the knights staying weren't really sympathetic to him, either. And then there was Mariah...

Astra appeared to have thought about this, too. She nodded slowly. "Perhaps I'll lend you my bow."

Astra:

It was mid-morning when Astra, Asher, Delnor, and Ivinon left the camp. Astra did not want to enter the village too early, lest it be obvious they had camped nearby. They cut through the woods to the open road, where Astra stopped the group.

"Asher, Delnor, you two will go first." Astra instructed. "When you reach the village, you will split up. Both of you act like you are buying supplies for your families. Buy as much food and clothing as you can without looking suspicious."

The two nodded before Delnor began dividing the money Keeshiff had given him. In turn, Astra began parceling out her squares of fabric. When she had realized that they did not have enough money for all of the needed supplies, she had turned to the dresses she had worn in Melye. The fabric was expensive enough to be of enough value for trading. So, all too gleefully, Astra had pulled all the seams and then cut the fabric into squares.

"Ivinon and I will do the same, but we will wait half an hour so as to be less noticeable." She said. "Leave at different times and use a different road to get back. We will meet here and then go back so that we leave fewer trails back towards the camp."

Everyone agreed to the plan, and the first two knights departed. Astra and Ivinon waited their allotted half hour in silence. The girl was the first to speak, only asking, "Are you ready?" when it was time.

Ivinon nodded, and they both set out.

It took a little while, but Ivinon finally struck over some sort of conversation. "So, Princess Astra, is it true you fought in the final battles of The War?" His brow was furrowed incredulously.

Astra wondered at the sudden curiosity, and more so wondered if it was good or not. "Yes," she said simply, pausing before adding: "And there is no need to use my title unless you wish to."

Ivinon nodded at this, and continued, "Forgive me, I just find it hard to believe that you were there. I tried so hard to keep my own brother from The War—and he is older than you."

Ah. He was confused at how Ent would have allowed her to fight. "It's alright," Astra said. "Your question is understandable. My own brother would not have allowed me to fight either, but he had no such option. We were separated for a long time and I was pulled into The War by myself. When we were reunited, there was no way that he could keep me out of it."

Ivinon thought on this. "That makes sense," he said.

Astra now switched topics, both wanting to deflect further curiosity and satisfy her own. "Where are you and your brother from?"

"A little village two days north of Melye," Ivinon replied. "My mother still lives there."

Astra heard what was unsaid, and did not have to ask to know that Ivinon had no father. Whether he had died or had left was not her place to ask. She thought of how hard it must be for Ivinon and Farian to leave their mother alone, without the security of knowing her husband was there to care for her. Astra was thankful that her parents and brother were all well-looked after.

"What led you to become a knight?" she asked, thinking the question safer than the others she thought of.

"The income." Ivinon's voice held the slightest tension, and Astra was surprised that he was so openly honest. "But that is a problem all Merimeethians have—unless you're like Lucian, but he had money problems in a different way, you could say." A smile tugged at his lips.

Astra cocked her head. "A different way?" She tried to recall what she knew of Lucian, but knew little beyond his strong, quiet character.

Ivinon's smile was slightly mischievous. "Yes. He scorned his rich palace and servants to come live among the peasants. That's why he hated Keeshiff so much at first. But he found out he really isn't that bad when you get to know him." He paused, looked at her, and frowned. "You really do have to try, though." Then he quieted. After a brief moment of silence, he spoke up again, this time very sincere and serious. "Keeshiff is not as bad as he makes out to be. Being around his family is hard, and the shock of everything has made him irritable. I'm sure it will pass soon." He huffed out a breath of air and readjusted the sword by his side. He seemed to be unsure if he should have spoken, and almost regretful—as if betraying the confidence of a friend.

Astra walked in silence a moment. Yes, this was hard on Keeshiff, too. True, she had many times been harsh towards him; it was hard for her to side with him when she had to daily watch the way he treated Louko. This wasn't to say that Astra had never noted the other side of the eldest prince. That side of Keeshiff was just one of his men, not the irritable royal. That side had so much potential to grow and do good and lead well. It made Astra wonder if Keeshiff put on just as much of an act as his brother. If Ivinon was right about Keeshiff struggling with having to be near family, perhaps Omath had merely found another way to abuse him from how he had abused Louko.

"I hope you are right," Astra said, quiet. "I think he has more ability than he realizes. When he finds it, he could prove himself admirably."

"For now, we should be thankful for Merimeethians' lack-luster for politics. I think it is one of the reasons we have not been caught." Again Ivinon smiled, but more wryly than before.

Astra knew he was likely right. None of the knights ever mentioned Omath except for the fact of his murder. The common folk of Merimeethia would have even less reason to care.

But before she could say anything, the two came in view of the village. They both knew their cover and their mission, and so fell into mutual silence. They took their time in the village, knowing that rushing would catch notice. Thankfully, many travelers stopped here before going through the pass, so Astra and Ivinon were not especially noticed, nor pried for the rare bit of news.

The two wandered from stall to stall and bought as much clothing and food as they could give excuse for. Then they took a meandering route back to the meeting place. Their purchases were heavy and unwieldy to bear through the forest, but neither complained. When they reached it, Asher and and Delnor were already waiting.

"Do you think the camp will still be standing?" Ivinon asked, apparently trying to make a joke.

Asher didn't seem to find it funny. Astra silently hoped it was only a joke, and that Mariah had done nothing to Louko.

Delnor gave a sigh and said, "Thinking of who we left there, who knows? They quarrel worse than my children."

"I have met your children," Asher said. "And if Mariah and the rest are truly that bad, I say we hurry back."

Delnor gave Asher a slight, playful shove, and Ivinon just chuckled. Not truly part of the joke, Astra just shouldered her things and started to lead the way back to camp.

This time the silence did not last long, and soon the three knights were talking amongst themselves.

"Are you planning to send for your family when we reach Nythril, Delnor?" Ivinon asked.

The older knight let out a long breath as he walked. "I don't know," he admitted. "My wife has doubtlessly taken the children to her parents', but I don't know whether it is safer to leave them there or bring them with me. I cannot, in good conscience, bring them if it puts them at risk."

Astra listened with a sadness. She knew very well how much it hurt for a family to be separated. For a father to not even know if he could protect and provide must be a cruel form of torture. Astra thought of her own father; the years he had been imprisoned without even knowing whether or not his family was alive still haunted him. The thought made her recall her conversation with Louko yesterday, and her sorrow turned to confusion.

It was Asher who spoke to comfort Delnor. "Perhaps you will never even have to choose," he said. "Maybe one day you will be able to go home to them."

Delnor scoffed, "If we don't get ourselves killed first."

That's when Astra stopped them.

"What is it?" Asher asked in an undertone.

"I hear raised voices," she replied, listening intently.

"But shouldn't the camp be just ahead?" Ivinon asked.

Astra nodded.

Quietly, the group crept forward to investigate.

***

I dismiss a servant and return to my desk. I know that I've received all the notes from my informant that I will get before they come in person, but it can be trying to wait for news. I always prefer to do the job myself. Still, this person has proved immensely useful thus far; I don't think they will stop till they see it through. Too bad they will hate themselves for the result.

CHAPTER XVII

Louko:

"What exactly do you think you're doing??" Mariah stood before Farian and Louko, who had just been trying to do a little sparring match. *That* had apparently been a mistake.

"Mariah—"

"Shut up." She spat.

"Princess Mariah, please, this is hardly your business." Farian came to Louko's defense in a surprising development.

"See? See? Keeshiff, he's turning everyone against you." She caught poor Keeshiff, who had just come out of his tent to see what the noise was. Louko gave a deeply apologetic glance to his brother, secretly wishing Keeshiff would help him... just once. That's all he wanted. But he knew Keeshiff wondered just as much as the others whether Louko was really innocent or not.

"Mariah, calm down, I've got it under control." Keeshiff's voice sounded weary.

"Come on, Keeshiff, don't you see how he's worming his way right back into your life so *he* can control *you*?"

"That's *enough*." Keeshiff was shockingly firm, and even Louko was caught off guard. "We are not going to keep bringing this up, Mariah. Right now, the priority is to survive, not point fingers."

"But think about how close the patrols are getting!" Mariah yelled back, of *course* equally stubborn. "He and Astra could be planning something!"

Louko wished he could disappear, but there were no tunnels to hide in here. Only open space and exposure.

"Come now, don't be ridiculous, Mariah." While Keeshiff deescalated what he saw as a petty argument, Louko had this horrible feeling that Mariah knew something.

"What's ridiculous is that you somehow believe him—" Mariah jabbed a finger in Louko's direction. "—over me! Since when could you trust *him*? Or Astra, for that matter? She may have the title of a princess, but she's hardly more than a peasant. Even her own family tossed her out as soon as they could."

Keeshiff stopped short. "What did you say?"

Mariah feigned innocence. "Oh, didn't you know?" She looked over shoulder at Louko. "I bet *he* could tell you all about it. Astra was exiled after nearly killing half the nobles of Litash—her brother included." The clearing went silent. "Oh, I don't know if she meant to or not..." Mariah let the sentence trail before adding, "Some people think she's just unstable and easily manipulated." Another glare towards Louko.

Louko's blood ran cold as he saw that Mariah had everyone's attention. "Would you stop it, Mariah?" Too late he realized he'd snapped.

"Why?" The sweet way she asked the question meant she knew that she was getting to him. "Don't like to have your plans made public? What did you promise Astra, anyway? To help her get revenge on her brother? Or maybe just a place in your new castle?"

Louko was too aghast to respond immediately, and in doing so allowed the other knights to react.

And that wasn't exactly a good thing.

"What?" It was Rufio, naturally, the first to jump into an argument against Louko. "What are you talking about, Mariah?"

"I'm talking about how none of you seem to see how Louko and Astra are obviously in on something together," Mariah took on a nearly pleading tone, like she had always done to win her point with Omath. "Don't you see? He killed Father, Astra tried to kill her brother, and now we're letting them lead us to Nythril—a place where Louko has other political ties. Isn't it clear that they are scheming to take over Merimeethia?"

"She has a point, Keeshiff... Didn't Lord Aelor Ven almost start a war trying to force Mariah and Louko back to Nythril?" Coryn spoke up hesitantly.

"What?" Louko was so stressed now he couldn't breathe. Were they seriously going to do this *now*? When any hesitation would get them killed? "Do you think you are *helping,* Mariah? You realize if we *don't* get to Nythril we will all die!" His voice was dangerous from frustration and almost panic. *Idiot.* He should have kept his head down. He should never have taken up Farian's offer. He never should have tried to *actually* get involved with anyone. What in Eatris had he been thinking?

Rufio started to say something in return, only to get cut off by Farian. Coryn tried to calm the two, and only made it worse. Lucian went to his aid to no avail. If that wasn't bad enough, Mariah was now raving on about murder and secret plans—not that Louko could hear the specifics. The now shouting knights next to him made that impossible. This was bad. This was very bad. They were too close to the village for

351

this.

The combination of movement in his peripheral vision and the voice that followed made Louko turn around.

"What is going on here?" Astra's question, though even in volume, was enough to still the tumult. Apparently, the knights had noticed all their comrades returning.

Louko just gave her a desperate look.

"Just explaining your *exile*," Mariah spat like a toddler. Louko found himself almost wishing they'd just left her somewhere to go crawl back to Melye. She was going to get Keeshiff and the rest killed.

Well, aren't you a lovely soul?

Astra looked perfectly calm from the outside, but Louko saw the way one hand itched to go to her wrist. "What about it?" she asked, scanning the crowd before looking at Mariah again.

"Mariah, stop it, we can discuss all of this nonsense *later*," Keeshiff spoke for the first time in a while, having lost all control once the noise had erupted. "You are going to get us all killed. I don't care about Astra's exile, and at the moment *your* uncle is probably the only one that doesn't want to get us killed, so would you please shut up and let me think for once in your life?"

Mariah stared at him, open-mouthed in shock.

For a moment, Louko thought that it had worked. That Mariah would actually stay quiet. But then he saw her eyes narrow and her hands formed fists and he knew he was wrong.

"You're siding with *him?!* Since when?!" Mariah's whole face was red. "Or have you always been on his side? Maybe that's it. Maybe you just played along so that Father wouldn't hate you, too. Maybe you know Louko killed him, but you just don't *care*. Just like you apparently don't care that he killed Mother." Her voice was low and sharp.

Louko's throat was closing in on itself. This needed to stop. Keeshiff looked equally upset.

"Do *not* make me gag you, Mariah." The words were dangerous as they came from Keeshiff's mouth. His face was twisted in a strange mix of emotions that rarely had ever shown.

There was a short silence, where Louko could see Mariah evaluating Keeshiff's resolve. Apparently she believed the threat. She straightened her shoulders and lifted her chin in a haughty fashion, saying, "Fine. Have it your way. I'll be quiet and let you *think*." She smirked. "As if you ever did that for yourself. I guess Louko will do it for you, now." She shrugged and turned away towards her tent, calling back over shoulder. "You might just want to watch yourself. He may not be as forgiving as you think he is."

Nothing was said for a long time, and for a long while Louko found himself staring at Keeshiff. But what was off was the way he was staring back—and Louko wondered if he was imagining the regret in his eyes.

Astra:

Funny that, after being so careful with the secret of her exile, its reveal to the entire camp should be secondary in Astra's thoughts. Indeed, as she stood there watching the two princes, it barely bothered her at all. Mariah turning her sharp tongue on Keeshiff had been so unexpected that it left everyone stunned—including Astra.

"Everyone needs to be on alert," Keeshiff's voice had an odd twinge as he spoke—he was still staring at Louko, "Who knows who heard that nightmare. We need to move on soon."

There were nods and grunts of agreement all around the camp.

"Did you want to inspect the supplies that we bought first?" Astra asked, quietly bringing things back to business.

Finally, Keeshiff's eyes left his brother and he turned to Astra. "Yes." Turning to some of his men, he continued with, "Bandon, Lucian, do a perimeter search to make sure Mariah didn't draw the attention of our pursuers. Ivinon, make sure the horses get some water."

The two nodded and set off.

Astra, Delnor, Asher, and Ivinon all brought their supplies to the center and untied the various bundles so that Keeshiff could go over everything. Since Delnor was in charge of rations and Asher the medicine, Astra decided she wasn't needed. She had already gone over all the mountain wear. So she went to find Louko.

He was standing rather awkwardly in the back, watching everything and clearly trying to keep an eye on where Mariah was. He flinched a greeting as Astra approached, but said nothing.

"Are you alright?" Astra asked, even though she knew the answer. Louko looked tense enough to snap.

"I do not know," he murmured.

The simple fact that he had not said 'I'm fine' meant it had to be bad. But Astra didn't know what to say next. What would help? She toyed with a few ideas, then just got it over with.

"What happened?" She supposed it would be better than Louko going over and over it in his head.

"I made a mistake," he replied simply. "And Mariah…" he trailed off, but the way in which he did it sounded almost more pensive than anguished. Something was on his mind.

"What is it?" Astra prompted.

"I don't know…I just… that went far," he whispered, but Astra's blood ran cold as he added, "She's smarter than she acts. Even Mariah would know better than to go on yelling that loudly at a time like this."

The only reason that Astra caught what Louko was implying was because she had had the same thought before. "She has a purpose in it. And it would seem Keeshiff was getting in the way of whatever that was."

Louko ran his hand through his hair, face hard as stone in apprehensive thought. "Yeah." The one word was said breathlessly, holding a burdened meaning.

Both stood, not speaking as their minds ran through all the implications. If Mariah was working with someone in Melye, there was only one person that could be…

"Louko," Astra said suddenly, looking him in the eyes. "Just promise me that you will be careful, alright?" Mariah had never bothered to hide her hatred for her younger brother. He was the most at risk.

With a roll of his eyes, the prince replied with, "I'm always careful."

Astra didn't look away. "I'm serious."

"I know." Louko's voice rang sincere.

Astra held his gaze a moment longer. Just until she was sure that he really would be cautious. Then she looked to where Keeshiff was helping the others hand out the heavy mountain coats. He still seemed to be in shock, his movements oddly delayed and his voice quiet.

Then, almost on cue, he turned and locked eyes with Astra, "Would you and Louko go find some firewood? I'm guessing that there won't be much for us to forage in the mountains.."

Astra dipped her head in a nod, glad Keeshiff had provided his brother with an escape.

With a sigh Louko added, "Yeah," and ran his hand through his hair again. "I suppose that's probably a safe job…" the last bit was mumbled.

They headed off and, while Louko didn't say anything, his posture could have written a book. It was a similar mixture of emotions to what Astra had seen the last time Mariah had driven him into the center of attention. Astra was disgusted with how much Mariah accused Louko of trying to have a claim to attention and prestige, when all he ever wanted was to be left alone in the shadows. As Astra dug through piles of brush to look for anything dry, she forced herself to swallow her anger. Louko didn't need that.

"So how did it all start?" Astra asked as she broke a branch in half to make it easier to carry.

"Farian asked me to spar," he replied, sounding almost bitter.

"And she got angry over that?" She kept her voice calm, even as the pettiness of it all threatened her resolution to hold her temper.

Louko did not reply, but the forceful way in which he snapped a large twig he had grabbed was answer enough.

Astra added another bunch of sticks to her little armful while she tried to think of something to say. She hoped that, one day, Mariah would finally understand all the harm she inflicted on her own family.

"I am glad Keeshiff stepped in," Astra finally commented. At least Louko now had one sibling willing to do something besides let him take the fall.

"Yes." This reply was more quiet and less tense, but still simple. "I think everyone sees her a little more clearly now."

"Let's hope so, because she seems intent on getting everyone killed."

The topic stirred up Astra's suspicions again. Mentally, she debated the question before finally asking, "Do you think he would work with her? Tyron, I mean." She stumbled over saying his name aloud.

Louko froze, then said slowly, "I don't know. But something is definitely not right."

Astra agreed. Then something occurred to her. "Mariah was the one who told them of my exile, wasn't she?"

After a pause, Louko nodded.

"How would she have known? Ent made sure that knowledge didn't leave Litash."

"*Someone* told her. Seeing as not even Keeshiff knew, it had to be someone who isn't just a royal or visiting noble... I didn't even know you were exiled, and I was *in* Litash... I don't know..." he trailed off.

Fear curled in Astra's stomach and she forced stiff fingers to keep searching for firewood. Tyron always had his sources, his various ways. "I suppose all we can do is keep a close eye on her and make sure she doesn't contact anyone outside the camp." Were there ways to do that via Gifting? Not that Mariah had any. But if Tyron's was enough... Astra rued her own ignorance.

"Yes," Louko agreed, "We're so close... all we have to do is get into the mountains, then we'll be safer." Astra couldn't tell who he was trying to reassure.

Either way, she wanted to reinforce the rare attempt at optimism. "Exactly. And when we reach Nythril, we can sit down and figure this out."

"Yeah."

The conversation died, but there was still more wood to be gathered. So Astra tried again on what she hoped was a safe topic.

"What is your uncle like?"

"I don't really know. I haven't seen him since I was pretty young, I think… though from his letters he is a very... opinionated person," Louko replied in a sort of reminiscence.

Astra barely caught herself from saying that opinions seemed to run in the family. Instead she asked, "Do you think he will be willing to help? Not just with shelter. But with this whole mess."

Louko gave a stiff shrug. "Perhaps if I help. But I don't think he likes the idea of Keeshiff being on the Merimeethian throne."

Ah. So things would be tense there, too. "Maybe this change of character will be enough to convince him otherwise," Astra suggested, though having no surety in her words.

Louko's laugh was dry. "My uncle is a prejudiced man. In fact, I'm more worried his hatred of Litashians will get in the way..."

"Why does he hate Litashians?" Considering how few ever left the country, Astra wondered how the man could have even met one.

"Oh. He met Tyron, when I was little." Louko looked uneasy.

"Oh."

Louko fell silent, rummaging under a tree for some more fuel for their future fire.

In another minute or two, both had their arms full and were heading back. Before they reached the rest of the group where he was less likely to answer, Astra quietly asked,

"Is there anything I can do to help?"

"I don't do...sympathy...or kindness...or hugs..." The suddenness and awkwardness with which he said the disjointed list was almost humorous if it hadn't been so odd.

"...hugs?" Astra stopped in her tracks, confused. She glanced down at her armful of brush, trying to comprehend how hugs would even be possible—much less on Louko's mind.

"Um, I mean, er," he stumbled a moment, muttering 'idiot' under his breath, "I am just listing general signs of affection—just covering my bases, I suppose..."

Astra nearly smiled, now taken by the humor of the conversation. "Is affection such an issue?"

"If it includes hugs, then yes, definitely." He seemed to also catch the air of amusement, and Astra watched with satisfaction as his shoulders ever so slightly relaxed.

"Alright, I'll be careful to remember that," Astra said, with no small amount of sarcasm, as they continued walking. "What about without hugs?"

"Still doubtful, depends on the situation, I suppose." Louko shrugged.

"And what about gathering wood makes it so distasteful?"

"Because, it's rough." He looked pleased with himself for some reason.

Astra raised a brow. "The wood or my attempt at conveying affection?" Wait, no, that sounded wrong...

Louko blinked at least fifty times, looking uncomfortably perplexed, "Um...The wood…" He said at last, each word pulled out with a slowness that could put the dead to shame.

Cheeks now burning, Astra mumbled something along the lines of, "Just checking."

"Well," Louko cleared his throat, "Good thing we are back at the camp." he said as they walked back into the clearing where the group was still mulling about in what appeared to be preparation to leave..

All of the men were busy packing their bought and gathered supplies and talking amongst themselves. Astra and Louko handed off their loads to Coryn and Ivinon, who were loading up the horses.

"I have never been this close to Nythril. I'm beginning to not hate our weather so much," Ivinon said with a reluctant laugh as the conversation the group had apparently been holding continued on.

Coryn nodded. "We may get constant rain, but at least we don't get snow," he said. "I've never set foot in the stuff, but I hear it can make drifts several feet deep."

Astra stayed out of the conversation, sticking to tying the firewood into bundles

"It's not so bad." Lucian spoke now. "You just have to watch out for when all of it slides."

Ivinon looked confused. "Slides? It's just snow. How bad can it be?"

"It is like mud, just lighter. If it gets warm enough to begin to melt, it can be dangerous." Asher answered from where he was loading a leather satchel.

Ivinon nodded in understanding.

Of course Merimeethians would understand mud.

And that's when Keeshiff returned from where he had been talking to Mariah in the farthest corner of the clearing. Astra noted he looked exhausted and frustrated and, by the red on his cheeks, Astra guessed it hadn't gone well.

"How did it go with the witch?" Lucian asked, and promptly received an icy glare from Keeshiff.

"She will keep quiet for now," he replied sternly.

Astra noticed how Louko had turned away and pretended to be busy with a piece of tack.

"What are we going to do about her?" Gavin posed the question. "And with..." his gaze drifted towards Astra and Louko as his sentence dropped away.

"We do nothing. We get to safety." Keeshiff sounded stressed to the breaking point.

The following quiet was only broken by the uneasy shuffling of feet.

Bandon's murmur came from the back. "We can't afford to be heard."

"And she shouldn't have spoken to you like that," Farian burst out. The poor knight hadn't stopped his nervous fiddlings since the argument. "All that happened was I asked to spar with Louko!"

"Are we going to start the yelling again, Farian?" Keeshiff's voice was the kind of calm that you say through your teeth.

Farian's head immediately bowed, and he started rubbing his temple with one hand.

Keeshiff began inspecting the supplies that had been fastened to the horses, "Leave Mariah to me. I talked to her already and warned her she should stop giving her opinions so readily."

"I doubt that will hold her long." Asher's comment was factual rather than derogatory. "She takes every chance she can get to deride Louko and Astra. And now that *you've* interrupted her, she seems all too willing to go after you, too."

This only frustrated Keeshiff more, and he sighed. "Well, I am open to suggestions." His voice held a sour tang.

There were a few grumblings under their breath, but no one said anything.

"Just tell her she'll cause an avalanche if she speaks—we're close enough to the mountains." Everyone was startled by Louko's reply, as everyone had apparently forgotten he was there.

Farian looked at Ivinon. "Is that actually true? Can you really start an avalanche by being too loud?" His question was voiced in an undertone.

When Ivinon seemed at a loss for reply, Astra answered. "No, but Mariah needn't know that."

"Well, that's better than nothing," Keeshiff agreed with the suggestion, "and no one else seems to have come up with something. We might as well try."

This seemed to turn the mood from tense to jesting. Many of the knights clearly enjoyed the thought of Mariah keeping quiet out of the fear of, well, nothing.

But Astra knew that it wouldn't be enough. Even if the other princess held her vicious tongue, what was to keep her from continuing her betrayal? Her gaze wandered towards Louko. Who would help him if Mariah pulled off whatever it was she was scheming? Astra couldn't help but fear who Mariah might be working with. There was no way to find out for certain. All that she knew for certain was that, no matter who it was or how Mariah did it, Astra was not going to let Louko take the fall.

***

The Game is set.

CHAPTER XVIII

Astra:

The night was bitter cold. Astra fought the wind for her cloak, pulling it around her as an extra layer over her coat. She wished yet again for a fire, even as she knew that it wasn't worth the risk of being found. Without the trees to hide them—not to mention how reflective the snow was—a flame would be visible at a long distance from their current campsite.

So Astra huddled in the little crevice of stone, peering out into the moonlit night as she kept her watch. The only sound was the whistling and cracking of the wind over rock. That was, until there was the soft sound of snow crunching underfoot. Astra's head snapped towards the sound, and she saw a black shape against the white background. It slipped out of a tent and away towards the edge of the camp.

Astra might not have thought much of it if it had been one of the knights. But the shape was too small and too intent on staying out of sight. Besides, Astra knew whose tent that was—Mariah's.

There were only seconds of delay before Astra made her decision. Leaving her cloak in the cleft of rock lest its flapping give her away, she tightened her grip on her bow and got to her feet. Noiselessly, she crept through the camp and followed the footprints. The girl was careful to keep far enough back so as not to be seen, while still close enough to know exactly where Mariah was. Whatever Mariah was up to, Astra wanted to catch her in the act.

For nearly ten minutes, Astra followed, noting how the trail was starting to double back towards the Merimeethian side of the pass. Two minutes more, and Mariah had reached the same path they had used that very day. The slough left behind by knights and horses made it impossible to single out Mariah's footsteps and Astra was forced to keep a little closer than she would have liked. She was so busy watching the shadow of a figure that it was another five minutes before she realized that there were far more tracks in the snow than could possibly belong to the knights. Astra froze, instinctively crouching low as she realized her mistake. Her heart sunk.

Too late. It was too late. *Idiot!* Already she could hear the faint choir of footsteps building. Astra had walked into the very trap she had warned Louko of, and all because she had been too stupid to realize that she was the bait. One look around the bare ridge told her there was no way out. The only hiding places had been used to conceal the ring of soldiers that was tightening around her.

In deliberate motions that hid the panic she felt, Astra forced numb fingers to pull an arrow from her quiver and set it to her bowstring. She held it there, still crouching low, ready to draw; waiting for the first person to crest the edge of the ridge. Then a close-sounding footfall behind her made her spin around, instinct aiming her arrow towards the source of the noise. But the figure's raised hands stayed her shot.

"Please, Princess, none of that," came the deep voice. "There are too many of us for you to possibly take. Why kill without cause? Lay down your weapon."

The first thing Astra registered was the familiarity of the voice. This was the same captain that Keeshiff had let go after the skirmish in the forest.

The second thing Astra registered was that the captain knew who she was.

The third, and most sickening, was that the captain was right. Now that most of his men were in view, Astra did not need to count them to know that there were at least four times as many as before. They well outnumbered even Keeshiff and all the knights.

"What will you do with me if I do?" Astra asked, stalling for time in the hopes that she could think of a way out.

"Escort you back to Melye," the captain replied. "Steward Kaeden will make the decisions after that. I suppose it will be between your country and his."

Back to Melye. Right to Tyron.

Astra's arm began to ache with the weight of her bow but she willed the wood not to lessen the draw. "What of the others?"

The captain now sounded exasperated. "They will all be taken back and given fair trial. Now come, Princess, lower your weapon—you have no chance. Would you obstruct justice? Would you rob Merimeethia of the chance to find out who murdered their king?"

He was right: she could not escape. However, no matter what he said, Astra could *never* go back to Tyron. And she could never give up and so let Louko and the others be captured.

Slowly, Astra relaxed her bowstring and set the weapon on the ground. She let the arrow drop point-first into the snow.

"Thank you," came the captain's voice, calm once more. "Now please raise your hands above your head."

Astra did not heed the command. She glanced sideways and

noted Mariah standing beyond the ring of soldiers. Then Astra turned her gaze up the ridge where an overhanging crag was heavy with glistening snow.

"Princess, put your hands above your head." The order grew more stern.

Astra reached one hand to her wrist and removed the bronze cuff, tossing it aside.

"Stop her!" Mariah's warning came too late.

Astra directed the blast of energy upwards, rippling through snow and stone and air. The impact nearly shattered the face of the crag. The cracking, splintering, shattering sounds were only interrupted by cries to run. But it was too late for them now, too. The snow came tumbling down with a roar that drowned out every possible thought. The last thing Astra remembered doing was picking up her bow, crossing her arms over her chest, and taking the deepest breath she could before the avalanche hit her.

Louko:

Louko had awoken by a cold draft. The nights were getting more frigid than he had ever been used to, and so the slightest extra breeze was enough to stir him awake. He thought of Astra, and suddenly wondered if she had told anyone to relieve her. She had that nasty habit of 'forgetting'.

So, stiff from the freezing night, Louko got up, strapping the sword and readjusting his coat before leaving the tent. He looked over to where Astra had been perched right before he had agreed to turn in, and to his dismay found that she was not there—only her cloak. Neither was there anyone on guard.

Panic swelled a little, and then was stifled as he noticed her disappearing around a face of rock on the opposite side of the camp.

Where in Eatris was she going? Clearly it wasn't something to raise alarm, as she would have done so... but why leave her post?

Still concerned, Louko followed after, far enough behind and quiet so that even her hearing wouldn't catch his steps. The War in Litash had taught him how to outstealth an Elf, if nothing else.

But such maneuvers required being very far back—and too late did he realize she was heading for some sort of ambush. He noticed the multiplying footsteps and so picked up the pace to warn her, but moments later he heard footsteps and voices and had to dive behind a snow drift. No no no no. What had Astra gotten herself into?? What had they *all* gotten themselves into? As he watched the group of men passing, it was clear this was far more than a small patrol. How had they found them so quickly? And dispatched this number of men? Surely Kaeden would not have sent so many here unless he'd been certain he would know where they were, and he would have had to know for possibly weeks.

"Please, Princess, none of that," came the deep voice. "There are too many of us for you to possibly take. Why kill without cause? Lay down your weapon."

The voice was barely audible, but recognizable as Killyan—the patrol captain. Oh, no. Louko didn't know what to do. He was back far enough that he could escape and warn the others to make a run for it... but then he would be leaving Astra. *Astra.* His friend. His only friend. He wasn't about to just leave her.

But she would kill him if he stayed and they were all caught.

No sooner had he forced himself into a bitter sort of reality than the rumbling began. The deep, resounding, rumbling was echoed by the shaking of the very ground.

"Stop her!" Louko barely had time to be angry at the recognition of Mariah's voice before the snow came toppling down on top of them. He may have been farther back, but the avalanche didn't care as it came steamrolling over the scrubby trees and heaving down on top of everyone. With only seconds before he was hit, Louko spotted a large out-jutting rock and threw himself at its mercy, hoping it would shelter him enough to keep him from drowning in the white death.

At least it would help him know which way was up. The roar was deafening, and the screams barely audible above it as the world shattered to pieces around Louko, forcing him to cover his ears and tuck himself in so that snow and shards of wood wouldn't hit his face. Everything was rumbling, and panic turned to a feverish kind of nightmare as he wondered if Keeshiff and the others had even avoided this. Or even if Astra had gotten somewhere safe.

The questions were wiped away by the buffeting of snow against his back. It seemed the rock was protecting his head, but it did nothing to stop the noise. The vibration seemed to shake the entire mountain, filling him with a sensation of inescapable sound. There was no hiding from it. Only waiting and hoping that it would end.

Louko had no idea how long it lasted, but it felt like an eternity. When the adrenaline began to subside and the noise was far away, he started to get up. That's when he found out he couldn't. The snow, even though it hadn't covered his face, had filled up too much of the space around his legs and back until he couldn't move them. He was all but completely buried.

For a moment, blind panic overtook him, and Louko struggled wildly. He *needed* to move, to free himself. It took the icy sensation of snow on his face to bring him to his sense. *Stop it, you idiot. You're just going to bury the rest of you and suffocate.* He needed to be patient and to think—not panic.

"Louko? Astra? Mariah?"

The names echoed above him, and filled him with hope. Keeshiff and the rest must have been woken by the avalanche, and had been far enough away after all.

"Here!" Louko tried to shout, but worried the snow would smother any sound for help.

He heard a commotion from outside and voices nearby, prompting him to shout until his voice failed from hoarseness.

"Here!" Asher's voice sounded faraway, though in truth it couldn't be much farther.

The sounds of digging followed, and soon Louko felt something hit up against his back. Then several pairs of hands dragged him upwards, and the blinding white of the snow was replaced by the dark sky above.

"Astra, where's Astra?" He stood up, only to realize he couldn't see a thing.

"You need to sit down, Louko." It was Asher, and Louko felt a hand on his shoulder. But still he could see nothing.

"He looks unwell.""

371

"Louko? Louko!"

The young prince was unsure exactly when he had fallen or how, but the last thing he remembered was someone catching him as his legs gave out.

***

Empty. Louko had never felt so blank and void as he did now, and time felt endless in passing until it was maddening. And then, finally, he heard voices.

It was Keeshiff, and he sounded nervous. "Is he going to wake up?"

Louko became aware that he could actually feel his extremities, and tested the ability to move his fingers back and forth. The movement was sluggish at first, but with it came his vision.

"Yes. I think he is now, actually." Asher had been kneeling by Louko, and got up quickly as Louko jolted into a sitting position, eyes riveting on his brother, who was standing a little farther back.

"Where's Astra?" Louko asked Keeshiff desperately, who was still regarding him with a shocked sort of relief.

But Louko was too busy realizing they were in a tent… how long had it been? Or had they been caught?

Keeshiff's face grew colder than snow at the question. "Thernyn, one of the soldiers we dug up, said Captain Killyan sent Mariah and another group to bring her back to the capitol and left the others to search for survivors." As he finished speaking, his lips pressed tightly together in a grave line.

If Louko's blood hadn't been cold before, it was now. "We need to find her. We need to get her." The younger prince was in a frenzy, but found getting up was hard to do without falling.

Asher grabbed his arm and forced him firmly back down. "Careful, you have been unconscious for nearly two days," he chided.

Two days??

This only made Louko more frantic, and he pushed Asher away with surprising force. The young prince knew who Kaeden was, and while he held no fear of him, he had seen what had happened to Astra at his hand. He couldn't let that happen again.

Keeshiff must have guessed his intentions. "You can't go back. That would be idiotic. You would be caught and executed! The worst that will happen to Astra is that she'll get sent back to Litash." The foreign emotion of concern in his brother's voice was not for the princess. "Knowing her, she'll beat us to Nythril. But you're not even in shape to get back over these mountains without keeling over, let alone go back to Melye."

"No." Louko was firm, though taken aback by his brother's concern. "You don't understand. She's not going to get sent to Litash, Keeshiff." Didn't he get it? How would Kaeden have known how to subdue her in the first place? There was no way a group of soldiers could keep her under control after she came to consciousness, and there was no other explanation of how they were going to be able to keep her captured, unless Kaeden was not who he claimed to be.

"What don't I understand?" Keeshiff's question was exasperated. "The depths of your death-wish?"

"Kaeden won't hurt me, Keeshiff!" Louko shouted this much

louder than he intended, "In fact, I don't even think he *is* Kaeden. At least, he isn't who he claims. How else could he manage to capture someone like Astra? Do *you* know how to catch a Litashian like that? You saw how powerful she was in The War. He *isn't* going to let her go, and I can't live with myself if something happens to her. I can't leave her." There was no time to explain about who Kaeden *really* was. Every moment they sat here talking was a moment for the soldiers to get further away with Astra, and Louko knew Keeshiff wouldn't easily believe him if he *did* share his reasonings. "Now I am going. With or without your permission. I can't leave her."

Keeshiff looked startled. He opened his mouth to argue, then shut it. He set his shoulders and said, "Fine. Then we're coming with you."

There was a brief second where Louko wanted to agree. For the first time in his entire life—that he could recall—Keeshiff had just offered help. The gravity of that was enough to catch him off guard, and renew the undying wish he had always had to hear Keeshiff say that.

But then it was drowned by reality "And start this whole thing over again? We didn't even make it out of Merimeethia unscathed the first time. No. Keeshiff, you can't. I'm sorry. I have to go alone. There isn't another way."

"But why you?" Keeshiff was already shaking his head. "You could be *executed*. Let one of the knights go instead. Asher has his connections. So does Rufio. You aren't safe with Kaeden, any more than I am."

"I know that castle better than anyone else alive, Keeshiff. I'm the only chance at getting in and out unnoticed, and I'm sorry, but

Kaeden is *not* going to kill me. I need to go…" He began feeling more and more fidgety as the minutes swept by around him. Every minute was one he lost.

Keeshiff grit his teeth, and his hands formed fists. "And what if something happens? How would I even know?"

"Well. If I'm not at my uncle's house within three weeks of you arriving there... then, there's your clue." Louko replied grimly. "It will be fine. When was the last time I got caught doing something?" He rolled his eyes as he said this, trying to ease his brother's uncharacteristic worry for him. It was slightly unnerving.

It looked like Keeshiff really wanted to say something. He fought with himself a moment, then just shook his head again. "It wasn't that long ago," he grumbled. Then he let out a long breath. "Fine," he finally said. "Go. But be careful and take some supplies. And if you aren't back in two weeks, I'm coming after you."

"Three." Louko corrected. "If you come too early, you could pass by us without ever knowing, and then we would be in even worse trouble." He regarded his brother earnestly. "Thank you."

Keeshiff looked far from pleased. "Three," he relented begrudgingly. Then he softened. "Go. Be quick—and be careful." He hesitated, looking almost like he was going to clasp Louko on the shoulder. Instead he turned towards Ivinon, who was calling his name.

And then came the awkward throat clearing from Asher, "I still need to clear you to ride, first. And as attending physician, I outrank your brother."

Louko was desperate, "Please, Asher she could get herself killed. You know she's been exiled now. What if she *does* get sent back?"

There was a dark expression on the physician's face. "I know," he said simply. "But you won't be much use to her dead. I can't stop you, but if you want to get there alive, you'll wait until I have done a final examination and given you something to help keep you from getting ill."

Though Louko's heart beat at a rate that could have thrown it from his chest, the prince nodded, hoping every second lost wouldn't be one that mattered. And yet, he knew it was, and that only made it worse.

Asher was quick and yet thorough, not entirely pleased with Louko's condition but seeming to guess Louko's determination to leave. At long last he gave a gruff nod, and said, "Just make sure you drink this, please? I don't need you to collapse somewhere of pneumonia." Asher thrust a small vial into Louko's hand, and the prince quickly obeyed. That done, Louko was allowed to leave—after being given more medicine with daily instructions.

"Is he ready?" Keeshiff's voice came from outside the tent.

Asher looked to Louko, clearly not wanting to reply. So Louko was the one who said, "Yes. I'm coming." And stepped outside the tent.

Keeshiff was wringing his hands and looking uncharacteristically out of sorts as he said, "We...we found her horse. But she won't let anyone really near her. She's just been hanging around. I thought maybe she'd let you ride her. I mean, she's fast, after all. And she at least likes you better than the rest of us."

"Thank you," Louko whispered, already setting eyes on the skittish mare that stood on the outskirts of the assembled camp that had been made in the wake of Louko's unconsciousness.

With time a non-existent commodity, Louko didn't waste any

more words, quickly—yet carefully— making his way over to where the mare was and putting his hands up when she pinned her ears.

Somehow, he thought talking to her would work. "Alright...So don't kill me...but she's gotten caught...and I'm going to go save her, alright?" Louko knew Dannsair was his best bet at catching up, and hopefully Dannsair would realize that too… He was only glad she hadn't taken off already. Fortunately, the horse appeared to realize hooves would only get her so far in trying to save her master. After a few skittering evasions, she let him catch her. The mare was covered in sweat and her ears flicked restlessly in different directions. Her nostrils flared with her ragged breathing.

Hesitantly, Louko petted her neck, whispering, "I know. We'll get her back, promise."

***

Dannsair carried Louko like the very wind was chasing her. Louko had never ridden an Elvish horse, and he wondered if they all had this much stamina, or if Dannsair was just so focused on getting Astra back that she would run until she died.

Whatever the reason, Louko found that Dannsair made incredible time. And yet, even though he rode into the night and began before dawn each day, they still did not catch up to Astra and her captors. They had apparently been making quick work of time as well, most likely equally as dedicated to getting back to Melye.

They made it to the capitol in a little over a week's time. It was much faster to take a direct route and to do it alone. It wasn't hard getting in. Now that they had been engaged at the border, no one would expect one of the princes to return. It would be suicide…for Keeshiff, maybe. But Louko had never been permitted outside the castle walls and was therefore unrecognizable to anyone who didn't live within them.

Louko stabled Dannsair at a local inn, and promised the horse he would return with her master. The streets, as always, bustled with people, making their way in and out of various houses. Everyone seemed almost…happier. Deceit or no deceit, it would appear Tyron had made many positive changes. He heard the whispers of others as he passed them by, how they marveled at better street-lighting and more attention to the needs of the people—nobles and poor. How odd that Tyron—whose very name was enough to cause disgust to rise before them—was the one giving them all these changes. And they didn't even know.

It did not take long to make his way through the passersby and reach the palace. He didn't bother to wait and figure out a plan, mind too clouded by fear, panic, and the strongest sense of longing. What would Tyron do? What would he be like? Louko had not set eyes on the man since he was seven or eight, but now, apparently, he had been with him for almost nine years. Nothing made sense. One minute he was a murderer, the next he was helping Merimeethia. But was the loss of Omath so terrible? Louko had not heard one person bring it up since he'd gotten to Melye…

Slipping into the servants' passage by the guard house, he swiftly made his way through the walls of the castle. Where would they be keeping Astra? What if Louko had somehow missed them, and had arrived first after all? Perhaps then Louko would have time to talk

Kaeden—Tyron—out of whatever he would do to Astra.

It was settled, then.

Louko was careful to use the less known and traveled passages, not wishing the alarm to be raised. Tyron might not mind seeing him, but if a guard caught sight, Louko wouldn't get a chance. He wanted to talk to Tyron alone.

Slowly, Louko visited each room Tyron could be in. The Library —nothing. Tyron's room—no. He now stood in front of the servant's entrance that led to the throne room. Louko's hand moved to the latch, but he did not take hold of it. Perhaps Astra was wrong—or maybe Louko had misinterpreted her. Maybe Kaeden was not Tyron after all. Maybe he *was* just Kaeden? Would that be so terrible? But Louko brushed that silly doubt away. No. He knew now it was true. All the conversations, the hints, the sparring lessons. It was all Tyron, and Louko knew he could not doubt.

But now, standing only a door away, he hesitated. The stories he'd heard…Louko had passed some of them off as Euracia, but others…Surely Tyron would have a reasonable explanation? Louko remembered expressing his anger to Kaeden…but now could not remember Kaeden's reaction. What if it had all been a mistake? Louko would soon find out.

With a deep breath, Louko grabbed hold of the latch and listened as the metal rang through the passage. He was about to come face to face with probably the closest thing to a true father he had ever had, only… that father was his friend's worst nightmare.

"Hello, Louko," came the voice, as Louko entered the throne room.

It was Kaeden. He was in the great hall alone, bent over a table of charts and maps. Louko noticed that the table was the only change to the throne room, besides the plain wooden chair that sat next to the throne. It would seem he had not made any attempt to crown himself king.

Kaeden himself looked only slightly different. Perhaps simply more tired. He straightened, looking Louko over with those intense green eyes.

"Are you alright?" Kaeden asked, worry barely lacing his voice. He always hid it well. "You haven't come to any harm, have you?"

Louko's voice stuck in his throat as he stared Kaeden in the face. The last time he had seen the advisor, a knife had been plunged into the king's back. And now, with the way Astra had danced around the subject—and Louko's own doubts—he wondered who he was really standing in front of. All over again, Louko felt like a lost little boy, standing in the dark and just waiting to be rescued. And here, in front of him was... was...

"It's you, isn't it?" The words echoed through the empty hall. "You came back." The last bit was choked out, thick with emotion.

The small question seemed to hit hard. Kaeden started to speak, but had no breath to do so. His brow furrowed in grief and one hand began to run through his hair. Then he forced his hand down as he let out a long breath. "Yes, it's me."

Any plan Louko had flew out the window after that. Any words he had formed in his head, any idea he'd come up with. All he had was the word, "Why?" It tumbled out, laden with the years of desertion and heartache—the one question that had wracked Louko's conscience for what felt like centuries.

Louko had seen a shape-shifter change skins many times before. Never had it taken his breath away. But as the guise of Kaeden melted away, the one who stood there was enough to do just that. He looked worn, thin, face nearly gaunt. His once jet-black hair showed grey at the temples. But those green eyes were exactly the same. Still unbearably sad.

"What would have happened to you if you had known?" he asked softly.

"We could have left." The words were so softly said as Louko felt one tear run down his cheek. One more than he had allowed in years. "We could have disappeared—no one would have cared." The words were so desperate.

"And then you would have been hunted for the rest of your life." Tyron's voice was nearly raspy. "Do you think that I *wanted* to leave you here? Under your father?" The unusual show of emotion was only curbed when Tyron looked away, running his hand through his hair again.

"He wouldn't have looked that hard." Louko didn't stop. "Maybe then you wouldn't have—" He broke off, overwhelmed by the memories of what he had seen during The War. Astra. He suddenly remembered why he was there.

"Louko, you were seven," Tyron said gently. "Where could I have taken you where you would have been safe?"

"Cadbir, Krysophera, Rednimaen," Louko was still desperate, but now the worry for Astra had dimmed his emotions. Dimmed, but not subdued. "But no, you had to leave with Euracia and for what? To torture some teenager and her brother? To starve and kill hundreds of innocent people. *Why*?"

Tyron went completely still, gaze glued on some distant object that Louko couldn't see. "I had no choice," he murmured. "I had no choice." He swallowed and looked down, hands falling open in a helpless manner. "I did not go with him willingly. But if I didn't do what he wanted..." He closed his eyes and shook his head. "It doesn't matter. I have no excuse. All I can say is that, in the matter of, of, what happened to Astra, if I did not do it, Euracia would have done it himself." Tyron opened his eyes and gave a bitter smile. "She would not have survived that."

"But what about now? Where is she? The soldiers took her *here*." Louko's breathing became more rapid as everything just became more confused and out of sorts.

A nearly amused expression crossed Tyron's face. "If you truly believe that a few of your father's foot soldiers could hold Astra all the way back from the border, you have a higher opinion of them than you should."

She was safe... Louko's breath let out so quickly he didn't know what to do. Here he was... with Tyron... Keeshiff was safe... Reality washed in around Louko until he was drowning. Sense told him Tyron was not the same—it called back the memories of the horrors in The War. But his heart... oh, how his heart hurt. His heart told him there was no longer any reason for Louko to leave. Tyron had simply rationalized... tried to protect what he could under his brother. But now, now they could disappear—start again. Maybe they could both have a life.

Tyron turned his head as if he had heard something. The burden of worry returned in an instant, and he looked back to Louko. "You shouldn't stay long. I don't know that you want to be seen with me," he said in quiet shame. "I, I am trying to convince them that it wasn't you. I'm almost there. It's almost safe. Just give me a few more weeks and I will make this right."

Louko felt like he would pass out at any moment, and yet still the irrational words came out of his mouth: "We could leave right now... No one would know we were gone until we were far away. Keeshiff wouldn't send anyone after us—he already was half convinced I'd killed Omath and he still didn't do anything."

Tyron stared at him, lips parted in wordless shock. "You want me... to come with you?" He spoke as if barely able to believe he was saying it aloud.

"Why not? We can just leave, can't we?" Louko had devolved to desperate motions, waving to the door.

The conflict that raged so openly on Tyron's face was hard to watch. He seemed nearly as despairing and hungry for hope as Louko felt. Then his countenance fell. "I... I can't." Tyron struggled to say the words. "There is no one here who could rule. They wouldn't call for Keeshiff. Not yet. The whole country would fall to pieces." He shook his head more vehemently now. "I cannot be responsible for that again."

"But he's with my uncle. Keeshiff is more capable than people give him credit for." Louko, though desperate to fly, was already feeling Tyron's words sink in. "Staying would mean you confessing; it's the only way to fix this, Tyron. You've already died once—please don't do that to me again." What was he saying?! Louko had promised himself he would

383

never cross this line again, but here he was, just a desperate little boy with his arms wide—crying for Tyron not to leave him again. The only person besides Astra who had ever looked past all his faults. He didn't have enough in him to do this again, but he didn't have enough in him to pretend anymore, either.

Tyron's entire expression crumpled and he looked away. Both hands went to his head, tugging at hair that was greying too early. "I can't," he nearly shouted the words, as if crying out against his own situation. "If 'Kaeden' confesses, all his work will be undone. That is far more than you realize. And if I confess, it does not end here. I would have to confess in Alarune and Litash, and you know how that would end." He threw up his hands as if in defeat. "My only hope was to let Kaeden convince Merimeethia of your innocence. Then I could let him 'retire' and I could let myself disappear."

"*Mine*?" Louko was repulsed by the inkling of confusion and fear. He was hung up on semantics. Of course, Tyron didn't mean just him, "Keeshiff too, surely."

That look of utter shame returned and Tyron hung his head. *No...*

"You have studied enough of history to know that everyone wants someone to blame, Louko," came the soft explanation. "I was left with the choice: you or him. I chose who I believed was most fit to lead a nation."

"Lead?" Louko repeated in anguish and confusion. "Tyron, I don't want to lead, I want to *leave*. You—You're just going to leave Keeshiff in exile? His men have families, Tyron, actual families— families here. Families they are separated from. Families that can't just

384

follow them to Nythril. And of course Keeshiff will tell them to go back to them. And if they do? Keeshiff will be all alone in a country that hates him with no one but Mariah for company. What in Eatris are you *thinking*?"

"Thinking was exactly what I was doing. Thinking, not feeling." Tyron looked up now, one hand marking his point in the air. "I had a choice between two men: one with the habit of keeping quiet to save his own skin, of letting other people do his thinking for him, of allowing the weak to suffer so long as the strong still served him; the other had not only a sharp mind and knowledgeable background, but also the desire to help *everyone* around him—even the very ones who had wronged him." The breathless words came to a sudden halt. Then came the challenge: "Look it at it from the view of logic and tell me that you would have done any differently."

"Logic. Is that it?" Louko was shaking his head. "No. Leaving Keeshiff is one thing; but I will not lie. I can't—and I thought you wouldn't have either... Logic alone is as cold as a dead man's bones, Tyron. Please don't."

Tyron tried to hide his shaking hands. "I have to do this," he nearly whispered. "I can't have any more blood on my hands. I followed my heart before and it cost too much in the end. I have to follow my head this time." Tyron's self-control seemed to crack even further before Louko's eyes. "Please," he pleaded. "I know, I know I am the furthest person from deserving it, but please trust me. Just give me a little more time. Please."

Louko just stood there, staring at the man he had looked up to almost his entire life. He had no idea what to do. None. All he knew was how much he yearned to give in. Could he rationalize this?

Astra:

Astra was mere feet from Louko. Her throat was sore from screaming, her wrists from fighting the chains that bound her. But it was all in vain. Tyron had used Gifting so that she would neither be heard nor seen. No matter what she did, Louko had no idea she was there.

Astra had woken up only yesterday, having been drugged the whole way to the castle so that she couldn't escape. She had been in the same red bronze shackles that held her so tightly now. She'd had even been forced to swallow some of it in liquid form. Astra knew that her Gifting would not help her escape. She was trapped. And Louko was falling for Tyron's bait.

So great was her despair that Astra almost wished Louko would accept Tyron's offer. At least then she knew that he would not suffer the same fate that no doubt awaited her. Yet Astra knew that if Louko did so, he would be corrupted the same way Tyron was and it would be his downfall. That was why she was so terrified to hear how much Louko clearly longed to give in.

"But then what? How long? A few weeks? What if that's not long enough? Years?" Louko sounded so tortured.

"Three weeks," Tyron replied firmly. "I promise. And then you will be in charge and you can do what you think best. Even bring back Keeshiff after a little while. Merimeethians have short enough memories."

Louko hesitated. "And what will you do then?"

Tyron bowed his head ever so slightly. "You will be in charge. I will do whatever you ask."

387

"And if I ask you to stay?"

"Your word is my command."

Astra cried out in defeat.

EPILOGUE:

<u>Entrais:</u>

Ent was pacing wildly in the empty throne room, open letter in his hand. It was the last one he had received from Astra—and it was dated from almost two months ago. She'd always been good about keeping him updated—every month the letters had come. The knot in Ent's stomach grew. "Oh Slip... where are you," he murmured, her troubled, sorrowful eyes in the forefront of his mind.

"What is it, Ent?" Ent's brother-in-law, Soletuph, asked as he slipped in from a side passage.

Ent had asked Soletuph to meet him here. Soletuph was one of the few outside the Court that knew of Astra's exile, and he was someone who could be trusted to be discreet. They had to do something. What if Astra really had been right... but what if Tyron had found *her* first? Oh, Ent never should have allowed her to go! If only he wasn't king; if only he could leave right now and go find her himself! And why not? Why not? Why did Ent even care if the Court dethroned him? Look what it had cost him. Look what it had done to Astra! Why had Ent thought he could deal with it himself?

"Ent?" Soletuph's voice held the barest hint of concern in it.

"It's Astra." Ent barely registered that it was his own voice that broke the silence. Astra. He'd abandoned her—the thing he had *sworn* never to do. Never to let her go again.

Instantly, Soletuph snapped to attention and muttered, "I told you it was a terrible idea."

"I know...I know..." Ent went back to pacing, panic rising in his throat. He should have figured something out—*anything* else. "I'm sorry... I never should have let her go. I should have fought harder. She could be..." *dead.* Only, Ent didn't have the guts to say the word out loud. After everything Tyron had done to her, and what had Ent done? What had he done? Nothing. He'd abandoned her. Left her in the trust of Louko without any explanation. "You were right."

Soletuph looked grim, but did his best to comfort. "Well? What do you plan on doing?" His anger was evident, and Ent didn't blame him. He had been weak, stupid, and a fool.

"I haven't heard from her in two months, Soletuph. She had been sending them very regularly, at the beginning of the month." Ent resumed his pacing.

"Are you sure that she isn't just in a place where she can't send letters?"

Ent stopped and faced the shape-shifter. "She would have told me. Last she had contacted, she and the Merimeethian princes were almost to Nythril. She should be established there by now with Louko's uncle, and the only way I can think of that she wouldn't be able to send letters would be..." if Tyron had her.

Soletuph let out a long breath. "So what do you want me to do?"

As the captain and the most powerful of the Ethian Guards, Soletuph would have the best chance of rescuing Astra if she truly was captured. "Go to Nythril and find out where she is." *Find out if she was alive...* But saying that out loud would only make the possibility feel so much more real. He couldn't think she was dead. She *couldn't* be dead.

All of the sorrow they had gone through in The War—the

heartache, the sacrifice—was this their reward? Where was the hero's welcome for Astra? Where were the songs of bravery and tales of heroics? Astra had sacrificed more than any other person, and it had not been enough that the very people she had helped free had turned her away! Now… now her own *brother* could have sent her away to her… her…

"Write to me when you get there. Find out what happened." Ent forced himself to speak, if only to turn his mind from his plummeting thoughts.

With a nod and a slight bow, Soletuph said, "As you say." He left the room with a hand on his dagger.

Ent had lost Astra again…and it was all his fault. He only hoped it wasn't too late.

And so it begins.

Next book in A Daughter's Ransom series:

TO TAKE A WORLD: THE GHOSTMAKER

There's not much left in the world of Baeno. With two Watchers dead and the third turned against the world she was supposed to protect, chaos reigns for near a decade as Skayla rules with the strange beasts called Drogans.

And then there's Baey. Rescued by the last act of The Watcher, Sven Mara, she now stays hidden in the mansion of Valdon, where the last Gifted of Baeno stand as a pitiful defense for the City of Kaedna. The last promise of The Creator says she--an Esmer (or one with wings)--will free Baeno from the grips of Skayla and the mysterious beasts that aid her. However, doubts haunt Baey and even the others at Valdon seem to doubt her destiny. But one thing keeps her strong: the ring she was given by Sven Mara, a trinket no one but her can see.

But when a stranger appears on Valdon's doorsteps, everyone doubts his motives and the message he carries. Little do they know what he stole, and little do they know how close Valdon is to ruin.

About the authors:

NIAMH SCHMID:

Born in Clifton Park New York, Niamh is (unfortunately) a human being. She would much rather be off in some pretend world battling an ogre or taming a rabid pegasus, but instead is currently engaging in completing a bachelor's in Piano Performance. In her spare time she cares for her two mini ponies (or monsters), Freddie and Taffie, as well as her Dorkie (dachshund/yorkie mix) Tobie. She also loves to compose, collect stamps, and dabble in being a very mediocre artist.

REBECCA SCHMID:

Though many seem to miss the fact, Rebecca is actually *not* Niamh. She is a separate human being, who just so happens to also be from upstate New York, also be a pianist, also love animals and literature and art, also have the last name Schmid.... Oh well. Perhaps she's a lot like Niamh. Rebecca lives with her husband and horde of dogs, and spends her time practicing piano, maintaining too many hobbies, and drinking way too much coffee.

Made in the USA
Columbia, SC
14 September 2021